W9-BLU-574

Praise for the Alice-Miranda series

'Alice Miranda's optimism and determination is infectious. An immediately lovable character that young girls are going to want to be or be with.' Deborah Abela, bestselling author of *Max Remy*

'What's the worst thing about reviewing kids' books? When you find a book so enchanting that you want to ignore your own child to keep reading it! A modern story with a touch of the classics about it.' Megan Blandford, Kids' Book Review blog

'Full of humour and with very likeable characters, this book sets a benchmark for a fantastic new series.' Donella Reed, *Read Plus*

'Alice-Miranda is a powerhouse of positive thinking, a problem solver and a friend to all – she's quite simply unstoppable.' *Maitland Mercury*

'It is a welcome change to read about a small child who changes adults' lives . . . even though she never changes, everyone around her does, for the better.' *Sydney's Child*

'Her generosity of spirit, enthusiasm and ultra well-heeled practicality endear her to the reader.' Katharine England, *Adelaide Advertiser*

'A great book for ages 6 and up.' Kate O'Donnell, *Magpies Magazine*

'Ever since reading the first Alice-Miranda book, I've been dying to read the second book. Finally, here it is, and I love it . . . Now I want the third book.' Matilda Murrihy (11 years), *Herald Sun*

'In the best tradition of Pollyanna, Pippi Longstocking and Milly-Molly-Mandy . . . A modern fairytale, *Alice-Miranda On Holiday* is a delightful read full of quirky characters and events, plenty of chuckle-worthy moments, and a wonderful sense of fun.' NSW Association for Gifted and Talented Children website

WYNDHAM CITY
LIBRARY SERVICE
P.O. BOX 197
WERRIBEE VIC. 3030

Alice-Miranda Takes the Lead

Jacqueline Harvey

RANDOM HOUSE AUSTRALIA

A Random House book
Published by Random House Australia Pty Ltd
Level 3, 100 Pacific Highway, North Sydney NSW 2060
www.randomhouse.com.au

First published by Random House Australia in 2011

Copyright © Jacqueline Harvey 2011

The moral right of the author has been asserted.

All rights reserved. No part of this book may be reproduced or transmitted by
any person or entity, including internet search engines or retailers, in any form
or by any means, electronic or mechanical, including photocopying (except
under the statutory exceptions provisions of the Australian *Copyright Act 1968*),
recording, scanning or by any information storage and retrieval system without
the prior written permission of Random House Australia.

Addresses for companies within the Random House Group can be found at
www.randomhouse.com.au/offices.

National Library of Australia
Cataloguing-in-Publication Entry

Author: Harvey, Jacqueline
Title: Alice-Miranda takes the lead / Jacqueline Harvey
ISBN: 978 1 86471 849 2 (pbk.)
Target audience: For primary school age
Subjects: Girls – Juvenile fiction
          Boarding schools – Juvenile fiction
Dewey number: A823.4

Cover illustration by J.Yi
Cover design by Mathematics www.xy-1.com
Internal design by Midland Typesetters, Australia
Typeset in 13/18 pt Adobe Garamond by Midland Typesetters, Australia
Printed in Australia by Griffin Press, an accredited ISO AS/NZS 14001:2004
Environmental Management System printer

10 9 8 7 6 5 4 3 2 1

FSC
www.fsc.org
MIX
Paper from
responsible sources
FSC® C009448

The paper this book is printed on is certified against the
Forest Stewardship Council® Standards. Griffin Press holds
FSC chain of custody certification SGS-COC-005088.
FSC promotes environmentally responsible, socially
beneficial and economically viable management of the
world's forests.

For Ian and Sandy

For Linsay and Kimberley

Chapter 1

Twelve pairs of eyes widened in unison, awaiting Miss Ophelia Grimm's next move. She stood in the corner of the room, a scarlet flush creeping up from her neck to her cheeks. Her blonde hair sparked with static and her lips drew tightly together.

'Out!' Her shrill voice shattered the silence. 'Get out and don't come back, you horrid little monsters!'

Eleven girls reeled backwards in terror, their hands clutching pallid faces. Millie's cinnamon freckles turned white and Jacinta's mouth gaped open. Only Alice-Miranda dared to smile.

'And that, my dears, was how I got rid of the two cheeky chimps who had taken up residence in our room!' Miss Grimm smiled and plonked herself down in the striped armchair beside the fireplace in her study. Dressed casually in jeans and a pretty orange shirt, Ophelia Grimm was a picture of happiness.

The girls exchanged quizzical looks and then disintegrated into fits of giggles. Mr Grump, who was sitting in the armchair opposite, roared with laughter.

'You should have seen those poor monkeys.' Aldous Grump grinned at his new wife. 'They didn't have a hope with Ophelia after them. Ran for their lives, they did – thought they'd be better off taking their chances with the lions out on the game reserve.'

'Very funny darling,' Miss Grimm admonished. 'I was just tired of the little brutes raiding my make-up purse, that's all. I hadn't realised chimps were fond of lipstick and blush until I caught them giving each other a makeover at the dressing table after we returned from breakfast one morning.'

'We must have stayed at the same lodge when we were on safari last year,' said Alice-Miranda, 'because the very same thing happened to Mummy. The manager, Mr Van Rensburg, said that his chimps had collected enough stolen lipstick to start their own beauty parlour. Apart from that, it does sound like you had a lovely time.'

'We most certainly did,' Mr Grump nodded.

Millie took the last sip of her hot chocolate, up-ended the delicate blue-and-white mug and allowed a sodden marshmallow to slide into her mouth.

'Mmm, yum!' she exclaimed.

'All done?' Miss Grimm asked.

Millie nodded.

'Well girls, I think you had better be heading off. School tomorrow and we have loads of exciting things planned for the term.' Miss Grimm stood up and walked towards the mahogany door.

'But can't we stay and hear more?' Jacinta grumbled. 'I want to know what happened to the baby elephant you saw on safari. Did he escape from that crocodile?'

'Next time,' Miss Grimm promised. 'And girls?' She tapped her finger to her cheek as though she had just remembered something important. 'We have a new student starting tomorrow. She'll be rooming with you, Jacinta, so I expect you to make her feel *very* welcome.' Ophelia arched her eyebrow and gave Jacinta a meaningful look.

Jacinta nodded like a jack-in-the-box.

'A new girl? That's lovely,' Alice-Miranda replied. 'I can't wait to meet her. What's her name?'

'Sloane. Sloane Sykes,' Miss Grimm replied. 'Now, off you go, girls.'

Alice-Miranda was the first to stand. She said goodnight to Mr Grump, who was still sitting in his armchair. Without warning, the tiny child leaned forward and gave him a peck on his stubbly cheek.

'Now what was that for?' Aldous asked.

'Just because,' Alice-Miranda replied, before skipping over to Miss Grimm to give her a warm hug too. Miss Grimm smiled at her youngest student with the cascading chocolate curls and eyes as big as saucers.

'And you know something?' Alice-Miranda scanned the walls either side of the door. 'I simply love your photographs. That one of you and Mr Grump is gorgeous, and that one of the elephant is too cute – you could enter it in a competition.'

The previously bare walls now played host to

more than a dozen pictures: Miss Grimm and Mr Grump's wedding, their honeymoon and even some casual shots of Miss Grimm with girls around the school. There were faces and places and memories.

'Do you remember, Miss Grimm, when I first met you, I said that what this room needed was some photographs? And now look – it's perfect!'

'Yes, young lady, I certainly do recall that was one of your recommendations, among rather a few others,' Miss Grimm teased. Alice-Miranda grinned and leaned forward to give the headmistress another quick hug.

The group of girls behind her took turns saying goodnight to Miss Grimm and Mr Grump. It was amazing how much things had changed at Winchesterfield-Downsfordvale in the past few months. Who would ever have thought that Alice-Miranda Highton-Smith-Kennington-Jones, along with eleven of her friends, would enjoy an hour in the headmistress's study, hearing all about her recent honeymoon safari to Africa?

Alice-Miranda smiled to herself. She couldn't wait to see what excitement the new term would bring.

Chapter 2

Alice-Miranda led the charge across the cobble-stoned courtyard towards Grimthorpe House. From her position on the dimly lit veranda, the house-mistress Mrs Howard peered out into the darkness, a flurry of bother frothing on her lips.

'Oh, thank heavens!' she exclaimed. 'I was worrying myself into an early grave. Where on earth have you been? Dinner was an hour ago. Now hurry up inside, it's cool out and the last thing I need is a house full of coughs and splutters.'

The girls poured into the hallway, one after the

other. Mrs Howard gathered them around her like a mother hen, locked the front door and turned to face her charges.

'Sorry Mrs Howard, we should have phoned you,' Alice-Miranda began. 'Miss Grimm and Mr Grump invited us back to the study for hot chocolate and marshmallows and we lost track of the time. Miss Grimm was telling us about their honeymoon in Africa. It all sounded so wonderful. They went on a safari and they saw elephants and lions and hippos . . .'

'And guess what, Howie?' Millie interrupted as she rushed through from behind Alice-Miranda. 'Two monkeys invaded their bedroom and stole Miss Grimm's lipstick and when she was telling us about it, I almost jumped out of my skin. She's good at scary stories, that's for sure.'

Mrs Howard rolled her eyes. 'Imagine that! Well, run along girls and brush your teeth. I'll be in to turn the lights off in ten minutes.'

The girls began to disappear through doorways along opposite sides of the long corridor. Alice-Miranda and Millie were headed towards their room when Jacinta whispered Millie's name. She then opened and closed her hands, signalling the number ten. 'Ten minutes. Okay?' Jacinta asked.

Millie gave two thumbs up.

'What was that fo–?' Alice-Miranda began. Millie promptly put her hand over Alice-Miranda's mouth and gave her a gentle shove into their bedroom.

Millie shut the door and flopped down onto her bed. 'Midnight meeting in Jacinta's room.'

'Midnight! What fun! But it's school tomorrow,' Alice-Miranda said as she unbuttoned her shirt. 'Won't that upset Mrs Howard? I don't think she was very happy about our staying out late tonight.' She retrieved her pyjamas from under her pillow and began to get changed.

'Don't worry about Howie,' Millie replied. 'She was just pretending to be annoyed. She could have phoned the kitchen if she was *that* worried. Anyway, the girls on the corridor always have a "midnight meeting" on the first night back.'

'We didn't last term,' Alice-Miranda replied.

Millie explained that this was because Alethea wouldn't allow anyone except *her* friends last term. Apparently the meeting was not really at midnight anyway, more like quarter to nine and usually someone fell asleep by quarter past and everyone got off to bed by ten at the latest. After holidays where the girls got to stay up later, it was hard to go back to the routine of 8.30 pm bedtime for at least a couple of nights.

'We can talk about what we did on the holidays,' Millie informed her friend.

'But Millie, there are some things we *can't* talk about from the holidays,' Alice-Miranda reminded her.

During the school holidays, Alice-Miranda, Jacinta and Millie had far more adventure and excitement than any of them had bargained for. Jacinta had gone to stay with Alice-Miranda for the whole break. The two girls quickly found themselves at the mercy of a rather cranky boy and a dastardly stranger. When Millie arrived to join in the fun for Aunt Charlotte's birthday party, things went from bad to worse. A case of mistaken identity saw dear old Aunty Gee kidnapped by a gang of rogues intent on getting their hands on the Highton-Smith-Kennington-Joneses' cook and her formula for Just Add Water Freeze-Dried Foods. The fact that Mrs Oliver and Aunty Gee looked like twins had a lot to do with the confusion. In the end Aunty Gee returned safely and Alice-Miranda's bravery ensured that the crooks were captured, but the girls had been sworn to secrecy. Since Aunty Gee also happened to be the Queen, her future freedom depended on their silence. Indeed, she would never be allowed anywhere on her own again if news of such misadventures reached the palace.

'Do we take snacks?' Alice-Miranda asked. 'Because Mrs Oliver packed a whole tin of her chocolate fudge.'

'Yum.' Millie licked her lips. 'Treats are always welcome. But don't expect to have any leftovers.'

Alice-Miranda and Millie finished changing into their pyjamas, grabbed their toothbrushes and hurried to the bathroom at the end of the hallway. The place was a hive of activity as all of the girls from the ground floor readied themselves for bed.

Not five minutes later, the bathroom was empty and Mrs Howard was patrolling the corridor, poking her head into each room, saying her goodnights and flicking off the lights.

Alice-Miranda and Millie lay in the dark, watching the clock as the minutes ticked by slowly until 8.45 pm.

'It's time,' Millie whispered as she pushed back the covers and sat up, swivelling her legs around to scoop her slippers from the floor.

Alice-Miranda hopped out of bed and pulled on

her dressing-gown, then slid her feet into her pink slippers. 'This is such fun!' she smiled. Her tummy was full of butterflies. 'Are you sure Mrs Howard won't mind?'

'Trust me,' Millie replied. 'It's a first night tradition. Well, most of the time.' She grabbed Alice-Miranda's tiny hand and they scampered to the door.

Chapter 3

The corridor was empty. Alice-Miranda followed her friend as they tiptoed along the softly lit hall to Jacinta's door. Other doors were opening and it wasn't long before there were at least ten other girls headed to the same place.

'Password?' Jacinta's voice murmured on the other side of the door.

'Dead,' Millie replied, louder than she had intended.

'That's not it,' Jacinta whispered back.

'No, but that's what you'll be if you don't hurry up and let us in,' Millie threatened.

Jacinta giggled and opened the door.

The stream of visitors poured into the room, finding themselves comfortable spots on Jacinta's bed and the spare bed that was to be Sloane Sykes's as of tomorrow. Alice-Miranda and Millie sat cross-legged on the Persian rug in the middle of the timber floor and Alice-Miranda offered the fudge tin around.

Just as the group got settled there was a shuffling sound outside the room, followed by a booming voice.

'Jacinta Headlington-Bear, turn off that light, or I will be in to turn it off for you,' Mrs Howard instructed. The girls froze. Jacinta had left her bedside lamp on so everyone could see their way in.

'Just doing it now, Howie,' Jacinta called back.

The girls remained silent until they heard the housemistress's footsteps on the stairs at the end of the hall.

'That was close,' Susannah whispered as the group let out a collective breath.

Jacinta grabbed her torch from the bedside table, held it under her chin and flicked on the switch, doing her best impression of a ghost. 'Welcome to

Grimthorpe Hoooooouse.' Everyone giggled.

'So what do we want to talk about?' Danika asked. Now that she was officially Head Prefect she thought she had better take the lead. 'What did everyone do in the holidays?'

Ivory, Shelby and Ashima all complained about having to stay at home and being totally bored.

'Well, I saw Alethea,' Susannah began. 'She was walking out of Highton's in the city with her mother and she almost knocked me over.'

'Please, can we talk about more *pleasant* things?' Lizzy replied as she glanced at Shelby and Danika. The three girls had once been Alethea's best friends until they realised how incredibly horrid she was.

Alethea Goldsworthy had been Head Prefect at the beginning of the year, until it was revealed that she was a cheat and a liar, and had consequently left the school in a terrible hurry. She had treated Alice-Miranda especially badly.

'Well, I feel sorry for her,' said Alice-Miranda.

Millie turned to her. 'Why? She's totally evil. And after what she did to you, she deserved everything she got.'

'I'm sure she's not mean and awful all the time,' Alice-Miranda replied.

'You're too nice, Alice-Miranda, that's your problem,' said Ivory, smiling at her little friend.

'No, I'm not.' Alice-Miranda shook her head.

'No, she's *really* not,' Jacinta agreed. 'You should have seen what she did to Mr Blu–' Millie and Alice-Miranda shot Jacinta a stare that would halt a river of lava. 'Oh, never mind.'

Danika practically pounced on Jacinta. 'What were you about to say?'

'Nothing, nothing at all,' Jacinta lied. 'Umm, does anyone know where that secret passage is off the Science room?'

The girls shook their heads.

'Don't you remember Alethea saying that she'd found a secret passage but she was the only one allowed to go there?' Jacinta continued.

'Knowing Alethea, she was probably just showing off,' Lizzy said. 'But we should look for it. You never know – maybe she was telling the truth for once in her life.'

'O-o-o-o-h-a-a-a-h,' Alice-Miranda yawned and rubbed her eyes. 'Sorry, I'm really tired. I might go to bed.'

'No!' Jacinta wailed. 'It's too early. I know, let's tell ghost stories.'

Millie clasped her hands together. 'I love ghost stories.'

'No, not ghost stories,' said Madeline, shaking her head. 'I think we should tell Alice-Miranda a true story – about the witch in the woods.'

'A witch in the woods?' Alice-Miranda frowned. 'What do you mean?'

'I suppose we never got around to telling you about her last term because there were too many other things going on,' Madeline began. 'But now you *need* to know.'

'Definitely . . . yes . . . for sure,' the other girls chorused, nodding their heads.

'But I don't believe in witches,' Alice-Miranda smiled. 'They're only in fairy stories.'

'Well, you should believe this – because it's absolutely true.' Susannah wriggled forward to the edge of the bed. 'Come and sit up here next to me.' She patted the bedspread.

The youngest child stood up and moved in beside Susannah and Ashima on the bed. Millie stayed on the floor looking up at the storyteller.

'All right, you'd better start at the beginning,' Alice-Miranda directed.

'Well.' Susannah lowered her voice. 'In the woods

not far from here, there's a witch. She lives on her own in a gigantic house, overgrown with vines and hidden by the forest. There's no one there except her and about a hundred cats, all meowing and calling and scratching and fighting.'

The girls began to shift uncomfortably. Alice-Miranda's brown eyes were wide.

'Have you seen her?' Alice-Miranda asked. 'I mean, anyone could make that up. Some of the children who live at Highton Mill, the village near our place, probably tell the same stories about Granny Bert – and she's not scary at all.'

'I disagree! She's mad,' Jacinta disputed.

Madeline leaned over and took the torch from Jacinta, and held it under her chin. 'This witch is tall, possibly the tallest woman you'll ever meet and she has enormous hands like a man and she wears the same black clothes every day and her teeth, well the ones she has, are rotten and crooked and there's a fang . . .'

The girls were now on the edge of the bed leaning in towards the storyteller.

'But the worst thing is her face,' Madeline whispered. 'It's . . .' Madeline grabbed her cheeks and pulled one up and one down, splaying the flesh between her fingers.

At that same moment, a branch scratched against the window outside and the room erupted into squeals which continued for at least a minute.

'Quiet everyone, shush,' Alice-Miranda commanded, trying to quell the fuss. 'Mrs Howard will –'

Without warning Jacinta's bedroom door flew open.

'Mrs Howard will what, young lady?' The housemistress panted. 'What a ruckus.'

There in the doorway, in an orange chenille dressing-gown with a floral shower cap perched atop her head, stood Mrs Howard. Her gaze moved from one girl to the next until it came to rest on Jacinta.

'Jacinta Headlington-Bear, was this *your* idea?'

Jacinta gulped, looked up and nodded slowly.

'Well, tomorrow we'll talk about what you can do to make it up to me. I was about to hop into the bath when I heard such a racket that would wake the dead. I've run all the way from the flat upstairs thinking there was a prowler or the like. And it's just you and your silly "midnight meetings" at nine o'clock. Off to bed, girls, NOW!'

The party began to break up. No one dared to say a word, except Alice-Miranda.

'Mrs Howard, please don't blame Jacinta. No

one made us come and apparently it's a bit of a tradition to have a meeting on the first night back. Well, except last term, but that doesn't matter. Please don't be cross. I promise we will make it up to you tomorrow. What about we bring you something extra special for your tea? I can ask Mrs Smith if she can make your favourite. It's apple cinnamon bun, isn't it? Is that what you'd like?'

Howie did her best to maintain her furrowed brow, but in the end could barely restrain the smile that was spreading across her face.

'Oh, dear girl, wherever did you come from?' She shook her head. 'Now, off to bed quickly. And no more of this, all right?'

The girls nodded in unison and scampered off to their rooms.

Within a very short time, all that could be heard was the sound of Jacinta's snoring, competing with some rather loud snorts from the flat upstairs.

Chapter 4

Alice-Miranda was awake long before Mrs Howard's clanging bell roused the rest of the house. She was sitting up in bed reading when Millie yawned and rolled over.

'Good morning,' Alice-Miranda greeted her friend.

Millie sat up and rubbed her eyes. 'I wish it was still holidays,' she grumbled.

'Oh, I don't,' Alice-Miranda replied. 'I mean, I love being at home but there are so many things going on here and I can hardly wait to hear about Miss Grimm's plans for the term.'

Millie shook her head. 'One day, Alice-Miranda, when you're as old as me, you'll be completely *over school.*'

Alice-Miranda giggled. 'I can't imagine what it's like to be as ancient as ten. But I don't think I'll ever be over school. I simply love it – and I know you're only teasing me because secretly you love it too.'

'Well, just don't tell anyone,' Millie smiled, 'or you'll ruin my reputation.'

At the opposite end of the corridor, Mrs Howard's shrill morning call began. 'Rise and shine, girls, rise and shine. Time to get up, time to sparkle. Chop, chop, choppy chop.' Her chorus continued along the hallway, punctuated with loud bursts of bell ringing. She stopped outside the girls' door and knocked firmly before entering.

'Good morning, ladies. I trust you slept well after your *late night.*' Mrs Howard placed her bell on Alice-Miranda's desk and set forth retrieving uniforms from the wardrobe.

'Good morning,' they replied in unison before Millie yawned loudly.

'Run along now to your showers, you don't want to be late for breakfast,' Mrs Howard instructed.

'No, that's for sure.' Alice-Miranda threw back the covers, leapt out of bed and gathered up her toothbrush and towel. 'Mrs Smith's making creamy scrambled eggs with crispy bacon this morning as a welcome back treat. And I'll ask her for something extra special for your tea this afternoon, Mrs Howard, to make up for last night.'

Mrs Howard shook her head, picked up her bell and followed the pair into the hall. 'Off you go now,' she smiled.

The dining room was abuzz with chatter as the students caught up on all the happenings of the holidays. Clattering cutlery was momentarily stilled when Miss Grimm arrived to take up her seat at the head table alongside Miss Reedy and Mr Plumpton. Although things had changed remarkably in the past term, the girls were still only getting used to seeing their headmistress on a daily basis. This morning, dressed in a stylish pale pink suit and with her hair pulled back into a low ponytail, Miss Grimm looked much younger than her thirty-seven years. On the way through the dining room, she greeted the students and grinned broadly.

'So what do you think Miss Grimm has in store for us this term?' Jacinta asked as she loaded her fork with another mouthful of scrambled eggs.

'I hope it's something fun, like a trip away, or maybe a school fair or a carnival,' Millie replied. 'We've never had anything like that since I've been here.'

'Maybe it's a gymkhana. Miss Grimm seemed keen for girls to bring their ponies back to school this term,' said Alice-Miranda.

Jacinta pulled a face. 'Oh, I hope not. You know I can't stand horses. That wouldn't be any fun at all.'

'Well, we've got assembly this morning so maybe she's going to tell us then,' said Millie.

Alice-Miranda changed the subject. 'Has Sloane arrived yet?'

Jacinta stared blankly. 'Who?'

'Your new room mate. Sloane Sykes?'

'Oh, no. There was no sign of her before I left the house.' Jacinta frowned. 'She'd better be nice.'

'I'm sure she will be,' Alice-Miranda assured her friend.

'But what if I don't like her?' Jacinta pushed a stringy piece of bacon around her plate.

'Of course you'll like her,' Alice-Miranda said.

'I'm not like you, Alice-Miranda. I just can't *like* everyone. It's not in my nature. And maybe I'm not always the easiest person to get on with either,' Jacinta admitted.

'Come on, Jacinta – I haven't seen you throw a tantrum in, what, at least a month now?' Millie suppressed a giggle.

'Millie,' Alice-Miranda chided.

'I have been trying hard to be better.' Jacinta looked serious. 'I thought I was pretty well behaved in the holidays, wasn't I?'

'Of course you were. Stop worrying, Jacinta,' Alice-Miranda soothed. 'I'm sure Sloane's lovely and I'm positive you'll be great friends in no time.'

But Jacinta was not yet convinced. 'You'd better be right.'

The girls finished breakfast, cleared their plates and charged outside into the crisp morning air. Charles Weatherly, the school's head gardener, was tending to the newly planted roses in the quadrangle.

'Hello Mr Charles.' Alice-Miranda ran and gave him an unexpected hug.

'Well, hello to you too, my girl.' Charlie's cornflower-blue eyes twinkled. 'It's been rather quiet around here these past two weeks.'

'I can see you've been busy. The garden looks lovely,' Alice-Miranda replied. 'Mr Greening sends his regards.'

Charlie nodded. 'He's a good fellow. I'd best be off, lass. Mrs Derby's after some roses for Miss Grimm's study. These are just about perfect.'

'Yes, they're lovely.' Alice-Miranda nodded at the bunch of iceberg blooms in Charlie's hand. Just at that moment she remembered that she had promised to organise that special treat for Mrs Howard's afternoon tea. Alice-Miranda ran back to Millie and Jacinta and informed them that she was going to see Mrs Smith before the bell.

'Oh, drats,' Millie scowled. 'I've left my pencil case back at the house. I've got English first up after assembly so I'd better go and get it.'

'I'll come with you,' said Jacinta. 'Anyway, I want to see if my room mate has arrived.'

'See you later then.' Alice-Miranda waved goodbye to her friends and strode across the quadrangle to the kitchen door.

'Hello Mrs Smith!' Alice-Miranda called as she entered the room. In the cavernous space with its rows of stainless steel benches, Mrs Smith was checking through the luncheon menu. She promptly put the paper down and turned with outstretched arms to give her tiny visitor a warm hug.

'Hello there, young lady. How are you this fine morning?'

'Very well,' Alice-Miranda nodded. 'Thank you for breakfast. It was delicious.'

'My pleasure, dear,' Mrs Smith replied. 'Now, to what do I owe this early visit?'

'I'm on a special mission.' Alice-Miranda climbed up onto the kitchen stool to sit opposite the cook.

'Oh dear – should I be worried?' Mrs Smith frowned. 'It doesn't involve any spontaneous trips does it, this plan of yours?'

'No, not at all. It's just that last night the girls on our corridor had a midnight meeting . . .'

'Midnight! My dear girl you'll be asleep in your arithmetic,' Mrs Smith scowled.

'Well, except that it wasn't midnight at all. It was only nine o'clock and it's a first night tradition, but then Madeline decided that she would tell us a story about a witch in the woods and the girls got a bit scared, and then a branch scraped against the window and everyone squealed, and Mrs Howard came running and she was a bit cross, especially with Jacinta, but I asked her not to be because it was all our faults, and then I said that I would ask if you could fix something special for her afternoon tea,' Alice-Miranda babbled.

'Slow down, young lady.' Mrs Smith shook her head. 'So you've come to see if I might make her an apple cinnamon bun?'

'However did you know?' Alice-Miranda asked.

'My dear, everyone knows that's Howie's favourite. And it just so happens . . .' Mrs Smith stood up and walked to the other side of the kitchen, returning with a tea-towel covered tray. 'Ta-da!' She pulled the cloth away to reveal the most magnificent apple cinnamon bun Alice-Miranda had ever seen.

'Perfect.' Alice-Miranda grinned and clapped her hands together.

'Now, what was that you were saying about a witch in the woods?' Mrs Smith asked.

'Just a silly story, that's all,' Alice-Miranda replied. 'There's no such thing as witches.'

'No, of course not.' Mrs Smith shook her head. She knew Alice-Miranda was right but Doreen Smith had heard the same story – about a witch in the woods – before. And although she knew better, she wasn't entirely convinced that there wasn't a grain of truth in there somewhere.

'All right, young lady. Housemistress pacification seems to be taken care of so you'd better be off to class,' Mrs Smith instructed.

'Thanks, Mrs Smith – you're the best!' Alice-Miranda hopped down off her stool and scampered out into the sunshine.

Chapter 5

Meanwhile, Millie and Jacinta had made their way back to Grimthorpe House, where Millie quickly retrieved her missing pencil case.

As they walked down the hallway, a shrill voice coming from inside Jacinta's room caught their attention.

'Look, Sloane, look at this. Isn't that Ambrosia Headlington-Bear? She must be your room mate's mother. Imagine always being in magazines and newspapers. She's like royalty. You'd better make friends with her daughter – you never know what you might get us all invited to.'

Millie and Jacinta stood outside. Millie pressed her ear up against the door while Jacinta leaned down to peer through the keyhole.

'Ooh, and make sure you introduce her to your brother as soon as you can. They might get married.'

Jacinta's eyes almost popped out of her head. 'Married! What are they talking about?'

'And look at this, Mummy,' a young voice added. 'All those beautiful dresses and we're the same size. I'm sure she won't notice if one or two go missing.'

'What are they doing in there?' Millie whispered, straining to hear.

'Planning a wedding and raiding my wardrobe, by the sound of it.' Jacinta's face was getting redder by the second. 'Right, that's it.'

Jacinta flung open the door, ready to pounce. Millie almost fell over and just managed to steady herself. Sloane and her mother spun around.

'What are you doing?' Jacinta demanded. 'Are you looking through my things?'

Sloane slammed the wardrobe door shut and kicked a dress under the nearest bed.

'No, of course not,' the young girl replied. 'I'm just moving in.'

'You must be Sloane Sykes.' Millie marched forward to stand beside Jacinta.

'Yes, and you are?' the girl asked, arching her eyebrows.

'I'm Millie and this is Jacinta. She's your room mate – the one whose things you were just ferreting through.'

'Ahem.' The woman cleared her throat.

'And you must be Mrs Sykes.' Millie's lips drew tightly together in a straight line.

'Yes, but you can call me September,' the woman replied, crossing her arms over her ample chest and striking what seemed to be a modelling pose.

'Did Mrs Howard let you in here?' Jacinta asked.

'Yes, she told us to make ourselves at home and so we were just unpacking, weren't we, darling.' Mrs Sykes pointed at the suitcase still lying closed on the bed.

'Yes, Mummy.' Sloane smiled at her mother like a piranha in a goldfish bowl.

September Sykes wore skyscraping gold heels and a metallic blue dress so tight and short she must have been vacuum-packed into it. Her waist-length platinum hair bounced in loose curls and her make-up appeared to have been applied with the aid of a cake decorator's spatula.

Sloane Sykes, in a crisp new uniform, was shorter, thinner and wore only slightly less make-up which, on an eleven-year-old, was more than a little disturbing.

'And what's *your* surname, Millie?' September smiled, revealing a set of dazzlingly white teeth.

'McLoughlin-McTavish-McNoughton-McGill,' Millie replied.

'Oooh, that sounds important,' September cooed.

'No, not at all,' Millie frowned.

Mrs Howard appeared in the doorway, with Mrs Derby, the headmistress's secretary, in tow.

'Millicent and Jacinta, what are you doing back here? You know you're not allowed to return to the house after breakfast,' Mrs Howard chided.

'Sorry, Howie,' Millie apologised. 'I forgot my pencil case.'

'And it was just as well we came back, seeing as you've left these two in here alone going through my things,' Jacinta snarled.

'Jacinta Headlington-Bear, mind your manners. That's no way to treat your new room mate.' Mrs Howard spun around to face Sloane and her mother, and then turned back to the girls.

'But it's true,' Millie nodded.

Mrs Howard's eyes widened in disbelief. 'You two can apologise, please. NOW!'

Millie and Jacinta scowled. With heads bent towards the floor they both muttered a half-hearted 'sorry'.

'That's not like you at all, Millicent. You, on the other hand, Jacinta – well, I hope we're not heading back to the bad old days,' Mrs Howard tutted. 'I'm sure the girls will make it up to you, Sloane.'

'Don't fuss, Mrs Howard,' September grinned. 'Jacinta and Sloane are bound to become best friends. Or rather, BFFs – isn't that what you girls call them these days?'

Jacinta rolled her eyes.

'Yes, well, her manners had better improve by this afternoon. Now, off you go, you two. Lessons are about to start and you don't want to be late on your first day. Mrs Derby will bring Sloane over in a little while, once she's had a chance to get properly settled.' Mrs Howard's forehead wrinkled like pintucking on a blouse and she gave Millie and Jacinta one of her best ever death stares.

The girls marched off. Not a word was spoken until they reached the safety of the veranda.

'What was that?' Jacinta demanded. 'Who is that woman? And that girl – I've never seen anyone her age with make-up like that!'

'Don't worry, Jacinta.' Millie put her hand on her friend's shoulder. 'I wouldn't want to be in her shoes when Miss Grimm and Miss Reedy spot her. She'll be wiping that mascara off in no time.'

'But she's awful, and I don't see why I have to be in the same room as her.' A fat tear wobbled in the corner of Jacinta's eye.

'It's all right,' Millie replied. 'She's probably just nervous about being at boarding school.'

Millie couldn't believe their bad luck. Alethea Goldsworthy had left big shoes to fill when it came to being the school bully. But if the few moments that Millie had spent with her were anything to go by, Sloane Sykes, it seemed, had very big feet.

Chapter 6

The whole school was seated in the Great Hall for the first assembly of the term. Millie and Jacinta sped into their seats a moment before the staff processional began, with Miss Grimm at the head of the line. She glided down the aisle, a gratified smile on her face as she led the other teachers behind her.

Mr Trout's organ accompaniment of the school song rose and fell with the fervour of a crashing symphony. But his improvised flourishes at the end of each verse seemed to cause Miss Grimm's mouth to twitch and her grin to disappear.

Ophelia reached the microphone. 'Thank you, Mr Trout, for your rather, mmm, how to put it, *extravagant* recital. Perhaps you'd like to talk to me about that later?' She looked up at him in the organ gallery, arched her left eyebrow, then turned back to face the students. 'Good morning, everyone.'

'Good morning, Miss Grimm,' the students chorused.

'I'd like to welcome you all back for a new term and a very exciting one at that. There are some birthday announcements from Miss Reedy and then I'll tell you about a wonderful project we'll be working on over the coming weeks.'

Ophelia Grimm sat down and Miss Reedy read the names of girls who'd had birthdays over the term break. They were invited to come up on stage and receive a garland of flowers hand-picked from the garden, which was placed ceremoniously on each head by Miss Grimm. This was followed by a rousing rendition of 'Happy Birthday'. Ashima and Susannah were joined on stage by the sports teacher, Miss Wall. Her buttercup-yellow wreath clashed horribly with her cerise-and-blue velvet tracksuit, but she seemed to enjoy the attention all the same. The birthday wreaths had been a long-held school tradition until Miss Grimm had banned the practice along with flowers in general. But things were different now at Winchesterfield-Downsfordvale and happily both the flowers and wreaths were back.

With the celebrations over, Miss Grimm again took to the microphone. 'Girls, Miss Reedy has been very busy over the break. She's met with Mr Harold Lipp, the head of English at Fayle School for Boys on the other side of the village. We've decided that it would be timely for us to join forces for a drama production. I do hope you'll take up this opportunity and I particularly look forward to the splendid play we'll all be able to enjoy towards the end of term. Miss Reedy has the details about auditions and the like and will also explain exactly what you'll be performing.'

A ripple of excitement reverberated around the hall. 'That's so exciting . . . my mummy told me they used to do plays with the Fayle boys when she was here . . . I hope I get a part . . . what fun . . . I wonder what play it is?'

Alice-Miranda leaned forward and tapped Jacinta's shoulder. 'You know, I think Lawrence is trying to get Lucas a place at Fayle at the moment.'

Jacinta swivelled her head and smiled at her friend. 'Well, we have to get parts in that play – then we'll be able to see him more than just at the weekends. If he gets to come, of course.'

Lucas Nixon had caused quite a fuss when Alice-Miranda and Jacinta first encountered him. Sent to live with his Aunt Lily and Uncle Heinrich, who managed the farm at Alice-Miranda's home, Highton Hall, he seemed to spend most of his time lashing out at everyone around him. But a lot of things had changed very quickly over the holidays: Lucas's absent father turned out to be none other than the famous movie star Lawrence Ridley, who became engaged to Alice-Miranda's beloved Aunt Charlotte. Jacinta and Lucas couldn't stand one another to begin with but, after a couple of weeks, they realised they had much more in common than they could ever have imagined. Jacinta thought it would be wonderful to see him again.

Miss Reedy stood up and walked to the microphone. 'Girls, the play we'll be performing is *Snow White and the Seven Dwarfs*. There are plenty of roles and I'm looking forward to seeing lots of girls try out. Of course, girls can try for boys' roles and vice versa. It should be loads of fun.'

Miss Reedy announced that there would be more details about the play up on the noticeboard before the end of the week. Just as she was explaining that if girls were interested in auditioning for parts, they needed to pick up copies of the script from her office that afternoon, a small commotion erupted at the back of the hall. 'Ohhhh, did you hear that darling? A play! How wonderful.'

From her position in the rear seats, Alice-Miranda turned to see what was going on. A tall woman with long blonde curls was pointing at the stage and talking rather loudly to a young girl standing beside her who looked remarkably similar.

'Excuse me, can I help you?' Miss Reedy glanced up from her notes and peered over the top of the spectacles perched on the end of her nose.

'Look, Sloane, look at the headmistress and the teachers up there. Oh, they're so cute – like in *Harry Potter* or something,' the woman giggled. The child ignored her, instead splaying the fingers of her left hand and admiring her scarlet nail polish.

With her perfect view of the hall, Miss Grimm had also become aware of the new arrivals. Endeavouring to make them feel welcome, Ophelia decided to introduce the pair to the whole school.

'It's all right, Miss Reedy.' Miss Grimm motioned for the English teacher to take her seat, then moved towards the microphone. 'Girls and staff, you may have noticed we have some guests. Not guests, in fact, but new members of the Winchesterfield-Downsfordvale family. Please welcome Mrs Sykes and her daughter Sloane.'

One hundred pairs of eyes swivelled from Miss Grimm back to the newcomers.

'Hello everyone. Call me September – Mrs Sykes sounds so old and, well, I'm not old, am I? This is my daughter, Sloane. She's lovely, isn't she?' September wrapped her arm around the girl's shoulder. 'We can't wait to meet you all, can we, Sloane? And Sloane's very clever and a fantastic actress. I just heard you saying something about doing a play? Sloane's had acting lessons since she was two and she's the best dancer ever. So, of course, she should be top of the list for the lead role.'

Sloane looked up and smirked.

'Yuck, she's even more revolting than I first thought.' Millie buried her head in her hands.

'Yes and she's my room mate,' Jacinta whispered.

'No, not Sloane,' Millie replied. 'I meant her mother.'

40

'Oh,' Jacinta grimaced.

Miss Grimm's welcome was losing its gloss as September continued to babble.

'Would you like to take your seat, Sloane?' Miss Grimm pointed towards the front of the hall, near the older students. 'And please see me after the assembly as we'll need to have a chat about your . . . face.'

'What about my face?' Sloane asked, to no one in particular.

'Make-up,' Ashima whispered as Sloane took her seat. 'We're not allowed.'

Sloane rolled her eyes. 'Pathetic.'

'And Mrs Sykes, if you'd like to stay for the remainder of the assembly you're welcome to sit in the row there just next to you.'

September tottered towards the pew, caught her foot on an uneven flagstone and almost fell into Alice-Miranda's lap.

Alice-Miranda caught hold of Mrs Sykes's arm.

'Ow!' September grimaced. 'That hurt.'

'I am sorry. I was just trying to help.'

'Well, don't bother next time.' September Sykes glared at Alice-Miranda, then smoothed her dress and sat bolt upright in her seat. How she could breathe was anyone's guess.

Alice-Miranda turned towards her and smiled. 'Hello, my name's Alice-Miranda Highton-Smith-Kennington-Jones,' she whispered and held out her tiny hand. 'And I'm very pleased to meet you.'

September Sykes's ears pricked up. 'Did you say Highton-Smith-Kennington-Jones?'

'Yes,' Alice-Miranda nodded. 'Do you know my mummy and daddy?'

'Well, sort of, but I'd looove to get to know them better,' September simpered, her pearl-white smile widening. She took Alice-Miranda's dainty hand in hers. 'It's very nice to meet you too.'

September Sykes could not believe her luck. Today was turning out even better than she had hoped.

Chapter 7

The arrival of Sloane and September Sykes caused quite a stir among the girls and staff. At the conclusion of the assembly, Mrs Sykes seemed very eager to speak with Sloane's teachers and joined the staff as they left the hall. As she bumped in beside Mr Plumpton, his red nose took on an even brighter glow, particularly when Mrs Sykes linked her arm through his. Miss Reedy glowered and bit her lip. She wasn't used to such ostentatious displays.

September Sykes didn't notice Miss Reedy's

glares. She was too busy loudly describing her glorious modelling career and explaining that Sloane's father regularly appeared on television, although in what capacity she didn't reveal. Mr Plumpton coughed awkwardly as September leaned in and whispered that, thanks to her step-mother-in-law making provisions for the children's education, Sloane and her older brother Septimus were finally exactly where they belonged, at Winchesterfield-Downsfordvale Academy for Proper Young Ladies and Fayle School for Boys.

With a flutter of her lashes, September released Mr Plumpton's arm and trotted after Miss Grimm 'for a little chat'. She was convinced that this was only the start of much bigger things for the Sykes family. In her mind, they'd struggled quite long enough and it was about time she had everything she wanted, including that oversized Prada handbag she'd seen on Ambrosia Headlington-Bear's arm in a magazine photograph. Now that she and her children were mixing in the right circles, she was sure life was about to become a whole lot more interesting.

As for the students of Winchesterfield-Downs-fordvale, the girls had hurried off to their first lessons aflame with curiosity about the new girl and her remarkable mother. Amid much chatter and speculation, they seemed to have quite a deal of trouble concentrating on their morning classes.

At half past ten, Alice-Miranda was on her way to meet Millie in the dining room for morning tea when she saw Sloane standing on her own near the entrance to the library.

'Are you lost?' Alice-Miranda smiled. 'You're Sloane, aren't you? My name's Alice-Miranda Highton-Smith-Kennington-Jones and I'm very pleased to meet you.' She offered her tiny hand.

Sloane looked down at her and glared. 'No, I'm not lost. I'm just waiting for, what's her name, Dinka or something.'

'Oh, you mean Danika. She's the Head Prefect. I suppose Miss Grimm has asked her to show you around. Are you having a good day?' Alice-Miranda continued, 'I just love school. And wait until you see what Mrs Smith has made for our morning tea.'

Sloane stared at Alice-Miranda as if she had been promised a roast pork dinner but was served pickled pigs' trotters instead.

Finally she spoke. 'Are you always like this?'

'Like what?' Alice-Miranda's eyes widened.

'So . . . happy and bouncy and *enthusiastic*.' Sloane's monotone voice could barely hide her distaste.

'Oh, yes. I can't imagine a reason not to be happy and bouncy and enthusiastic. Winchester-field-Downsfordvale is simply the most splendid school ever and our teachers are lovely and so clever and Miss Grimm, well, she's the best headmistress in the whole world.'

Sloane slowly shook her head. 'Good grief!' she muttered under her breath. 'And my mother expects me to be friends with someone like you.'

'Oh, yes, I'm sure we'll be friends too.' Alice-Miranda smiled.

'You can go now.' Sloane flicked her hand. 'I'm fine and you don't want to be late for your tea.'

'Oh, all right, I think Danika's coming now anyway.' Alice-Miranda looked over Sloane's left shoulder. 'See you in a minute.'

The younger girl waved, and then skipped off in the direction of the dining room. As soon as Alice-Miranda's back was turned, the older girl's tongue shot out like a lizard's. Unlike her mother, Sloane Sykes was not the least bit impressed by her new surroundings or the people who inhabited them.

Chapter 8

'Yum, is that strawberry sponge?' Alice-Miranda licked her lips as she slid into her seat beside Millie in the dining room.

'Sure is.' Millie pushed a plate of the sticky confection towards her friend.

'I've just had a lovely chat with Sloane,' Alice-Miranda announced.

'I can't imagine how,' Jacinta glowered. 'You didn't see what she and her mother were doing when we went back to the house before.'

'What were they doing?' Alice-Miranda quizzed.

'Going through Jacinta's things,' said Millie. 'And getting awfully wound up about Jacinta's mother, for some strange reason.'

'Oh.' Alice-Miranda rested her fork against the side of her plate. 'Well, I'm sure they were just excited about being at school. It's such a great adventure being a boarder.'

Millie agreed. 'That's what I said, but I have to admit that I have a bad feeling about those two. I think Sloane's trouble with a capital T and her mother is even worse.'

Alice-Miranda frowned. 'I'm sure they'll be fine. Sometimes it just takes a little while to settle into somewhere new.'

Jacinta and Millie smiled at their little friend and shook their heads. She could always be relied upon to think the best of everyone.

The bell rang to signify the end of morning tea and Alice-Miranda, Millie and Jacinta took their dirty plates and cups to the sideboard.

'Are you going to try out for the play?' Alice-Miranda asked the girls.

'Yes, of course,' said Millie.

Jacinta nodded. 'I wonder if one of the dwarfs could be a gymnast? And what about you Alice-Miranda? Will you audition?'

'I think so – I'm going to get a script from Miss Reedy after school. I can get copies for both of you as well.'

The girls parted company, heading off to their various lessons. Alice-Miranda and Millie decided they would take a walk to the stables at lunchtime to see how Alice-Miranda's pony, Bonaparte, was getting on. Jacinta tried not to wrinkle her nose and said she planned to do some gymnastics training instead.

Alice-Miranda had been thrilled that her parents agreed to let Bony come back to school with her. After all, she had settled in so well and there was no doubt Bonaparte could do with being ridden more often. Hopefully his new surroundings would keep the little monster out of trouble. At least while he was at school he would stay out of Mr Greening's prized vegetable patch at Highton Hall.

There was only an hour of class time before lunch. Alice-Miranda had her favourite English class with Miss Reedy while Millie was at PE and Jacinta had Mathematics. Just after 1 pm, Alice-Miranda and

Millie met at the dining room where they collected some sandwiches to take with them to the stables.

They bounded off across the oval and down the lane, chatting between bites of lunch.

'Hello there Bonaparte,' Alice-Miranda called, as she and Millie entered the cool brick stable block.

A loud whinny pierced the air as Bonaparte spun around and thrust his head over the half door of the stable.

'Are you starving again, you poor man?' Millie fetched a loose carrot from the feed room and held it out to him. 'Steady on there, greedy guts,' she scolded, as Bonaparte almost inhaled her hand along with the carrot.

Alice-Miranda picked up a brush, opened the stall door and walked inside. She began giving the pony a quick rub down. A young lad pushing a wheelbarrow full of straw entered the building and plodded towards them.

'Hello miss.' The boy put the barrow down and addressed Millie. 'Is he yours?' He motioned at Bonaparte's stable, where Alice-Miranda was hidden from view.

'No,' Millie replied. 'Definitely not.'

Alice-Miranda scrambled onto the stall door, her

feet dangling in the air as she hoisted herself up with her arms. 'He's mine.'

'Goodness, miss, you do surprise me,' the boy replied.

'Why is that?' Alice-Miranda asked.

'Well, he's a bit of a monster, that one – you take care in there.'

'Oh dear, have you been a bad boy already, Bonaparte? I'm sorry if he's given you any trouble. He's really very sweet but he seems to be a bit set against young lads. Our poor Max at home cops it all the time. Just be firm, that's the trick.' Alice-Miranda slid down the door. She emerged from the stable and brushed Bonaparte's grey fuzz from her uniform.

'Hello,' she said, holding her hand out to the young man. 'My name is Alice-Miranda Highton-Smith-Kennington-Jones, and I'm very pleased to meet you, Mr . . .'

'It's Wally, Wally Whitstable.' The boy reached out slowly and shook her hand.

'And this is Millie,' said Alice-Miranda. Millie reached forward and shook his hand too.

'Are you new here, Wally?' Millie asked. She noticed he had the most brilliant emerald-green eyes and a shock of red hair to rival her own.

'Yup, Charlie put me on last week – said that there were lots of ponies coming for the term and he needed some help. I like horses, I really do. I'm hoping to be a strapper if I can. I don't imagine race-horses could be any more difficult than that bloke.' Wally motioned his head towards Bonaparte.

'That sounds like fun,' Alice-Miranda smiled. 'And I am sorry about Bony. I hope in time you might learn to like him a little bit. He's really quite lovable when you get to know him.'

'Do you have a pony, miss?' Wally asked Millie.

'Yes, his name's Chudley Chops.' Millie shook her head and rolled her eyes. 'I know, like the dog food. Everyone thought it was a very funny joke when I decided to call him Chudley and then Dad added Chops because he thought it was hilarious. Anyway, we just call him Chops for short and he's arriving very early on Saturday morning.'

'Well, I'll be pleased to make the acquaintance of old Chudley Chops. Now, I'd best get off and finish mucking out, and I think by my watch it must be time for your afternoon lessons.' Wally excused himself.

Alice-Miranda nodded. 'We'll see you soon, Wally. And you behave yourself, Bonaparte. Stay out of trouble.'

Bonaparte whinnied loudly in reply and shook his head up and down as if to agree.

'So, you will be a good boy,' Alice-Miranda laughed.

'Yes and I'll believe that when I see it,' Millie grabbed her friend's hand and they charged off to class.

Chapter 9

The rest of the week passed by in a blur. Classes were busy and most of the girls spent any spare time learning lines in preparation for the upcoming auditions. Alice-Miranda, Jacinta and Millie were each trying out for several different parts, but Sloane informed them that there was only one decent role in the whole thing and there was no doubt it would be hers.

Sloane didn't seem especially keen to make friends with anyone, in spite of her mother's insistence that she and Jacinta would become BFFs. Her attempts at conversation usually involved questions about what the girls' parents did and where they lived and if they had a holiday house or a yacht. Alice-Miranda said that Sloane was probably just nervous and not good at making chitchat, but Millie thought she was a bit on the nosy side.

Jacinta and Sloane had come to an uneasy truce. With no further evidence of Sloane meddling with her things, Jacinta decided she would give her a chance. But it wasn't always easy, especially when she overheard Sloane talking to her mother on the telephone and the whole topic of conversation seemed to be her own mother and what she was reportedly up to that week.

At Friday's afternoon tea, which consisted of the most delicious apple pie, Millie asked around to see who would like to go out on a riding party on Saturday.

'Count me in,' Alice-Miranda nodded.

'Me too,' Susannah agreed.

'Urgh, me not.' Jacinta pulled a face. 'I've got training and you know how I feel about horses – I'd rather file my nails.'

The other girls laughed.

'What about you, Sloane? Would you like to come riding?' Alice-Miranda asked.

'Um, yes, of course, but my new horse, Harry, hasn't arrived yet. He should have been here but Mummy messed up the transport,' she sulked.

'That's all right. I think there are a couple of spare ponies that Mr Charles is looking after for someone in the village. I'll ask him if you can ride one of those,' Alice-Miranda offered.

Sloane hesitated. 'Oh, okay.'

'They're pussycats, believe me,' said Alice-Miranda. 'I rode a gorgeous fellow called Stumps last term because Bonaparte was still at home. He's the sweetest little man.'

'A *little* pony? I don't think he'll be good enough for me.' Sloane seemed to have regained her confidence.

'Oh, he might be small, but he's fast, especially going uphill,' Alice-Miranda smiled.

Sloane gulped. 'Well, it's just that I'm used to having a really big proper horse, not some dinky pony. I'm just not sure . . .'

'Oh, come on, Sloane – if you can handle proper horses, I'm sure you'll have no problems with old Stumps,' Millie grinned.

And so it was all arranged. Alice-Miranda and Millie marched off to find Mr Charles and tell him of their plans. A quick visit to Mrs Smith ensured there would be a picnic feast fit for a king. She insisted that they should have egg sandwiches and tea and scones with jam and cream. The group would ride as far as Gertrude's Grove where Wally would deliver their spread in time for lunch.

Chapter 10

Just before 10 am on Saturday, Sloane Sykes asked her room mate if she had a spare pair of riding breeches she could borrow. And a shirt and helmet and gloves, if possible, as hers were still at home, along with the elusive new horse that was due to arrive any day now. Although Jacinta hated riding, her mother had insisted that she have a complete outfit, just in case she changed her mind. This time Jacinta found herself handing over her belongings quite happily.

'You know, if you don't like to ride, you should just say so,' Jacinta offered.

'It's not that at all.' Sloane stood admiring her reflection in the long mirror behind their bedroom door. Certainly the outfit suited her.

'Well, there's no shame in saying what you really think,' Jacinta tried again.

'I *love* riding and I'm *very good* at it,' Sloane said, almost too emphatically.

'Okay then, have a good time.' Jacinta pulled on her tracksuit pants and sat down to lace up her shoes. 'I'll see you after training.'

Sloane was halfway out the door when she turned back. 'Does your mother come and take you out at the weekends?'

Jacinta looked up and frowned. 'You're kidding, aren't you? I think *your mother* knows more about where my mother is from week to week. I haven't seen her since Christmas.'

'Oh,' Sloane mouthed. 'So I guess I won't be able to meet her anytime soon. My mother was hoping they could have tea together when she comes to collect me for mid-term.'

'Well, unless every last one of my mother's friends suddenly wind up in hospital or worse, I can pretty much guarantee that I'll be staying here for mid-term, so tell your mother that if she had hoped to meet the oh-so-famous Ambrosia Headlington-Bear, she's going to be sorely disappointed.'

Jacinta picked up her gym bag and pushed past Sloane. She was very glad she wasn't going riding. Horses weren't the only thing she found irritating.

Sloane was beginning to wonder what the point of being at boarding school really was. So far, she hadn't met anyone remotely famous and her room mate's mother was turning out to be a huge disappointment. As for being invited away on holidays, she hadn't any prospects yet. School was okay – the lessons were quite good and the teachers seemed to know their stuff, but what use was it if you didn't get to meet the right people?

Her mother promised that boarding school would change her life. In fact, both Sloane's parents had been thrilled when her step-granny Henrietta had arranged for her and her brother to go to boarding school. The old woman didn't have any children of her own, so when she married Sloane's grandfather, Percy Sykes, rather late in life, she inherited Sloane and Septimus as grandchildren. When Percy died last year and left Sloane's parents his grocery shop with the flat above, they sold the lot quick smart, even though Henrietta was supposed to be able to live there for as long as it suited her. In September's opinion, Henrietta was both ancient and dotty, so she convinced her husband that the elderly lady would be better served in an aged person's home. It hadn't been too hard for them to shuffle her off to a place called Golden Gates. The nurses told September and Smedley that Henrietta kept asking to see her family. But Henrietta didn't have any other relatives, so clearly, thought September, the old woman *was* losing her mind!

Sloane had started to wonder if her mother thought she was an inconvenience too, just like Granny Henrietta. She glanced at her watch and went to telephone her mother. September insisted that she call home every day for an update.

'Hello Mummy.' Sloane sounded less than excited.

'Well, how are you getting on then? Where have you been invited to?' her mother asked.

'Nowhere. It's completely dull here and I want to come home,' Sloane nagged. 'The girls are all so boring and they don't do anything fun. Jacinta told me her mother won't even be coming to get her at mid-term.'

'Well,' said September, changing tack, 'try some-one else then. You know the little one's parents are completely loaded. I think you'll find they're richer than the Queen – and most likely related.'

'Good grief, no. She's the most painful Pollyanna I've ever met. She smiles *all* the time and she's happy *all* the time and she never complains about anything, not ever. It's just not normal,' Sloane grouched. 'And when are you sending my horse? I'm going riding today and I have to borrow this horrid little pony – and I had to sponge Jacinta's riding gear as well. If you want me to fit in here, I can't be borrowing things all the time.'

'Sloane, you know we can't afford a horse,' her mother whispered. 'What with your grandfather only leaving us such a dreadful, cheap little shop and flat. But don't worry; your father's new business is going to be a licence to print money. It won't be long until we can buy you everything you could possibly want. But for now, you know there's no harm in borrow-ing. If the girls offer, it would be rude not to.'

Sloane hung up the phone. In her opinion, life simply wasn't fair.

Chapter 11

Millie, Alice-Miranda and Susannah were already in the stables when Sloane appeared. She looked the part in her borrowed gear and the girls all commented on her beautiful riding jacket. Sloane didn't tell them it was actually Jacinta's – she couldn't see the point.

Wally Whitstable had been busy helping the girls saddle their mounts. Bonaparte was now standing beside Chops, flicking the older pony with his tail. They'd already had a mighty squabble that ended with Bonaparte giving Chops a nasty nip on the neck.

'He seems to be in a bit of a mood, miss.' Wally gave Bonaparte a friendly pat on the backside and was nearly kicked for his trouble.

'I don't know what's gotten into him.' Alice-Miranda shook her head. She looked her pony in the eye. 'Bonaparte Napoleon Highton-Smith-Kennington-Jones, you stop that behaviour at once or there will be no treats and no ride.'

At the mention of treats, Bony whinnied loudly.

'No, I said, *no treats* – you need to understand the difference,' Alice-Miranda tutted.

'Hurry up, Sloane,' Millie directed. 'That's Stumps in there. You'll need to put his bridle on.'

Sloane entered the stall. Stumps was already saddled with his lead rope tied loosely to a hook on the wall. There was a bridle hanging on the back of the stall door. Sloane grabbed it and tried to work out what went where.

'Okay, let's put this on,' she muttered under her breath. Sloane approached the pony and began to force the bridle over his head. Unfortunately she hadn't yet undone the straps and it was proving more than a little difficult.

Wally had just finished helping Susannah with her pony Buttercup, when he spotted Sloane.

'Would you like some help there, miss?' he asked.

'Yes, you should have done it already.' Sloane let go of the bridle and it fell to the ground. 'I haven't got time to be fussing around with that silly thing.'

'Well, if you want to go riding then I think *that silly thing* is rather important.' Wally retrieved the bridle from the floor and undid the throat lash. 'Would you like to give me a hand?'

'No, not especially. Isn't that what *you* get paid for?' Sloane sneered at the lad.

Alice-Miranda walked over to Stumps's stable. 'If you're nervous, Sloane, that's perfectly all right. My daddy says that it's good to be wary around horses no matter how well you know them. Bonaparte always keeps me on my toes.'

'I'm not nervous. Don't be ridiculous. It's just that stupid silver thing – it's not the same as the one I have at home.' Sloane pouted.

Millie and Susannah joined them.

'You mean the bit, is that what you're talking about?' Millie's suspicions that Sloane wasn't a rider were beginning to ring true.

'Yes, of course I meant the bit – what else would I be talking about?' Sloane's eyes drilled into Millie.

Wally finished bridling Stumps and led the pony out into the passageway. 'Well, he's all yours, miss.' He handed the reins to Sloane.

'This is going to be such fun.' Alice-Miranda pulled a stool up beside Bonaparte and nimbly hopped onto his back with the expertise of someone who had been riding most of her life. Millie didn't bother with the stool and easily hauled herself onto Chops's back. Susannah's much larger horse, Buttercup, swayed lazily as she put her foot into the stirrup and swung gently into the saddle. This left Sloane marooned beside Stumps.

'Would you like a leg-up, miss?' Wally offered.

Sloane shook her head and pulled a stool up next to the pony.

'Excuse me, miss,' Wally began. 'You're not going to get on from there are you?'

'Why?' Sloane looked around. The other girls were sitting atop their mounts waiting for her.

'Because that's the far side of the horse and you never get on that side. Usually scares them.'

Sloane gulped loudly. 'Well, at my riding school, we always get on from this side. My riding teacher went to the Olympics and he rode the Spanish dancing horses too.'

'Gosh, that's amazing,' Alice-Miranda gasped.

'Weird, more like it,' Millie added. 'I've never heard of anyone who's been in the Olympics *and* with the Spanish dancing horses.'

'Well, it's true,' Sloane snapped. 'And if you don't believe me, I won't bother coming.'

'Of course we believe you, Sloane,' Alice-Miranda soothed. But Alice-Miranda had a strange feeling that something wasn't quite right – and if there was one thing she was usually right about, it was her strange feelings.

Stumps began to snort. As Sloane attempted to throw her leg over his back, he spun around and butted her bottom with his head. She fell to the ground with a thud, right in the middle of a freshly steaming pile of manure deposited moments ago by Bonaparte.

'Ahh,' she cried. 'You little beast. Look at me!'

Sloane's white riding breeches now resembled the patchy hide of a Guernsey cow.

'There, there, miss.' Wally grabbed the pony's reins and wheeled him back around. 'I think the poor fellow just got a bit nervous. Perhaps if you try getting on the usual way? An old bloke like Stumps is not used to fancy Spanish riding habits.'

Sloane picked herself off the floor. She was sorely tempted to tell the other girls she wasn't feeling well.

'Are you all right, Sloane?' Millie asked. 'You know, you don't have to come if you don't want to.'

But Sloane took Millie's comment as a challenge and she was determined to prove the little brat wrong.

'I'm fine,' she spat and this time, standing on the near side of the pony, she swung herself into the saddle. Stumps stood perfectly still – not even an ear twitched.

'Well, come on then everyone, let's go!' Alice-Miranda clicked her tongue and the group moved off into the bright sunshine.

Chapter 12

Millie and Chops led the group as they made their way down the lane into the woods. Sloane spent most of the time watching how the other girls managed their ponies. She'd been on a horse only once before, at the local show on a lead rope. But no one needed to know that now and besides, she seemed to be doing quite well.

The group walked and then trotted for a while. When Millie called out that they were going to canter, Sloane yelled back that she thought Stumps was tired and they could go on without her if they wanted.

'Of course we won't race off.' Alice-Miranda slowed down and rode alongside her.

Millie rolled her eyes. She was bursting to take Chops for a proper gallop. As if reading her mind, Alice-Miranda suggested that Millie and Susannah have a race to Gertrude's Grove. She and Sloane would meet them there in a little while.

Millie didn't need any more encouragement.

'Thanks, Alice-Miranda,' she called. 'See you there!'

Chops and Buttercup hit their strides within seconds, leaving Alice-Miranda and Sloane doddling along together.

'Bonaparte's tired too,' Alice-Miranda smiled. 'Do you have any brothers or sisters, Sloane?'

'I have a stinky brother who's a year older than me,' she replied.

'That's lovely,' Alice-Miranda nodded. 'Not that he's stinky, but that you have a brother. I'd love to have a brother or sister but Mummy says that it wasn't to be. So there's just me and Mummy and Daddy at home. Oh and Mrs Oliver and Shilly, and Max and Cyril and the Greenings and Lily and Heinrich and Jasper and Poppy and Daisy and, of course, Granny Bert.'

'Do they *all* live with you?' Sloane asked in astonishment.

'Oh no, not at all. Daisy and Granny live at Rose Cottage and the Bauers live down the lane and the Greenings live in the gatehouse. Max and Cyril have a flat over the stables so only Mrs Oliver and Shilly live in the Hall with Mummy and Daddy and me.'

'Where do you live?' Sloane asked.

'Near a lovely little village called Highton Mill. It's terribly pretty. Our house is called Highton Hall,' Alice-Miranda replied.

'Is it very big?' Sloane continued.

'It's certainly not as big as some of our friends' houses but there's plenty of room. Tell me about your brother. What's his name?'

'Septimus,' Sloane smirked. 'He's foul.'

'I'm sure he can't be that bad,' Alice-Miranda smiled. 'Does he go to school close by?'

'He's at Fayle,' Sloane replied, then giggled. 'He'll probably fail at Fayle.'

'I don't think so,' Alice-Miranda said. 'It's against the school charter. It's such a funny name for a school, isn't it? I asked Miss Reedy however it came to be called that and she told me that the man who started the school was Mr Frederick Erasmus

Fayle and he wrote a strict charter, which is sort of like a set of rules, I think, about the importance of academic standards. Do you know, the school motto is "*Nomine defectus non autem natura*", which means "Fail by name, not by nature". That's terribly clever, don't you think? If more than twenty-five per cent of boys fail any test, the school has to close immediately and whoever is next in line in the Fayle family can do with it whatever they choose. Wouldn't that be a terrible shame? A grand school like that closed down. Mr Fayle must have been a very proud man to make that rule. Anyway, Millie, Jacinta and I have a friend who we hope might be starting there soon. His name's Lucas, and his father is going to marry my Aunt Charlotte. Maybe he and your brother will become friends?'

'Whatever.' Sloane stared off into the distance. 'Do you think we could trot for a while? I'm hungry.'

'Of course,' Alice-Miranda clicked her tongue and Bonaparte picked up the pace. She rose and fell with the trot. Sloane just bounced along on top of Stumps.

When the girls finally reached Gertrude's Grove, Wally had already met Millie and Susannah with a basket and picnic rug and driven away again. Sloane threw her right leg forward over Stumps's neck and slid off the pony, hitting the ground with a thud.

'That was a fancy dismount,' Alice-Miranda admired. Sloane raised her nose in the air and did her best attempt at stalking off towards the picnic. Trouble was, she could barely stand, let alone walk gracefully.

'Do you want some help with Stumps?' Alice-Miranda offered.

'Yes, you can tie him up for me, can't you?' Sloane didn't even look back. Alice-Miranda grabbed Stumps's reins and looped them over the nearby gate. She made sure Bonaparte was far enough away that he couldn't get up to any mischief. It was never a good idea to tether him within reach of another pony.

'You took your time,' Millie called, as she looked up from where she was rummaging through the wicker basket. 'We've been here for ages but Wally just arrived with the food a few minutes ago.'

'There's a lovely stream over there beyond the willows,' Susannah added. 'We had a competition skimming stones.'

'And I won.' Millie smiled.

Sloane hobbled over and gingerly lowered herself down onto the edge of the picnic rug. Her grimace said it all.

'Sore backside, hey?' Millie queried. 'Usually happens when you haven't been on a horse for a while.'

'I'm fine,' Sloane retorted. 'And who said I hadn't been on a horse for a while?'

'Well, it's dead obvious –' Millie began.

'And what's that supposed to mean?' Sloane snapped, a crimson rash rising up her neck.

Alice-Miranda arrived just in time to survey the delicious-looking spread that would be their lunch. 'Ohh, look at that!' she gasped, interrupting Millie and Sloane's exchange.

Susannah had unwrapped a stack of sandwiches; there was egg and lettuce, ham, cheese and tomato, turkey, brie and cranberry, not to mention roast beef with a touch of horseradish. From the bottom of the basket, Susannah retrieved four plump scones, a pot of jam and another of cream, and four large slices of devil's food cake. There were two thermos flasks, one filled with tea and the other hot chocolate.

Sloane reached forward and helped herself to a slice of cake.

'Would you like to have a sandwich first?' Alice-Miranda offered.

'No, I hate sandwiches. Unless they're fully organic and I can't tell so I'd rather not have any,' Sloane replied.

Millie raised her eyebrows. 'But it's all right to have a huge piece of chocolate cake?'

'What's it to you?' Sloane bit into the cake.

It seemed that the school's newest student didn't have the easiest nature, but Alice-Miranda was determined to make her feel part of the group, and hurriedly changed the subject.

'You know, I came through here when I was on my hike last term,' she commented. 'And then I headed over the stream and up into the mountains. It was so lovely.'

'I still can't believe you had to do it.' Susannah smiled. 'I would have been so scared.'

'Well, I was a little bit nervous but I knew that there was nothing out here to hurt me,' said Alice-Miranda.

'Except the witch,' Susannah lowered her voice and widened her eyes.

'A witch. As if!' Sloane scoffed. 'You're such a baby. I'm not going hiking. Ever!'

'Miss Grimm will have something to say about that,' Millie replied.

'Really? I don't think so. Mummy says hikes are for tomboys and I'm hardly that, am I now?' Sloane spat.

'Would you like something else to eat Millie?' Alice-Miranda hurriedly handed her friend a jam-smothered scone.

'Thanks.' Millie rolled her eyes at Sloane, who fortunately was looking elsewhere.

The scrumptious lunch had a soothing effect and the girls had a lovely time eating and lying about in the warm sunshine. The ponies were behaving themselves too, with barely a snort or grunt out of any of them. Amid the chirping of birds, the only other sound was the tearing of clumps of grass as Bony and his friends enjoyed the sweet tastes of the meadow.

'I'm so full!' Millie patted her hand on her stomach and lay back with her head in Alice-Miranda's lap.

'Me too,' wailed Susannah.

The girls had all but demolished Mrs Smith's feast, leaving only a couple of half-sandwiches and one lonely scone.

'Look.' Alice-Miranda pointed at the gate. 'There's Wally.'

The clattering of the old school Land Rover filled

the air and Wally Whitstable pulled up beside them. The engine shuddered to a halt and he hopped out of the vehicle.

Wally eyed the remains of the picnic. 'Goodness, you lot must have been famished.'

'Yes, but now we're all as full as ticks,' Alice-Miranda sighed.

'Not me.' Sloane turned up her nose. 'Some of us watch how much we eat.'

Millie sat up and offered Wally a leftover sandwich.

'Thanks, miss,' he said. 'I'm a bit hungry myself. It's been a busy morning. I've been giving some riding lessons to a couple of the girls who aren't very confident. Perhaps you'd like to join them next time, Miss Sloane?'

'Why?' bit Sloane. 'I don't need lessons with beginners.'

'Well, the offer's there.' Wally wolfed down the roast beef sandwich.

Alice-Miranda and Susannah set to, packing the thermos flasks and other bits and pieces into the picnic basket. Millie picked up the rug and tried to fold it but she couldn't quite get the two ends lined up. Sloane ignored her.

Millie let out a shuddering sigh. 'Do you think you could give me hand?'

'Oh, all right,' Sloane replied, grabbing at the other end of the rug. Anyone would have thought she'd been asked to scrub a toilet with a toothbrush.

'Here, Miss Millie, I'll do that,' Wally said.

'It's all right, Wally. Sloane's helping me,' said Millie with narrowed eyes.

'Then let me carry that basket to the car,' he offered, as Alice-Miranda and Susannah struggled with the enormous wicker hamper.

When the rug was finally folded and stowed in the four-wheel drive, Wally said, 'I'd best be off, girls. Are you heading straight back?'

'Yes, I think so,' Millie replied. 'We need to learn our lines for the auditions next week.'

'Well, be careful.' Wally hopped into the driver's seat. 'Oh, and by the way, Miss Sloane, just watch Stumps – I've heard he can be a bit of a bolter on the inbound run, but I'm sure an experienced rider like you won't have any trouble with him. Just don't mention the "h" word.' Wally winked at Millie, who smothered a smile.

'What do you mean, the "h" word?' Sloane called

out over the clattering engine of the four-wheel drive. But Wally was halfway up the hill.

'You just have to make sure you keep a tight rein on him, that's all,' said Alice-Miranda. 'Don't worry. I'll ride with you the whole way. If the other girls want to race, that's fine. I won't leave you.'

Susannah and Millie walked off to get Chops and Buttercup from where they were tied up further down the fence line. Alice-Miranda hauled herself up onto Bonaparte and watched as Sloane attempted three times to get onto Stumps. Thankfully, he really was a dozy old fellow and didn't even flinch when, on the fourth attempt, she landed a thumping blow to the side of his ribs with her right boot. Alice-Miranda wasn't concerned about Stumps's alleged habit of bolting for home. Whenever she rode him last term, he was the gentlest chap she'd ever met.

Millie and Susannah joined Alice-Miranda and Sloane. The four of them were standing abreast when Sloane leaned forward and asked, 'Well, are we heading straight *home* or what?'

With the mere mention of the word, Stumps let out an ear-piercing whinny. He threw his head back and forth, pawed at the ground and then took off, from zero to gallop in barely a second.

'Ahhhhhhhhhhhhh!' Sloane screamed as she leaned forward and clutched Stumps's shaggy mane. Millie, Alice-Miranda and Susannah knew they had to catch up – and fast.

'Hold on, Sloane, we're coming,' Alice-Miranda called as she dug her heels into Bony's side and urged him after the runaway horse.

Stumps flew across the open meadow, through the stream and towards the woods. Sloane continued screeching as the girls raced to catch up. Millie and Chops were the fastest – his little legs pumped as Millie sat glued to the saddle.

As they neared the woods, Susannah yelled, 'Keep your head down, Sloane.'

Sloane ducked just in time as a branch grazed the top of her riding helmet. The ponies were flying through the undergrowth, snorting and puffing.

Up ahead, Sloane could just make out the shape of a fallen tree. She realised that Stumps was not about to stop and braced herself as the pony flew through the air and cleared the trunk with no trouble. Surprisingly, she was still on his back when he landed. Millie and Chops easily managed the jump with Susannah and Alice-Miranda close behind. The ponies raced on. Stumps was increasing his lead. Who would have thought the old boy had it in him?

The woodland gave way to a clearer path, lined on either side by thick undergrowth. Sloane's screams echoed through the forest. The trail narrowed and then, without warning, split into two paths. Sloane and Stumps were nowhere to be seen. Chops and Buttercup headed left and, despite Alice-Miranda's best efforts to follow them, Bonaparte veered to the right. Alice-Miranda jerked the reins as hard as she could. She ordered Bony to stop, but a small child of seven and a half is no match for a pony on a mission. As Chops and Buttercup thundered on in the other direction, with Sloane's shrieks fading in the distance, Alice-Miranda was aware of Bonaparte sniffing the air around him. In spite of his pace, he was lifting his head and inhaling wildly. Alice-Miranda knew this could only mean one thing – cabbages!

Chapter 13

Alice-Miranda and Bonaparte thundered on through the woods until Bonaparte finally came to a halt outside what must once have been a gigantic vegetable patch. Bounded by a tumbledown fence still high enough to keep the pony out, Alice-Miranda had just managed to stop herself flying over his head when Bony stopped dead in his tracks. She could see the overgrown rows of gardens, a jumble of weeds sprouting from the hardened earth – rather like Mr Trout's uncontrollable clumps of ear hairs, she thought to herself.

'It's about time you stopped, Bonaparte Napoleon Highton-Smith-Kennington-Jones,' Alice-Miranda panted. 'Thank goodness for that fence. You're a very naughty pony. And there are no cabbages here anyway, you silly old boy. I don't know where we are or how far we've come. And poor Sloane – I hope she's all right.'

Bonaparte whinnied and pawed at the ground, eager to see for himself whether there was anything worth having in the patch. But Alice-Miranda had had enough. She was a very good rider, although no child her age could match Bony's strength when he decided there were free vegetables on offer.

Alice-Miranda looked about her. She had been so preoccupied with getting Bonaparte to stop, she hadn't really taken much notice of where they were. But she did recall passing through a set of enormous derelict gateposts. As Alice-Miranda wheeled Bonaparte around, she noticed a large outbuilding in the distance. She decided to see if there was anyone who might be able to help her find her way back to school.

Digging her heels in, Alice-Miranda urged Bonaparte forward. But he stayed put. She tried again, giving him a sharp kick to the left flank, but he refused to move. There was only one thing for it. She fossicked about in her jacket pocket and found five slightly crumbled sugar cubes. Alice-Miranda dismounted and pulled the reins over Bonaparte's head, then showed the greedy pony one cube. He whinnied loudly and reached out to snaffle the treat from her outstretched hand.

'I have some more, Bony,' Alice-Miranda informed him. 'But only if you follow me.'

Bonaparte might have been stubborn but he was not stupid and decided that it was better to have *some* treats than none. He followed Alice-Miranda back towards the outbuilding. She stopped every twenty paces and offered the little beast another cube, which he greedily gulped.

Along the gravel pathway, ancient urns on tall plinths poked through the undergrowth. Alice-Miranda thought they looked quite like some she had at home at Highton Hall, except for their state of decay.

As the tiny girl and her pony reached the building, she realised that there were, in fact, several separate structures bounded by a high brick wall. The entrance to the complex was through a magnificent stone archway, now flecked with mould and decay. Alice-Miranda imagined that in the past it had seen the coming and going of many a splendid carriage. In the forecourt there was a small yard, which she decided would be a perfect pen for Bony while she had a look around.

The main structure had been a very handsome stable block, now in tumbledown disrepair. The slate roof looked like a patchwork quilt and the timber doors were missing several panels.

Alice-Miranda coaxed Bonaparte over the cobblestones and into the enclosure and handed over the last sweet reward.

'Now you stay here,' she glared, 'and don't you get any thoughts about going back to that patch.'

Alice-Miranda checked twice that the rusted chain was secure. Just as she was about to head inside the main building, a large tabby cat appeared and started rubbing against her leg, purring loudly. She turned around to check on Bony and noticed that three more cats, in shades of ginger, grey and black, were now taking up various positions around the yard. One on a windowsill, another atop the wall that enclosed the stable block and the other had bravely sidled up to Bonaparte, who was now engaged in a 'sniff-off' with the black intruder.

'What a lot of cats,' Alice-Miranda said to herself. 'You be nice to that moggy, Bonaparte,' she warned. 'He's probably got a good old set of claws on him.'

Alice-Miranda left the yard and entered the stable block. Immediately her nostrils were assaulted by the smell of damp hay and horses.

'Hellooo,' she called. 'Is there anyone here?'

The musty brick building creaked and groaned as if apologising for its current state. She soon realised that there were no animals inside any of the stalls, but the open booth at the end of the passageway was full of ancient saddles and bridles, their leather split and dry, brass fittings tarnished and bits blackened with the passing of time. Several pairs of long riding boots were lined up on a shelf alongside a selection of moth-eaten velvet hats and helmets all coated in thick dusty webs. It didn't look like anyone had been in the tack room for a very long time.

In what would have been the feed room, a row of timber hoppers stood open, their contents of oats and barley long gone. A few loose remnants of straw littered the floor and a large open vat of molasses contained an array of grasshoppers and bugs, fossilised in their amber trap.

'Helloooooo?' Alice-Miranda's voice echoed through the rafters. She wondered if there might be a flat above the stables just like they had at home. But she couldn't see a staircase. Her voice brought no human reply, but the yowling of several cats filled the air.

Alice-Miranda decided that a stable block such as this would no doubt belong to a large house. She wanted to keep exploring but her watch said that it was now half past two. Millie, Susannah and Sloane should have been home by now. Perhaps they would come looking for her.

Emerging into the afternoon sunshine, Alice-Miranda shielded her eyes and waited for them to adjust to the light. Bonaparte acknowledged her presence with a snort. He was dozing against the gate with one eye open, watching the black cat who had now taken up residence on top of the feed bin which hung over the gate.

'All right, Bony, there's no one here. But I see you've got plenty of friends to keep you company, so I'm off to find the house that must belong to these stables.' Alice-Miranda patted the top of another ginger cat's head as it rubbed its neck up and down her riding boot.

The estate was dotted with handsome trees, claret ash, oak and fir, many of which Alice-Miranda recognised from her outings with her own gardener at home, Mr Greening. He loved that she asked him so many questions about the names of the plants and although she was still only seven and a half, Alice-Miranda's knowledge of botanical species was something Mr Greening was secretly very proud of.

As she walked further along the driveway, the grassy edges were replaced with a cobblestoned guttering, a sure indication that somewhere up ahead there would be a house. No one would go to that much trouble for a road to nowhere, Alice-Miranda was certain. Through the jungle of branches, she spied an overgrown lawn. A huge ornate fountain sat partially hidden by the mass of weeds and waist-high grass.

'Hellooooo,' she called again. The only reply was the meow of a cat. Alice-Miranda looked down to see that the tabby from the stables had joined her on her walk. 'Oh, hello puss.' She reached down and patted the top of his head. 'Fancied an outing, did you?'

All of a sudden, Alice-Miranda had a strange feeling that she was being watched. She turned around to see that her tabby friend had been joined by at least ten more cats padding along silently behind her.

'Goodness me, there are an awful lot of you indeed,' she addressed her feline audience. 'Do you *all* live here?'

An uneasy recollection invaded her mind. 'Cats, lots of cats,' she said aloud, before dismissing the thought. Alice-Miranda didn't believe in witches. They were only in fairy stories.

Chapter 14

Like the Pied Piper with his merry followers, Alice-Miranda continued her way up the drive. She rounded a sweeping bend, where the foliage was so thick it created an arch like a giant's ribcage from one side of the road to the other. Another set of iron gates, hanging open from their limestone columns, beckoned her to enter. There was a name on the left-hand pillar, obscured by a tangle of ivy stuck fast to the tarnished brass plate. She reached up as high as she could and tried to pull back the greenery. It was tricky but Alice-Miranda caught a handful of leaves and wrenched hard. She traced the blackened outline of the words *Caledonia Manor*.

Alice-Miranda knew the house couldn't be too far away. She began to jog, anxious to find out if there was anyone at home who could set her in the right direction. Her furry friends circled around her, some racing in front as if they knew exactly where to go. Up ahead, she could have sworn she saw a black figure scurrying into the bushes.

'Hellooooooo,' Alice-Miranda called. 'Can you help me, please? I seem to be lost.' But the figure disappeared and so Alice-Miranda continued on her way.

At last, the trees thinned out and there it was in front of her. 'Goodness.' She drew in a sharp breath. 'What an amazing house.'

Caledonia Manor was indeed an amazing house. Its ancient limestone blocks glinted in the sunshine. Four Ionic columns formed a magnificent portico with five steps leading to the most enormous double entrance doors Alice-Miranda had ever seen. Her own house, Highton Hall was renowned as one of the most beautiful homes in the country, but surely Caledonia Manor could once have been included in the same company.

On closer inspection, Alice-Miranda could see that the manor was at the mercy of silent invaders. Tendrils of Virginia creeper grew across some of the upstairs window frames and grass as tall as Alice-Miranda peered through the downstairs casements. Alice-Miranda could not even see the whole house, so dense were the bushes at the far end. But she could smell smoke and that had to be a good thing. It meant there was a fire in a hearth somewhere close by.

She marched up the front steps and pressed the discoloured brass buzzer beside the door. Then she listened for any sound from within. Nothing. Alice-Miranda clasped the lion's head knocker in the centre of the door with both hands and attempted to loosen it from the grip of time. But it was rusted in place and the door was firmly locked.

She looked around to see that her feline followers had disappeared, except for one last tabby who she spied heading around the corner of the building. Surely the cats would know best where to find the house's owner? After all, they were a well-fed looking bunch, and that couldn't just be the result of mousing in the stables.

The windows were thick with grime, giving no opportunity at all to see inside. As she beat a path around the side and came to the back of the building, she realised that the house was a vast U-shape, with an open terrace at the rear. The land behind the manor was far less densely vegetated than at the front. There was evidence of an expansive lawn stepping down from one level to the next, with rows of stone balustrade still zigzagging across its width.

It was only now, when she could take in the whole building, that Alice-Miranda noticed the entire roof of the wing opposite was missing. Blackened rafters poked from the top and the long wall bore holes like Swiss cheese where once there had been windows.

Alice-Miranda scampered to the top of the terrace and saw her furry friends milling about together at the end of the veranda.

'Hellooooo,' she called as the cats meowed, rubbed against each other and wound themselves in and out of her legs. 'Is anyone home?'

Alice-Miranda moved towards what looked like the kitchen door. There was still no sign of anyone, but when she tried the door handle this time, it opened. Without a second's hesitation, Alice-Miranda marched inside. Indeed she was right. A large AGA stove dominated the room. The old-fashioned iron cooker sat beside an open fireplace, where a small bundle of kindling was well alight. There was a huge double Butler's sink and taps that looked like they had come straight from a museum. Saucepans hung on treacherous-looking hooks above the fireplace and a kettle boiled on the stovetop. Someone was home, somewhere.

Chapter 15

Sloane's knees stopped trembling for the first time since she was unceremoniously dumped by Stumps in yet another pile of manure. Her face, as pale as parchment, was beginning to regain some colour as she sat on a straw bale, moaning softly to herself.

'Are you feeling any better?' Susannah asked, patting Sloane on the shoulder.

'Don't touch me!' Sloane spat. 'My legs hurt, my backside hurts and I think I might die.'

'Well, Miss Sloane, I did try to warn you not to

mention the "h" word,' said Wally Whitstable as he handed her a cup of hot cocoa.

'How was I to know what you meant?' Sloane sniffed.

Millie spun around to face her. 'Well, if you're half the rider you say you are, you'd know exactly what that meant.'

'At my riding school, we don't know about that because our horses aren't ill-tempered enough to do what that little brute did.' Sloane slurped her drink and cast a death stare towards Stumps's stable.

Millie glanced at her watch. 'Alice-Miranda should be here by now. I thought she was right behind you, Susannah.'

Susannah frowned. 'I thought she was too, but then, do you remember that fork in the road? I wonder if she might have gone the other way.'

'She wouldn't have done it on purpose,' said Millie. She was starting to worry. Although she knew Alice-Miranda to be a very capable rider, she was also aware that Bonaparte could be a little monster. 'Wally, do you think I should go and look for her?'

'Let's give her a few more minutes,' he replied.

Charlie appeared at the stable door. 'Let's give who a few more minutes?' he asked.

'Alice-Miranda,' Millie said. 'We rode out to Gertrude's Grove this morning but on the way back Sloane said the "h" word and Stumps bolted. We were all chasing after her but then Alice-Miranda disappeared. She should have been back by now.'

'Yes, she said that she would ride back with me the whole way, the little liar.' Sloane pouted.

'Oh, do be quiet, Sloane. Just because you're the most pathetic rider I've ever seen! Consider yourself lucky not to be in hospital.' Millie stood with her hands on her hips.

'Now, now, Miss Millie, that's not like you,' Charlie chastised. 'Don't worry about the little one. We'll give her another ten minutes and then we can take the Land Rover out and have a look. You know she's smart. Bonaparte's probably thrown a shoe and she's walking him back so he doesn't go lame.'

'Yes, that's probably it,' Millie nodded, glad that Charlie had thought of such a sensible explanation. But Millie had a niggling feeling about Alice-Miranda being out there in the woods on her own. Even though it was still only mid-afternoon, the sooner Alice-Miranda was back home safely the better, as far as Millie was concerned.

Chapter 16

Alice-Miranda called out three times before she decided she'd have to venture further inside Caledonia Manor in order to find its occupants.

She exited the kitchen through a door which led to a long passageway. At the end, the ceiling opened up double height to a stately entrance hall dominated by an elegant carved staircase. It was truly a magnificent piece of craftsmanship, rising in one broad flight before splaying left and right to an enormous gallery landing above. Most of the furniture in the hall was hidden under yellowed sheets, while a thick lashing of dust covered the flagstone floor. Alice-Miranda noticed that the only footsteps unsettling the grime were her own, so she decided that whoever lived in the house did not use that route to get to the second floor. She returned to the kitchen, thinking she might find a set of back-stairs like the ones at home.

Alice-Miranda tried another door off to the left. She turned the handle and was surprised to find it locked.

'Hello?' she called. 'Is anyone in there? I need some help, please. You see, I'm lost and I don't know how to find my way back to school.'

There was no reply.

She tried another door opposite. The handle turned. Alice-Miranda opened it to find that the passage led to a smaller hallway with a much plainer staircase.

'Helloooo, is anyone up here?' she called as she climbed, every step creaking more noisily than the one before. At the top of the stairs, Alice-Miranda could see that she was at the far end of the landing she had spied from the front hall. She was about to explore further when there was a loud crash downstairs.

Alice-Miranda ran as quickly as she could down the backstairs and into the kitchen, where she glimpsed a flash of black scurrying through the door which had previously been locked.

'Stop!' she called. 'Please, come out. I'm lost and I'd really like to talk to you.' She heard the door click shut. And then she saw it: a large brass key in the door lock.

Alice-Miranda knocked on the door and then turned the tarnished brass handle. She wasn't sure what to expect, but had in her mind something like the side sitting room at home with its comfortable couches and television in the corner. This room, however, bore no resemblance.

It was a large space with a threadbare maroon-velvet chaise longue, just the right size for a child. There was also an impressive cedar bookcase which took up the entire length of the wall opposite the windows. A miniature pair of wingback chairs faced the garden and, in between them, on a low inlaid table, a tiny children's tea set in delicate blue-and-white china was laid out perfectly as if guests were expected. Underneath one of the windows stood a huge Victorian doll's house and a white rocking horse. A wicker pram full of porcelain dolls completed the picture. Alice-Miranda noticed at once that, unlike the front hallway, there was not a skerrick of dust on the furniture and she could see her reflection in the gleaming timber floor.

'I know someone's here. I'd really like to meet you,' Alice-Miranda called as she walked around the room. She reached into the pram and examined one of the china dolls. Its brilliant blue eyes opened and closed slowly when Alice-Miranda picked her up. 'I need to talk to you. I'm lost and I have to find my way back to school!'

Alice-Miranda was sure she had seen with her own eyes the same figure dressed in black she'd spied earlier in the garden disappear into this room. Trouble was, there didn't seem to be any other doors and there was certainly no one inside.

She checked behind the chairs and near the doll's house. The bookcase laden with hundreds of stories beckoned and Alice-Miranda read the titles on the leather-bound spines. *Treasure Island* and *Alice in Wonderland* stood alongside *Moby Dick* and *Great Expectations* and hundreds of other classics. Alice-Miranda walked along the length of glassed-in shelves before coming to an open section.

Reaching up to take a closer look, she put her hand on the slim volume of *Ali Baba and the Forty*

Thieves and realised immediately that it wasn't a real book at all. It was made of wood, as was every other one beside it. Alice-Miranda knew that could mean only one thing.

She pushed and prodded every title along the line. It was only when she reached *Pride and Prejudice*, second from the last, that there was a loud click and the wall pivoted. It revealed a small windowless room containing a narrow single bed, dressing table and small sofa. A giant wardrobe stood against the far wall. Alice-Miranda could make out the sound of gentle weeping coming from inside.

'Please come out,' Alice-Miranda soothed. 'I really do need your help.' She approached the wardrobe and turned the handle. As Alice-Miranda opened the door, there was a jagged scream and a tall figure within cowered, shielding its face.

'Please, don't be afraid,' Alice-Miranda begged.

She stepped back to allow whoever was inside the cupboard to come out. It was clearly an elderly woman, dressed in black from head to toe. Her blouse, long skirt, tights and shoes – all black – gave her the appearance of a bent stick of liquorice. Atop her head was a black velvet bowler hat with a long black veil that reached down to her waist. The woman sniffed several times in quick sucession, then slowly stood up.

'Hello,' Alice-Miranda said. 'My name's Alice-Miranda Highton-Smith-Kennington-Jones and I'm very pleased to meet you, Miss . . .' Alice-Miranda extended her small hand.

The woman kept her head bowed and managed to stumble from the cupboard, steadying herself on Alice-Miranda's outstretched arm.

'Do you have a name?' Alice-Miranda asked. 'I'm so sorry if I startled you. I really just need some help. Why don't you come along with me and I'll make us both a nice cup of tea.'

And with that, Alice-Miranda hurried away to the kitchen and busied herself finding the necessary ingredients to put the pot on. She was already pouring two cups of strong black tea when finally the woman appeared in the doorway.

'Oh, there you are.' Alice-Miranda set the cups down at the kitchen table. 'Please sit down. You still haven't told me your name though, miss, and I'd so like to know with whom I'm about to have tea.'

The woman manoeuvred her crooked frame into one of the antique timber chairs without a sound.

'I simply adore your house,' Alice-Miranda continued. 'It's terribly big and very beautiful, although I see perhaps you haven't had any help in the garden for a while. It's hard to keep such a huge place in check, isn't it? My mummy has an army of help and she still spends hours each week making sure things are just so. Do you live here on your own? Because that would be impossible . . . to keep on top of things, I mean. I'd so love to know your name.'

Silence enveloped the house. Alice-Miranda grew aware of the ticking of a clock and glanced around the kitchen, searching for it.

'Aren't you afraid of me?' the woman asked quietly.

'Of course not.' Alice-Miranda smiled. 'Why would I be? In fact, I thought you seemed rather afraid of me – which is very silly indeed.'

'Because . . .' the old woman faltered. 'I'm the one . . . I'm the one they call the witch.'

'Oh really? I had wondered about that. I met lots of cats on the way up here and the girls at school told me a story a few nights ago about a witch in the woods with hundreds of cats, but I don't believe in witches. Everyone knows they're only in fairy stories – unless perhaps you really are a witch, in which case it's a pleasure to meet you, being the first real witch I've ever met.' Alice-Miranda paused and sipped her tea. 'Anyway, I really should tell you how I came to be here. You see, I was out riding with my best friend Millie and another friend Susannah and a new girl called Sloane and well, Sloane was riding Stumps and he's one of those ponies who you should never mention *home* to because, well, as soon as she did, he bolted and we all gave chase but my naughty little Bonaparte could smell your old vegetable patch and so they went one way and I went the other and that's how I ended up here at Caledonia Manor.' Alice-Miranda finished her one-sided conversation and took another sip of tea.

'Oh,' the woman spoke. There was a long pause. 'My name's Hephzibah.'

'What a delicious name.' Alice-Miranda clapped her hands together. 'I'm so glad we've met properly. Now we can truly be friends.'

'Friends?' Hephzibah's voice quivered.

'Are you all right?' Alice-Miranda asked. 'Why don't you take your hat off and then I can see you properly?'

'I can't,' Hephzibah wheezed. 'I can't.'

'Of course you can,' Alice-Miranda insisted. 'I know it's important to wear sun protection outside but we're inside and I'd so love to see your face.'

Hephzibah hesitated, fearing this would be a terrible mistake. But something about this child made her feel different. There was something comforting about her – something she hadn't felt since . . .

Hephzibah slowly lifted her veil before taking her hat off and placing it on the table beside her cup. She looked up at Alice-Miranda, her mouth drawn tightly into a thin line. With the fingers of her left hand, she gently traced the outline of her scarred face. A tear formed in her right eye and slid silently down her cheek, dropping onto her lap.

'Oh, you have such pretty eyes.' Alice-Miranda smiled.

All at once, Hephzibah broke down into shuddering sobs. Alice-Miranda slipped from her seat, pulled the chair around beside her new friend, and immediately climbed up and placed her arm around the elderly woman's shoulder.

Chapter 17

Armed with a hand-drawn map tucked safely into her breast pocket, Alice-Miranda returned safely to school with Bonaparte that afternoon, to the great relief of all. Mr Charles and Susannah had gone out in the Land Rover to look for her while Millie and Wally had taken the horses and retraced the girls' journey from Gertrude's Grove. Sloane said that there was no way she was going out looking for anyone – she had lines to learn (and a very sore bottom).

Alice-Miranda and Bony had met Millie and Wally

at the fork in the road. She explained Bonaparte's wilful behaviour, saying that he had sniffed out an old vegetable patch and simply couldn't be held. Thankfully, she added, there weren't any cabbages, but she had pulled up a few woody carrots for Bony and then waited until he was in a better mood before heading for home. She didn't like telling untruths but she had a feeling that the real story might cause undue concern.

Millie nodded after hearing her friend's tale. She well knew about Bonaparte's predilection for cabbages – and any other vegetable on offer.

Wally pointed towards the pathway where Bony and Alice-Miranda had come from. 'You know, miss, the witch lives down there?'

'I'm sure there's no such thing, Wally,' Alice-Miranda chided.

'It's true, you know. She's scary as. I once went there with my mates – we was daring each other. It was just on dusk with the light fading fast and then we saw her – dressed from head to toe in black and this veil thing covering her ugly head. She screamed blue murder and set her feral cats on us. I ran so fast, I thought my heart was going to burst right out of my chest.'

'Oh dear,' Alice-Miranda whispered. 'Poor Hephzibah.'

'Anyway, looks like you survived, miss. Now, we'd better get these ponies home. I'll call Charlie and let him know you're safe and sound.'

The group met at the stables. Alice-Miranda recounted the same story to Susannah and Charlie who seemed satisfied with her explanation.

Millie, Alice-Miranda and Susannah walked back to the house.

'Well, you took your time getting back.' Sloane glanced up at the girls from where she was lying on the couch in the sitting room, rehearsing her lines for the audition. 'Did you have a fall?'

'Hello Sloane,' Alice-Miranda began. 'I am sorry about the ride. I know I said that I wouldn't leave you at all but my Bonaparte had other ideas, I'm afraid, and once he has a sniff of a vegetable patch, he's pretty much unstoppable.'

'Well, now that I know how unreliable you are, I won't depend on you again.' Sloane buried her head in the script.

Millie rolled her eyes. Susannah didn't say a word but headed straight to her room.

'Come on, Alice-Miranda,' Millie said. 'Let's go and get changed and then we can help each other learn our lines.'

Sloane looked up and pouted. 'I need someone to practise with too. Jacinta's off doing stupid gymnastics training or something. Anyone would think she wants to go to the Olympics.'

'She does,' Millie replied.

'She does what?' asked Sloane, pulling a face.

'Want to go to the Olympics.'

'She's incredible and I'm sure that she'll get there. She trains almost every day.' Alice-Miranda smiled.

'Whatever.' Sloane flicked her hand dismissively. 'I need someone to rehearse with.'

'We're busy,' Millie informed Sloane as she grabbed her friend's hand and headed for their room.

'We could include Sloane, you know,' Alice-Miranda said to Millie as they were getting changed.

'She's awful,' Millie replied. 'I thought Alethea was spoiled and horrible but Sloane's just as foul.'

'I'm sure she's just getting used to being at school, that's all,' Alice-Miranda replied. 'Don't you remember what it's like being the new girl?'

'Well, I hope I was never like her,' Millie frowned.

Alice-Miranda and Millie spent the rest of the afternoon in all manner of poses and positions, learning their parts for the *Snow White and the Seven Dwarfs* auditions. Alice-Miranda decided she would try for the lead as well as some of the supporting roles, while Millie had her heart set on either Doc or the Magic Mirror.

Later that evening, Alice-Miranda skipped off to call her parents.

'Hello Mummy, how are you?' she asked.

'I'm fine, darling – and how are you finding things back at school?' her mother fussed.

'Wonderful, Mummy – so please don't start crying. You know that I'm perfectly all right and if you cry, I won't call you any more,' Alice-Miranda scolded.

'Oh, don't be cross. Anyway, I have some marvellous news for you, sweetheart,' her mother offered. 'You know that Lawrence had made some enquiries about getting Lucas into Fayle? Well, first he was told that there were no spots at all and Lucas would have to go on the waiting list – which I think, between you and me, he didn't mind one bit. But Lawrence just called a little while ago and apparently there are twins leaving to do some travelling with their parents, so Lucas has a spot. He'll be starting next week. In fact, I think he might be there tomorrow afternoon.'

'That's fantastic, Mummy. I can't wait to tell Jacinta. She'll be over the moon. Does that mean Aunt Charlotte and Lawrence will be bringing Lucas down? Will they have time to come and visit?' Alice-Miranda asked.

'Of course, darling. I'll phone Cha and let her know you're looking forward to seeing them.'

Alice-Miranda wanted to tell her mother about Hephzibah but something told her that now was not the right time. She knew that her parents would want to help, but she didn't know if Hephzibah was ready for the full force of the Highton-Smith-Kennington-Joneses just yet.

She had promised to visit Caledonia Manor again and knew that the only way she could go would be to take a friend with her, as students were not allowed to ride on their own. Of course she would take Millie, but she'd wait for just the right moment to tell her. Hephzibah hadn't asked to be kept a secret but Alice-Miranda understood that there was something very special about her new friend – and just now, a strange feeling told her that their meeting would be best kept to herself.

Instead, she spent a few minutes telling her mother all about the excitement the play was causing. 'I'd better go, Mummy. Millie and I are rehearsing for the auditions. I'd love to have a role – then I'll be able to see Lucas much more often.'

'All right, darling. Love and hugs from Daddy and me, and Shilly just said to say hello and Dolly wants to know if you enjoyed the fudge.'

Indeed, Alice-Miranda could hear Shilly and Mrs Oliver calling out in the background.

'Tell Mrs Oliver that her fudge was the best ever,' Alice-Miranda replied. 'Give everyone a big hug from me and I'll talk to you soon. Love you.' She put the phone back into its cradle and ran off to find Jacinta and tell her the good news.

Chapter 18

In the late afternoon sunshine, Smedley and September Sykes reclined on their brand-new lay-z lounges in their brand-new back garden, sipping brand-new champagne and indulging their fantasies about where they would take the children for holidays once Smedley's brand-new property developing business took off.

Although it wasn't the warmest of days, September was working on her tan, in a terrifyingly tiny leopard-print bikini. Her husband gazed admiringly at his wife, who he worried spent rather more time at the beauty salon than he could currently afford. Being a vacuum cleaner salesman, even on the home shopping channel, did not exactly bring in the big bucks. But Smedley believed with great certainty that their fortunes were about to change.

'Have you talked to the children today?' Smedley asked.

'Yes, Sloane called this morning. She's getting on soooo well with the other girls. I told her to make friends with that Highton-Smith-Kennington-Jones child. Imagine us being invited to their mansion for the weekend! They must be almost the richest people in the whole country,' September babbled. 'I haven't spoken to Sep but I'm sure he's fine. I just hope he's making some friends – that boy needs to get his head out of those dull old science textbooks and start paying attention to the important things in life, like whose father owns that gorgeous sky-blue Rolls-Royce I saw turning out of the Fayle driveway when I was dropping Sloane at school the other day.'

'Don't you worry about Septimus – he's just a bit shy, that's all. You keep working your magic, sweetheart, and I'm sure we'll be top of everyone's invitation list before long.' Smedley grinned, revealing a dazzling white smile to match that of his wife's. A handsome man, Smedley had once harboured dreams of a career as a talk-show host. Unfortunately, things never quite came together and the closest he had come to being a TV star was plying his trade in vacuum cleaner technology on infomercials.

'You know, we'd be far further up the social ladder if your father hadn't been such a dreadful cheapskate. The reading of his will was the most disappointing day of my life – fancy only leaving us his hideous old grocery shop and that poxy flat. I'd have thought a man of his supposed intelligence would have had some other investments,' September moaned.

'Well, at least Step-Mummy Henrietta's taken care of the school fees,' Smedley said with a wink.

'Yes, I suppose so, but I wish that wretched nursing home would stop calling. You know I haven't got the time. I don't look like this –' September paused to bounce her curls – 'by sitting on my rear end all day. There's the gym and the nail salon and the hairdresser and the beautician. And I think I should probably join the Village Women's Association too. I might be able to run some workshops for all the fashion victims around here.' September rolled her huge blue eyes. 'Golden Gates phoned four times yesterday. Apparently the daft old bat's been asking for some suitcase that was left in the shed at your father's place. I don't know where it is and I haven't got the time to go looking. I've no idea what happened to any of that rubbish. For all I know, it went to the tip.'

Smedley sighed and stood up. As he stalked off towards the shed at the far end of the garden, his mobile phone rang. He disappeared into the shed and re-emerged with a large blue suitcase in his left hand, all the while continuing his conversation.

September could only hear snatches of the exchange.

'Yes, yes, that's great. How much? Fantastic, I'll put the money in the account tomorrow.' Her husband gave her the thumbs up, then strode back towards the terrace where she was sitting.

September sat up. 'What was all that then?'

'Everything's a go for the offshore property deal.' Smedley put the suitcase down by the back door before picking up the champagne bottle and topping up both their glasses. 'Won't be long now until we're living life in the fast lane.' He raised his glass and tried to chink it against September's, except that it thudded instead, being made of plastic. 'And I think that's Step-Mummy Henrietta's suitcase.' He pointed at the battered leather bag.

'Well, I haven't got time to deliver it. You'll have to take it. And you'd better be right about this deal because I have just bought two pairs of designer jeans and a gorgeous leather jacket – and someone has to pay for them. I've got my eye on a new fridge with a built-in ice-maker and you know we *have* to buy a fountain for the garden. I can't possibly work any more, what with the children and their hectic schedules,' September griped.

Smedley had rather hoped that now Septimus and Sloane were busy at boarding school, September might get a few odd modelling jobs here and there – but after what happened earlier in the year, he was reluctant to bring up the subject again.

A few months ago Smedley had heard about a new agency that was recruiting and had been stupid enough to read the ad aloud to her. 'Models required! All ages, sizes, shapes and talents welcome.'

September had gone very white for a moment and then flown into a blistering red rage. 'You might as well say I'm a fat old cow with a head like a robber's dog! Is that what you mean, Smedley?' she had screamed.

'No darling, of course not. It's just that, well, you're not quite the little thing you were before the children, now are you? And I hear there's very good money in catalogue work for the more mature lady.'

Smedley had dug himself a hole that took two whole months to get out of. No end of flowers and shoes, and shoes and handbags, and handbags and flowers had been able to thaw September's icy mood until one day he walked into the kitchen and threw a set of car keys on the bench.

'For you, darling.' He looked at the keys and glanced up at his wife.

'If you think getting my car washed is going to see you back in the good books, Smedley Sykes, then you're even thicker than I thought.'

'Have a look at the keys, my lovely,' Smedley cooed. 'I think you might find that the "car wash" had rather a transforming effect.'

Sloane picked up the keys. She examined them carefully and realised that the key ring certainly wasn't that of her old sedan.

'Oh my gosh, Smedley, what have you done?' September squealed. 'Is it new?'

'Of course, darling, nothing less would do for you, my sweetheart.' Smedley laid on the charm so thick you could have eaten it on toast for breakfast. He held out his arms, waiting for September to rush to his embrace. His wife, however, had other priorities and ran straight past her husband to the garage to hug her new baby sports car.

Smedley had hoped that would do the trick and might even encourage September to give the modelling another thought. Goodness knows, the jobs were hardly taxing and usually paid more money than he saw in a month. But she would have none of it and he hadn't been brave enough to mention it again, although he was thinking about it – a lot.

Smedley sat back down beside his wife and pushed his sunglasses onto the top of his head.

'Smedley, is this deal really going to come off?' September glared. 'I'm so sick of being poor. I just don't deserve this life,' she wailed.

'Don't you worry your pretty head, my lovely. Soon enough the Sykeses will have more money than God.'

September smiled broadly. 'But how do you know how much money God has?' she asked, tilting her head and looking thoughtful.

'Oh, trust me, darling – I'm sure he has loads,' said Smedley.

Chapter 19

The Fayle school campus spread out over a thousand glistening acres, with magnificent Victorian buildings surrounded by sports fields, a swimming pool, sailing lake and stables. From the road it was almost completely hidden from view, no doubt the result of clever planning by generations of gardeners. McGlintock Manor, named after its founder's beloved wife, Helena Louise McGlintock, was renowned as the most beautiful of any school building in the country and had been extended over the years to house most of the classrooms, administration areas and the headmaster's residence.

Septimus could hardly believe his luck when he heard that his step-grandmother Henrietta had arranged for him and his sister Sloane to go to boarding school. It had been his dream – and one that he'd shared with his beloved grandfather Percy on the rare occasions that he'd been allowed to visit and the even rarer ones he was able to stay the night. Three years ago, Septimus had pinned a list of schools he would have liked to attend to his bedroom wall, with Fayle being his first preference. He'd heard that it was an outstanding institution, where being smart was revered, rather than reviled. And if there was one thing Septimus most certainly was, it was smart.

In his family, Sep had always felt like the odd one out. The only person who truly understood him was Grandpa Percy, and now that he was gone, life seemed like a lonely place. Septimus adored reading – about science and history and politics. His mother, on the other hand, only ever flicked through the pages of *Women's Daily* and *Gloss and Goss*, his father pored over the racing pages at the back of the newspaper, and his sister thought reading was something you only ever did if the television was on the blink.

He loved his mother and father but, quite simply, he thought they could have been from another planet.

So when Septimus arrived at Fayle, he found that it was even better than he had dreamt of. Although just twelve years of age, Sep had learned early the difference between what you hoped for and what you expected. While he hoped the students would be kind, the teachers brilliant and the school perfect, what he expected was very different.

At his last school, on the very first day the kids had branded him Septic Sykes and it had stuck. He expected the teachers at his new school to be strict in the extreme, perhaps even carrying canes or some other medieval devices of punishment. But so far, Fayle was different. No one said anything about his name. When he told the boys that everyone called him Sep, they believed him without question and Sep it was. And the teachers, while perhaps a little on the vague side, were incredibly knowledgeable and kind, with no sign of any instruments of torture. He couldn't believe that there was absolutely nothing to be disappointed about – and that made him happier than he had been in his entire life.

Now that he was a fully fledged member of Fayle, Septimus vowed to make the most of every minute.

Within the first few days, he'd signed up for the school newspaper, the science club, the athletics squad and swimming training. At assembly, Professor Winterbottom announced that, for the first time in over ten years, Fayle would be teaming up with the girls from Winchesterfield-Downsfordvale to put on a play. Drama wasn't something he had any experience with, but he was willing to give it a go all the same.

On Saturday afternoon, Sep was on his way to the running track when the headmaster called out to him from across the quadrangle.

'I'd like a word, young man.' The professor walked towards him, peering over the top of his spectacles.

Professor Wallace Winterbottom had been the headmaster at Fayle for a very long time. The school was his life and, although his long-suffering wife Deidre often hinted that she thought it might be time they took off and saw the world, Wallace was deaf to her suggestions. Deidre enjoyed school life too, but carried a long-held desire to visit the pyramids and Greece. In fact, she had an extensive list of places she wanted to see, which curiously enough she carried with her everywhere, in her right shoe.

The three loves of Wallace's life were Fayle, of course, his beloved West Highland Terrier named

Parsley, and his wife Deidre, possibly even in that order. He had started his teaching career at Fayle as a young English master and gained the role of head very early on. So, in all, he'd been at the school for more than forty years – almost a record, but not quite. Hedges, the gardener, beat him by a long shot, having started at age fourteen; he was now seventy-four and showing no signs at all of slowing down.

'Yes, sir,' Septimus replied as he reached the old man.

'We've got a new boy starting tomorrow and I was thinking he might go in with you,' Professor Winterbottom began. 'Name's Lucas Nixon. He's had a rough trot lately, so I need someone who'll look after the lad. Can I rely on you?'

Sep nodded. 'Of course, sir. I'd be pleased to have a room mate. It's been a bit quiet.'

'Very good. That will be all.' The professor came as close to a smile as anyone might ever have seen.

Septimus was looking forward to the arrival of a room mate. He'd already made friends with several of the boys and although he enjoyed his own company, it would be good to have someone to talk to after lights out.

Chapter 20

'Guess who starts at Fayle tomorrow?' It was now Saturday evening and Alice-Miranda and Millie had just joined Jacinta in the dining room dinner line.

'Lucas?' Jacinta asked, wide-eyed.

The other girls nodded.

'That's fantastic. I can't wait to see him,' Jacinta gasped.

Millie rolled her eyes. 'Three weeks ago, you couldn't stand him. 'Now I think you're seriously "crushed".'

'No, I'm not,' Jacinta protested. 'We just under-stand each other, that's all.'

'Well, I don't think we'll get to see Lucas tomorrow.' Alice-Miranda shuffled along, edging closer to where Mrs Smith was pushing out plates of steaming hot roast beef, crispy potatoes, beans and cauliflower cheese covered with lashings of thick gravy. 'But Mummy said that she would see if Aunt Charlotte and Lawrence can pop in and say hello once they've got Lucas settled.'

'Ohhhh,' Jacinta sighed. 'Imagine, Lawrence Ridley – here – at Winchesterfield-Downsfordvale. Best keep that between us, or the poor man will be mobbed. He's sooo dreamy.'

Millie and Alice-Miranda giggled.

'I'm sure you'll look after him, Jacinta,' Millie grinned.

'Yes, of course I will. He's a national treasure and in my favourite ever movie.'

The girls hadn't noticed Sloane, who had slipped into the line behind Millie and was eavesdropping on their conversation.

'Did you say Lawrence Ridley?' Sloane asked. 'As in Lawrence Ridley, the movie star?'

'Oh, hello there, Sloane,' Alice-Miranda leaned around Jacinta and Millie so that she could see her.

'Yes, that's right. Jacinta did say Lawrence Ridley.'

'How do you know him?' Sloane demanded. 'If you actually do, that is.'

'Oh yes, I really do. We all do. Lawrence is my Aunt Charlotte's fiancé and his son Lucas is starting at Fayle tomorrow. Do you remember I told you about them when we were out riding this morning?' Alice-Miranda smiled.

'No, you didn't. You didn't say anything about Lawrence Ridley. I'd have remembered that,' Sloane replied.

'Well, I thought I did but perhaps I didn't. Anyway, he's the loveliest fellow and terribly handsome too.'

'Will I get to meet him?' Sloane demanded.

'Quite possibly, if he and Aunt Charlotte come over tomorrow once they've dropped Lucas off.' Alice-Miranda picked up her knife and fork as the group moved along the servery.

'You have to introduce me,' Sloane insisted. 'Meeting Lawrence Ridley is definitely on my "to do" list.'

'You're well organised, having a "to do" list. Oh, hello Mrs Smith.' Alice-Miranda reached the front of the queue. 'It looks like you've outdone yourself tonight. Dinner smells delicious.' She picked up her plate and held it under her nose. 'And thank you for the picnic today – it was scrumptious. That chocolate cake was one of the best ever.'

'My pleasure. Dolly gave me a few pointers with my cauliflower cheese so I'm hoping that it's up to scratch. I know there's no one makes it like she does but I am trying.' Mrs Smith pushed another plate forward, which Millie scooped up.

'I think it looks perfect,' Alice-Miranda nodded.

Mrs Smith smiled. It seemed to be her automatic response whenever Alice-Miranda appeared.

The girls moved off to find a table. Sloane followed rather more closely than Jacinta was comfortable with.

'Are you going to sit with us, Sloane?' Alice-Miranda turned and asked her. 'You're most welcome.'

Millie and Jacinta exchanged frowns.

Sloane gave a half-hearted nod. Although she would have preferred to be with some of the older girls, she wanted to find out more about Lawrence Ridley. It really didn't seem fair at all that the painful little brat would end up with a movie star for an uncle.

The dining room hummed as girls swapped stories of their day. Alice-Miranda was so pleased to see Miss Grimm and Mr Grump sitting with Mr Plumpton and Miss Reedy, chatting and smiling. Mr Plumpton's red nose glowed like a beacon as he roared laughing at something Mr Grump had just shared with the group. This was exactly what school should be like, she thought to herself. But there was something worrying her too and it was all to do with her new friend Hephzibah.

Sloane interrupted her thoughts. 'So what's he really like?'

'Who?' Alice-Miranda looked up from where she had just pushed her knife through a plump potato.

'Lawrence Ridley, of course.' Sloane rolled her eyes. 'Don't you ever listen?'

'Oh, he's a darling,' Alice-Miranda replied.

'But what else?' Sloane quizzed.

'What do you mean, what else?' Alice-Miranda asked.

'Well, he's a movie star. He must have loads of girlfriends and go to parties all the time and get himself into lots of trouble,' Sloane purred.

'No, I don't think so. He's really just an ordinary person,' said Alice-Miranda. 'More handsome than the average fellow, but perfectly normal as far as I can tell.'

Sloane sneered. She was clearly disappointed by Alice-Miranda's response. 'Well, he doesn't sound like any of the movie stars I know,' she huffed.

'And who do you know?' Millie queried.

Sloane glared at Millie. 'Loads of people.'

'Really? Such as?' Millie invited.

'You wouldn't know them.' Sloane picked up her plate and stalked off to sit at another table.

'You know she's lying.' Millie shook her head. 'I'm sure she doesn't know anyone.'

'Give her a chance, Millie,' Alice-Miranda replied. 'She's just trying to fit in.'

Towards the end of the meal, Miss Reedy stood up from her seat and moved to the podium.

'Ahem,' she cleared her throat. 'Girls, I just wanted to remind you all that auditions will commence tomorrow afternoon at 2 pm in the Great Hall. The schedule has been posted on the noticeboard. Please take note of the time you have been allocated and don't be late as we have a lot to get through.'

'That's so exciting,' Alice-Miranda gasped when Miss Reedy finished her speech.

'Yes, let's just hope that "you know who" doesn't get the main role.' Jacinta nodded her head towards Sloane, who had taken her dessert off to yet another table. 'Her head's big enough already.'

Alice-Miranda came to Sloane's defence. 'If she does, she'll have earned it. You know Miss Reedy doesn't play favourites.'

The girls finished their butterscotch puddings and raced off to check the time of their auditions. Millie ran her finger down the list, finding Alice-Miranda at 2.30 pm, Jacinta at 2.45 pm and her own name at 3.00 pm.

'I'd better let Mummy know to tell Aunt Charlotte not to come until afternoon tea time so we can all be finished,' Alice-Miranda said, as the three girls skipped back to Grimthorpe House and an early night.

Chapter 21

An hour after lights out, Alice-Miranda lay awake in bed, her mind a whirl. She was excited about the auditions tomorrow but there was something else. She couldn't stop thinking about Hephzibah. She knew her friend wasn't ready for one of her parents' rescue missions – not just yet. Alice-Miranda wanted to visit again in the morning, but she couldn't go riding on her own. It wasn't allowed and for good reason too. There was only one thing for it. She had to tell Millie.

'Millie,' she whispered. 'Are you awake?'

Millie rolled over and faced her friend. 'Yes, I thought *you* were asleep. I've been trying to remember my lines and now I can't stop thinking about them.'

'I can't sleep either – but it's not because of the auditions. I have to tell you something, but you must promise not to tell anyone else. It's terribly important.'

'Of course,' Millie replied, as she wriggled out from under the covers and propped herself against her pillow.

Alice-Miranda sat up and hugged her knees under her chin. A shard of moonlight fell through the window, creating a soft half-light.

'What is it?' Millie looked at her friend. She couldn't remember Alice-Miranda ever looking so serious.

'Well, you know this afternoon when Bonaparte bolted?' Alice-Miranda began.

'Yes, little monster. I think that pony of yours has bionic smell power.' Millie giggled at her own joke.

'That's for sure. But it's just that I didn't tell you the whole story,' Alice-Miranda continued.

Millie raised her eyebrows. 'The whole story?'

'I met someone and they helped me find my way back to the fork in the path.'

'Who was it?' Millie asked. 'Was it a gypsy or a tramp or someone?'

'No, of course not,' Alice-Miranda shook her head.

'Well, why are you being so secretive about it?' Millie frowned. 'Did they hurt you?'

'Goodness no,' Alice-Miranda gasped. 'We're friends. I want to go and visit her again tomorrow and I'd like you to come with me.'

'Of course I will,' Millie replied. 'We'll go early, just after breakfast.

'You must promise that you won't be scared,' Alice-Miranda added.

'Why would I be scared if she's your friend?'

'Well, it's just that there are stories. You see, she has a rather large number of cats.'

Millie's eyes widened. 'No,' she gasped. 'You didn't . . .'

Chapter 22

'Are you going riding *again*?' Jacinta moaned as Alice-Miranda and Millie arrived at the breakfast table dressed in their jodhpurs, shirts and boots. Millie placed her plate down opposite Jacinta while Alice-Miranda slid in next to her.

Ignoring the question, Millie looked up and asked Jacinta if she was training that morning.

'Of course,' she replied.

'Then why are you whining about us going riding?' Millie frowned. 'You don't have time to play anyway.'

'Oh, good point.' Jacinta took a mouthful of cereal.

'Hello Sloane.' Alice-Miranda smiled as the school's newest student set her plate down at the end of their table.

'Don't expect me to come riding with you two again,' Sloane grouched when she noticed the way Alice-Miranda and Millie were dressed. 'After what you did yesterday, I'll wait until Hugo arrives, thank you very much.'

'Well, for your information, we weren't going to ask you anyway,' Millie replied. 'And I thought you said that your horse was called Harry?'

'No, I didn't.' Sloane narrowed her eyes. 'You just don't listen.' She stuck her nose in the air, picked up her plate and headed off to sit with Ivory and Ashima, who didn't exactly look pleased to see her.

The girls tucked into their breakfast.

'Yum, that was delicious.' Alice-Miranda licked her lips. 'I love Sundays – Mrs Smith always does something extra yummy.'

Millie stabbed at the last piece of pancake on her plate and popped it into her mouth.

'We should get going,' Alice-Miranda suggested. 'We don't want to be late getting back.'

'If we come back.' Millie raised her eyebrows meaningfully.

'What's that supposed to mean?' Jacinta quizzed.

'Nothing,' Alice-Miranda smiled. 'Millie's just being dramatic. Isn't that one of the lines in your audition piece?'

'Ha ha!' Millie replied, her face deadly serious.

'I'll see you both later then.' Jacinta scraped the last of her cornflakes from the bowl before starting on her pancakes.

'Bye,' Millie gulped.

'See you soon, Jacinta,' Alice-Miranda called.

The two girls headed for the stables where they promptly set about saddling Bony and Chops. It was Wally's day off so, according to school rules, Alice-Miranda scratched a note on the old chalkboard which hung at the building's entrance, saying what time they were heading out and when they thought they'd be back. It was also one of the rules to say where they were going. Without wanting to lie, Alice-Miranda jotted down – *Millie and Alice-Miranda, same as yesterday.*

The girls mounted their ponies and walked lazily out of the stable block and into the warm morning sunshine.

'You must have had a good sleep Bonaparte – you do seem to be in a better mood today.' Alice-Miranda squeezed her legs and the pony sprang to life, jogging down the path towards the gate which led to the forest beyond the school's boundaries. Millie was unusually quiet as she trotted alongside her friend.

Finally, she spoke. 'Are you sure she's not . . . you know?' Millie asked for at least the tenth time since Alice-Miranda had shared her secret the night before.

'Millie, I promise, she's not. But if you don't want to come in, you don't have to,' Alice-Miranda reassured her.

Millie wanted to believe her tiny friend. But she'd heard the story about the witch a few times since she started at the school. It was hard to believe that it wasn't true. Deep down, she wasn't sure if she actually believed in witches at all, but the witch in the woods had been folklore at Winchesterfield-Downsfordvale for generations.

The girls continued through the woods, following the map Hephzibah had drawn for Alice-Miranda the day before.

As they approached the estate, Bony thrust his nose in the air and whinnied. Alice-Miranda held the reins as tightly as she could. 'I don't think so, mister – you're not running off today. There are no vegetables in that old patch anyway.' Alice-Miranda guided Millie towards the first set of gates, which yesterday had been a passing blur. Two limestone pillars, an indication of the grandeur of the estate contained within, towered next to an unwieldy yew hedge. The rusted gates, held hostage by years of untended foliage, bore an intricate pattern.

'Look at that.' Alice-Miranda pulled on the reins and Bonaparte stopped in the middle of the entrance. 'Can you see that, Millie?' she pointed at the gate on the left-hand side. 'It looks like a giant C wrapped into the iron.'

Millie nodded, too in awe to speak.

'Oh, and look there, on the other gate – there's an M . . . CM – of course, Caledonia Manor! Gosh someone went to a lot of trouble with this place,' Alice-Miranda prattled.

'And look at that,' Millie's voice trembled. There was a weathered sign covered with vines poking out of the bushes. It read, 'Keep out! Trespassers will be prosecuted.'

'Are you sure we should go in?'

'Of course,' Alice-Miranda replied. 'Don't pay any attention to that silly old thing.'

The girls continued on their journey up the over-grown drive, past the ancient vegetable patch with its weedy scarecrows. The ponies clip-clopped towards the dilapidated stable block with its missing slates and grimy walls. A black cat with huge green eyes appeared on the top of the outer wall and was imme-diately joined by three of his friends – a ginger, a tabby and a grey.

'Good morning, pussycats,' Alice-Miranda addressed the row of felines. They responded with a cacophony of meows. 'How sweet – a welcome song from the Kitty Chorus,' Alice-Miranda giggled.

It didn't even raise a grin from Millie. Her mouth seemed plastered shut as she took in their surround-ings.

'We'll leave the ponies here.' Alice-Miranda slid down off Bonaparte and took the reins forward over his head. She scrounged around in her pocket for a sugar cube, which Bony nibbled from her out-stretched hand.

Millie found her voice. 'Why can't we ride the whole way?'

'I think it's safer to tie them up here than some-where near the house. This is where I left Bony yesterday,' Alice-Miranda replied. 'I don't want him getting any more ideas about that vegetable patch. It's perfectly safe.'

Millie hopped down from the saddle and followed Alice-Miranda into the outside stall. Both girls looped their reins through the bridles so the ponies could move freely around the yard. A heavy overnight downpour had half-filled a smooth stone water trough in the corner that Bonaparte rushed straight for.

'Are you sure they'll be all right?' Millie followed Alice-Miranda out of the enclosure.

'Positive,' her friend nodded, checking the latch. 'It's not too far to the main house. Just wait until you see it, Millie – it's amazing.'

Millie was not convinced. So far, the stables and the gardens looked like a picture from one of her old Grimm's fairytale books. She seemed to recall that the owner of *that* house had some rather nasty magical powers.

Alice-Miranda took off up the drive with Millie in tow. This time, the cats from the stables seemed happy to stay where they were, lolling about in the sunshine, keeping one eye on their equine friends.

As the girls reached the second set of gates, Alice-Miranda noticed that the ivy she'd pulled from the gatepost only the day before had already begun to reattach itself to the brass nameplate.

'Caledonia Manor, more like Creepy Manor if you ask me,' Millie muttered under her breath as she looked around at the fossilised garden urns and enormous derelict fountain overgrown with weeds. She half-expected a giant or troll or some other fairytale creature to emerge from the thicket beside them at any moment.

The girls rounded the final bend and there in all its tumbledown splendour was Caledonia Manor. Millie gasped as Alice-Miranda had done the day before. 'It's huge,' she breathed.

'Yes, it's amazing, isn't it?' Alice-Miranda replied. 'Such a lovely house.'

'Lovely?' Millie questioned. 'I can think of some other words that would better describe this place.'

'Oh, I know it's far from perfect,' Alice-Miranda began, 'but if you look past the flaky paint and the grubby windowpanes, there's a real beauty underneath.'

Millie was not so sure. The house was enormous, that was true. But as for beautiful, she was not at all convinced.

'Come on,' Alice-Miranda called, as she ran towards one side of the building.

Millie gasped again when the girls emerged from the tangled undergrowth and onto the open lawn at the rear of the house.

Alice-Miranda continued on her way, jogging up the stone steps with their zigzag balustrade. 'Hurry up,' she called. Millie's heart hammered in her chest. Her mouth was dry, as if she'd eaten a bucket of rocks.

Alice-Miranda reached the back porch and waited for Millie to catch up.

Five black cats lazed in various positions along the terrace. Millie hesitated when she saw them. She was quite convinced their eyes were following her every move.

'I might wait here,' Millie gulped.

'Oh, all right, if you're sure.' Alice-Miranda tapped on the glass panel of the kitchen door. There was no answer. 'But I might be a little while.'

'Wait, I'll come.' Millie ran to stand beside her friend.

Alice-Miranda knocked again, then turned the handle and walked into the kitchen.

'Helloooo?' she called. 'Are you here, Miss

Hephzibah? It's me, Alice-Miranda. I've come to visit and I've brought a friend.'

The door to the room off the kitchen, which Alice-Miranda thought of as the playroom, was closed. There was a rustling sound coming from within. The tiny child knocked gently and called again. Then she opened the door and poked her head inside.

Millie stood on the other side of the kitchen. In spite of the warmth of the day, she shivered beside the lit stove.

'Hello Miss Hephzibah,' Alice-Miranda spoke. 'I'm going to put the pot on and I've brought some lovely cake for your morning tea.'

Millie tried to see inside the room but her feet seemed set in concrete.

'If you'd rather take your tea in here,' Alice-Miranda continued, 'I can bring it in for you in a minute.'

From where she stood, Millie heard no reply. Alice-Miranda closed the door and walked back across the kitchen where she busied herself filling a battered copper kettle, which she placed on the stove top.

Millie hadn't moved an inch. 'Is she . . . is she in there?' Millie whispered.

'Oh yes. I think she's feeling a little tired so I said that I would take the tea in for her,' Alice-Miranda smiled. 'Are you all right? You look a bit pale.'

Millie's freckly face had drained of colour. Her red hair looked like firelight against her porcelain skin.

'Are you really going in there?' Millie pointed at the closed door.

'Of course. Will you come with me?' Alice-Miranda asked, as she removed three china cups and saucers from the pine sideboard.

Millie shook her head.

'That's all right. You can stay here if you'd prefer.'

Millie's eyes darted all over the place as she took in the kitchen and its ancient contents. There was another doorway to her left and a further entrance-way at the opposite end of the room.

'There's a back staircase just through that door beside you.' Alice-Miranda filled the teapot with boiling water. 'I went upstairs yesterday, but I haven't had a proper look around because I heard a clatter down here and that's when I found Miss Hephzibah. I was rather hoping we might be able to explore properly sometime.'

Millie peered at the doorway. Her mind raced. Perhaps it was safer to join Alice-Miranda in the other room. She didn't fancy being alone in the cavernous kitchen with its creaks and groans and doors to who-knows-where.

'I'll come,' Millie blurted.

'That's lovely. But you mustn't be frightened. Other than me yesterday, I don't think Miss Hephzi-bah has seen anyone for a long time and she's very shy.' Alice-Miranda poured three cups of black tea. From her backpack she produced a container of milk and three large slices of butter cake. When she'd asked Mrs Smith for three pieces this morning, the cook had automatically assumed that Millie and Alice-Miranda were taking one of the other girls with them on their ride. Alice-Miranda hadn't corrected her.

'Is that a tray over there?' Alice-Miranda pointed at a cabinet next to where Millie was still rooted to the spot.

Millie spun around, moving for the first time since the girls had entered the kitchen. She bent down and retrieved an ornate timber tray, its faded decoration hinting at the once grand house's glory days. She handed it to Alice-Miranda, who loaded it up with the three cups and plates.

'Can you open the door for me, please?' Alice-Miranda picked up the tray and walked towards the playroom door.

'Oh.' Millie swallowed hard. 'Okay.' She walked forwards slowly as if at any moment she might turn and flee.

'It's all right, really it is,' Alice-Miranda reassured, as Millie reached up and turned the handle.

Chapter 23

That afternoon, Millie, Jacinta and Alice-Miranda milled about outside the assembly hall, waiting for their turn to audition. Millie and Alice-Miranda couldn't help exchange knowing glances as they recalled their morning's adventure. Fortunately, Jacinta was far too engrossed in reading over her lines to notice their strange looks. Ashima emerged from the building.

'How did you go?' Alice-Miranda asked.

'Okay, I think. You can go in now, Alice-Miranda. Miss Reedy asked for you. Good luck.'

'Thanks!' Alice-Miranda bounced into the hall.

'Hello there, young lady,' Miss Reedy smiled. 'I see you're auditioning for two parts this afternoon. May I introduce Mr Lipp?' Miss Reedy nodded at the gentleman sitting beside her. They each had a pile of papers in front of them. Mr Lipp was dressed in a very dapper mustard-coloured suit with a multi-coloured cravat. His handlebar moustache was neatly groomed, however his eyebrows resembled two hairy caterpillars crawling across his brow.

'Hello Mr Lipp.' Alice-Miranda walked towards him and held out her hand across the table. 'My name is Alice-Miranda Highton-Smith-Kennington-Jones and I'm very pleased to meet you, sir.'

Mr Lipp peered over the top of his spectacles and gently shook Alice-Miranda's tiny hand. 'Pleased to meet you too, young lady.'

'Now, where shall we start?' Miss Reedy glanced at the list in front of her.

'If I may, Miss Reedy, I'd like to read for Snow White first.' Alice-Miranda walked up the side steps and onto the stage.

'Very well,' Miss Reedy agreed. 'Why don't you commence from the part where the huntsman is taking Snow White into the forest with the intention of killing her. That should give you a bit of dramatic scope.'

Alice-Miranda stood in the middle of the stage and gathered her thoughts. She imagined that the assembly hall was now a dark forest and that the hunter was standing right in front of her.

'Please, sir, don't kill me. If you let me go, I promise I'll tell no one. I will find somewhere to live and I won't ever return to the palace,' Alice-Miranda pleaded with her imaginary foe.

Miss Reedy read the part of the huntsman. 'But I . . . I have a job to do. The Queen will . . .'

'Sir!' Alice-Miranda interrupted before letting out a heart-wrenching sob. 'I beg you.' The tiny child fell to her knees.

'Then go. Go far away and never return. I will take the Queen the heart of a boar and make her believe that it was yours,' Miss Reedy read passionately.

Alice-Miranda looked up slowly. 'Thank you, kind sir. Thank you with all my heart. Your generosity will never be forgotten.' And with that, Alice-Miranda fled into the wings.

Mr Lipp brushed his eye and sniffed. Miss Reedy threw him a curious glance and he at once protested,

'Dust, I think. Yes, very dusty in here.' He stuck his finger in his eye as if to remove the offending object.

Alice-Miranda returned to the stage where both Mr Lipp and Miss Reedy clapped vigorously.

'Well done, my dear, that was wonderful,' Miss Reedy enthused.

'Thank you.' Alice-Miranda smiled and gave a little bow. 'May I read for the part of the narrator now?' she asked.

Mr Lipp and Miss Reedy lowered their voices.

'No, I don't think so,' said Mr Lipp finally.

'But Mr Lipp, I'd like to give myself a chance as the narrator.'

'Alice-Miranda, there's no need. You're the final girl auditioning for the part of Snow White and we've decided that the role shall be yours,' Miss Reedy announced. 'But if you would please keep that to yourself until the cast is announced on Wednesday, we'd greatly appreciate it.' She raised her eyebrows and then paused, thinking. 'Unless of course, Mr Lipp, you have any boys who have put their names down for that role? I'd almost forgotten. We still have to see the Fayle boys tomorrow afternoon.'

'Ahem,' Mr Lipp cleared his throat. 'No, I don't know of any boys who have expressed a desire to play the role of Snow White,' he grinned. 'Although, last year when we were flying solo on the school play, one of the lads did a very good job of Maid Marian in Robin Hood.'

Alice-Miranda giggled. Miss Reedy did too.

'It looks like the part's yours, young lady,' Miss Reedy nodded her head. 'But –' the teacher raised her forefinger to her lip – 'until Wednesday.'

'Of course, Miss Reedy. Thank you so much. I promise I won't let you down.' Alice-Miranda skipped out of the hall and raced off to meet Millie and Jacinta, who were waiting outside.

Chapter 24

'**I** am a complete failure,' Jacinta wailed. 'Mr Lipp didn't appreciate my improvisations of Happy turning cartwheels at all. He said that, as far as he knew, dwarfs weren't renowned for their gymnastic abilities.'

'Don't worry, Jacinta. I'm sure you did just fine,' Alice-Miranda comforted her friend. 'And you auditioned for the role of the narrator as well, didn't you?'

'Yes,' Jacinta pouted. 'I couldn't even tell what Miss Reedy and Mr Lipp thought about *that*.'

'There's always stage crew,' Millie added.

'Stage crew – for losers who couldn't get a proper part in the play,' Jacinta moaned.

'No, that's not true, Jacinta. The stage crew is very important. If there weren't a stage crew, then the actors would have to slip in and out of character as they carried trees and buildings and magic mirrors and things on and off the stage. Just imagine – the Evil Queen finishes her lines and then has to pick up the mirror and struggle off with it – that would be terribly silly,' Alice-Miranda grinned.

'I suppose you're right.' Jacinta managed a half-smile. 'Hopefully I'll get a part, but if I don't, stage crew will have to do.'

'What about you, Millie, did your audition go well?' Alice-Miranda asked.

'I think so. I'm not sure which part I'd prefer though. Doc's pretty funny, but I love that the Magic Mirror gets to give it to the Queen,' Millie replied. 'How do you think you went, Alice-Miranda?'

'Okay, I think,' she replied.

The girls were on their way to the front of the school to meet Charlotte and Lawrence, who had phoned to say they would be at Winchesterfield-

Downsfordvale in time for afternoon tea. Sloane was stalking about in the garden.

'Oh, hello Sloane,' Alice-Miranda called when she spotted her lurking behind the rose bushes. 'What are you doing over there?'

Sloane looked up. 'I was just, um, waiting for my mother,' she replied. 'She's coming to visit.'

'That's convenient,' Millie whispered to Jacinta. 'More likely she told her that Lawrence was stopping by. She'd better not cause a scene.'

'Why don't you come over here and wait with us?' Alice-Miranda asked.

Millie and Jacinta huffed.

Sloane walked over to the group.

'Did you enjoy your audition?' Alice-Miranda asked.

'I suppose so,' Sloane replied.

'What did you try out for?' Jacinta asked.

'The only role worth having, of course,' she scoffed.

Alice-Miranda felt a flurry of butterflies in her tummy. Sloane would be very disappointed when she missed out on the part of Snow White.

'So you tried out for Snow White, then?' Millie pressed.

'Good grief, no,' Sloane replied. 'Who'd want to be that sappy little do-gooder? I'm going to be the Evil Queen. That's the only part that's any good in this pathetic little fairytale.'

Alice-Miranda exhaled softly. Her butterflies flapped their wings and flew right away.

In the distance, the girls could hear the low rumble of a sports car engine. A shiny silver vehicle entered the driveway.

'They're here!' Alice-Miranda ran down the steps of Winchesterfield Manor to greet her beloved aunt and soon-to-be uncle.

'Oh my gosh, it's really him!' Sloane gasped.

'Of course it is,' Jacinta replied. 'Did you think Alice-Miranda was making it up?'

'No,' Sloane spat. 'I believed her.'

The car grumbled to a halt in one of the recently added visitor parking spaces. Only a matter of months ago, parents and other family members were strictly forbidden from visiting the school at any time other than to drop off and pick up their daughters at the beginning and end of term. But, of course, that had all changed now and Miss Grimm had come to see the importance of family dropping in whenever possible.

'Hello.' Alice-Miranda launched herself at her Aunt Charlotte as soon as she was out of the car.

Charlotte scooped the little child into her arms and peppered her face with kisses – cheeks, forehead and, lastly, the tip of Alice-Miranda's nose. It had been done that way for as long as either of them could remember. Alice-Miranda hugged her tightly.

'And how is my favourite niece?' Charlotte set the child down. Lawrence emerged from the rear of the car and snuck up behind Alice-Miranda, tickling her wildly before twirling her over his shoulder and depositing her back on the ground.

She squealed with delight. 'I'm . . . very . . . well . . . thank . . . you,' Alice-Miranda gasped between giggles.

Millie chuckled and Jacinta almost fainted.

'Hello Millie and Jacinta.' Charlotte ran up the steps and kissed both girls on the cheek. Lawrence followed, with Alice-Miranda holding tight to his left hand.

'And how are my favourite adopted nieces?' He leaned down and hugged Millie then Jacinta. Jacinta's legs turned to jelly.

'Great thanks, Mr Ridley,' Millie replied. Jacinta

said nothing but stood looking rather goggle-eyed. A quick jab to the ribs from Millie seemed to bring her back around.

'Well, very, thank you.' Jacinta shook her head. 'I mean, very well, thank you.'

Sloane had remained a few steps away from the group, taking it all in. She wished she really had phoned her mother to come and see this. In fact, she knew she'd be in huge trouble for not telling her. It was just that her mother had a way of making it all about her, and this was Sloane's opportunity to meet a real live movie star without her mother being in the way.

'And who do we have here?' Lawrence turned his hypnotic smile to Sloane.

'Excuse me for being so rude.' Alice-Miranda grabbed Sloane and brought her closer to the group.

'This is Sloane Sykes. Sloane, this is my Aunt Charlotte and soon-to-be uncle, Lawrence Ridley.'

'How do you do, Miss Sykes?' Lawrence bowed his head.

'It's lovely to meet you, Sloane,' Charlotte nodded.

'Gosh, you're gorgeous!' Sloane had clearly fallen for Lawrence's charm. 'I mean, it's a pleasure to meet you too, Lawrence.'

Sloane ignored Charlotte altogether as she stood mesmerised by the movie star.

'You're just in time for afternoon tea,' Alice-Miranda informed them. 'Mrs Smith was so excited when I told her that you were coming, I think she's cooked enough to feed a small army.'

The group headed for the dining room. Sunday afternoons were often quiet as girls were out and about, enjoying their weekend freedom. Yet this afternoon the room was packed and even the teachers had turned up.

'Did you tell everyone they were coming?' Jacinta hissed at Sloane.

'No,' she replied innocently. 'Why would I do that?'

Jacinta shook her head and Millie's face crumpled into a frown. The appearance of Lawrence caused a near riot. Girls were shouting out, asking him to come and sit with them. It was only when Miss Grimm took to the microphone that things settled down.

'Girls, please be quiet.' Her ice-cold stare had the desired effect. 'We have visitors for afternoon tea and yes, one of them is a wee bit famous and the other is an Old Girl of the school. However, that is no reason for the sort of behaviour I have just witnessed. Mr Ridley and Miss Highton-Smith are here as guests. Please do not pester them or ask for autographs. As your headmistress, I promise I will get an autograph which will suffice for all,' Ophelia smiled.

The hush that had fallen over the room was maintained as Miss Grimm invited Lawrence and Charlotte to find a seat. She then hurried over and produced what appeared to be a rolled-up poster for his latest movie, *London Calling*, and a thick black texta, which she handed to Lawrence. He signed the poster and when Mr Grump appeared with a camera, Lawrence posed for several photographs with the headmistress.

Miss Grimm chatted with Lawrence and Charlotte for what seemed like ages. Finally, Alice-Miranda interrupted them and asked if anyone would like tea.

'Oh, I am sorry, Alice-Miranda.' Ophelia blushed. 'I know your aunt and uncle have come to see you. I'll be off now.'

'You have to try some of this cake.' Millie pushed a piece of passionfruit sponge towards Charlotte.

'So, how is Lucas?' Jacinta asked.

'Yes, how did he seem when you left him at school?' Alice-Miranda quizzed. 'You know, we're doing a play with Fayle and the rehearsals and everything will be over in their new drama theatre. We've all tried out, so hopefully we'll be able to see Lucas a lot.'

'He was okay,' Lawrence nodded. 'When I went to Fayle, it was a great school – never had any problems with bullies or the like. And his room mate is a really impressive young man.'

'What's his name?' Sloane asked.

'Sep,' Charlotte replied.

Sloane almost choked on her tea.

'Sep, as in Septimus, as in my brother, Septimus Sykes?' she babbled. 'My brother is sharing a room with your son?!'

'Oh, that's great,' Lawrence smiled *that* smile. Half the girls in the room almost fainted.

'Isn't that lovely?' Alice-Miranda grinned.

Jacinta wasn't so sure. She hoped that Septimus Sykes wasn't at all like his sister. Otherwise Lawrence's recollections about bullies at Fayle might prove nothing more than a long-distant memory.

Chapter 25

Sloane Sykes stalked off to telephone her mother. She was furious. Anyone would have thought Alice-Miranda was the movie star, the way the girls had all mobbed her after her aunt and Lawrence Ridley had left. Just watching the whole display turned Sloane's stomach. Life simply wasn't fair. Why couldn't her mother have married someone like Lawrence Ridley instead of her loser vacuum-cleaner salesman father? Sloane dreaded the other girls finding out about that. She'd never live it down. At least she had proof of her mother being a successful model, even if it was a hundred years ago.

'Hello Mummy,' Sloane spoke.

'Are you having a good time?' her mother asked.

'No, not especially.'

'You just need to make some friends, that's all,' her mother cooed. September was enjoying her new-found freedom with her children away. It was lovely not having to do the daily school run – now she could loll about in bed until 9 am and spend the rest of the day pleasing herself. The last thing she wanted was for Sloane to come home again.

'Septimus has got a new room mate,' Sloane drawled.

'That's nice. I'm glad you're keeping in touch with your brother. I was worried he wouldn't make any friends, being the strange little fellow that he is,' said September, admiring her French manicure.

Sloane offered the smallest titbit of information. 'His father's a movie star.'

September dropped the phone. There was a rustling sound as she fumbled about retrieving it from the floor. 'What did you say?'

Sloane repeated herself, slowly. 'Septimus's new room mate's father is a movie star.'

'Oh my gosh, are you kidding?' Her mother steadied herself on the bench, then had to sit down.

'No, Mummy, I'm not kidding,' Sloane said.

'Well, who is it then?' September demanded.

'Some kid called Lucas,' Sloane teased.

'I don't care about him,' September spat. 'Who's his father? Who's this movie star?'

'Umm, well, I just met him a little while ago,' Sloane continued.

'Sloane Sykes, hurry up and tell me. Or do I have to drive over there and drag it out of you?' her mother demanded.

'Oh, it's Lawrence Ridley,' Sloane sighed.

There was a dull thud at the other end of the line. September had fallen off the chair and was now picking herself up from the kitchen floor. Sloane could hear her mother's squeals and wondered if perhaps she was having a heart attack.

'Are you there, Mummy?' she asked. 'Mummy, are you there?'

There was the sound of deep breathing – more like huffing and blowing – until September finally gathered herself together enough to speak. 'Sloane Sykes, you'd better not be having me on.'

'I'm not, Mummy. He was just here a little while ago, having tea.'

'Then why didn't you call me? I could have been there in an hour. You just don't think, do you, Sloane? And now I've missed my chance to meet Lawrence Ridley.' There was another thud. Sloane rolled her eyes. She waited for her mother to come back on the line.

'Mother, I have to go.'

'No, no, you don't. Tell me about him.' September gathered herself together. 'What's he like?'

'He's handsome and charming and he's marrying Alice-Miranda's aunt,' Sloane grouched.

'Really? What's she like?' September asked. 'Is she pretty?'

'She's okay, I suppose. But totally wrong for him.' Sloane scratched at her pinkie nail.

'Not glamorous enough, it happens all the time. Movie stars always marry beneath them.' Her mother clicked her tongue. 'He needs someone more like . . . well, like me, I suppose.'

'That's what I thought,' Sloane replied. 'But I have to go, Mummy.' Sloane glanced up at the queue of girls who were waiting to use the telephone. Mrs Howard had appeared and was tapping her watch and giving Sloane very dark looks, before bustling out of the room with an armful of towels.

'Call me tomorrow,' her mother demanded. 'Is he coming back again soon?'

'Who?' Sloane asked.

'Lawrence Ridley, of course.' September wondered where her daughter got her brain sometimes.

'I don't know,' Sloane replied.

'Well, you'd better find out. Maybe we'll get invited to the wedding,' September squealed.

'Yeah, maybe, if he goes through with it.' Sloane turned her back to the line of girls waiting for the phone.

'Bye, darling.' September hung up.

Sloane continued talking into the phone for at least another three minutes before she finally put it down.

'Sorry girls, important business.' She smiled like a toad in a swarm of flies.

'Sloane Sykes.' Mrs Howard reappeared. 'In here, young lady. NOW!'

Sloane huffed and walked to Mrs Howard's little office, which was across the hallway from the sitting room.

'Close the door,' Mrs Howard commanded.

The girls waiting to use the phone listened intently as Sloane got a very solid telling off for being so inconsiderate of others.

Chapter 26

On Wednesday morning, just as Miss Reedy had promised, the cast list for the play was posted to the noticeboard outside the Great Hall. As morning tea finished, the girls spilled out of the dining room to check if they had secured a role.

'Alice-Miranda's Snow White,' Millie squealed and hugged her little friend. 'And Jacinta – you got the narrator.' Jacinta breathed a sigh of relief. A group of taller girls had pushed in close. Millie was standing on tiptoe but had no chance of viewing the board.

'Millie, what are you?' Alice-Miranda asked.

Danika turned around and grinned at the smaller girls. 'Millie's the Magic Mirror.'

'That's great.' Alice-Miranda smiled and squeezed Millie's hand.

Sloane was standing back from the group.

Jacinta turned to her room mate. 'What about you, Sloane?'

'I'm in no hurry,' she sneered. 'Seriously, who else could play the Queen like me?'

Jacinta muttered under her breath, 'You've got that right.'

'What was that?' Sloane glared.

'Um, nothing, I just said yes, it's a part with real bite.' Jacinta blinked innocently.

Ashima and Susannah linked arms. 'Hi ho, hi ho, it's off to class we go,' they sang, thrilled with their parts as Dopey and Doc.

Ivory was excited to be named head of the stage crew and Danika was in the group working on costume design.

'I wonder who my Prince will be?' Alice-Miranda thought out loud.

'It says here, Sep Sykes.' Shelby turned around from the board, disappointed that she'd missed out on being one of the dwarfs, but consoled by her role as the lead tree in the forest.

'That's great,' Alice-Miranda smiled. 'Did you hear that, Sloane? Your brother is playing the Prince!'

'How lovely for you,' Sloane drawled.

The taller girls dispersed, leaving Sloane, Alice-Miranda and Millie to check through the complete list. Sloane moved forward and ran her finger down the page.

'Told you so,' she said aloud. 'Evil Queen – Sloane Sykes.'

'I guess it won't be a stretch just playing yourself,' Millie quipped.

'Millie, that wasn't very kind,' Alice-Miranda berated her friend.

'Sorry,' Millie apologised. 'It's just that I couldn't imagine you having a more suitable part either, Sloane.'

'Look!' Alice-Miranda gasped. 'It says that the Woodcutter is Lucas Nixon. I'm so glad he arrived in time to audition.'

'Good on him,' Millie smiled. 'There's no better way to fit in at school than to get involved . . .'

Sloane rolled her eyes at Millie.

'Well, that's what Miss Reedy's always saying.' Millie pulled a face back at her.

The first read-through with the cast was to take place the following afternoon. The girls were to meet Miss Reedy and walk with her to the other side of the village to Fayle, where all of the rehearsals would take place. The school had recently built a state-of-the-art drama facility, which would be perfect for the play.

'We'd better get to class.' Alice-Miranda said goodbye to Millie and Jacinta and strode off to Science with Mr Plumpton. She always looked forward to his lessons as they usually involved some type of experiment – which rarely went according to plan.

'Shall we go riding after school?' she called to Millie.

'That would be great.' Millie winked. 'Meet you at the stables at half past three.'

Chapter 27

'So where are you two going this fine afternoon?' Wally Whitstable was sitting in the middle of the stables on a bale of straw, oiling an old saddle.

'Hello Wally,' Alice-Miranda smiled. 'We're just going for a loop over to Gertrude's Grove and home again.'

She placed a small backpack outside Bonaparte's stall. Mrs Smith had happily handed over three large slices of hummingbird cake and three chocolate brownies when Alice-Miranda had earlier appeared at the kitchen door. She explained that they were going out riding and wouldn't be around for tea.

'That's quite a long way, girls. Make sure you're back before dark. That forest gets awful creepy once the light fades,' Wally warned.

'We'll be fine,' Millie said as she grabbed Chops's bridle from the tack room wall.

'Watch that bloke of yours today, miss.' Wally pointed at Bonaparte's stable. 'I was giving 'im a nice rub down before and the little monster nipped me on the ear. Drew blood, he did.'

'Bonaparte.' Alice-Miranda shook her head. 'I just don't understand your lack of manners. You've grown up with some of the best-tempered horses I've ever met and still you behave like a spoilt little boy. I am sorry, Wally. One day he might learn to behave but I am afraid I have my doubts.' Bonaparte looked at his mistress with the sad eyes of a child in trouble.

'I haven't seen Miss Sloane down here again,' Wally grinned. 'I think Stumps might have put paid to her riding career.'

'She says that she's waiting for her horse to arrive. Do you remember what she said his name was?' Millie asked.

'Yes, didn't she call him Harry?' Wally replied.

'That's what I thought. Then, the other day, she said that she was waiting for Hugo. I think her horse might be a figment of her overactive imagination.' Millie pursed her lips.

'Don't be too hard on her, Millie,' Alice-Miranda said. 'Maybe she really wants a horse but her parents can't afford one. It costs a lot of money to come to a school like this and ponies are very expensive.'

'But her mother's a model and her dad's on television – or so I heard.' Millie lifted her saddle down from the post on the wall and walked over to where she had Chops tied up in the stable.

'Television did you say, Miss Millie? What's Miss Sloane's surname then?' Wally asked.

'Sykes, she's Sloane Sykes,' Millie replied.

'You know, that name does ring a bell.' Wally stopped polishing the leather and tapped his lip thoughtfully. 'I know. There's a bloke on the 'ome shopping channel called Smedley Sykes. My old nan's always got that on. She thinks he's a bit of a looker.'

'There you are then. That could be him,' said Alice-Miranda as she led Bonaparte out of the stall, his shoes clip-clopping on the cobbled floor.

'But what does he *do* on the home shopping channel?' Millie asked.

'I think he sells gym equipment.' Wally poured some more polish onto the cleaning cloth. 'No, that's some other bloke Nan likes looking at too. Hang about. It's, um, oh, that's it. He sells vacuum cleaners. They're beauties too. I bought one for Nan last year for Christmas and she loves it. She sucked Uncle Alf's rug right off the top of his bald head one day when he wouldn't lift his feet off the carpet.'

Millie roared with laughter, imagining Wally's uncle losing his toupee up the vacuum cleaner.

'Well, Mr Sykes isn't exactly the television star that Sloane would want everyone to believe,' Millie giggled.

'I don't think Sloane ever mentioned that he *was* on television. Didn't one of the other girls say that? I think it was Ashima who said that she overheard Mrs Howard talking to Mrs Derby about Sloane's parents,' Alice-Miranda replied as she pulled up a stool and hauled herself onto Bonaparte's back.

'Maybe,' Millie replied. 'She's probably embarrassed. I'd die if my father was on the television lifting bowling balls with a vacuum.'

'No, you wouldn't,' Alice-Miranda said. 'There's nothing wrong with being in sales. I mean, look at my mummy and daddy. Our family livelihood depends on department stores and supermarkets.'

Chops and Bonaparte were ready to go.

'Take care there, girls. See you soon.' Wally stood up and gave Bonaparte a friendly pat. The pony repaid his kindness by trying to bite his finger. 'Off with you then, you little monster.'

Alice-Miranda and Millie trotted to the gate. Once on the other side, they cantered across the field and into the woods towards Caledonia Manor. Just as they had done on Sunday, the girls left the ponies in the stall outside the stables. Alice-Miranda led the way as they raced up the driveway to the house.

'Hello Miss Hephzibah,' Alice-Miranda called as she knocked, then walked straight into the kitchen with Millie behind her. 'We're here and we've brought cake and brownies too.'

The old woman emerged from the playroom and Alice-Miranda ran to give her a hug. Hephzibah didn't know how to respond, having lived for such a long time without human affection. She gently patted the child on the back. Millie was more cautious, saying hello from where she stood.

'Hello,' Hephzibah nodded. 'Please come.' Her left palm was outstretched, indicating that they would sit at the pine table in the middle of the kitchen. There were three cups and saucers with matching plates out ready. 'It's good to see you again . . . so soon. I . . . I wasn't sure that you would come . . .' Her voice faltered.

'Of course we were going to come and see you.' Alice-Miranda unpacked the contents of the backpack and busied herself distributing Mrs Smith's sweet treats. 'But I'm afraid we can't stay for too long or Wally will send a search party.'

Hephzibah was dressed in the same black clothes with her hat and veil shielding her scarred face. When Alice-Miranda had visited last time with Millie, the old woman had not removed either and had kept her face hidden. Hephzibah had seen in Millie the fear of a child who had been told the witch stories, and she was anxious not to cause further alarm. There was something lovely about Millie's red hair and sprinkling of freckles like paprika that reminded Hephzibah of someone long ago. Someone she had loved with all her heart.

The trio sat down to their afternoon tea party.

'We're doing a play with the boys at Fayle,' Alice-Miranda began. 'Millie's going to play the part of the Magic Mirror.'

'And Alice-Miranda's Snow White,' Millie added.

Hephzibah looked up at the girls with a flicker of a smile hiding on her lips.

'A play, how wonderful. When I was a girl, I played the part of Snow White too,' she spoke softly. 'It was marvellous.'

'That's amazing,' Alice-Miranda gasped. 'You can help me learn my lines.' The tiny child beamed.

Hephzibah clasped her bony hands in front of her. 'That was a million years ago – another lifetime – I was a different person then.'

'But it will be fun,' Alice-Miranda insisted. 'Anyway, next time we come, we can bring our scripts, can't we Millie?'

Millie took a bite of chocolate brownie and nodded.

Alice-Miranda sipped her tea. She placed her cup back on the saucer and, for a moment, there was complete silence between the three of them.

'Have you always lived here?' Alice-Miranda asked.

Hephzibah rested her cake fork on the side of her plate. Something about this tiny child with her cascading chocolate curls and eyes as big as saucers made her feel safe.

'Yes,' Hephzibah replied. 'Would you like to have a look around?'

'Yes, please.' Alice-Miranda stood up. 'That would be wonderful.'

Chapter 28

September Sykes sat on the couch watching her favourite television game show, *Winners Are Grinners*. A painful memory invaded her thoughts. Smedley had auditioned to be the host of that show fifteen years ago. He made it to the final two and then Cody Taylor, who she was now watching on the television, was given the job.

At the time, September had begged Smedley to change his name. She'd been keen on Saxon, but he wouldn't hear of it. Cody Taylor was now one of the most sought after presenters in the country. He owned an island and fourteen sports cars and his real name was Wilfred Thicke.

Life simply isn't fair, September thought to herself. At least things were changing for the better.

For a start, September was thrilled that Septimus was rooming with the son of the most handsome movie star on the planet. And if she wasn't free to marry Lawrence Ridley herself, at least she could get herself and Smedley invited to Lawrence's star-studded celebrity wedding. She could imagine what the girls at the gym would say about that. And then there was Smedley's new business. He'd used the proceeds from the sale of his father's shop to buy into a company building condominiums for cashed-up retirees chasing the sun overseas. He'd shown her the brochures – the apartments were gorgeous and the whole scheme was certain to turn a handsome profit. The kids were tucked away at boarding school and September simply didn't have a minute to miss them. Life was certainly on the way up.

The last contestant had just blown it. 'Oh, you silly cow,' September shouted at the television. 'Everyone knows that it's God who's richer than the

Queen.' She pressed the 'off' button on the remote before seeing the answer, which actually named a famous children's author as the correct response.

September picked up the phone and dialled the common room at Fayle.

'Hello,' she purred. It's September, Septimus's mother.'

'Oh, hello Mrs Sykes,' the housemaster, Mr Huntley, replied.

'Please, call me September,' she smiled down the phone. 'Is my darling Septimus about?'

'I'm sorry Mrs Sy–, I mean, September, but Sep is, er, at . . .' He ran his finger down the list of names on the sheet which gave him the whereabouts of all the boys at their afternoon activities. 'Your son is currently at football training.'

'Football? That doesn't sound like Sep at all,' September replied.

'Well, I can assure you, that's where he is. Would you like me to have him phone you when he gets in?' Mr Huntley enquired.

'Yes, I've called four times now since the weekend but he's never available,' September moaned. 'Anyone would think he loves that school more than his own mother.'

'No, I'm sure that's not true at all. Sep is doing a great job of settling in. I don't remember a boy so enthusiastic about being involved in . . . well, just about everything. There's nothing to worry about.' Horatio Huntley was losing his patience and thanking his lucky stars that it must have been one of the other residents who had taken Mrs Sykes's calls on the previous three occasions.

'Well, I haven't got time to keep phoning, Mr Hunter,' September tutted.

'It's Huntley, Horatio Huntley, madam,' he corrected her.

'Whatever. Perhaps you can tell me about his new little room mate?'

'Yes, of course. He's a good lad, name's Lucas Nixon. I think they're getting along extremely well. Both keen on their sports and their studies and they've both won themselves parts in the school play that we're doing with the girls from Winchesterfield-Downsfordvale,' Mr Huntley offered.

'So he's an actor, just like his father.' September grinned to herself and checked her reflection in the refrigerator door.

'I'm sorry, September, but I'm not at liberty to discuss the boy's family,' Horatio sighed.

'Well, of course you can, Horatio,' September assured him. 'You know I won't tell anyone – and he is sharing a room with my son. I'd like to know that his parents are good eggs. Don't want to find out darling Sep is sleeping next to the son of an axe murderer or something.'

Horatio had just about had enough. 'Mrs Sykes, I'm terribly sorry, but I must go. One of the boys has just superglued his finger to his science project. I'll let Sep know you called.' And with that, he hung up.

'Rude,' September huffed.

Smedley arrived home just as the call finished. His brow looked like ten rows of pearl-stitch knitting and he was as pale as a pint of milk.

'You have to call the headmaster at Fayle, Smedley, and make a complaint about that rude housemaster, Mr Huntley.' September opened the fridge and retrieved two large pre-packed tubs of potato salad. 'He just hung up on me.'

'Really?' Smedley looked at his wife. 'Why?'

'Some stupid brat had superglued his finger to his science project or something. Surely he could have waited,' she complained.

September took the lids off the plastic tubs and emptied their contents onto two plates.

'Oh, we're not back on that again, are we?' Smedley screwed up his face. 'A man can't live on potato salad alone. Can't we have some meat?'

'No. I've just started the carbo-salad diet and if I have to suffer, you do too.' September pushed the plate in front of her husband.

Smedley glanced at the pile of letters on the countertop and sighed loudly.

'I have to go out,' he gulped.

'Why?' September demanded.

'Business.' He grabbed his briefcase and jammed the letters inside.

'When will you be back, then?' she pouted.

'Later.' Smedley strode out the back door.

September heard the car door slam and the tyres squeal as he backed out of the driveway. As she sat at the kitchen table picking her way through the potato salad, she noticed a letter that must have fallen on the floor when Smedley grabbed the pile off the bench.

She reached down to get it and noticed the words 'Private and Confidential' emblazoned across the top. Her stomach did a backflip. 'What's all this then?'

September marched over and flicked the switch to start the kettle.

Chapter 29

Alice-Miranda bounced along beside Miss Reedy all the way to Fayle. The steel-grey sky was threatening rain but, armed with their raincoats and umbrellas, Miss Reedy knew that a brisk walk was just the thing to get the girls settled before the first read-through of the play. The group marched in two straight lines through the tiny village of Winchesterfield: past the Victorian terraces, past the butcher, baker and post office and past the little grocery shop with the flat above, which used to belong to Sloane Sykes's grandfather Percy.

The longest part of the walk was down the hedge-lined driveway at Winchesterfield-Downsfordvale and back up the even longer driveway at Fayle.

'What a lovely school,' Alice-Miranda remarked, as they walked along a pathway bordered on both sides by clipped camellia hedges. On the way over, Miss Reedy and her smallest charge had chatted about all manner of things – books they'd read, Miss Reedy's recent trip to the city and ideas for some of the scenes in the play. Miss Reedy had written the adaptation herself and was keen to see it come together. When at last the main school building came into view, Alice-Miranda couldn't help feeling as if she'd been there before.

Millie caught up to her friend. She'd spent the walk chatting to Jacinta. Only a few months ago, the two barely spoke at all, but since Alice-Miranda had arrived at school, Millie had come to realise that although Jacinta was a little highly strung, she was really very good fun.

'It's huge, isn't it?' Millie looked up at the building, with its four Ionic columns and grand portico. Then she thought for a moment. 'You know what this place looks like?' Millie tilted her head to one side

Alice-Miranda nodded. 'Yes. That's it. It's almost exactly the same.'

'The same as what?' Miss Reedy asked, glancing down at the tiny girls.

'Oh, the same as a friend's house,' Alice-Miranda smiled.

'Goodness, you do have fortunate friends to live in a house like this. It's beautiful, isn't it?' Miss Reedy admired the detailed plasterwork.

One half of the double front doors swung open and Mr Lipp emerged. His red suit stood out against the dreary day.

'Good afternoon, ladies,' he nodded. 'We'll head straight to the drama centre. The boys are gathering there now.'

Millie and Alice-Miranda fell to the rear of the group as they took in every detail of the mansion. A shiny brass nameplate beside the front doors bore the building's name: McGlintock Manor.

'Come along, girls,' Mr Lipp called, as he waited for the group at a stone archway. 'We must get started posthaste.'

Alice-Miranda and Millie ran to catch up.

The drama centre, though apparently brand new, looked as if it had been part of the school forever. The girls were ushered through an opulent foyer and into the top of a large theatre, with curved rows of tiered seating and a stage area below. They walked in single file down to the bottom two rows. The girls were directed to take a seat on the left-hand side, while the boys from Fayle sat on the far right. Jacinta spotted Lucas first of all. She waved frantically. He looked up and raised his left hand.

'Which one is your brother?' Alice-Miranda asked Sloane, who had sat down beside her.

Sloane gazed over at the group of twenty or so boys. 'There he is.' Sloane shuddered. 'Next to that boy waving.'

'Oh, that's Lucas. They must be friends already.' Alice-Miranda stood up and waved to her soon-to-be cousin. 'He looks just like his dad, doesn't he?'

Sloane peered across at the boys and nodded. He certainly did.

'Jacinta adores him,' Alice-Miranda stated. 'I do too, but not in *that* way. They didn't like each other at all a few weeks ago, but then they had a long chat and "voila", they became great friends.'

Sloane decided right there and then what she must do. Jacinta was no match for her charms. If Sloane played her cards right, Lucas would be falling all over her in no time at all.

Mr Lipp and Miss Reedy stood side by side on

the stage, looking up at the assembled students. It was Miss Reedy who spoke first, about the importance of learning lines and being on time for rehearsals. Her stern voice rang out through the theatre, apparently coming as quite a shock to some of the boys, whose faces took on a pale tinge.

Her message was loud and clear. 'Tardiness will *not* be tolerated, inappropriate behaviour of any sort will *not* be tolerated and missing rehearsals for any reason other than extreme illness will *not* be tolerated. This is the first time that our two schools have joined forces in over ten years. I would like this to become an annual tradition once more, as would you, Mr Lipp, I presume.' She frowned at the teacher beside her, who nodded his head like a jack-in-the-box. 'As we enter a new age of cooperation, I look forward to nothing less than a performance of the highest standard. And, above all –' her voice softened – 'I hope that you will have a lot of fun in the process.'

'Fun? Is she kidding?' Lucas whispered behind his hand to Sep. 'She's terrifying. Glad she doesn't work here.'

'What was that, young man?' Miss Reedy glared up at Lucas.

'Nothing, miss. I was just saying I can't wait to get started,' he lied.

Sep had not taken his eyes off Miss Reedy, who apparently had a built-in tracking and radar system capable of picking up even the softest of sounds and most minuscule movements. He thought she'd be a valuable asset to the FBI with those skills.

Mr Lipp then handed out the scripts. Each student's name was printed clearly at the top and their lines had been highlighted throughout.

'Oh, and please don't lose those,' Miss Reedy added, 'or you will be writing them out again by hand.'

There was an audible gulp from the group.

The read-through began. Several of the students decided to try out different accents, with varying degrees of success. One young lad, playing the role of Sneezy, sounded like a breathless old man and was told under no circumstances could he keep that voice, until Mr Lipp pointed out to Miss Reedy that it was, in fact, his real voice. The poor lad was suffering terribly with allergies, which Mr Lipp thought added to the authenticity of the part.

An hour passed, and Miss Reedy and Mr Lipp seemed pleased with the students' efforts. They indicated that the children could head up to the foyer for a few minutes while the teachers conferred on some matters.

The girls and boys left the theatre. They walked up opposite aisles and milled about in two separate groups, until Alice-Miranda marched over to say hello to Lucas.

'There you are,' she smiled. 'How are you getting on?'

Lucas nodded. 'Fine. Yeah, it's good.'

'Jacinta, Millie,' Alice-Miranda called. 'Come and say hello.'

The two girls walked over to join the pair. Jacinta was just about to say something, when Sloane Sykes appeared.

'Hello,' she purred. 'You must be Lucas. I feel soooo sorry for you.'

'Why?' Lucas replied.

'You have to share a room with my disgusting brother,' she grimaced.

'Oh, so you're Sloane,' said Lucas.

'Yes.' She fluttered her eyelashes.

'There's no need to feel sorry for me. Sep and I are getting on great.' He grinned – and there it was, that million-dollar smile, just like his father's.

Sloane smiled back. 'I met your dad the other day.'

'Yeah, me too,' Lucas smirked. Alice-Miranda, Jacinta and Millie giggled. Sloane laughed too, though she had no idea what she was laughing about.

'Next time we come over to Fayle, you'll have to show us around,' Jacinta spoke.

'Yeah, that'd be great. Although there are heaps of places I don't know yet either,' Lucas replied.

Septimus Sykes was standing on the other side of the room, hoping to avoid his sister. She was bound to make a scene. Lucas spotted him and motioned to his friend to join them. Sep didn't move.

'Hang on a minute,' Lucas told the girls and waved again at Sep. Septimus was reluctant, but he didn't want to disappoint Lucas and seem rude. He walked over to his friend.

'Hello.' Alice-Miranda held out her tiny hand. 'My name is Alice-Miranda Highton-Smith-Kennington-Jones and I'm very pleased to meet you, Sep.'

Septimus couldn't help but smile.

'These are my friends, Millie and Jacinta,' she nodded at the girls. 'And I think you know Sloane.'

Millie and Jacinta smiled but Sloane just curled her lip into a snarl.

'Hello,' Septimus said to Millie and Jacinta. He glanced at his sister. 'I see you're in a good mood, as usual.'

'All the better for seeing you, big brother,' Sloane bit back.

Miss Reedy and Mr Plumpton appeared in the foyer.

'Come along, girls, we must be going,' Miss Reedy boomed. 'You'll need to put your raincoats on.'

'See you soon.' Alice-Miranda gave Lucas a quick hug. His face turned the colour of Mr Lipp's suit.

With the exception of Sloane, the other children exchanged polite goodbyes. 'Bye . . . see you tomorrow . . . nice to meet you . . .'

Miss Reedy stood tall at the head of the line. Outside, it had started to drizzle.

'It's so cold,' Sloane grouched. 'I don't know why we couldn't have taken the bus.'

'Moral fortitude, young lady.' Miss Reedy's bionic hearing had kicked in again. 'Stop complaining or we'll go the long way around.' The teacher glanced at Alice-Miranda beside her and winked.

Alice-Miranda giggled as they set off through the damp air for home.

Chapter 30

September Sykes was seething. She had just arrived home from her daily work-out at the gym and checked the phone messages. She had hoped to hear from Septimus but, instead, Golden Gates had left four messages asking her if she could get in touch to organise the return of her step-mother-in-law's suitcase.

'What's in that thing?' she grouched. 'Gold bars?'

Things were not going as planned in the Sykes household. Steaming open her husband's private and confidential letter had sent Sloane into an incandescent rage. It seemed that Smedley's 'can't lose, licence to print money' retirement-villa scheme was already in trouble. Apparently the construction company had hit a sewer line the previous week when drilling the foundations, spilling thousands of litres of raw sewage into the street and flooding several houses. The clean-up was going to cost thousands and the insurance company refused to cover it. She had confronted Smedley when he arrived home, but he simply told her that it was all going to be just fine and he'd already sorted it out. She didn't believe him.

September had a shower and changed into her favourite pink leisure suit. She made herself a cup of coffee using the shiny silver machine Smedley had given her for Christmas, opened a packet of choc-chip biscuits and pranced out to the back garden to soak up the sun. She needed something to take her mind off her stupid husband and his bodgie business deals. She remembered that she'd left the latest copy of *Gloss and Goss* on top of her gym towel on a pile of laundry. She jumped up to get it and stubbed her toe on the battered blue suitcase Smedley had left beside the utility room door.

'Oh, blast and blast,' she yelled. 'My toe!' Plump

tears wobbled then spilled down September's perfectly made-up cheeks. 'Smedley, you idiot!' she yelled. At that moment, the telephone rang. September hopped inside on one leg to pick it up.

'Hello,' she said, wincing.

'Oh, hello, Mrs Sykes, is it?'

'Yes,' September grouched.

'It's Matron Payne from Golden Gates. I am terribly glad to find you at home. I've been calling and calling and I wasn't sure if you'd received any of my messages.'

'What do you want then?' September rubbed her big toe.

'Well, Mrs Sykes, it's your mother-in-law,' Matron Payne began.

'She's my step-mother-in-law.'

'Of course, your step-mother-in-law.' Matron Payne was not enjoying September's tone at all.

'Has she died?' September asked.

'No, she's as well as can be expected under the circumstances.' It was fortunate September couldn't see the matron, who was quivering in disgust.

'What is it then? I'm very busy. I don't have all day.' September was thinking about her coffee getting cold.

'Your step-mother-in-law has been asking about a blue suitcase. Apparently it's very important to her. As you know, she hasn't been able to speak since the stroke and her writing is awfully wobbly, but this morning she spent rather a long time creating a message which indicated that she is fretting terribly for it. The doctor says it would most likely help speed her recovery if it were found and returned to her immediately,' Matron Payne explained.

'I have no idea what you're talking about.' September walked to the patio doors and looked directly at the suitcase which she had just tripped over.

'Well, Mrs Sykes, could you please have a look for it? I know your step-mother-in-law would be very grateful.' Matron Payne was fast losing patience.

'I'll tell my husband and he can bring it round, if he finds it, that is. I have to go.' September hung up.

'Mrs Sykes,' Matron began, then realised that the line was dead. 'I'm sure your step-mother-in-law, Henrietta, one of the loveliest ladies I've ever had the pleasure to care for, would be happy to have some visitors,' she whispered into the beeping handset.

September had already decided midway through the conversation that the battered blue suitcase must contain something of value. Why else would the old girl be so desperate to have it back? She dragged the case towards the outdoor setting and lifted it onto the table. A rusty padlock guarded its contents. September went to the shed and found a pair of pliers with which she mangled the lock until it snapped in two. It was only tiny and came away quite easily. As she unzipped the case and pushed open the flap a smell of mildew, mouldy socks and Stilton cheese rose up and hit her in the nostrils.

'Pooh!' September held her nose and waved her hand. 'So where's the treasure?'

At first glance, it seemed that the contents were nothing more than a pile of old papers. There were some photographs and faded newspaper clippings, but no gold bars or bags of diamonds. September continued rummaging and found an antique pipe and a framed photograph of a man from long ago.

'What a lot of sentimental rubbish,' she said out loud. She was about to close the lid when something caught her eye. It was a piece of yellowed parchment written in fancy lettering. The name at the top was familiar. *Fayle*. She pulled it from the pile and laid it on the table. It was a family tree; the bottom left-hand corner was missing and there were some holes in the page, but it was unmistakable. It was the Fayle family tree. September wondered if it had anything to do with the school.

'Here it is.' She followed the trail with her finger. 'Frederick Erasmus Fayle, founder of Fayle School for Boys, married Helena Louise McGlintock. They had one son and they lived at McGlintock Manor, which it says here is the school house. George McGlintock Fayle married Edwina Elena Rochester. They had one son called Erasmus McGlintock Fayle. Gawd, what a terrible name! They lived at the school house too. Then Erasmus married someone called Willow Caledonia Henry and they had, well, of course, this part's missing, isn't it? D-A-U-G-H – it must have been a daughter. Here it is then. Henrietta McGlintock Fayle. *Our Henrietta?* September screwed up her nose. 'Granny Henrietta was a Fayle?'

September wondered what else she might learn about her step-mother-in-law. All this time and the old duck had never said anything. September was sure her name was Henrietta McGlintock, but she'd never mentioned being a Fayle. And the only thing she'd ever paid for was the children's new school fees, which September now decided she likely got for free anyway, seeing as though she probably owned the school. September tutted and rolled her eyes. As she did so, she spotted another piece of paper in the case. She snatched it up and unfolded it. It looked much older than the first document and was also damaged at the bottom. She couldn't tell how much of it was missing. Again, she read aloud.

'"Fayle School Charter. This document outlines the rules by which Fayle School for Boys is herewith established. Number one: the school motto will henceforth be *Nomine defectus non autem natura – Fail by name, not by nature*." That's a bit stupid, isn't it? "Number two: boys will be trained in academic, artistic and athletic pursuits" – isn't that what all schools do?' September shook her head. '"Number three: only teachers of the highest calibre will be employed at the school. Number four: Fayle will remain on the site purchased by the school's founder, Frederick Erasmus Fayle, on one thousand acres of land in the village of Winchesterfield." Boring – blah, blah, blah.' September ran her finger down the remainder of the list. 'What's this? . . . "Number twenty-nine: failure at Fayle is not acceptable. Should more than twenty-five per cent of boys fail ANY examination, the headmaster incumbent –"

I wonder what that means "– must invoke clause thirty of the Fayle School Charter . . ." Well, what's that rule?' September scanned further down. 'Ah, here it is.' She tapped her red talon on the page. '"The school must be closed within twenty-eight days and all land, buildings and other assets be returned to the oldest living relative of Frederick Erasmus Fayle."'

September's eyes almost popped out of her head. She re-read the paragraph. Then she re-read the family tree. One child, that's all the Fayles ever had. One child in every generation. If this were true, then Smedley's step-mother would be the next in line to the Fayle family fortune. And she was old and sick, and probably wouldn't live for much longer.

'Oh, this is the answer to all our problems!' September folded the charter and family tree, stuffed the rest of the papers back into the suitcase and zipped it up. 'I don't think we ever did find that bag,' she said to herself, as she dragged it into the house. 'I think that bag must have gone missing some-where.' She stopped in the hallway and pulled down the attic ladder. Her mind was racing. A wicked plan was brewing and she knew just the girl to help her with it.

Chapter 31

The girls arrived back at school in time for tea. Mrs Smith had decided to expand her catering repertoire this term, with themed dinners once a week from countries around the world. Tonight she had whipped up butter chicken with rice, naan bread and a mild beef vindaloo curry. Dessert was a delicious sweet dumpling dish.

'What's this muck?' Sloane pushed her food around the bowl. 'It's disgusting.'

'Don't you like it?' Alice-Miranda asked. 'I think

it's scrumptious. Last year, when Mummy and Daddy took me to visit their friend, Prince Shivaji, I fell in love with Indian desserts. But I can tell you this *gulab jamun* is the best I've ever tasted. Mrs Smith is so clever.'

'She's certainly improved, that's for sure,' Jacinta nodded. 'You don't remember, but her food used to be awful.'

'All that time with Mrs Oliver must have improved her technique. Now there's a great cook.' Millie rubbed her tummy and shovelled another spoonful of the sticky treat into her mouth.

'Your brother's lovely, Sloane.' Alice-Miranda set her spoon down inside the empty bowl.

'My brother's a pig,' Sloane replied.

'I wish I had a brother,' Alice-Miranda said. 'But at least I'm getting a cousin.'

'So, when's the wedding?' Sloane asked.

'I'm not sure. It will depend on Uncle Lawrence's film schedules and Aunt Charlotte's work, too.'

'Will there be lots of famous people there?' Sloane didn't want to sound desperate but she simply had to get an invitation.

'I don't know really. I mean, Aunt Charlotte and Uncle Lawrence have lots of friends, but I'm not sure if they're famous,' Alice-Miranda said thoughtfully.

'Of course they'd be famous. Don't famous people only hang out with other famous people? I mean, look at your mother, Jacinta. She's always with beautiful people doing important things in interesting places,' Sloane informed the group.

'I don't really know what my mother does or who she's friends with.' Jacinta's lip quivered. 'And it's not really any of your business either.'

'You're kidding, aren't you? Your mother is in every edition of *Women's Daily* and *Gloss and Goss* I've ever seen. She's practically their poster girl for famous people doing fun things with other famous people.'

'I don't care,' Jacinta glowered. 'What my mother does is entirely up to her.'

'If my mother was as famous as that, I'd talk to her every day and I'd tell everyone where she'd been and who she was with.'

'Good, I'll tell her to adopt you. Perhaps we can trade mothers.'

'Now you really are kidding, aren't you?' Millie laughed. Jacinta smiled too. That was a terrible thought.

'What's wrong with my mother?' Sloane fizzed with anger. 'She's beautiful and she was a famous model too. What does your mother do, Millie?'

'Millie's mother is a vet,' Alice-Miranda contributed. 'And she's awfully good. You know, Chops had a mystery virus and he could have died, but Millie's mother solved the puzzle and cured him. And she started an animal shelter for unwanted pets.'

'Wow,' said Sloane sarcastically, rolling her eyes. 'And what's your dad? A lion tamer?'

'He's a farmer,' Millie replied.

'Double wow,' Sloane drawled.

'Well, at least my father doesn't flog vacuum cleaners on the home shopping channel for a living.' Millie couldn't help herself. It was out of her mouth before she had time to think.

'Why, you little brat!' Sloane screamed and stood up. She picked up her bowl of *gulab jamun*, marched around to where Millie was sitting, and tipped the entire contents over her head.

Millie bellowed. She grabbed Sloane by her long blonde ponytail and yanked as hard as she could.

'Ow, you brat!'

The chinking of cutlery died down as the other girls turned to see what was going on.

'Millicent Jane McLoughlin-McTavish-McNoughton-McGill and Sloane Sykes, come here, NOW!'

Miss Grimm bellowed across the room. Her general demeanour may have changed for the better but she could still silence an entire dining room in a second.

Millie lifted the upended bowl from her head and set it back on the table. She turned to face her attacker, then marched towards the head table, where Miss Grimm stood with her arms folded in front of her. Sloane followed at a distance.

Miss Grimm lowered her voice and glared at the culprits. '*What* was that?'

'She started it,' Sloane began to sob. 'She said awful things about my mother and father.'

'I did not,' Millie retorted. 'She's a bully, Miss Grimm.'

'Bully is a very strong word, Millicent, and not one we throw around willy-nilly.' Miss Grimm was inclined to believe her red-headed charge, but she had to keep an open mind. From where she and Miss Reedy were sitting, it did look as though Millicent had pulled Sloane's hair. But there was the indisputable evidence of the upended dessert. Millie was dripping dumplings onto the floor right in front of them.

Ophelia realised that the room was still silent. She looked up and addressed the girls. 'Please go on with your dinner. Talk among yourselves. This is now a private matter and I will settle it with Millicent and Sloane. I will see both of you,' she said, staring them down, 'in my office, tomorrow morning at 7 am. Do not be late and remember, I *will* find out what happened so it will be much easier if you tell me the truth. Off you go. You can sit at your table until the end of teatime.'

Millicent glanced up at the clock on the wall. It was only a quarter past six. They didn't go back to the house until 7 pm. Her hair was beginning to set like concrete on the side of her face. She opened her mouth to speak.

'I would also suggest that you remain silent,' Miss Grimm commanded.

Ophelia thought it was probably punishment enough that the girls had to stew on things for the night. She wasn't planning anything especially severe – perhaps some additional gardening duties with Charlie or mucking out the stables. She had a niggling feeling about Sloane Sykes though and, after what had happened with Alethea Goldsworthy, she didn't plan on being fooled again.

Chapter 32

Back at the house, Millie sped straight for the showers to wash her hair. Sloane Sykes went straight for the telephone. She called her mother and immediately began to cry.

'Darling, what's the matter?' September fussed. 'Why are you so upset?'

'I got into trouble with Miss Grimm. It wasn't my fault. Millie said mean things about you and Daddy,' Sloane sobbed.

'Oh sweetie, what did she say?'

Sloane began to wail even louder.

'Don't you worry your pretty head about that nasty little brat. I'm so glad you called, though. I have something important to tell you.' Sloane's mother smiled to herself. 'Your father's not here, and that's a good thing, because this is a special secret just between you and me. Septimus doesn't need to know either, okay?'

'What is it, Mummy?' Sloane perked up.

'Did you know that if twenty-five per cent of the boys at Fayle fail any test, the school has to close immediately?'

'Yes. Alice-Miranda told me that. She says everyone knows it. But the boys at Fayle don't fail and so nobody's ever worried about that silly rule,' Sloane replied. 'Why do you ask?'

'Well, sweetie, do you know what would happen to all that lovely land and those gorgeous buildings if the boys failed and the school had to close?'

'Yes. It gets sold off or something.' Sloane twisted a long blonde strand of hair around her index finger.

'Well, yes and no. The school has to close immediately but the land and the buildings go to the next living relative of the school's founder – some fellow called Frederick Erasmus Fayle.' September was enjoying this.

'Big deal, Mummy. I don't see what any of this has to do with us. We're Sykeses not Fayles.'

'I see what you mean. But did you know what Granny Henrietta's surname was before she married Grandpa Percy?' September asked.

'No, Mummy. Why would I know that?'

'I don't suppose you would.' The mother was toying with her daughter like a kitten with a string. 'But I do.'

'Mother, get to the point. I have to go and paint my toenails,' Sloane snapped.

'Sloane, I have recently learned that your darling step-granny was once known as Henrietta McGlintock Fayle. And guess what? She's an only child.' September waited for Sloane to realise what she had just said.

Sloane was not impressed. 'Yeah, so what, Mummy? Granny Henrietta gets the school if the boys fail – which they won't, because they don't.'

'But what if they did?' September lowered her voice. 'What if they failed and Granny passed away? Work it out, sweetheart.'

Sloane pondered for a moment. 'That would mean Fayle, and all those beautiful buildings, and

all that lovely land would go to . . . oh . . . Daddy!'
She cupped her hand to the telephone. 'Oh my gosh,
Mother, you're a genius!'

'Thank you, darling.' Possibly for the first time
in her life, September felt like a true genius too.

'But Mummy, the boys at Fayle don't fail – not
ever.' Sloane reminded her mother.

'Well darling, you see, that's where you come
in . . .'

Chapter 33

Alice-Miranda sat up in bed. 'Good morning, Millie.' She looked over at her friend. 'How are you feeling?' Alice-Miranda had set her alarm for 6 am. She was planning to use the extra time to practise her lines for the play.

'Terrible,' Millie sighed. 'I didn't sleep much at all. Miss Grimm's probably going to kick me out of the play.'

'I don't think so,' Alice-Miranda reassured her. 'She's changed so much, remember, and I'm sure if you apologise to Sloane, Miss Grimm will accept that. Sloane *was* being a bit tricky.'

'Yes, but I have to keep my temper under better control.'

The two girls hopped out of bed. Millie didn't want to be a second late for her appointment with Miss Grimm.

'Good luck.' Alice-Miranda gave Millie a quick hug. 'Just tell Miss Grimm the truth – that's all you can do.'

It was a quarter to seven when Millie departed for Miss Grimm's study. The corridors of Winchester-field Manor were particularly foreboding in the early morning light. Millie glanced at the portraits of the former headmistresses with their stern looks. She felt like they were all frowning at her.

Mrs Derby hadn't yet arrived for the day but Miss Grimm had obviously opened the office door for the girls. There was no sign of Sloane and, come to think of it, Millie hadn't seen her back at the house. Surely she wasn't stupid enough to miss the meeting?

Millie sat in one of the chairs positioned outside Miss Grimm's study to wait until 7 am. She watched the grandfather clock against the wall. Tick . . . tick . . . tick . . . The rhythm of the grand old timepiece was like a slow march. Every minute seemed like an hour. In an effort to take her mind off her impending doom, Millie stood up and walked over to have a look at Mrs Derby's row of photographs perched on the marble mantelpiece. There was a lovely picture of her and Constable Derby on their wedding day and another of Millie and Alice-Miranda as flower girls. In fact, Mrs Derby had involved all of the girls in her celebration, each wearing pretty dresses in a rainbow of colours with floral garlands in their hair. Millie's own red locks stood out like a beacon compared with the other girls.

Millie walked back over to the mahogany chair and sat down. According to the clock, it was two minutes to seven. At 7 am precisely, she would knock.

Ding dong dong ding, dong ding ding dong . . . The clock rang out its merry tune.

Millie waited until the last chime before she reached up to tap on the mahogany door.

'Come!' Miss Grimm's voice boomed from within. She was sitting at her desk, but stood up and indicated that Millie should take a seat on the leather chesterfield sofa near the fire.

'Is Sloane with you?' Miss Grimm asked.

'No, Miss Grimm,' Millie replied.

'Well, she'd want to hurry.' Miss Grimm glanced at her watch and the clock on the wall opposite her desk.

Ophelia sat down in one of the wing-backed armchairs opposite Millie. 'Millie, would you like to explain to me, please, what happened last night?'

'I'm sorry, Miss Grimm. My behaviour was unacceptable. I didn't mean to pull Sloane's hair. It's just that when she poured the *gulab* over me, I couldn't control my temper.' Millie stared at the Persian carpet on the floor in front of her, mesmerised by its intricate pattern.

'All right, well, you can apologise to Sloane – when she gets here,' Miss Grimm advised. 'You might like to tell me the events that led to Sloane depositing her dessert on your head.'

'Yes, Miss Grimm. Sloane was talking about Jacinta's mother and saying that if she were her mother, she'd tell everyone how famous she was and who she was with. Jacinta was a bit upset because, well, she never really sees her mother very much. Then Jacinta made a joke and said that she could trade mothers with Sloane, and I said that she had to be kidding, and Jacinta and I laughed. Sloane got angry and asked why we were laughing.'

'And why were you laughing?' Miss Grimm asked. Her mouth was drawn into a tight line.

'Well, I suppose we thought it would be even worse having Sloane's mother,' Millie admitted.

'And why do you think that?' Miss Grimm asked.

'I don't know exactly. It's just that Sloane's mother seems awfully caught up with who people know and what they look like. I suppose we laughed because we all know Jacinta's mother isn't exactly in the running for mother of the year and the idea of her swapping her mother for Sloane's was really silly.'

'Indeed.' Miss Grimm drummed her fingers on the arm of the chair. She couldn't agree with Millie more, but it wasn't appropriate for her to say so. She caught Millie looking up at her sheepishly. 'Was there anything else?' Miss Grimm asked.

'Yes. Sloane made fun of my mother when Alice-Miranda said she was a vet, and then she asked if my father was a lion tamer, and that's when I blurted out that at least my dad wasn't a television vacuum-cleaner salesman.' Millie hung her head.

'And is that Sloane's father's job?' Miss Grimm asked.

'Yes, I think so. Wally said that he'd seen a man called Smedley Sykes selling vacuum cleaners on the home shopping channel.'

'I see.' Miss Grimm was beginning to get a clearer picture. 'Well, it sounds to me, Millie, like you've realised your mistake. I think perhaps you could spend a couple of afternoons helping Wally with the mucking out down at the stables. And you can apologise to Sloane, if she ever bothers to arrive,' Miss Grimm instructed.

'You mean, I can keep my part in the play?' Millie looked up at Miss Grimm.

'Yes, of course,' Ophelia nodded. 'That was never in doubt.'

'Oh, thank you, Miss Grimm,' Millie launched herself at the headmistress and gave her a hug.

'Steady on there, Millicent,' Miss Grimm smiled. 'I see you're taking your cues from your room mate these days.'

Millie let go of Miss Grimm and sat back down on the couch.

By now, the clock on the wall indicated that it was ten past seven. There was a loud rumpus in Mrs Derby's office and a knock on the study door. Miss Grimm went to open it.

'You're late, Sloane.' The headmistress was stern.

Sloane made no apology. 'I couldn't get my hair-dryer to work.'

'Sit there.' Miss Grimm pointed at the couch next to Millie. 'You're a very brave girl, Sloane Sykes.'

'Thank you, Miss Grimm,' Sloane replied. 'I've been subjected to the most awful bullying.'

'I didn't mean that.' Ophelia took up her position on the chair opposite. 'You obviously don't believe in punctuality. Is that correct?'

Sloane had to think. *Punctuality.* Was that the same as punctuation? She couldn't remember.

'Yes, I do, Miss Grimm. I always use full stops and capital letters,' Sloane replied at last.

Millie had to clamp her hand over her mouth for fear of bursting out laughing.

'Sloane, Millie has something she'd like to say to you.' Miss Grimm chose at this stage to overlook Sloane's ignorance. But it had given her a plan that would be most satisfactory.

Sloane looked at Millie with an air of righteous indignation.

'I'm sorry that I insulted you, Sloane, by laughing about your mother and saying that your father had a silly job,' Millie blinked.

'And?' Sloane glared.

'And what?' Millie was puzzled.

'And what are you going to do about it?' Sloane insisted. 'Like, are you going to do my house chores for a week or carry my books or something?'

'She most certainly will not, Sloane Sykes.' Miss Grimm's temper was beginning to fray. 'Now, young lady, what do you have to say to Millie?'

Sloane shook her head. 'Nothing. I didn't do anything. She started it and it was her fault she ended up with pudding on her head,' she spat.

Ophelia's temperature was rising.

'I don't think so, Sloane. There are two sides to every story and unless I hear an apology, heartfelt, from you in the next ten seconds, I will be handing your role in the school play to . . . Wally Whitstable, for all I care,' Miss Grimm roared.

Sloane's mouth gaped open.

'Ten, nine . . .' Miss Grimm began counting. She'd reached two when Sloane finally found her voice.

'Sorry, Millie,' she seethed.

'Sorry for what?' Miss Grimm was secretly enjoying this a little.

'Sorry for tipping that goo on your head,' Sloane added.

'Well, it was an apology, but I have to say I don't much believe you, Sloane.' Miss Grimm shook her head. 'This is not the first time your lack of manners has been brought to my attention. You can keep your part in the play for now, but if I hear one word, one single word, that says you have been less than kind or gracious or caring to anyone at this school, Wally will have that script in his hand before you have time to say "mirror, mirror". Do you understand me?' Miss Grimm stared at Sloane.

'Yes,' Sloane replied.

'Yes, what?' Miss Grimm demanded.

'Yes, Miss Grimm.'

'Better.' Miss Grimm stood up. 'Off you go now, Millie. Just report to Wally this afternoon and I'm sure he will find you some jobs to do.'

Sloane stood up to follow her.

'Where are you going, young lady?' Miss Grimm asked.

'Breakfast,' Sloane replied. She wasn't a very fast learner.

'I don't think so,' Miss Grimm said. 'I'll have some porridge sent up for you. You have work to do.'

'What work?' Sloane huffed.

'Well, for a start, I think we'll spend some time on the dictionary. At your age, you should definitely know the difference between punctuality and punctuation. I suspect copying out the entire P section of this will help.' Miss Grimm pulled an enormous leather-bound Oxford Dictionary from her bookcase. 'You will report to my study every morning at seven and will remain here until lessons commence at half past eight, for as long as it takes.'

'But that's child abuse!' Sloane wailed.

'Oh no, my dear girl.' Miss Grimm shook her head. 'Think of it as extra tuition, for free, and with the headmistress, no less. Now, why don't you sit yourself down over there.' Ophelia pointed at the writing desk opposite her own. 'I'll bring you some paper and a pen.'

Chapter 34

Sloane appeared to be on her best behaviour for the rest of the week. She attended her morning lessons with Miss Grimm and, despite looking like she'd sucked on a lemon, didn't complain at all – well, not to the other girls or teachers. She saved it all for her mother who decided that her plan to bring Fayle unstuck was not only brilliant, it would also save her darling daughter from the clutches of the evil Miss Grimm.

During rehearsals, Sloane spent as much time with Lucas as she could.

'You're a brilliant Woodcutter,' she complimented him.

'Thanks.' Lucas didn't quite know what to make of his room mate's sister. Sep said that she was shallower than a kiddie wading pool, but she seemed okay.

'So, have you had a lot of tests lately?' she asked.

'We have a Maths test every Tuesday. And there was a Science exam yesterday,' Lucas explained.

Sloane's brain was ticking. She needed to get her hands on a set of test papers.

'What's your Maths teacher like?' She batted her eyes at Lucas.

'Really smart,' Lucas replied, 'but mad as a hatter. He's always forgetting things and bringing the wrong books, and I think last week he couldn't find our test papers.'

'Oh really? He does sound a bit crazy,' she smiled. 'So on Tuesdays you have a test? That means you had it this morning.'

'Yes,' Lucas nodded. 'I probably should be doing my homework between scenes. Sorry, it's just that we have quite a few assignments.'

'I've got a much better idea.' Sloane grinned like a fox in a henhouse. 'Why don't you show me around a bit? Miss Reedy said that we won't be needed for at least another thirty minutes.'

'I really should stay here and go over some grammar.' Lucas picked up a textbook from the bag at his feet.

'Oh, but I'd really love to have a look around and Sep won't take me,' Sloane pouted.

Lucas didn't want to leave the auditorium at all. But he'd also heard about Sloane's legendary tantrums and the thought of her causing a scene was worse. 'Okay, but it has to be quick,' he agreed.

'Fine by me. Why don't you show me your class-rooms?' Sloane purred.

Jacinta looked up from her position on the stage to see Sloane loop her arm through Lucas's, and the pair head out of the theatre. Her heart felt like a pounding lump of rock in her chest. The blinding lights didn't allow her to see that just as quickly as Sloane had grabbed him, Lucas had managed to pull his arm away, pretending he had an itchy nose.

Lucas showed Sloane around the classrooms in the main building. She seemed particularly keen to see where they had Maths and Science, which he thought a little strange, given that Septimus said she was not keen on academic studies at all.

Sloane lingered outside one of the rooms. 'Can we go in?'

'I don't think we should.' Lucas was keen to get back to the drama theatre.

'Is there an alarm or something?' Sloane peered through the glass at the top of the door.

'No, it's just that the teachers don't really like us being in there when we don't have lessons,' Lucas replied.

'All right,' Sloane agreed. 'Let's go back. This is boring.'

Lucas was relieved. The pair walked along the corridor.

'Is there a ladies' loo around here anywhere?' Sloane asked.

'Um, I think it's back there, past the foyer,' Lucas sighed. He didn't particularly want to wait for her.

'It's okay,' Sloane smiled. 'Why don't you go back and I'll join you shortly.'

Lucas couldn't help himself and returned her smile. Maybe she wasn't really that painful after all.

'I'll see you in a bit,' said Lucas.

Sloane turned and walked back towards the foyer. She waited until Lucas disappeared around the corner before rushing to the room where he'd said they had their Maths lessons. The door was unlocked.

On the teacher's desk at the front of the room, atop a towering pile of papers, Sloane found exactly what she was after. 'The Weekly Quiz'. Trouble was, she didn't have time to sit and change the papers now. She'd have to do that later in the privacy of her own room – perhaps when Jacinta was at gym training. She leafed through the stack and gathered up the tests from today. Fortunately, the professor was every bit as disorganised as she had hoped – his desk looked like an explosion in a paper factory. Sloane spent a couple of minutes rearranging papers from one side to the other – hopefully, by the time she had made the changes and returned the tests, the silly old man would be none the wiser. Sloane stuffed the papers into her backpack.

She smiled smugly. This was as easy as falling off a log.

Chapter 35

On Friday morning, Septimus Sykes and Lucas Nixon headed off to their Maths lesson. Their teacher, Professor Pluss, welcomed the class with a smile that stretched from one side of his red face to the other. The boys couldn't remember ever seeing him look so happy.

'Greetings and salutations, lads.' The Professor moved to the front of the room. He walked over to his desk where he put his hand on top of the pile of papers. 'Today is a momentous day in the history of this fine school,' he began.

'What's he talking about?' Lucas turned and whispered to Sep.

'Beats me,' Sep replied.

'Today you have made me the proudest old prof on the planet. You see, boys, for the first time, certainly since I have been the Mathematics master at this outstanding institution, which is over twenty years, every single member of this class has scored one hundred per cent on the weekly quiz.'

The boys smiled and laughed and congratulated themselves and one another.

'Quiet down, please. You must have all thought long and hard about your answers. By gosh, there was a good deal of crossing out, but even you, old Figgy –' Professor Pluss grinned at the oafish lad in the back row – 'you must have been listening all that time I thought you were gazing longingly at the football pitch.'

Lucas was puzzled. Figgy hadn't scored above fifty per cent in the past four tests. And there were a couple of really tricky problems he was sure he'd messed up too.

Professor Pluss handed the papers back, then turned to the board where he began to explain, in great detail and without time for any questions, how to find the circumference of a circle.

Sep put his paper to the side of his desk. Lucas leafed through his. It looked like his writing, but there was an answer he couldn't remember filling in. In fact, now that he was looking at it again, he was fairly certain he'd left that section blank.

'Excuse me, sir?' Lucas put up his hand and waited for the old man to turn around.

'What is it, Nixon?' The professor peered over the round spectacles perched on the end of his nose.

'Sir, I don't think this is all my work.' Lucas held the test paper aloft.

Some of the other boys began to make similar noises.

'Nonsense, Nixon, you're not giving yourself enough credit there.' The professor turned back to the board.

'But sir, I'm pretty sure I left this answer blank,' Lucas offered.

'Is there an answer there now?' The professor spoke with his back turned to the boys.

'Well, yes, sir,' Lucas tried again.

'So you didn't leave it blank. Tell me, Nixon,' the professor spun back around to face the group, 'tell me, what did you do at eleven minutes past two yesterday afternoon?'

Lucas thought for a moment and wondered if this was some kind of trick question. 'I was in Science class,' he replied.

'Yes, but what *exactly* were you doing at eleven minutes past two? Were you listening or speaking or marvelling at the laws of gravity or the fact that we live on a spinning lump of rock in the middle of the universe?' the professor continued.

'I can't remember, sir.' Lucas wasn't sure where this was heading.

'There you have it. Proof.' The professor turned back to the board.

'I'm sorry, sir. Proof of what, exactly?' Lucas was feeling more and more confused by the second.

'My dear boy. Proof that you could well have written an answer on that page.' He marched towards Lucas and picked up his paper. 'And you probably forgot. We all forget things. In fact, we will forget far more than we ever remember. Did you know that statistically . . .' The professor was about to start one of his long lectures.

Lucas decided it was better to be quiet and leave things alone. But something wasn't right. The boys at Fayle didn't need to cheat. By and large, they were a smart enough bunch. They studied pretty hard too –

it was just the way things were there. So why would anyone want to cheat just so the whole class scored one hundred per cent?

'Why would anyone cheat for us?' Lucas asked Sep when they were on their way to English class.

'I don't know.' Sep shook his head. 'Make the old prof feel like a hero?'

'Yeah, maybe.' The boys reached the entrance foyer. The classrooms in McGlintock Manor ran east and west with Science and Maths on the west and English, History and Geography on the eastern side. A magnificent staircase stood in the centre of the building's entrance hall, rising in one flight before splitting left and right. On the right-hand wall were portraits of Frederick Erasmus Fayle, the school's founder, and his successors. There were two more Fayles, and another man, before the picture of the current headmaster, Professor Winterbottom, whose portrait must have been painted early in his tenure, as his beaming face was wrinkle free. On the opposite wall in a large gilt frame, the Fayle School Charter was in full view for all to see.

'Oh blast.' Sep grimaced, as they were about to climb the stairs.

'What's the matter?' Lucas asked.

'I forgot my assignment. It's in my locker. Will you wait? I won't be a minute.' Sep handed Lucas his pile of books and sprinted back down the corridor.

Lucas set the tower of texts down on a high-backed chair that resembled a throne. He walked over to the charter and read from the top. He smiled at the school's motto – it was pretty funny, after all, to name a school Fayle. But it wasn't until he reached the bottom, clauses twenty-nine and thirty, that alarm bells began to ring. Lucas had an uncomfortable feeling that perhaps cheating had been happening for quite a while – but, this time, the culprit had got rather carried away with themselves.

Sep returned and the two lads had to run to get to class before the bell. Lucas would have to wait to share his suspicions with his friend.

Chapter 36

September Sykes could not have been prouder when Sloane told her what she'd done.

'Oh yes,' she gloated to her mother, 'it won't be long now before the word gets out that more than twenty-five per cent of boys have failed at Fayle. But it took loads of work, so you'd better thank me for it, Mummy,' she hissed. 'And I almost got caught taking the papers back.' Sloane was whispering into the telephone. Although she thought she was alone in the common room, she never knew when someone might come in and overhear her conversation. 'How's Granny?'

September attempted to sound sad. 'Not doing too well, I'm afraid. I went to see her yesterday afternoon and she looked rather peaky indeed. She seemed quite upset, poor old dear. But she did sign some very important documents for me. Have you heard of something called a power of attorney?'

She neglected to tell Sloane that the reason Henrietta had become so upset was that September had all but revealed her dastardly plan. She had told her about the suitcase, and that it was just so unfortunate that they'd found it but now it was gone again. Vanished out of sight. Puff – like magic. September thought the old bag might up and die right then and there, but her heart held out and it was only when her step-daughter-in-law promised another visit that Henrietta's face reddened and she looked set for another stroke.

'What shall we do with all that money?' September gloated, rubbing her manicured hands together.

'For a start, Mummy, I think we should go somewhere sunny – for good.' Sloane smiled at the thought of her and her mother in their matching bikinis, lying in the sun with a butler attending to their every need.

Howie entered the common room. She frowned at Sloane, who seemed to have that phone perpetually stuck to her ear.

'Prep,' Mrs Howard ordered.

'But I've got play practice in ten minutes,' Sloane smirked.

'Oh no you don't,' Mrs Howard replied. 'Haven't you read the schedule, young lady? This afternoon, only Alice-Miranda, the Prince and the Woodcutter are needed. Oh, and Millie and Jacinta.'

'Why does Millie get to go? She's *my* Magic Mirror,' Sloane grouched.

'I don't know. But it says so on this here piece of paper.' Howie waved the notice under Sloane's nose. She was still on the telephone.

Mrs Howard took the handset from her. 'Hello Mrs Sykes, it's Mrs Howard. I'm afraid Sloane has to go to prep so I'll tell her you said goodbye, will I?' And with that, Mrs Howard hung up the phone.

'You've got no right . . .' Sloane began, steam rising from her nostrils.

Mrs Howard raised her eyebrows. Miss Grimm had asked her to keep a close eye on their newest student after the incident with Millie. She knew that any cheek, and Sloane would be out of the play. 'Are you sure you want to say something?'

'I'm going.' Sloane stalked off to her room.

Alice-Miranda, Jacinta and Millie were required on set for an extended rehearsal that afternoon. The group had walked to Fayle, but Miss Reedy had arranged for Charlie to pick them up in the school bus when they were finished, as it would be dark.

Miss Reedy was keen to get some of the lighting in place and, although the girls knew their parts well, she had decided it was easier to practise some scenes separately so the cast were completely confident. Lucas and Sep were also required to be there. The children had been rehearsing well but, as it was getting close to performance time, things needed to step up a little.

'Girls, I hope you don't mind, but we'll get started straightaway and then break for tea with the boys later. Then we'll do another hour or so and call it a night.'

'That's lovely, Miss Reedy. It will give us a chance to catch up properly with Lucas and get to know Sep a bit better too,' Alice-Miranda smiled.

Mr Lipp greeted the group as they entered the auditorium. Today's suit made him look like a bloated canary.

'Hello girls, Livinia.' He had taken to using Miss Reedy's Christian name, which caused her to frown.

'Mr Lipp,' Miss Reedy nodded.

'Ready for some hard work?' Mr Lipp asked.

'Oh yes, sir,' Alice-Miranda beamed. 'Where would you like to start?'

'I thought we'd go from your scene, Alice-Miranda, with the Prince,' Miss Reedy directed.

And so the rehearsal began.

An hour later, the group trooped off to the dining room. The children sat together, while Mr Lipp invited Miss Reedy to sit on the head table with Professor Winterbottom and his wife.

'I think old Hairy's got a thing for your Miss Reedy,' Sep grinned.

'Really?' Millie screwed up her nose. 'Well, that's gross. Anyway, she has a thing for our Science teacher, Mr Plumpton. You should see the two of them — he looks like a little beach ball and she's a string of spaghetti but it's quite plain they adore one another.'

'Perhaps they'll get married,' Jacinta beamed. 'I do love a wedding.'

'Well, I imagine the next one you'll attend is my father's and Charlotte's,' Lucas offered.

'Will I get invited?' Jacinta asked, wide-eyed.

'I should imagine so,' Lucas grinned. And there it was again. Jacinta's heart fluttered in her chest.

'So, how are you all getting on with my sister?' Sep asked the group.

'Let's just say that she and I are hardly best friends,' Millie replied.

'I think Sloane's a bit complicated,' said Alice-Miranda. 'I'm sure she has a heart of gold.'

'You're kidding, Alice-Miranda,' Jacinta snorted. 'Sorry, Sep, but your sister isn't my favourite person either.'

Septimus Sykes looked concerned. 'Has she actually done anything wrong over there?'

'Well, she tipped her dessert on my head last week,' Millie explained. 'But I probably deserved it.'

'And I caught her and your mother going through my things on the day she arrived,' Jacinta added. 'But they were probably just unpacking.'

'I think you're both being far too kind.' Sep shook his head. 'You don't know her like I do.'

'But she's your sister, Sep, you should stick up for her,' Alice-Miranda said.

'I wish I could,' Sep began. 'She should be more grateful. The only reason either of us is at boarding school is because of our step-grandmother Henrietta. She's paying for the lot. She's the sweetest lady and my mother and father and sister treat her like garbage. I just wish I could see her.'

'Where does she live?' Alice-Miranda asked.

'Well, that's the thing. She was meant to be able to stay in the flat over Grandpa's old grocery shop, here in the village, for as long as she wanted. But Mum and Dad sold it and then she had a terrible stroke and now she lives in a retirement home called Golden Gates.'

'But do you write to her?' Alice-Miranda asked.

'Yes, but she can't write back because of the stroke,' Sep explained. 'My sister is so hateful to her. But Grandpa adored her and so do I.'

Alice-Miranda's brain was already in overdrive. She would call her parents as soon as she could and arrange for Sep to visit his granny. 'Don't worry, Sep, I'm sure you'll get to see her very soon,' she smiled.

Septimus Sykes had never met a girl like Alice-Miranda. She was so small, but seemed incredibly kind and smart too. He wished that *she* was his sister.

Millie changed the subject. 'And how are you getting on with all the work, Lucas?'

'Good,' Lucas grinned at Sep, who raised his eyebrows. 'I scored one hundred per cent on a Maths test this week.'

'Well done!' said Alice-Miranda.

'Problem was, so did everyone else,' Lucas continued.

'What?' Mille wrinkled her nose. 'The whole class got full marks?'

'Was it an easy test?' Jacinta asked.

'No, that's just the point,' Lucas answered. 'There were some tricky questions.'

'Was it multiple choice?' asked Millie.

Sep rejoined the conversation. 'No. Lucas tried to tell Professor Pluss that the tests had been tampered with, but he would have none of it.'

'Tampered with?' Alice-Miranda gasped. 'Do you mean that someone changed the answers – they cheated?'

'Yes, someone cheated and we all got one hundred per cent,' Lucas confirmed.

'But why?' Millie asked.

'Well, Lucas and I have a bit of a theory,' Sep frowned. 'And it's probably been happening for years.'

'Really?' Alice-Miranda's eyes were wide.

The children leaned in close. Lucas explained about the Fayle School Charter. He and Sep had come to the conclusion that the teachers must be cheating to make sure that the school stayed open. Maybe this time, Professor Pluss just got carried away with himself and didn't realise that he'd changed all the papers.

'I asked Miss Reedy how Fayle came to be named and she told me all about the charter. That would be awfully sad, if what you say is true,' Alice-Miranda spoke.

'I'd bet poor old Mr Fayle would be turning in his grave,' Millie added.

But Alice-Miranda found it hard to believe that a school like Fayle, with its wonderful teachers and high standards, would allow such a thing. It would mean that the teachers were plotting together, and she simply didn't believe this to be possible. Goodness, all the teachers she knew were honest and responsible. There had to be something else going on. They just needed to find out what it was.

Chapter 37

September Sykes put the telephone down and cupped her face in her hands. She couldn't believe what she had just heard. She dialled the number for the common room at Grimthorpe House.

'Hello, it's September Sykes. I must talk to my daughter, Sloane, immediately. It's an emergency,' she informed Mrs Howard.

'May I ask what type of emergency, Mrs Sykes? I don't want to alarm your daughter,' said Mrs Howard.

'No, you may not ask, you nosey old parker,' September growled.

Howie had a mind to hang the phone up immediately, but thought better of it. September Sykes was the rudest, most vacuous mother she had ever come across in all her years in the boarding house. At times, that had been a hotly contested title, but this woman was the clear winner.

'Sloane.' Mrs Howard rapped on the door. 'Your mother would like a word. She says that it's important.'

Howie entered the dorm. Sloane was lying on her bed, admiring her nails.

'Can I take it in here?' Sloane noticed that Howie had the cordless telephone in her hand. Usually, it was strictly forbidden for the girls to take calls in their rooms but, this time, Howie relented and handed over the phone.

'Just don't be long,' Howie instructed. 'There are other girls who like to speak to their parents too.'

Sloane turned her back to the housemistress and waited until she had left the room.

'Hello Mummy,' she said.

'Are you a complete idiot?' September began.

'What are you talking about?' Sloane snapped back.

'I've just got off the phone from your brother and apparently he's been doing so well, he got one hundred per cent in his Maths test this week,' September informed her daughter.

'That's not possible,' Sloane griped. 'I changed all the papers.'

'Yes, and whose paper did you copy from?' her mother asked.

'Septimus's of course. Everyone knows he's as dumb as a rock,' Sloane snarled.

'Well, I'm afraid that's not true. You see, everyone in the class scored one hundred per cent!' September yelled. 'And what were you thinking, changing all the answers to the same thing? I'm sure they wouldn't be very suspicious about that, now would they?'

'How was I to know Sep's some kind of math-ematical genius? I think he's an idiot!' Sloane roared back.

'Clearly you're wrong.' September could hardly believe they were so close to their fortune and Sloane had made a complete mess of everything. 'You have to do it again. And this time, don't use your brother's paper to copy from.'

'Well, whose paper should I use then?' Sloane demanded. 'I don't know who's smart and who's not.'

'As it happens, your brother commented that some kid called Figgy almost never passes Mathematics tests but got one hundred per cent this time. So use his – but make sure that you mix them up a bit. For goodness sake, do I have to do everything for this family?' September growled.

'Where's Daddy?' Sloane changed the subject. 'I want to talk to him.'

'Your idiot father is overseas checking on the development. But I have a feeling that it's not going to plan either. Sloane – I don't have to tell you again what this will mean to our family. Now, can I rely on you this time?' Her mother's voice softened slightly.

'Of course, mother.' Sloane rolled her eyes. 'But I can't do anything until next week.'

'Why not?' September demanded.

'Because they only have their stupid test on Tuesday and it's the weekend. Duh!'

'There's no need to get smart with me, young lady. You'd better think about who you're talking to.'

'And you'd better remember who's in the driver's seat here, Mother,' Sloane snapped.

And with that, she terminated the call.

As it turned out, two more weeks passed before Sloane had her chance. Professor Pluss was so anxious about the boys not replicating their one hundred per cent result that he didn't prepare a test for the coming week and the week after that they had a sports carnival. But by the time they had their regular weekly quiz again, Pluss was confident the lads would not let him down.

Chapter 38

Professor Pluss stood outside the headmaster's study trembling. He couldn't believe that in a career spanning more than thirty years, this is what he would be remembered for.

The campus was abuzz. Pluss had asked two of his colleagues to re-mark the papers. They had both come back to him, faces solemn, heads bowed.

Someone must have leaked the news to Professor Winterbottom, who had summoned Pluss for an urgent meeting first thing this morning. Even old

Hedges, the gardener, had sneered as Herman Pluss took his walk of shame to the headmaster's study.

Miss Quigley, the headmaster's personal assistant, shuddered as he entered the room. She was poring over a large document and had just retrieved a gigantic magnifying glass from the bottom desk drawer.

A woman renowned for her confidential manner, she had been with Professor Winterbottom as long as he'd been in charge. 'How could you?' she murmured under her breath.

Herman thought his knees would buckle any moment.

'He'll see you now.'

For a moment, Herman wondered how she knew that the headmaster was ready for him, but he suspected that after almost forty years together, they likely shared some sort of telepathic messaging system.

The door opened and Professor Winterbottom asked Professor Pluss inside.

'Take a seat. There.' The headmaster pointed. Professor Winterbottom's dog Parsley, who spent his days curled up in a basket in the headmaster's study, growled as Professor Pluss sat down.

'I hear you have something to tell me?'

But Professor Winterbottom didn't have to ask. He already knew. The whole school knew. Something as monumental as this would never remain a secret. It had never happened before and it would certainly never happen again.

'I . . . don't know what to tell you, sir . . . my class . . . eighty per cent of them . . .' Herman gulped.

'Yes, eighty per cent of them have what?' Professor Winterbottom had so far managed to keep calm.

'Eighty per cent of them have . . .' Herman clutched his face in his hands, hardly daring to say the word. 'They've failed. There it is. I've said it.'

'How can a class go from one hundred per cent success two weeks ago to . . . this?' Professor Winterbottom held one of the offending papers aloft. 'Yes, I know all about it. Your colleagues would hardly keep something like this a secret. In fact, they all know – the boys, the teachers. Do *you* know what this means, Pluss?'

Herman Pluss looked up and nodded.

'You, you and your vanity, have brought this great school to its knees. Do you know what it says in that charter out there?' Wallace pointed at the wall where the Fayle School Charter hung in all its ancient glory. 'It says that if more than twenty-five per cent of students fail *any* test, the school must be closed within twenty-eight days.'

'But sir,' Herman shuddered. 'Surely, that can't really be true. Can it?'

'It most certainly is. I warned you, Pluss, about all those weekly quizzes. I told you they weren't necessary and that one day you might come unstuck. But you assured me. Your teaching methods were inscrutable. You were the best teacher this place had ever seen. Well, look what you've done.' Professor Winterbottom's head looked like a pressure cooker about to explode.

There was a knock on the door. It opened and Miss Quigley entered.

'Sir, may I interrupt?' she asked. 'I've found something.'

'Well, unless it will save the school . . .' Professor Winterbottom sighed so deeply it felt like a draught in the room.

'Well, sir, I think you will be very happy to see this.' Miss Quigley unfolded the original copy of the Fayle School Charter onto her boss's football-pitch-sized desk. She produced the magnifying glass from her skirt pocket and pointed her manicured finger at the very bottom of the page.

'There, sir.' Wallace Winterbottom and Herman Pluss leaned in closely to look.

'I can't see a thing. It looks like a squiggly line,' the headmaster complained.

'That's what I thought too. But sir, if you look closely –' She held the magnifying glass over the end of the line and read aloud. 'Clause thirty of the Fayle School Charter can be revoked at any time, at the discretion of the heir to the Fayle estate. In the event that there is no living heir, the school must close and be sold, with the proceeds going to the Queen's Trust for Children.'

'Heavens, that's it!' Professor Winterbottom grabbed Miss Quigley in a bear-like embrace. 'Woman, you're a genius!' He then quickly let her go, embarrassed by his uncharacteristic outburst of affection. 'But how did we miss this?'

'Well, sir, it's not on the charter in the foyer. I suspect that the edge of the page was cut off to fit in the frame,' Miss Quigley remarked. 'From the looks of this dusty old thing, it hasn't been out of the safe in many years.'

'But who is the heir?' Wallace Winterbottom paced the floor. Not that it was an easy thing to do in his office, which was crammed full of furniture, books and other paraphernalia, including a rather large cabinet containing a bizarre collection of taxidermic birds. He began to think out loud. 'Fayle was founded by Frederick Fayle and then the next headmaster was his only son George and then I think the next head was George's son Erasmus.'

'Sir, if I may say something?' Professor Pluss asked.

The headmaster was terse. 'What?'

'Didn't Erasmus, his wife and his daughter perish in some terrible accident? I seem to recall when I was a boy and lived in Downsfordvale, there was a story about the headmaster of Fayle and his family passing in tragic circumstances. I can't remember much else.'

'Yes, I've read about that somewhere too. There was another man who came in then. The headmaster after Erasmus was Rigby Lloyd. You'd remember him. He employed me. And that's how I became headmaster so early on. Rigby was working in here one night when the poor fellow dropped dead of a heart attack.'

'So are there any Fayles left, sir?' Miss Quigley asked.

'I think there was another daughter who survived. But she'd be very old – if she's still alive, that is.' Professor Pluss tapped his right forefinger to his lip.

'We'd better hope she's alive and well, and find her quick smart,' Professor Winterbottom announced.

'Helloooo?' a voice drifted in from the office outside. 'Is anyone home?'

Miss Quigley opened the study door.

'Oh, there you are. I need to see the headmaster.' September Sykes stood towering in the doorway on her six-inch red heels.

'Can I help you?' The professor had not yet had the pleasure of meeting Mrs Sykes, as it was Sep's father who had taken the boy for his entrance test and interview. September had been busy that morning at the nail salon.

'I'm September,' she cooed.

Professor Winterbottom had no idea what that meant at all, and responded with a blank look and a shake of his head.

'September Sykes. Septimus's mother,' she smiled.

'Oh, of course, Mrs Sykes,' said Professor Winterbottom apologetically. 'I'm afraid we're a little bit busy at the moment, Mrs Sykes. Is it an urgent matter you've come about?'

'You might think so,' September nodded. 'You see, I've really come to find out how much this is all worth.' She waved her arms around.

The headmaster looked confused. 'Worth? Do you mean the school fees?'

'No, no, no, silly headmaster.' September was enjoying this. 'I mean the school. Fayle. The whole place.'

'I have no idea what you're talking about.' Professor Winterbottom was growing very uncomfortable.

'It's just that, well, I know what happens when more than twenty-five per cent of boys at this school fail a test. And I've heard that's just happened. So I want to know what it's worth?'

'I can't for a moment imagine that's any of your business, Mrs Sykes.' The headmaster was appalled.

September Sykes entered the study. She walked over to the antique globe that stood under the window and gave it a spin. 'Oh, isn't that fun?' she giggled.

Professors Winterbottom and Pluss and Miss Quigley could not take their eyes off this woman with her long blonde curls and garish red dress which hugged every curve.

'Mrs Sykes, I think it might be best if you left,' the headmaster suggested.

'Now, why would I do that?' September walked towards the group, reached forward and grabbed Professor Winterbottom's tie, pulling him closer. Her sickly perfume clouded his head and he soon felt quite faint. She let go and walked around the desk, where she sat in his green leather chair. 'What do you think?' She placed the professor's reading glasses on the end of her nose. 'Does the school look suit me? No, no. Not my thing at all, teaching. Really just for dull old bores, education.'

'Mrs Sykes,' Professor Winterbottom regained use of his vocal chords. 'You need to leave immediately.'

'No.' September shook her head. 'You need to sit down and have a look at this.' She rummaged around in her oversized pewter-coloured handbag and produced what appeared to be a legal document. 'You see, I heard you before, when I was out in the other room there. You can stop looking for the heir to the Fayle family. Because you've found her. And this –' she waved the power of attorney under the professor's nose – 'is all the proof you need. Granny Henrietta Sykes – she's the one you were talking about – well, she married my darling husband's father just a few years back. She was a Fayle, you know. But she's not well, and she's very old, and she insisted I look after things for her. So there you are.'

'Oh, thank heavens, Mrs Sykes. We were worried that we'd never find the heir in time and then the school would have no choice other than to close at the end of the term. But now . . .'

'But now *what*?' September sneered. 'You'll be closing all right. I've arranged for the estate agent to meet me here this morning. I can't imagine how many millions this place is worth, but I'm going to have lots of fun spending them.'

Professor Pluss burst into tears. Miss Quigley had to suppress the urge to strangle September on the spot. The headmaster gulped.

'Professor Pluss – you need to go to class. Miss Quigley – some tea.' He indicated towards the door. 'Mrs Sykes and I have a lot to talk about.'

'No, we don't, unless you want to tell me how wonderful Septimus is. But if you think I'll change my mind, you're wrong, old man.' September folded her arms in front of her.

Chapter 39

Word had spread quickly about the trouble at Fayle. Professor Winterbottom had spent an hour with September Sykes trying to change her view about enforcing the school's closure, but he was no match for her when she had millions on her mind. He suggested that they ask Mr Sykes in to talk about things, but she said he was overseas working and couldn't be contacted. September was determined to show her husband a thing or two about making money.

At Winchesterfield-Downsfordvale, Millie and

Alice-Miranda were talking about the recent turn of events.

'None of this makes any sense at all.' Millie was lying face down on her bed with her arms tucked under her chin.

'It's strange, isn't it, that in one test the boys all score full marks, and then only a couple of weeks later they fail. I have a very bad feeling about all this,' Alice-Miranda decided. 'Sep and Lucas must have been wrong about the cheating.'

'And imagine the Sykeses being the heirs.' Millie rolled her eyes. 'I mean, Sep's lovely but Sloane, urgh.'

'Sep really loves it at school, too. Maybe he can talk his mother into keeping it open,' Alice-Miranda suggested.

At that moment, Sloane Sykes appeared in the open doorway. 'I don't think so. Mummy and I don't care about that stupid school. Sep will just have to find somewhere else to go.'

'Oh, hello Sloane,' Alice-Miranda smiled. 'Would you like to come in?'

'Why?' Sloane retorted.

'I thought you might like to work on your lines with us,' said Alice-Miranda.

'It's all right, Sloane, I'm sure you're way too busy working out how you'll squander all those millions.' The last thing Millie wanted was to spend any more time with Sloane than she had to.

'I suppose our play next week will be Fayle's last hurrah,' Sloane laughed.

'Well, perhaps not,' Alice-Miranda smiled. 'Maybe your mother will think about the school and how important it is, and all that history. I mean, it's a big thing to close down a place that has educated so many boys. It's strange, too, how one week the boys all scored one hundred per cent on their test, and then the very next test they failed.'

'Yes, I wonder how that could have happened?' Sloane couldn't help herself. Her voice was dripping with sarcasm. 'Amazing, isn't it?'

Millie sat up. She watched Sloane. There was something about the twitch around her mouth – Millie had taken to reading about body language and knew this could be a sign of lying. When Sloane scratched her neck (another dead giveaway), Millie couldn't keep quiet any longer.

'You did it, didn't you?' Millie leapt from her bed to confront the girl.

'What?' Sloane retorted. 'I didn't do anything.' Sloane's eyes darted around the room.

'I remember, when we were at Fayle a couple of weeks ago, you went missing for ages and we were supposed to practise our scene. When you came back, you told Miss Reedy that you'd got lost. I bet you were changing the answers on the papers.' Millie's face was blood red.

'You've got a very good imagination, little one,' Sloane snapped. 'And so what? Even if I did, you'll never prove it.'

'I'll tell Miss Grimm,' Millie threatened.

'Go ahead,' Sloane challenged her. 'You can't prove it, and then you're just going to look like a little snitch.' Sloane turned and stalked off.

Millie fizzed with rage. 'She's foul. We have to find a way to prove that she cheated.'

Alice-Miranda walked over and stood calmly beside her friend. She looked at the clock beside her bed. It was just after 2 pm on Sunday afternoon. 'I think we should go and see Miss Hephzibah. A ride in the countryside will do us both the world of good.'

'I agree. I don't want to hang around here with *that* next door.' Millie began to change into her riding gear.

Not half an hour later, the girls were sitting in the kitchen at Caledonia Manor having tea and scones.

'There's a terrible disaster at Fayle,' Alice-Miranda informed their friend.

'Really?' Hephzibah raised her veil slightly so she could sip her tea. She still hadn't taken it off in front of Millie, although the child seemed much more comfortable in her presence now.

'The boys in Professor Pluss's Maths class failed a test and now the school is going to be closed,' Alice-Miranda continued.

'Yes, it's to do with some silly old rule in the Fayle School Charter that if any more than twenty-five per cent of boys fail any test, then the school must close and be returned immediately to the eldest heir of Frederick Fayle's,' Millie added. 'And you wouldn't believe who that is . . .'

Hephzibah nodded thoughtfully.

'It's a family called the Sykes. Sloane Sykes started at our school just this term and she's awful,' said Millie. 'And it's more than likely that she took the papers and changed the answers, and the school's going to close because of her cheating. It's all so obvious, but there's just no way to prove it.'

Alice-Miranda chimed in. 'Her brother Sep is such a lovely boy. He's devastated about the school closing. But Mrs Sykes won't reconsider. She wants it all sold straight away.' Alice-Miranda shook her head. 'I telephoned Mummy and Daddy and asked if there was anything that could be done. Daddy even sent over to Fayle for a copy of the charter, and he said that there was a secret clause in the smallest of print saying that if the heir said the school could stay open then it would, and they could make sure the silly clause was revoked for good, but Mrs Sykes is determined that she and her husband want the money. They're only in line anyway because Mr Sykes's father married one of the Fayles. A lady called Henrietta –'

Hephzibah clutched her chest.

Alice-Miranda rose in alarm. 'Are you all right?'

'What were you going to say?' Hephzibah whispered. 'About the Fayle woman?'

'Well, she's in a nursing home now and the Sykeses have her power of attorney, which means that they get to make all the decisions for her about money and things like that.'

Hephzibah breathed freely at last. 'It sounds like someone needs to do something.' She stood and walked to the playroom and returned with a shoebox. She began to unpack its contents onto the table.

'I think it's time I told you girls a story,' Hephzibah said.

'Oh yes, I love stories.' Alice-Miranda clapped her hands together. Millie looked up from buttering her scone.

Hephzibah took a sip of tea, as if steeling herself for the task ahead. Then she began. 'Once upon a time, long, long ago, there was a little girl called Hephzibah Caledonia . . .'

Chapter 40

Alice-Miranda and Millie returned from Hephzi-bah's in a flurry of excitement. Alice-Miranda tele-phoned her parents immediately.

'Hello Mummy.' The tiny child was buzzing like a bee in a jar.

Cecelia Highton-Smith smiled to herself. 'Oh, hello darling, how are you getting on?'

'I'm very well, thank you, Mummy. How is everyone at home?'

'Wonderful, darling, although Granny Bert is getting rather forgetful. I popped in to see her the other morning and she kept calling me Charlotte. It's sad to see her getting old,' Cecelia mused. 'And Mrs Oliver's been making some excellent progress with her organic vegetables. Shilly's got the place shining like a gold watch and I saw Lily and the children yesterday. They can't wait for you to come home for the holidays. But everyone's going to the play at the end of the week.'

Alice-Miranda loved to hear all the news but that day she felt about ready to burst with her own. 'Mummy,' she interrupted, 'I need to talk to you about something very important.'

Cecelia was taken aback by her little daughter's tone. 'Are you all right, darling? Is everything okay there at school? Miss Grimm hasn't had a relapse, has she?'

'Oh Mummy, of course not. You are a funny one. Miss Grimm is very happy. Well, except about what's happening at Fayle. But that's why I'm calling. Millie and I need your help. You see . . .' Alice-Miranda spent the next ten minutes telling her mother a story that seemed more like something from a fairytale.

After some reassurances and promises from her mother, Alice-Miranda hung up the telephone. Perhaps there might be a way to save Fayle after all.

Chapter 41

Millie and Alice-Miranda decided to give Sloane another chance to confess. At the final dress rehearsal, they told Jacinta, Sep and Lucas what they suspected. Lucas said that it all made sense. Sloane had made him take her for a walk around the school a few weeks ago, and she had particularly wanted to know about the classrooms and the teachers and where they kept their marking. He'd told her everything he knew, and left her alone after she made the excuse that she needed to go to the toilet and insisted he go back to the rehearsal.

'If she admits it, then we can go to Professor Winterbottom and stop the school being closed,' said Sep.

'Have you talked to your father about any of this?' Alice-Miranda asked.

'No, he's away overseas working. I've tried to get in touch with him but the phone just rings out,' Sep replied. 'Dad might try and put a stop to it all. But I don't really know. Like I said, sometimes I think I was born on another planet and the aliens decided to leave me with the Sykeses as a bit of a sick joke.'

Alice-Miranda smiled. She couldn't imagine what it would be like to feel as if you didn't belong in your own family.

'I say we confront her today,' Millie decided.

They all agreed.

Right then, a scene with the dwarfs returning home from work was being rehearsed and Alice-Miranda, Millie, Sep and Lucas weren't required. Jacinta had to stay back; being the narrator meant she didn't really get a break the whole time. The others watched as Sloane walked away from where she had been sitting and wandered upstairs to the foyer. Seeing a perfect chance, the children followed her. As she emerged from the ladies' toilet, they surrounded her.

'What do you lot want?' Sloane stared through narrowed eyes.

'Sloane, you need to do the right thing about the tests,' Sep told her.

Sloane rolled her eyes and folded her arms in front of her. 'I don't know what you're talking about.'

'Yes, you do. You stole the tests and changed the answers. I bet that the first time, you decided to use my paper to copy from because you're always telling me how stupid I am. It must have upset you when everyone scored one hundred per cent.'

'You haven't got any proof. I didn't change your stupid tests. Anyway, it's too late to stop things now. Mummy said that she's already got a buyer for the place,' Sloane spat.

'You'll get what's coming to you,' Millie threatened.

Sloane laughed. 'And what's that, millions of dollars, you little twit?' She pushed her way through the children and strutted back to the hall. Sep and Lucas followed her.

Millie was grim. 'She's had her chance.'

Alice-Miranda agreed.

Chapter 42

September Sykes had refused to listen to the pleas of Professor Winterbottom, her own son, and even the gardener, who had all begged her to think again. But with Smedley safely out of the way working on the property business, there was nothing that would stand in her way. September didn't see any need for her husband to know a thing until the deal was done. Soon the Sykeses would be rich. They would be invited to the best parties, they would have the most important friends, and September could buy anything she ever wanted. No doubt there'd be an invitation to Lawrence Ridley's celebrity wedding too.

Meanwhile, the children had been rehearsing for weeks. But as the play drew closer, it seemed that a cloud of gloom had descended over the village of Winchesterfield. The cast all knew their lines by heart, the costumes were dazzling and the back-drops superb, but there was one thing missing – excitement. The usual theatrical buzz had all but disappeared.

The days leading up to the performance were almost unbearable as the students and staff contem-plated the closure of Fayle forever. Only Alice-Miranda and Millie seemed anything like their usual selves.

'Come on, everyone,' Alice-Miranda pleaded when the cast gathered together before the curtain went up on opening night. 'Cheer up! It's not the end of the world.'

'No, but it's the end of our school,' Grumpy the dwarf frowned.

'Well, maybe there's a bit of magic left in the old place yet,' Alice-Miranda smiled.

'Can I come to Winchesterfield-Downsfordvale next term?' the little boy playing the role of Happy asked.

'Hey, that's not as silly as it sounds!' Millie smiled and winked at Alice-Miranda. 'We can ask Miss Grimm. I'd love to know what she thinks about that idea.'

'I already have asked her,' Miss Reedy informed the group. 'Never say never.'

'Only so long as we don't have to wear dresses,' Lucas added.

There was a collective giggle and the mood began to lift.

'Well, come on, everyone, I can see all the parents arriving.' Alice-Miranda poked her nose through the side curtain. 'Look, there's Mummy and Aunt Charlotte and Mrs Oliver and Shilly and Daisy . . . Oh goodness, I think everyone's come to watch.' She squeezed Millie's arm.

'There's my mother and father too.' Millie winked at them through the gap in the curtains.

Jacinta looked over the top of the girls' heads. She'd heard earlier in the day that her mother had telephoned Mrs Derby to say she was stuck in Monaco. Her father had said that he would try to get there, but as yet there was no sign. It didn't matter anyway. She hadn't reserved them any tickets.

Jacinta turned to Alice-Miranda. 'Where's your father and Mr Ridley?'

'They'll be along soon. They're just getting something sorted,' Alice-Miranda replied.

Mr Lipp bustled onto the stage and began ushering the girls and boys away from the curtains. 'Come along now, children. 'Places. We're starting in five minutes.'

Miss Reedy and Mr Lipp had the children form a circle backstage.

'Well, girls and boys, this is it. You've been rehearsing for weeks now and I know you're all going to do a wonderful job this evening. You are a credit to yourselves and your schools.' Miss Reedy wiped a tear that had formed in the corner of her eye.

'I couldn't agree more, Livinia,' Mr Lipp began. 'It's been a pleasure working with you all. I will miss . . .' Mr Lipp began to blubber like baby.

Miss Reedy pulled a tissue from her pocket and handed it to him. He blew his nose like an off-key trumpet.

'And we've had the best time working with you too,' said Alice-Miranda, smiling at the teachers. She glanced around the circle at the other students. 'Now, I think we owe it to Miss Reedy and Mr Lipp to put on the best performance of our lives. Three cheers for the teachers, hip hip hooray, hip hip hooray, hip hip hooray! And one cheer for us – HOORAY!'

Chapter 43

'Break a leg,' Millie whispered to Sloane, as she took up her position behind the Magic Mirror.

'I hope *you* break *your* leg,' Sloane spat back.

Millie sat in the chair behind her mirror. Charlie had helped to build the props and he'd done an especially wonderful job with this. He'd used a reflective surface that allowed Millie's face to fade in and out whenever she spoke to the Queen. Mr Plumpton had also been involved, giving Mr Charles some new-fangled materials that he'd been working with.

Miss Grimm and Mr Grump took their seats beside Professor Winterbottom and his wife Deidre, in the middle of the third row. The theatre was almost full, except for one empty seat in the centre of the second row. The lights began to dim.

'Hang on a tick. I'm not in my seat yet!' September Sykes teetered at the top of the stairs. The entire audience swivelled their heads in unison to see the outline of a woman in a minuscule dress, with more hair than your average lion, trying to navigate her way to the front. 'Put the lights on, please,' September asked in a syrupy voice.

There was a gasp as the parents and teachers squinting through the darkness realised exactly who the woman in the too-tight dress was.

'That's her. The one who's making the school close . . . she's vile . . . it's disgraceful . . .'

When nothing happened, September asked again. 'Put the lights on, NOW!' This time, there was not even a touch of sweetness in the request.

The poor young teacher at the lighting desk almost jumped out of his skin. He brought up the house lights. The audience couldn't take their eyes off September. She bounced and flounced to the second row and edged past the seated guests all the way to the middle, trampling more than one set of toes as she went.

September took their gasps and groans as compliments.

'Thank you, thank you.' She finally reached her seat. 'You can turn the lights off now,' she shouted.

A drum roll rumbled and the curtains went up.

'Once upon a time, long, long ago, a beautiful queen wished more than anything to be blessed with a child,' Jacinta narrated.

'You might want to wish for something less bothersome,' September quipped.

Ashima, in the role of Snow White's mother, stood at an open window with her needlework. She ignored the heckle and continued with her lines. The scene finished and the curtains closed, amid hearty clapping from the audience.

'She wasn't that good,' September said under her breath.

As the curtains opened again, the Evil Queen stood in the centre of the stage, her back to the audience. Her Magic Mirror sat on an elaborate dressing table facing the audience.

'Sloane!' September called and waved. 'That's

my girl up there. Mummy's here, darling, front and centre.'

The audience were fast losing their patience with this horrid woman.

Sloane was perfect in the part. She primped and preened. She checked her nails and brushed her hair and spent rather more time than Miss Reedy remembered from the rehearsals before she spoke to the mirror.

'Mirror, mirror, on the wall, who is the fairest of them all?' Sloane gazed lovingly at her own reflection.

Suddenly the mirror swirled and Millie's face appeared.

'Thou, Queen, there is none fairer than you,' the mirror replied, and with that, Millie disappeared.

'Bravo, bravo!' September shouted.

'Keep it down, woman.' It was Hedges, Fayle's gardener, who had the dubious pleasure of sitting beside her.

The play continued. The audience clapped and cheered for Snow White at the end of her scene with the Woodcutter, and laughed and laughed when she was found by the dwarfs. In no time at all, it was interval.

September turned to the man sitting on her left. 'Isn't she adorable?'

'Yes, she's a special one that Snow White,' he replied. It was Charlie and, next to him, Wally from Winchesterfield-Downsfordvale.

'Not that brat,' September grizzled. 'I meant the Queen – my daughter. She's lovely.'

'That's one word for her,' Wally quipped. *But perhaps not the first one that springs to mind*, he thought silently.

Interval lasted just a couple of minutes. Alice-Miranda grabbed what looked to be a script from backstage and handed it to Jacinta. 'Use this one from now on. There's no time to explain. Just go with it at the end – and don't be frightened. It's very important.'

Jacinta had no idea what her friend was talking about. And she didn't have time to look either. In a blink, the sets were changed and the curtain went up again.

'I haven't even had time for a toot break,' September complained. 'No champagne either. What sort of a play is this?'

'A school play, love,' Hedges leaned over and whispered, rolling his eyes at the dim-witted woman.

The scenes with Snow White and the dwarfs were wonderful. Poor old Sneezy's allergies were playing up more than ever and at one point he sneezed fifteen times in a row before they could continue.

'And here he goes again, and again, oh, now for something different . . .' Grumpy's improvisations delighted the audience, who were in hysterics.

There were boos for the Evil Queen as she tricked Snow White into eating her poison apple and sniffles when Snow White was found by her little friends and lifted into her glass coffin. Charlie, Wally and Hedges all produced large handkerchiefs to catch their torrents of tears. And then the Handsome Prince arrived to save the beautiful princess. When she awoke, the auditorium filled with cheers. The Prince's proposal had all the ladies swooning. Sep made a very handsome suitor indeed.

At last, it was nearing the final scene. The Evil Queen appeared on stage, fawning about all over herself.

'Mirror, mirror, on the wall, who's the fairest of them all?' she demanded.

Sloane turned her back to the mirror and gazed out at the audience. There was a loud gasp. This time, it wasn't Millie in the mirror.

'Look!' Wally called out. 'It's the witch. It's the witch from the woods. Ahhhhh!' The young lad clung to Charlie beside him. The whole audience drew in a collective gasp.

There in the mirror was Hephzibah, her scarred face hidden by her black veil.

'Jacinta,' Alice-Miranda whispered off stage. 'Just say it.'

'Dear Queen,' Jacinta looked at the script. She was completely bewildered. 'Your cheating ways and evil lies, have earned you now the greatest prize, a dear, dear friend has come to speak, about the havoc you did wreak.'

'That's not how it goes.' Sloane looked over to where Jacinta was standing. Miss Reedy was on the other side of the wings, flapping her arms about wildly. 'Who are you, anyway?' Sloane demanded, as she turned back to the mirror.

'She's the witch from the woods,' Wally shouted. 'Everyone knows that!'

'What witch?' Sloane folded her arms in front of her.

And then the mirror spoke.

'I know what you have done, Sloane Sykes.'

'I haven't done anything,' Sloane gasped and

turned back to face her accuser. 'I don't know what you're talking about.'

'I'm afraid you do, Sloane Sykes,' Hephzibah continued. 'You changed those papers. You made the boys fail.'

The audience had no idea what was going to happen next. Sloane began to shake. She did not know who this woman was, but she certainly didn't like her tone.

'It wasn't me. I didn't do anything,' Sloane protested.

'I don't believe you, Sloane Sykes. And do you know what happens to little girls who tell lies? Would you like to find out?' Hephzibah was shaking too.

Sloane started to cry. She spun around and pointed straight at her mother. 'It was her. It was all her idea. She made me take the papers and change the answers. She said that we would be rich. Like all of you!'

September Sykes sat with her mouth open like a stunned goldfish. The young teacher on the spotlight wheeled it around and suddenly there was September: a deer in the headlights, in a tiny green dress with nowhere to go.

'I don't know what she's talking about,' September

blurted. 'She's such a liar. Aren't you, Sloane? Always telling lies. Why do you think I sent her to boarding school in the first place?'

The audience drew in another collective gasp.

'I hate you, Mummy,' Sloane screeched and fled from the stage.

Alice-Miranda coughed and nodded at Jacinta who could hardly believe what she had just seen. Hephzibah was gone and the mirror was just a mirror.

Jacinta cleared her throat. 'The Evil Queen was banished from the kingdom and Snow White and her Prince were married and lived happily . . . ever . . . after . . .'

There was a pause as the children gathered their wits about them and flooded back onto the stage for the wedding party. The music struck up and Snow White and her Prince danced left and right, to much cheering and stamping of feet.

The scene ended, the cast took their bows and the audience clapped loudly. As the noise died down, Alice-Miranda invited Miss Reedy and Mr Lipp to join the group, where they were both presented with enormous bunches of flowers. The cast bowed once more and then stood in two lines, facing an expectant audience.

Professor Winterbottom moved from his seat to the microphone.

'Ladies and gentlemen, girls and boys, I'm sure you will agree with me that we have seen an astonishing performance here this evening – not exactly as expected, but fantastic just the same.'

September Sykes was wondering how on earth she could get out of the building. She needed to find her snivelling daughter and they needed to leave, as quickly as possible.

'I'm sure you've all heard about the recent real-life dramas here at Fayle. For a while, we thought the school would be closing at the end of the term, but as you saw tonight, that's not going to happen. And I'd personally like to thank Mrs Sykes for that. You see, if she hadn't tested the waters, so to speak, we might never have read the very fine, fine print, which actually told us that clause thirty of the Fayle School Charter could at any time be revoked by the oldest living relative of Frederick Fayle. Therefore, I do hope tonight that we can repeal that somewhat silly old rule and, while I can assure you the boys at Fayle will not fail, we will no longer have that hanging over our heads.'

'But I have Granny Henrietta's power of attorney,' September spat. 'I made her sign it . . .

I mean, she insisted I have it.' September stood up. 'And I'm not changing that rule. There will come a day when these boys *will* fail and then all this –' she waved her arms like a model from *The Price Is Right* – 'will belong to me.'

'It may be true that you have acquired your step-mother-in-law's power of attorney, Mrs Sykes, but you should check your facts. It seems that Henrietta is not Fred Fayle's oldest living relative,' said Professor Winterbottom.

September gasped. 'What are you talking about, you silly old man?'

'If you'd take your seat, Mrs Sykes, I'd like to invite Alice-Miranda Highton-Smith-Kennington-Jones to speak to us. I think she might be able to shed some light on this mystery.'

Alice-Miranda stepped forward to the microphone. Professor Winterbottom adjusted it downwards.

'Thank you, professor. Hello everyone, it's so lovely to be here tonight. If you would allow me, I'd like to tell you a story. You see, on the first night back this term, the girls in my house at school told me a tale about a witch who lived in the woods. That weekend, I went out riding with Millie and Susannah and Sloane and, well, I have a very naughty pony who loves vegetables . . .'

'You can say that again,' Mr Greening, the Highton-Smith-Kennington-Joneses' gardener, called from the audience. He received a sharp jab in the ribs from Mrs Greening beside him.

'Well, we had a lovely ride and a delicious picnic, and then when we were all on our way home, Bonaparte sniffed out a vegetable patch, so the girls went one way and I went another, and I ended up meeting a wonderful lady and I'd like to introduce her to you all now.' Alice-Miranda looked to the wings and beckoned with her right hand. Millie helped Hephzibah walk slowly onto the stage. No longer dressed in black, Hephzibah wore a lovely dress of purple and red, with a dainty hat and small net veil covering her face.

'Everyone, this is my dear friend, Miss Hephzibah Caledonia Fayle. She'd like to say something to you all.'

The audience gasped.

'She's not a Fayle!' September blurted. 'I've got the family tree and she's not on it.' But a sick feeling rose in September's stomach as she remembered that there was a corner of the document missing.

Hephzibah stood beside Alice-Miranda, who turned and gave her a gentle hug. Professor Winterbottom reached forward and raised the microphone.

'Hello everyone.' Hephzibah's voice wavered. 'As you've just heard, my name is Hephzibah Caledonia Fayle.' She spoke slowly and deliberately. 'I am an old woman who has spent most of her life being frightened. I have hidden from the world, too scared to show my face. In fact, everyone believed that I had perished in the fire which claimed my beloved parents many years ago, and I was happy for them to think that. And so, I became a sort of legend – the witch in the woods with her hundreds of cats. But this little girl, this wonderful little girl . . .' Hephzibah leaned down and kissed the top of Alice-Miranda's head, 'has shown me how to live again. She has made me laugh and cry, she's fed me some delicious chocolate brownies, and introduced me to her delightful friend, Millie.

'You see, my younger sister Henrietta gave up the best years of her life to be with me. Together, we made a life – and never left our home. Percy Sykes, a kind and wise man, delivered our groceries for years. He thought Henrietta lived at the manor alone – you see, I always hid from view if anyone ever came in.

I hid in the playroom, of all places. It was where I felt safest. When Percy lost his own dear wife, over time he and my sister fell in love.

'After all that Henrietta had sacrificed, she deserved to be happy, but I told her that if she married Percy, I didn't want to see her again. You see, my scars had made me selfish and hard. But that's not how the story will end. Today, with the help of Alice-Miranda's father and uncle, I have visited my sister. She is recovering from a stroke. We sat and we held hands and we cried tears of joy. I would also like to say, that while my great-great-grandfather Frederick Fayle was obviously a clever and visionary man, he wrote a very silly charter and therefore I hereby repeal clause thirty from this day forth.

'So, I am sorry to disappoint all of the children in this village who know me as the witch. I have no magical powers and no broomstick, no cauldron or book of spells. But I do have rather a lot of cats.'

There was not a dry eye in the house. One by one, the audience rose to their feet, clapping and cheering. Alice-Miranda looked up at her friend. She hugged Miss Fayle, who hugged her right back.

And just in case you're wondering . . .

September Sykes eventually located her daughter who was sobbing madly in the rose garden. After a rather wild argument, they dashed straight over to Winchesterfield-Downsfordvale and packed Sloane's things. Within a week, the Sykeses' brand-new house had a large 'For Sale' sign in the front garden. September phoned Smedley in a terrible huff, but was soothed a little when he explained that his offshore developing business wasn't faltering after all. September told him that Sloane was being bullied mercilessly at school, so she'd decided to sell the house and the two of them were coming over to be with him. She neglected to tell him about anything else that had happened.

Septimus steadfastly refused to leave school. He loved Fayle and Fayle loved him. Granny Henrietta heard all about what had happened. She'd always thought Septimus was just like his grandfather. She vowed to take care of him financially while ever he was at school or university and, in return, Septimus vowed to visit Granny Henrietta every week.

Caledonia Manor was transformed. Mr Greening, Charlie, Wally and Hedges, with an army of students led by Alice-Miranda, had the garden looking ship-shape in no time. Hugh Kennington-Jones finally got to send the builders.

Henrietta moved back to Caledonia Manor to live with her sister. They had a nurse to take care of them, and a cook and housekeeper. Over time, they gained a lot more company. It was far too big a house for the two of them to rattle around in so, in honour of their great-great-grandfather Frederick Erasmus Fayle, Caledonia Manor became a training college for teachers. Alice-Miranda and her friends visited Granny Henrietta and Hephzibah at least once a week.

Miss Grimm and Professor Winterbottom declared the play a resounding success. Miss Reedy and Mr Lipp were already arguing over what they would put on next year.

Alice-Miranda thought long and hard about what had happened with the test papers and the Fayle School Charter. She decided that Sloane shouldn't be held accountable for the actions of her mother. So after much consideration and a long chat with Sep, Alice-Miranda decided to write to Sloane and see if she might like to be penpals. After all, everyone deserves a second chance – don't they?

Cast of Characters

The Highton-Smith-Kennington-Jones household

Alice-Miranda Highton-Smith-Kennington-Jones	Only child, seven and a half years of age
Cecelia Highton-Smith	Alice-Miranda's doting mother
Hugh Kennington-Jones	Alice-Miranda's doting father
Aunt Charlotte Highton-Smith	Cecelia's younger sister
Lawrence Ridley	Famous movie actor and Aunt Charlotte's fiancé
Dolly Oliver	Family cook, part-time food technology scientist
Mrs Shillingsworth	Head housekeeper
Mr Greening	Gardener
Mrs Maggie Greening	Mr Greening's wife
Granny Bert (Albertine Rumble)	Former housekeeper at Highton Hall
Daisy Rumble	Granddaughter of Granny Bert, a maid at Highton Hall
Bonaparte	Alice-Miranda's pony
Max	Stablehand
Cyril	Helicopter pilot

Friends of the Highton-Smith-Kennington-Jones family

Aunty Gee — Granny Highton-Smith's best friend, Cecelia's godmother and the Queen

Prince Shivaji — Indian prince and friend of the family

Winchesterfield-Downsfordvale Academy for Proper Young Ladies Staff

Miss Ophelia Grimm — Headmistress
Aldous Grump — Miss Grimm's husband
Mrs Louella Derby — Personal Secretary to the headmistress

Miss Livinia Reedy — English teacher
Mr Josiah Plumpton — Science teacher
Howie (Mrs Howard) — Housemistress
Mr Cornelius Trout — Music teacher
Miss Benitha Wall — PE teacher
Cook (Mrs Doreen Smith) — Cook
Charlie Weatherly (Mr Charles) — Gardener
Wally Whitstable — Stablehand

Students

Millicent Jane McLoughlin-McTavish-McNoughton-McGill — Alice-Miranda's best friend and room mate
Jacinta Headlington-Bear — Talented gymnast, school's former second best tantrum thrower and a friend
Danika Rigby — Head Prefect
Madeline Bloom, Ivory — Friends

Hicks, Ashima Divall,
Lizzy Briggs, Shelby Shore,
Susannah Dare
Sloane Sykes   New student

Fayle School for Boys Staff

Professor Wallace Winterbottom	Headmaster
Mrs Deidre Winterbottom	Professor Winterbottom's wife
Miss Quigley	Personal Assistant to the headmaster
Professor Herman Pluss	Mathematics teacher
Mr Harold Lipp	English and drama teacher
Mr Horatio Huntley	Housemaster
Hedges	Gardener
Parsley	Professor Winterbottom's West Highland Terrier

Students

Lucas Nixon	Lawrence Ridley's son
Septimus Sykes	Brother of Sloane Sykes

Others

September Sykes	Mother of Sloane and Septimus
Smedley Sykes	Father of Sloane and Septimus
Percy Sykes	Deceased grandfather of Sloane and Septimus
Henrietta Sykes	Step-granny of Sloane and Septimus
Matron Payne	Matron at the Golden Gates Retirement Home

About the author

Jacqueline Harvey has spent her working life teaching in girls' boarding schools. She's never met a witch in the woods but she has come across quite a few girls who remind her a little of Alice-Miranda.

Jacqueline has published six novels for young readers. Her first picture book, *The Sound of the Sea*, was awarded Honour Book in the 2006 CBC Awards. She is currently working on Alice-Miranda's next adventure.

For more about Jacqueline and Alice-Miranda, go to:

www.alice-miranda.com

and

www.jacquelineharvey.com.au

Want more Alice-Miranda?

Look out for

Alice-Miranda
At Sea

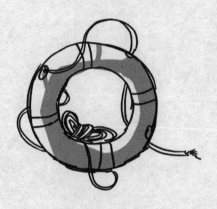

Coming soon!

W9-BKF-728

Praise for *New York Times* bestselling author RaeAnne Thayne

"[Thayne] engages the reader's heart and emotions, inspiring hope and the belief that miracles *are* possible."
—#1 *New York Times* bestselling author Debbie Macomber

"Entertaining, heart-wrenching, and totally involving, this multithreaded story overflows with characters readers will adore."
—*Library Journal* on *Evergreen Springs* (starred review)

"RaeAnne Thayne is quickly becoming one of my favorite authors…. Once you start reading, you aren't going to be able to stop."
—*Fresh Fiction*

"Thayne's realistic characterization grounds the hope of falling in love with the trials and tribulations that so often come with it."
—*BookPage* on *Serenity Harbor*

"RaeAnne has a knack for capturing those emotions that come from the heart."
—*RT Book Reviews*

"Her engaging storytelling…will draw readers in from the very first page."
—*RT Book Reviews* on *Riverbend Road*

"Tiny Haven Point springs to vivid life in Thayne's capable hands as she spins another sweet, heartfelt story."
—*Library Journal* on *Redemption Bay*

Also available from RaeAnne Thayne

HQN Books

Haven Point
The Cottages on Silver Beach
Sugar Pine Trail
Serenity Harbor
Snowfall on Haven Point
Riverbend Road
Evergreen Springs
Redemption Bay
Snow Angel Cove

Hope's Crossing
Wild Iris Ridge
Christmas in Snowflake Canyon
Willowleaf Lane
Currant Creek Valley
Sweet Laurel Falls
Woodrose Mountain
Blackberry Summer

For a complete list of books by RaeAnne Thayne,
please visit www.raeannethayne.com.

RaeAnne Thayne

SEASON OF WONDER

If you purchased this book without a cover you should be aware
that this book is stolen property. It was reported as "unsold and
destroyed" to the publisher, and neither the author nor the
publisher has received any payment for this "stripped book."

HQN™

Recycling programs
for this product may
not exist in your area.

ISBN-13: 978-1-335-94793-2

Season of Wonder

Copyright © 2018 by RaeAnne Thayne

All rights reserved. Except for use in any review, the reproduction or utilization
of this work in whole or in part in any form by any electronic, mechanical or other
means, now known or hereafter invented, including xerography, photocopying
and recording, or in any information storage or retrieval system, is forbidden
without the written permission of the publisher, HQN Books, 22 Adelaide St. West,
40th Floor, Toronto, Ontario M5H 4E3, Canada.

This is a work of fiction. Names, characters, places and incidents are either the
product of the author's imagination or are used fictitiously, and any resemblance
to actual persons, living or dead, business establishments, events or locales is
entirely coincidental.

This edition published by arrangement with Harlequin Books S.A.

For questions and comments about the quality of this book, please contact us
at CustomerService@Harlequin.com.

® and TM are trademarks of Harlequin Enterprises Limited or its corporate
affiliates. Trademarks indicated with ® are registered in the United States Patent
and Trademark Office, the Canadian Intellectual Property Office and in other
countries.

HQNBooks.com

Printed in U.S.A.

To Carly, for all the laughs, walks and joy. You are deeply loved!

SEASON OF WONDER

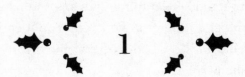

1

"This is totally lame. Why do we have to stay here and wait for you? We can walk home in, like, ten minutes."

Daniela Capelli drew in a deep breath and prayed for patience, something she seemed to be doing with increasing frequency these days when it came to her thirteen-year-old daughter. "It's starting to snow and already almost dark."

Silver rolled her eyes, something *she* did with increasing frequency these days. "So what? A little snow won't kill us. I would hardly even call that snow. We had way bigger storms than this back in Boston. Remember that big blizzard a few years ago, when school was closed for, like, a week?"

"I remember," her younger daughter, Mia, said, looking up from her coloring book at Dani's desk at the Haven Point Veterinary Clinic. "I stayed home from preschool and I watched Anna and Elsa a thousand times, until you said your eardrums would explode if I played it one more time."

Dani could hear a bark from the front office that likely signaled the arrival of her next client and knew she didn't have time to stand here arguing with an obstinate teenager.

"Mia can't walk as fast as you can. You'll end up frustrated with her and you'll both be freezing before you make it home," she pointed out.

"So she can stay here and wait for you while I walk home. I just told Chelsea we could FaceTime about the new dress she bought for the Christmas dance there and she can only do it for another hour before her dad comes to pick her up for his visitation."

"Why can't you FaceTime here? I only have two more patients to see. I'll be done in less than an hour, then we can all go home together. You can hang out in the waiting room with Mia, where the Wi-Fi signal is better."

Silver gave a huge put-upon sigh but picked up her backpack and stalked out of Dani's office toward the waiting room.

"Can I turn on the TV out there?" Mia asked as she gathered her papers and crayons. "I like the dog shows."

The veterinary clinic showed calming clips of animals on a big flat-screen TV set low to the ground for their clientele.

"After Silver's done with her phone call, okay?"

"She'll take *forever*," Mia predicted with a gloomy look. "She always does when she's talking to Chelsea."

Dani fought to hide a smile. "Thanks for your patience, sweetie, with her and with me. Finish your math worksheet while you're here, then when we get home, you can watch what you want."

Both the Haven Point elementary and middle schools were within walking distance of the clinic and it had become a habit for Silver to walk to the elementary school and then walk with Mia here to the clinic to spend a few hours until they could all go home together.

Of late, Silver had started to complain that she didn't want to pick her sister up at the elementary school every day, that she would rather they both just took their respective school buses home, where Silver could watch her sister without having to hang out at the boring veterinary clinic.

But then, Silver complained about nearly everything these days.

It was probably a good idea, but Dani wasn't quite ready to pull the trigger on having the girls alone every day after school. Maybe they would try it out after Christmas vacation.

This working professional/single mother gig was *hard*, she thought as she ushered Mia to the waiting room. Then again, in most ways it was much easier than the veterinary student/single mother gig had been.

When they entered the comfortable waiting room—with its bright colors, pet-friendly benches and big fish tank— Mia faltered for a moment, then sidestepped behind Dani's back.

She saw instantly what had caused her daughter's nervous reaction. Funny. Dani felt the same way. She wanted to hide behind somebody, too.

The receptionist had given her the files with the dogs' names that were coming in for a checkup but hadn't mentioned their human was Ruben Morales. Her gorgeous next-door neighbor.

Dani's palms instantly itched and her stomach felt as if she'd accidentally swallowed a flock of butterflies.

"Deputy Morales," she said, then paused, hating the slightly breathless note in her voice.

What *was* it about the man that always made her so freaking nervous?

He was big, yes, at least six feet tall, with wide shoulders, tough muscles and a firm, don't-mess-with-me jawline.

It wasn't just that. Even without his uniform, the man exuded authority and power, which instantly raised her hackles and left her uneasy, something she found both frustrating and annoying about herself.

No matter how far she had come, how hard she had worked to make a life for her and her girls, she still sometimes felt like the troublesome foster kid from Queens, always on the defensive.

She had done her best to avoid him in the months they had been in Haven Point, but that was next to impossible when they lived so close to each other—and when she was the intern in his father's veterinary practice, with the hope that she might be able to purchase it at the end of the year.

"Hey, Doc," he said, flashing her an easy smile she didn't

trust for a moment. It never quite reached his dark, long-lashed eyes, at least where she was concerned.

While she might be uncomfortable around Ruben Morales, his dogs were another story.

He held the leashes of both of them, a big, muscular Belgian shepherd and an incongruously paired little Chi-poo and she reached down to pet both of them. They sniffed her and wagged happily, the big dog's tail nearly knocking over his small friend.

That was the thing she loved most about dogs. They were uncomplicated and generous with their affection, for the most part. They never looked at people with that subtle hint of suspicion, as if trying to uncover all their secrets.

"I wasn't expecting you," she admitted.

"Oh? I made an appointment. The boys both need checkups. Yukon needs his regular hip and eye check and Ollie is due for his shots."

She gave the dogs one more pat before she straightened and faced him, hoping his sharp cop eyes couldn't notice evidence of her accelerated pulse.

"Your father is still here every Monday and Friday afternoons. Maybe you should reschedule with him," she suggested. It was a faint hope, but a girl had to try.

"Why would I do that?"

"Maybe because he's your father and knows your dogs?"

"Dad is an excellent veterinarian. Agreed. But he's also semiretired and wants to be fully retired this time next year. As long as you plan to stick around in Haven Point, we will have to switch vets and start seeing you eventually. I figured we might as well start now."

He was checking her out. Not *her* her, but her skills as a veterinarian.

The implication was clear. She had been here three months, and it had become obvious during that time in their few interactions that Ruben Morales was extremely protective of his family. He had been polite enough when they had met previously, but always with a certain guardedness, as if he was afraid she planned to take the good name his hardworking father had built up over the years for the Haven Point Veterinary Clinic and drag it through the sludge at the bottom of Lake Haven.

Dani pushed away her instinctive prickly defensiveness, bred out of all those years in foster care when she felt as if she had no one else to count on—compounded by the difficult years after she'd married Tommy and had Silver, when she *really* had no one else in her corner.

She couldn't afford to offend Ruben. She didn't need his protective wariness to turn into full-on suspicion. With a little digging, Ruben could uncover things about her and her past that would ruin everything for her and her girls here.

She forced a professional smile. "It doesn't matter. Let's go back to a room and take a look at these guys. Girls, I'll be done shortly. Silver, keep an eye on your sister."

Her oldest nodded without looking up from her phone and with an inward sigh, Dani led the way to the largest of the exam rooms.

She stood at the door as he entered the room with the two dogs, then joined him inside and closed the door behind her.

The large room seemed to shrink unnaturally and she paused inside for a moment, flustered and wishing she could escape. Dani gave herself a mental shake. She was a doctor of veterinary medicine, not a teenage girl. She could handle being in the same room with the one man in Haven Point who left her breathless and unsteady.

All she had to do was focus on the reason he was here in the first place. His dogs.

She knelt to their level. "Hey there, guys. Who wants to go first?"

The Malinois—often confused for a German shepherd but smaller and with a shorter coat—wagged his tail again while his smaller counterpoint sniffed around her shoes, probably picking up the scents of all the other dogs she had seen that day.

"Ollie, I guess you're the winner today."

He yipped, his big ears that stuck straight out from his face quivering with excitement.

He was the funniest looking dog, quirky and unique, with wisps of fur in odd places, spindly legs and a narrow Chihuahua face. She found him unbearably cute. With that face, she wouldn't ever be able to say no to him if he were hers.

"Can I give him a treat?" She always tried to ask permission first from her clients' humans.

"Only if you want him to be your best friend for life," Ruben said.

Despite her nerves, his deadpan voice sparked a smile,

which widened when she gave the little dog one of the treats she always carried in the pocket of her lab coat and he slurped it up in one bite, then sat with a resigned sort of patience during the examination.

She was aware of Ruben watching her as she carefully examined the dog, but Dani did her best not to let his scrutiny fluster her.

She knew what she was doing, she reminded herself. She had worked so hard to be here, sacrificing all her time, energy and resources of the last decade to nothing else but her girls and her studies.

"Everything looks good," she said after checking out the dog and finding nothing unusual. "He seems like a healthy little guy. It says here he's about six or seven. So you haven't had him from birth?"

"No. Only about two years. He was a stray I picked up off the side of the road between here and Shelter Springs when I was on patrol one day. He was in a bad way, half-starved, fur matted. I think he'd been on his own for a while. As small as he is, it's a wonder he wasn't picked off by a coyote or even one of the bigger hawks. He just needed a little TLC."

"You couldn't find his owner?"

"We ran ads and Dad checked with all his contacts at shelters and veterinary clinics from here to Boise, with no luck. I had been fostering him while we looked, and to be honest, I kind of lost my heart to the little guy and by then Yukon adored him so we decided to keep him."

She was such a sucker for animal lovers, especially those who rescued the vulnerable and lost ones.

And, no. She didn't need counseling to point out the parallels to her own life.

Regardless, she couldn't let herself be drawn to Ruben and risk doing something foolish. She had too much to lose here in Haven Point.

"What about Yukon here?" She knelt down to examine the bigger dog. Though he wasn't huge and Ruben could probably lift him easily to the table, she decided it was easier to kneel to his level. In her experience, sometimes bigger dogs didn't like to be lifted and she wasn't sure if the beautiful Malinois fell into that category.

Ruben shrugged as he scooped Ollie onto his lap to keep the little Chi-poo from swooping in and stealing the treat she held out for the bigger dog. "You could say he was a rescue, too."

"Oh?"

"He was a K-9 officer down in Mountain Home. After his handler was killed in the line of duty, I guess he kind of went into a canine version of depression and wouldn't work with anyone else. I know that probably sounds crazy."

She scratched the dog's ears, touched by the bond that could build between handler and dog. "Not at all," she said briskly. "I've seen many dogs go into decline when their owner dies. It's not uncommon."

"For a year or so, they tried to match him up with other officers, but things never quite gelled, for one reason or another, then his eyes started going. His previous handler who died was a good buddy of mine from the academy and I couldn't let him go just anywhere."

"Retired police dogs don't always do well in civilian life. They can be aggressive with other dogs and sometimes people. Have you had any problems with that?"

"Not with Yukon. He's friendly. Aren't you, buddy? You're a good boy."

Dani could swear the dog grinned at his owner, his tongue lolling out.

Yukon was patient while she looked him over, especially as she maintained a steady supply of treats.

When she finished, she gave the dog a pat and stood. "Can I take a look at Ollie's ears one more time?"

"Sure. Help yourself."

He held the dog out and she reached for Ollie. As she did, the dog wriggled a little and Dani's hands ended up brushing Ruben's chest. She froze at the accidental contact, a shiver rippling down her spine. She pinned her reaction on the undeniable fact that it had been entirely too long since she had touched a man, even accidentally.

She had to cut out this *fascination* or whatever it was immediately. Clean-cut, muscular cops were *not* her type, and the sooner she remembered that the better.

She focused on checking the ears of the little dog, gave him one more scratch and handed him back to Ruben. "That should do it. A clean bill of health. They seem to be two happy, well-adjusted dogs. You obviously take good care of them."

He patted both dogs with an affectionate smile that did nothing to ease her nerves.

"My dad taught me well. I spent most of my youth helping out here at the clinic—cleaning cages, brushing coats, walking the occasional overnight boarder. Whatever grunt work he needed. He made all of us help."

"I can think of worse ways to earn a dime," she said.

The chance to work with animals would have been a dream opportunity for her, back when she had few bright spots in her world. Besides that, she considered his father one of the sweetest people she had ever met.

"So can I. I always loved animals."

She had to wonder why he didn't follow in his father's footsteps and become a vet. None of his three siblings had made that choice, either. If any of them had, she probably wouldn't be here right now, as Frank Morales probably would have handed down his thriving practice to his own progeny.

Not that it was any of her business. Ruben certainly could follow any career path he wanted—as long as that path took him far away from her.

"Give me a moment to grab those medications and I'll be right back."

"No rush."

Out in the hall, she closed the door behind her and drew in a deep breath.

Get a grip, she chided herself. *He's just a hot-looking dude. Heaven knows, you've had more than enough experience with those to last a lifetime.*

She went to the well-stocked medication dispensary, found what she needed and returned to the exam room.

Outside the door, she paused for only a moment to gather her composure before pushing it open. "Here are the pills for Ollie's nerves and a refill for Yukon's eye drops," she said briskly. "Let me know if you have any questions—though if you do, you can certainly ask your father."

"Thanks." As he took the medication from her, his hands brushed hers again and sent a little spark of awareness shivering through her.

Oh, come on. This was ridiculous.

She was probably imagining the way his gaze sharpened, as if he had felt something odd, too.

"I can show you out. We're shorthanded today since the veterinary tech and the receptionist both needed to leave early."

"No problem. That's what I get for scheduling the last appointment of the day—though, again, I spent most of my youth here. I think we can find our way."

"It's fine. I'll show you out." She stood outside the door while he gathered the dogs' leashes, then led the way toward the front office.

After three months, Ruben still couldn't get a bead on Dr. Daniela Capelli.

His next-door neighbor still seemed a complete enigma to him. By all reports from his father, she was a dedicated, earnest new veterinarian with a knack for solving difficult medical mysteries and a willingness to work hard. She seemed like a warm and loving mother, at least from the few times he had seen her interactions with her two girls, the uniquely named teenager Silver—who had, paradoxically, purple hair—and the sweet-as-Christmas-toffee Mia, who was probably about six.

He also couldn't deny she was beautiful, with slender features, striking green eyes, dark, glossy hair and a dusky skin tone that proclaimed her Italian heritage—as if her name didn't do the trick first.

He actually liked the trace of New York accent that slipped into her speech at times. It fit her somehow, in a way he couldn't explain. Despite that, he couldn't deny that the few times he had interacted with more than a wave in passing, she was brusque, prickly and sometimes downright distant.

He had certainly had easier neighbors.

His father adored her and wouldn't listen to a negative thing about her.

She hasn't had an easy time of things but she's a fighter. Hardworking and eager to learn, Frank had said the other night when Ruben asked how things were working out, now that Dani and her girls had been in town a few months. *You just have to get to know her.*

Frank apparently didn't see how diligently Dani Capelli worked to keep anyone else from doing just that.

She wasn't unfriendly, only distant. She kept herself to herself. It was a phrase his mother might use, though Myra Morales seemed instantly fond of Dani and her girls.

Did Dani have any idea how fascinated the people of Haven Point were with these new arrivals in their midst?

Or maybe that was just him.

As he followed her down the hall in her white lab coat, his dogs behaving themselves for once, Ruben told himself to forget about his stupid attraction to her.

Sure, he might be ready to settle down and would like to have someone in his life, but he wasn't at all sure if he had the time or energy for that someone to be a woman with so many secrets in her eyes, one who seemed to face the world with her chin up and her fists out, ready to take on any threats.

When they walked into the clinic waiting room, they found her two girls there. The older one was texting on her phone while her sister did somersaults around the room.

Dani stopped in the doorway and seemed to swallow an exasperated sound. "Mia, honey, you're going to have dog hair all over you."

"I'm a snowball rolling down the hill," the girl said. "Can't you see me getting bigger and bigger and bigger."

"You're such a dorkupine," her sister said, barely looking up from her phone.

"I'm a dorkupine snowball," Mia retorted.

"You're a snowball who is going to be covered in dog hair," Dani said. "Come on, honey. Get up."

He could tell the moment the little girl spotted him and his dogs coming into the area behind her mother. She went still and then slowly rose to her feet, features shifting from gleeful to nervous.

Why was she so afraid of him?

"You make a very good snowball," he said, pitching his voice low and calm as his father had taught him to do with all skittish creatures. "I haven't seen anybody somersault that well in a long time."

She moved to her mother's side and buried her face in Dani's white coat—though he didn't miss the way she reached down to pet Ollie on her way.

"Hey again, Silver."

He knew the older girl from the middle school, where he served as the resource officer a few hours a week. He made it a point to learn all the students' names and tried to talk to them individually when he had the chance, in hopes that if they had a problem at home or knew of something potentially troublesome for the school, they would feel comfortable coming to him.

He had the impression that Silver was like her mother in many ways. Reserved, wary, slow to trust. It made him wonder just who had hurt them.

"How are things?" he asked her now.

For just an instant, he thought he saw sadness flicker in her gaze before she turned back to her phone with a shrug. "Fine, I guess."

"Are you guys ready for Christmas? It's your first one here in Idaho. A little different from New York, isn't it?"

"How should we know? We haven't lived in the city for, like, four years."

Dani sent her daughter a look at her tone, which seemed

to border on disrespectful. "I've been in vet school in Boston the last four years," she explained.

"Boston. Then you're used to snow and cold. We're known for our beautiful winters around here. The lake is simply stunning in wintertime."

Mia tugged on her mother's coat and when Dani bent down, she whispered something to her.

"You can ask him," Dani said calmly, gesturing to Ruben.

Mia shook her head and buried her face again and after a moment, Dani sighed. "She wonders if it's possible to iceskate on Lake Haven. We watched the most recent Olympics and she became a little obsessed."

"You could say that," Silver said. "She skated around the house in her stocking feet all day long for *weeks*. A dorkupine on ice."

"You can't skate on the lake, I'm afraid," Ruben answered. "Because of the underground hot springs that feed into it at various points, Lake Haven rarely freezes, except sometimes along the edges, when it's really cold. It's not really safe for ice skating. But the city creates a skating rink on the tennis courts at Lake View Park every year. The volunteer fire department sprays it down for a few weeks once temperatures get really cold. I saw them out there the other night so it shouldn't be long before it's open. Maybe a few more weeks."

Mia seemed to lose a little of her shyness at that prospect. She gave him a sideways look from under her mother's arm and aimed a fleeting smile full of such sweetness that he was instantly smitten.

"There's also a great place for sledding up behind the high school. You can't miss that, either. Oh, and in a few weeks we have the Lights on the Lake Festival. You've heard about that, right?"

They all gave him matching blank stares, making him wonder what was wrong with the Haven Point Helping Hands that they hadn't immediately dragged Dani into their circle. He would have to talk to Andie Bailey or his sister Angela about it. They always seemed to know what was going on in town.

"I think some kids at school were talking about that at lunch the other day," Silver said. "They were sitting at the next table so I didn't hear the whole thing, though."

"Haven Point hosts an annual celebration a week or so before Christmas where all the local boat owners deck out their watercraft from here to Shelter Springs to welcome in the holidays and float between the two towns. There's music, food and crafts for sale. It's kind of a big deal around here. I'm surprised you haven't heard about it."

"I'm very busy, with the practice and the girls, Deputy Morales. I don't have a lot of time for socializing." Though Dani tried for a lofty look, he thought he caught a hint of vulnerability there.

She seemed...lonely. That didn't make a lick of sense. The women in this town could be almost annoying in their efforts to include newcomers in community events. They didn't give people much of an option, dragging them kicking and screaming into the social scene around town, like it or not.

"Well, now you know. You really can't miss the festival. It's great fun for the whole family."

"Thank you for the information. It's next week, you say?"

"That's right. Not this weekend but the one after. The whole thing starts out with the boat parade on Saturday evening, around six."

"We'll put it on our social calendar."

"What's a social calendar?" Mia whispered to her sister, just loud enough for Ruben to hear.

"It's a place where you keep track of all your invitations to parties and sleepovers and stuff."

"Oh. Why do we need one of those?"

"Good question."

Silver looked glum for just a moment but Dani hugged her, then faced Ruben with a polite, distant smile.

"Thank you for bringing in Ollie and Yukon. Have a good evening, Deputy Morales."

It was a clear dismissal, one he couldn't ignore. Ruben gathered his dogs' leashes and headed for the door. "Thank you. See you around. And by around, I mean next door. We kind of can't miss each other."

As he hoped, this made Mia smile a little. Even Silver's dour expression eased into what almost looked like a smile.

As he loaded the dogs into the king cab of his pickup truck, Ruben could see Dani turning off lights and straightening up the clinic.

What was her story? Why had she chosen to come straight from vet school in Boston to set up shop all the way across the country in a small Idaho town?

He loved his hometown, sure, and fully acknowledged it was a beautiful place to live. It still seemed a jarring cultural and geographic shift from living back east to this little town where the biggest news of the month was a rather corny light parade that people froze their asses off to watch.

And why did he get the impression the family wasn't socializing much? One of the reasons most people he knew moved to small towns was a yearning for the kind of connectedness and community a place like Haven Point had in spades. What was the point in moving to a small town if you were going to keep yourself separate from everybody?

He thought he had seen them at a few things when they first came to Haven Point but since then, Dani seemed to be keeping her little family mostly to themselves. That must be by choice. It was the only explanation that made sense. He couldn't imagine McKenzie Kilpatrick or Andie Bailey or any of the other Helping Hands excluding her on purpose.

What was she so nervous about?

He added another facet to the enigma of his next-door neighbor. He had hoped that he might be able to get a better perspective of her by bringing the dogs in to her for their routine exams. While he had confirmed his father's belief that she appeared to be an excellent veterinarian, he now had more questions about the woman and her daughters to add to his growing list.

2

After a long, difficult day, following a long, difficult week, all Dani wanted was to pop a batch of popcorn, sit on the sofa and watch something light and cheery with her girls for a few hours. As she stood at the kitchen sink of their three-bedroom cottage drying the last of the dishes Silver had washed after school, she thought that what she would *really* like was a long soak in the tub. By the time her daughters were in bed most nights, she didn't have enough energy left to even run water in the tub.

The kitchen was small enough that cleaning it never took long. The house Frank Morales had provided as part of her internship compensation wasn't big but it was comfortable, with three bedrooms, a living room and a lovely glass-enclosed family room facing the lake, which had become their favorite spot.

Someday she'd like to have a little bigger house, maybe with an actual dining room, but that would have to wait awhile. She had thousands of dollars in student loans to pay back first. Meantime, this house worked well for their needs.

Her life could have been easier. Occasionally, she tormented herself by playing the old what-if game, wondering how things might have been different for her and her daughters if she had been able to ignore her conscience and taken money from Tommy.

If she had accepted the ill-gotten gains her late ex-husband had tried to give for child support, she might have been able to start her professional life as a veterinarian with a clean slate, even with a little nest egg, instead of feeling swallowed by debt. But she would have had to sell her soul in return and she wasn't willing to do that.

Yes, she was tired of the constant scrimping and saving and striving, but at least when she finally made her way to bed each night, she could close her eyes with a clear conscience.

Mostly clear, anyway.

She set the dish towel over the oven handle to dry and made her way to the family room. Silver was, as usual, on her phone while Mia was doing more somersaults, this time on the carpet, while their ancient little mutt Winky watched from her favorite spot on the floor, blocking the heater vent.

"Movie night!" Dani said cheerfully. "Who's ready? I'll make the popcorn. You two just need to pick a show."

"Yay! Movie night. My favorite!" Mia grinned from the floor.

"I think we should watch a Christmas movie. What do you say? *Elf*, *Grinch*, *Arthur Christmas* or something off the Hallmark Channel."

The previous Christmas, during Dani's rare moments off from school, they had binge-watched movies on the Hall-mark Channel. Dani had felt a little world-weary to truly appreciate the sweet happy endings but Silver had adored them.

It had been several months since Silver had been inter-ested in anything sweet. Right around the time she'd dyed her hair and started begging for the tattoo Dani would not let her get until she was eighteen.

"*Elf*," Mia declared without hesitation.

"Okay. One vote for *Elf*. What do you think, Sil?"

"I think you're going to have to watch without me." Her daughter rose from the sofa with the long-legged grace she had inherited from her father. "I've got to go. Some friends just texted me and they want to hang out."

Dani felt her temper flare at Silver's matter-of-fact tone but worked to keep it contained. "Are you asking me or telling me?"

Silver's jaw worked. "Asking, I guess. Can I go hang out with my friends?"

At thirteen, she seemed to think she didn't need permission these days for much of anything. Dani had a completely different perspective on the situation.

"Which friends? And what did they want to do?"

"Just friends from school," Silver said, impatience threading through her voice. "Why do you have to know every single detail about my life?"

"Because I'm your parent and responsible for you. I'm not asking for every detail but I have to know where you're going and who you will be with. Those are the house rules, kid. You know that."

Silver didn't appear to appreciate the reminder. "I thought you might lighten up a little once we moved to the middle of freaking nowhere. Instead, you're worse than ever."

Oh, Dani so did not want to deal with this tonight. Not after the day she'd had. "You're going to want to watch your tone and your attitude, miss, unless you would prefer to spend the night in your room instead of with any friends."

Her daughter glared for a moment and then, with her quicksilver moods lately, her expression shifted to one of resignation. "Fine. I'm going over to Jenny Turner's house. She's in my biology class. She was going to call some other friends so we could watch the latest Marvel movie that just came out. Is that okay with you?"

Dani knew Jenny and her parents. They lived just one street over and her family had two beautiful Irish setters who appeared well mannered and well loved.

"Will her parents be there?"

"Her dad is on a work trip but her mom will be home, she said."

She wanted to say no. Dani had been looking forward to spending a little time together with her daughters. The girls didn't have school the next day because of a teacher training thing and Silver could hang out all day with friends if she wanted while the babysitter was there with Mia.

But Silver had struggled to fit in socially and find good friends since they moved to Haven Point and Dani didn't want to discourage any progress in that area.

"That's fine, then. Do you want me to give you a ride?"

"No. I'll walk. It's just through the block. Can I stay until eleven?"

"Yes, since you don't have school tomorrow. Text me when you're done and I'll pick you up. It doesn't matter how close she lives, I don't want you walking around town so late."

"It's like a block away, Mom. And, again, we're in the middle of freaking nowhere, Idaho. Walking is good for me."

She sighed, choosing to pick her battles. "Watch for cars."

On impulse, Dani hugged her daughter, fighting the urge to wrap her arms around her and not let go. After a moment, Silver hugged her back but quickly pulled away and hurried out the door.

Dani watched after her, trying to ignore the niggle of worry.

How did parents survive these teenage years? She constantly felt like a raw bundle of nerves, always afraid she was going to say the wrong thing and set off an emotional meltdown.

She watched until Silver walked around the corner, then turned back to Mia.

"Guess it's just you and me, pumpkin. I'll make the popcorn. You pick the movie."

"Elf," Mia said without hesitation, which was just fine with Dani.

She was pouring kernels in the air popper when Mia came into the kitchen holding the Blu-ray.

"I found it."

"Good job. Why don't you grab some ice water so you don't have to leave in the middle of the show if you need a drink? Your glass with the elephants on it is still at the table from dinner."

Mia took her water glass and filled it from the refrigerator ice maker.

"Mama," she said, features pensive, after the rattling ice stopped, "why doesn't Silver like us anymore?"

Dani's heart cracked apart a little at the sadness in her six-year-old's voice, mostly because deep inside, she felt as bewildered and abandoned.

"She does, honey. She's just a teenager living in a strange town and trying to make friends. It hasn't been very easy for her."

"I think I liked the old Silver better."

Dani didn't want to tell her daughter that she did, too.

After she finished adding toppings to the bowl of popcorn, she and Mia settled onto the couch. With Mia snuggled against her, Dani felt some of the tension leave her, but she couldn't shake her worry about Silver. She wanted so desperately for her daughter to find good friends who were also decent human beings.

The movie was familiar enough that her mind began to wander. Not for the first time, she wondered if she had made a huge mistake by bringing her daughters to Haven Point.

It had seemed the perfect opportunity. She and Frank Morales had struck up an instant friendship her second year of veterinary school when she'd stayed after a seminar he presented at a conference to ask him some questions.

That initial meeting had developed into a semiregular correspondence. She had a feeling Frank had looked on her as a mentee of sorts. He had been unfailingly patient and kind with her questions about various aspects of veterinary medicine and what went into running a successful practice.

A month before her graduation, Frank had called her with a proposition. He was looking for another doctor to take some of the load at his veterinary clinic. If she liked it here in Haven Point after her year's internship was up, he wanted her to take over the practice.

It was an offer she couldn't refuse, beneficial to her professionally while being perfect for her little family on a personal level.

This was everything she used to dream about, the chance to raise her girls in a safe place surrounded by nice people who cared about each other. Here, people didn't know about Tommy, about his disastrous choices.

Of course, when she'd accepted the internship and moved here, she couldn't have known about the tragic sequence of events to come later, the horror story that unfolded across the country mere weeks after she came to town.

She felt the beginnings of panic again, just thinking about what would happen if news of Tommy's final moments were to filter through to everyone.

Frank knew, of course. She had to tell him. While he had been kind and understanding, she couldn't imagine the other people in town would accept the truth so easily.

Coming to Haven Point had sounded great in theory but the reality of making a life here was harder than she had imagined. The truth was, she didn't know how to socialize casually, which was a ridiculous thing for a thirty-year-old woman with a doctorate degree to admit.

She had married Tommy when she was seventeen. The years since, she'd been so focused on her girls, on school, on work and on simply *surviving* that she had gotten out of practice when it came to making and keeping friendships.

She didn't know how to relate to these people who were so darn *nice* all the time, and her awkwardness in the beginning had made her leery about accepting new invitations. Then Tommy had become a household name in the worst possible way. Dani knew she couldn't socialize now. She kept finding new excuses not to attend book club meetings or the Haven Point Helping Hands' regular luncheons and after a few months, the invitations had tapered off.

Her girls were struggling, too. Silver had all this attitude all the time, some of that from grief and shame over her father, Dani was certain. Even Mia, who hadn't even known

Tommy, had become painfully shy in public, though she was her usual warm, sweet self at home.

Dani had to fix this or they could never make their home here, but she didn't know the first place to start.

"Mama, you're not watching the movie," Mia chided her.

"I'm sorry." She forced a smile and reached for some popcorn. "I'll watch now."

She couldn't do anything at this moment but worry, so she vowed to put it aside for now and focus on something light and silly and fun.

And then maybe take that hour-long soak in the tub after Silver was home and her girls were both safely tucked in bed.

For about the twentieth time in the last fifteen minutes, Yukon went to the back door and peered through the glass toward the backyard and the lake at the edge of it.

Retired police dogs were a lot like retired police officers, in Ruben's experience. They sometimes had a difficult time remembering they weren't on the job anymore.

"Easy, buddy. What's going on?" Ruben scratched the dog's neck in an attempt to calm him but the dog still seemed to want to alert him to something out in the back.

Yukon pulled away and went to the door whining, his attention focused on something near the boathouse, something Ruben couldn't see. He could only hope it wasn't a skunk. He hadn't seen one around here in some time, but one never knew up here. It could also be a black bear or a mountain lion.

Yukon whined again and nudged at the door and Ruben

finally rose from the sofa and slipped his feet into the boots he kept by the back door. If the dog needed to go out, Ruben had to let him but he couldn't send him out alone if there might be a potential threat out there.

He pulled on his jacket and grabbed the dog's leash. Ollie trotted over, always ready for some fun, and Ruben had to shake his head at the little dog. "Not you. You've got to stay inside and watch the house while we do a little recon."

Ollie gave what sounded like a resigned sigh and plopped down on the rug to watch as Ruben clipped the leash on Yukon.

"All right, bud. Let's go see what's happening."

The night was cold, mostly clear, with only a few random clouds passing in front of the big moon that hovered just above the mountains. It was the kind of December night meant to be spent by the fire with a special someone.

Too bad he didn't have a special someone.

It had been almost a year since he had dated anyone remotely seriously, and that had been with a teacher in Shelter Springs.

He had met Lindsey while giving a self-defense class organized by Wynona Emmett, sister to his boss and close friend, Marshall Bailey. She had been sweet and warm and kind, but she also had been still in love with her ex-husband, something it had taken both of them six months of dating to fully acknowledge.

Ruben sighed. He missed Lindsey but he *really* missed hanging out with her kids, two cute little boys just a little older than Dani Capelli's youngest girl.

He supposed that spoke volumes about their relationship. His heart hadn't been committed yet, but he had definitely seen things moving in that direction eventually.

At least they hadn't gotten far enough for the situation to turn ugly, like it did for his brother Mateo, who was in the middle of a nasty court battle for visitation with the stepson he had raised from a baby.

Next time he decided to let his heart get involved, Ruben had vowed it would be with a woman who didn't have children. The only trouble with that philosophy was that he was getting older and so were the women who interested him. He had outgrown his attraction to dewy, fresh-eyed coeds when he was in his twenties. He liked a woman who had been around the block a time or two and had the wisdom and experience to prove it.

Someone like Daniela Capelli, for instance.

He glanced next door, toward her house. The lights were on and he thought he saw someone moving around inside.

He hadn't been able to stop thinking about the woman since he'd left the veterinary clinic earlier in the week. He was no closer to solving the mystery of her, though.

Too bad she had kids—a younger one who seemed afraid of him and an older one who treated him like he had a bad case of head lice every time she saw him.

Yukon whined and pulled in the direction of the boathouse again, which was really just a covered concrete slab where he kept his shiny new cabin cruiser, aptly named *The Wonder*.

Ruben could swear he heard whispers drifting to him on the wind. Was someone there?

Suddenly Yukon's whine turned to a bark and the whispers turned to shouts. Someone yelled, "Run," at the same moment the dog lunged away from Ruben and the leash slipped out of his hand.

He reached for it, but Yukon moved with single-minded speed toward the boathouse, barking away.

Surprised at the unusual behavior from his normally obedient dog, Ruben raced after him. He ordered the dog in Dutch—the language he was trained in—to stay. After only a moment's hesitation, Yukon reluctantly obeyed, too well trained to do otherwise.

"Good boy."

Ruben could hear rustling in the bushes around the boathouse as he drew closer.

"Whoever you are," he called out, "you're going to want to not move. My dog is trained to attack on command. I just have to say the word."

He heard a small sound of distress and aimed his flashlight in the direction of the dog, who had alerted onto a shape crouched close to the ground. The dog wasn't growling. In fact, his tail might even have been wagging, though it was too dark to be sure.

"I should also tell you, I'm a deputy sheriff and I'm armed."

He didn't add that he was armed with only a flashlight and can of bear spray. The intruder didn't need that much information.

"Don't shoot me. Please don't shoot me." The voice was

high-pitched and sounded terrified. Either it was only a kid or Ruben and Yukon had scared the cojones off somebody.

"Come on out from there. I won't hurt you. Neither will Yukon, as long as you don't make any sudden movements."

"Can you take his leash? Just in case?"

The voice struck a chord. He'd heard it before, and not that long ago. He tried to place it as he stepped forward to grab Yukon's leash, speaking in Dutch again to order the dog to stay.

"I have the leash but that probably won't help you. I was holding it earlier but he got away from me when he caught your scent."

He sensed the dog wasn't being predatory, he only wanted to play, but the intruder couldn't know that.

"Come on out."

After a long moment, the trespasser slowly rose from the ground, appearing ready to bolt at any moment. Ruben moved into position to block any escape route, and aimed his flashlight at the figure, clothed in a dark coat with the hood up.

Shock rippled through him. "Silver? Silver Capelli? What are you doing here?"

Of all the miscreants in town who might have it out for him—and it was impossible to avoid making a few enemies here and there in his line of work—he never would have pinpointed Dani's older daughter as someone who might trespass on his property.

"Um. Just taking a walk. That's all. I just wanted to, uh,

see the water, then your dog scared me and I freaked. I'll, uh, just be going now."

Did she really think he was that stupid? Her house was next to his. If she wanted to see the water, she only had to walk into her own backyard, not scale the fence to come into his.

"Hold on a second."

His flashlight gleamed on something metallic in the grass. He nudged it with his foot and saw it was a spray can. With a sinking suspicion, he turned the flashlight onto his new boat. Across the hull in glaring red letters he saw "Fascist Pi" written in two-foot-tall letters.

Either she had a thing against math equations or she hadn't had time to finish writing an inflammatory slur against police officers.

"Wow. Nice artwork."

"It was like that when I got here. I didn't see who did it."

He shined the flashlight on her. Again, did he look that stupid? "I can see the spray paint residue on your finger. I believe that's the very definition of red-handed."

She hid her hand behind her back, as if she were five years old and had been caught playing in her mom's makeup.

As he took a step closer, she stepped back, though she lifted her chin. Whether that was instinct or courage, he didn't know. One part of him had to admire her grit, even as he acknowledged that, ridiculously, his feelings were hurt.

What had he done to earn this kind of vitriol? He had tried to be nice to Silver since she and her family moved to Haven Point. He had talked to her a few times when he was making visits to the school and had even cracked a joke or two with her and her friends.

"I have two questions," he said as he flipped on the lights of the boathouse so he could get a better look at her handiwork. "The obvious one is why."

"What's the other question?"

"Answer the first one, then I'll ask the second."

She didn't meet his gaze. She still looked scared but he thought some of her abject terror seemed to be fading. She even reached down to pet Yukon, then faced him with an expression of defiance mingled with a shadow of guilt.

"I don't know," she finally said. "I guess it seemed like a good idea at the time."

It wasn't an uncommon excuse from kids who didn't always think through the consequences of their actions, who considered themselves invincible and were only interested in the thrill of the moment.

He had never personally been able to figure out the thrill of defiling someone else's property. Vandalism as a way to pass the time always annoyed the hell out of him.

"It wasn't. Obviously. It was a very, very bad idea. You see that now, right?"

She shrugged and looked down again without answering. When it became clear she wasn't going to respond, Ruben frowned.

"Second question. Who else did this with you?"

"Nobody," she said quickly. Too quickly.

He had heard other voices, had definitely heard that "run" command ring out across the backyard.

"You're in enough trouble, Silver. Don't compound it by lying to me. We both know that's not true. Who was here with you?"

She lifted her chin again and in the pale light, he saw defiance in her eyes. "Nobody. Only me."

"Why are you standing up for them? They were only too quick to leave you here to face the consequences—and Yukon—by yourself."

"You don't know anything," she snapped.

"I know that was a pretty rotten thing to do, letting you take the rap when you weren't the only one involved. Was this whole vandalism thing even your idea?"

She didn't respond, which he had a feeling was answer enough.

"What's going to happen to me?" she finally asked. "Are you going to arrest me?"

"That depends. Is my boat the only thing you've tagged tonight?"

She looked down at Yukon, as if hoping the dog could help her figure out how to answer.

"Silver?" he pressed.

"No," she finally said, her voice low. "You're going to find out anyway. I might as well tell you. We... I did two other things. A shed down the street where the mean old guy who always yells at kids lives, and Mrs. Grimes's garage door."

Gertrude Grimes taught English at the middle school and had been a cranky old crone back in the day when he went there. The intervening years hadn't improved her demeanor much.

"Are you going to arrest me?" she asked again. Her voice sounded scared and upset and, again, he caught that trace of guilt on her features.

He had the feeling Silver was having a hard time adjusting to life in Haven Point. Was this simply an outward sign of that, or was there more to it?

Technically they were within the town limits, which made this a case for Cade Emmett, the police chief of Haven Point. He could call for an officer and they would take Silver to the police station. She could be charged with criminal mischief and channeled into the juvenile justice system.

Sometimes that was absolutely the best course of action for a wayward teen, a firm and unmistakable wake-up call, but he wasn't sure Silver's actions justified that.

"First you're going to show me everywhere you hit tonight. With luck, we can talk to the owners and persuade them not to press charges as long as you promise to clean up after yourself. Then we need to go talk to your mother."

She opened her mouth as if to argue then closed it again, as if finally realizing just how much trouble she had created for herself.

"I'd rather you just arrest me than take me home," she said glumly. "My mom's going to freak."

"Either way, she's going to find out, Silver. Trust me, you're going to want to pick door number two, the one that doesn't include a trip to juvie."

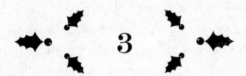

3

As Dani might have predicted, Mia fell asleep about half-way through the movie. Her youngest rarely made it all the way through a show. She would settle in, fully intending to persevere through the whole thing, but every time she curled up and drifted off.

Silver, on the other hand, couldn't bear not seeing things through to the end. If she started a movie, she would do whatever necessary to stay awake until the closing credits rolled past.

The girls had plenty of other differences. Mia loved dressing up, trying on Dani's few nice cocktail dresses and high heels, playing with dolls, drawing her own paper dolls and cutting them out. Silver had never done any of those things. When she was Mia's age, she loved soccer and hockey and watching the Red Sox, though at heart she was a die-hard Mets fan, even at six.

Despite their different personalities, Dani worried about her girls exactly the same.

As she sat in the darkened family room with her sleeping daughter on one side and their aging mutt on the other, Dani's thoughts circled back to her worries that she had made a grave mistake in moving to Haven Point.

All through those long, difficult years working on her undergraduate degree, then the even harder work to her doctorate, she had dreamed of raising the girls in a place just like this, somewhere rural and peaceful, a place of beauty and calm that might offer a tiny chance of protecting her girls from the ugliness of the world.

She wanted better. Better than the hardscrabble, uncertain life she had known growing up, better than the rough-edged world Tommy's family lived in.

With only one goal in mind, she had taken every scholarship that came her way, had worked double shifts, had taken out student loans. All so that she could provide a better life for her daughters doing something she loved.

Nothing was turning out the way she'd planned.

She sighed and nibbled her popcorn. Silver had become a distant stranger and Mia's sudden-onset shyness had become a crutch to her in every social situation. Her teacher said Dani's once bubbly, joy-filled daughter became withdrawn and silent the moment she walked into the school.

Dani wasn't exactly fitting in, either. Not only that, but the natural confidence and sharp intuition she had always felt around animals seemed to abandon her when she was the one making all the hard calls. Frank was so very kind and patient with her, but she still felt as if she was fumbling through everything.

Oh, she hoped this whole move wasn't a huge mistake. But really, what was one more? She'd been making mistake after mistake since she got pregnant with Silver at seventeen.

No. Her girls were her joy. Neither of them was a mistake, though Dani's choice of a man to be their father certainly was.

Mia stirred. "Is the movie over?" she asked sleepily.

"Yes. Come on. Let's get you to bed."

She scooped up her daughter, loving the poignancy of having her small, sweet-smelling shape nestled against her. Sooner than Dani wanted to think about, her baby would be too big for Dani to lift. She was growing so fast.

She carried Mia into her bedroom, decorated in her favorite colors, pink and lavender. After helping the girl under the covers, Dani pulled them up to Mia's chin.

"What about the movie? We didn't finish it," Mia said in a plaintive, sleepy tone, eyes mostly closed.

"Maybe you can watch the rest tomorrow with Silver while the babysitter is here or after I get home from work tomorrow night."

"Okay…" Mia's voice trailed off before she finished the word.

Dani stood beside the bed, Winky at her feet, watching her daughter sleep and feeling the weight of responsibility that had rested completely on her shoulders alone all of Mia's life.

"Come on, Wink," she whispered after a moment. The little dog led the way outside. In the hallway, the dog suddenly tensed, a small growl in her chest as she hurried to the door.

A moment later, someone gave a firm knock.

Dani glanced at her watch. It was after nine. Who would be coming at this hour? Silver had a key and would have let herself in.

Dani went to the door and peered through the peephole. At first, all she saw was a broad chest clad in a T-shirt and unzipped navy blue down jacket. Her gaze traveled up and she recognized the hard, masculine features of her next-door neighbor.

In the dim glow from her porch light, Ruben appeared dark and dangerous and as gorgeous as ever.

A slight movement caught her attention and Dani shifted her gaze, suddenly realizing he wasn't alone.

Silver stood next to him, eyes wide and nervous and her chin trembling as if it was taking all her energy not to cry.

Dani swore sharply and was glad Mia was in bed and didn't hear it. She had worked for years to clean up her street language but sometimes swear words slipped out in moments of high tension.

Her stomach dropped. *Oh, Sil. What have you done?*

Dani could think of a dozen reasons an officer of the law would be bringing back her child. None of them good.

She wanted to sneak away, to hide in her bedroom and pretend she didn't hear the doorbell, but she was a grown-up. She couldn't pull the covers over her head and ignore her law enforcement officer of a neighbor and whatever dire news he had to impart.

Trouble, like bloodhounds, will always track you down.

With a sigh and a prayer for patience, she opened the door. "Deputy Morales. This is a surprise. What are you doing here? And with my darling daughter, who was supposed to be spending the evening with a friend watching a movie."

"Apparently she found something else to do. May I come in?"

She wanted to say no. She wanted to bar the door against him and her baffling, frustrating child, but, again, adulting carried certain unavoidable responsibilities.

With no choice, she held the door open. Silver didn't meet her eye as she shuffled inside.

"I'm going to bed," she muttered, all prepared to flee toward her room across the hall from Mia's. She looked as if she wanted to be anywhere on earth but here in their living room.

"Guess again," Dani snapped. "What's going on? Why are you not watching a movie with Jenny? Why did Deputy Morales bring you home?"

She slumped into a chair, mumbling something Dani couldn't make out.

"What was that?"

"You're just going to yell."

"Silvia Marie Capelli. What did you do?"

Her daughter folded her arms across her chest and didn't answer. After a moment, Ruben answered for her.

"Instead of hanging out and watching a movie, Silver apparently decided it would be more fun to take a spray can around town and see what kind of mess she could make with it."

Dani's heart seemed to freeze. She stared at her daughter, shock rocketing through her. "A spray can!"

"She tagged three places in the neighborhood—a garage door at Gertrude Grimes's, an outbuilding at Tom and Mary Miller's, and my new boat."

Nausea churned through her, slick and greasy, and she was unable to think straight through the steady stream of swear words ringing through her head and the effort it was taking not to let them spew out.

Those names he gave were all neighbors and patrons of the veterinary clinic. She had treated one of the Millers' cats and Gertrude Grimes's rather unpleasant schnauzer.

"That's a strong accusation," she said, holding on to a fragile hope that he might be mistaken. "How can you be certain Silver was involved?"

"Show your mom your hand, Silver."

Her daughter gave a heavy sigh and thrust out her left arm, which earned her an amused look from Ruben.

"Nice try. The other one."

After a long moment, her daughter held out her right hand. The forefinger and thumb were covered in unmistakable red paint and Dani's heart sank.

"Silvia. What were you thinking?"

Her daughter remained stubbornly silent, answering only with her habitual nonchalant shrug that drove Dani absolutely crazy.

"In my experience, most of the time the kids involved *aren't* thinking. They get into a herd mentality kind of thing and nobody thinks to question whether what they're doing is a good idea or not."

She could understand that entirely too well. That sort of thinking had landed Tommy in jail when he was an irresponsible teenager and the pattern had continued through his short adulthood.

"Was this Jenny's idea?"

"I didn't go to Jenny's. That was a lie."

"So who was with you?"

"There wasn't anybody else. Just me," Silver said quickly. Too quickly.

"Really? All by yourself, you got it into your head that you would spend a cold December night vandalizing the property of our neighbors? Including a deputy sheriff?"

"Yeah. I guess I did."

"I'm not an idiot," Dani said flatly. "I know you're lying. I need the truth."

Her daughter lifted her chin. "Snitches get stitches. That's what Dad always used to say."

At the reference to her ex-husband, Dani glanced at Ruben, who was watching this interchange impassively.

She could feel heat soak her cheeks. Why did this particular man have to be involved? It was hard enough knowing he was a firsthand witness to her daughter's poor choices. She didn't need him knowing about her own.

"You, of all people, should have learned never to take to heart anything your father might have said," she said quietly.

She could never be quite sure if Silver hated her father or idolized him. The mood shifted constantly.

Since Tommy's violent death three months earlier, Dani was afraid Silver's memories of all those disappointments had begun to fade in the midst of a natural grief over losing her father, even after everything he had done.

"At least he never would have brought me to a stink hole in the middle of nowhere," she snarled back.

No. He would have just broken your heart again and again, until you had nothing left but shattered pieces.

"I happen to like this stink hole," Ruben said mildly.

"You would." Silver's voice dripped sarcasm and Dani stared at her, appalled at her daughter's rudeness to an officer of the law. She had taught both of her girls that nothing good ever came out of being disrespectful to people who were only trying to do their jobs.

"That's enough," she snapped. "Your father has nothing to do with this discussion. This is about you and your own mistakes. I can't believe you would do something like this. How could you?"

"It was easy. You just push the little nozzle on the spray can."

At Silver's flippant tone, Dani's anger spiked.

Sometimes being a parent really sucked.

She dug her nails into her palms to hold on to the fraying edges of her temper, drew in a deep breath and let it out slowly before she trusted herself to speak.

"How much damage did she do?" she asked Ruben.

"Hard to say in the dark. My boat will need some serious cleanup work. It will take the right solvent that won't damage the finish, so I'll need to talk to the marine supply places. We checked out the other places she hit and I'm thinking it would be cheaper in those cases to repaint."

Dani wanted to cry, to just sit right here in the middle of her living room and throw a good, old-fashioned pity party, with a healthy dose of temper tantrum thrown in.

Why couldn't anything be easy? It was hard enough trying to fit into a new place—a new school, a new neighborhood, a new town. Why did Silver have to go and make everything worse, for absolutely no reason Dani could see?

"We'll take care of all costs associated with the cleanup, of course."

Ruben was quiet, watching her out of those big, thick-lashed dark eyes. "Seems to me, Silver should be the one to put in the elbow grease and make it right."

"Me?" Her daughter's eyes widened and she looked appalled.

"Sure. Why not? If you can make the mess, you can clean up the mess. You could always share the burden by letting us know who else was with you tonight, so they can help in the cleanup."

Dani watched Silver's chin jut out with the stubbornness that was as much a part of her makeup as her green eyes and dimples. "No one was with me. How many times do I have to tell you that?"

"You can tell me as many times as you want but I heard voices and saw others running. None of your partners in crime will face the necessary consequences of their actions unless you come clean."

Silver folded her arms across her chest again. "I didn't have any partners in anything. It was only me."

Ruben shrugged. "That's fine. Then you alone can clean up the mess you created. Or I suppose I can go ahead and talk to the property owners and see if they've changed their minds about pressing charges."

Fear flashed across Silver's delicate features. For all her bravado, she didn't like being in trouble. She never had.

"Fine. I'll clean it all up by myself. Can I go to my room now?"

Dani wanted to keep her out there to yell at her some more but she figured some distance between her and her daughter wouldn't hurt right now while she worked a little harder to restrain her temper.

"Go shower and get your pajamas on. I'll be in to you in a minute."

Silver gave one last resentful look to the room in general— as if *she* had anything to be angry about!—and stomped to her room, leaving Dani alone with the deputy sheriff.

She never would have expected it, but she found the man far more intimidating when he was wearing jeans and a T-shirt under his down jacket, instead of his uniform.

The uncomfortable little sizzle of attraction didn't help matters any.

"I don't know what to say to you," she said after Silver's bedroom door closed. "I'm so sorry."

"It's not your fault—unless you were one of the people I saw take off running."

He smiled in response to her narrowed gaze. "Yeah. I didn't think so. In that case, you don't have any reason to apologize. You had nothing to do with it."

"Except I trusted her, when she told me she was going to watch a movie at her friend's house."

"Which friend was she supposed to go to? I can start there. You said Jenny? Which Jenny? I know a few."

She didn't want to answer him. Her tongue felt thick, the words tangled in her throat. Apparently her late ex-husband's disdain for snitches had worn off on her, too.

She sighed. She didn't know how to keep the girl out of it. "Jenny Turner."

"Sean and Christine's daughter."

"That's right. But Silver said she didn't go to her house and it wouldn't surprise me if she just used her name as an excuse, mainly because I know her parents. I can't imagine Jenny would have anything to do with this. I've only met her a few times but she seems very nice."

"She is. But nice doesn't have much to do with it. Even the so-called *good* girls can make mistakes with their friends egging them on."

Was Silver negatively influencing the whole neighborhood? Oh, she hoped not.

"I'm sorry," she said again. To her dismay, she could feel tears burning behind her eyes and blinked as hard as she could to keep them back. "She's never done anything like this before. I can't understand what got into her head."

Ruben's features softened in a way that made him seem far less intimidating. "Don't beat yourself up. She made a mistake and did something stupid. Probably won't be the first time or the last time."

Who would have guessed that she could take such comfort from the words of a tough deputy sheriff? She wanted to draw them close and hold on tight.

"I did plenty of stupid things when I was her age," he went on. "So did most of my friends. We even got caught a few times. Despite it, we all turned out okay. One's the county sheriff, one is an FBI agent and one is the town police chief. Don't worry. Silver will get through this."

"I suppose you're right. I just wish she had chosen something a little less destructive to the community for her first stupid foray into teenagedom."

"We can't change that now. The only thing she can do is try to make it right and then move forward. The good news is, the other property owners are pretty reasonable people. As long as she makes the effort to fix what she did, things should be okay."

She did *not* want to be in this man's debt but that was exactly where she found herself. He was being extraordinarily kind and she was well aware of just how much she owed him.

"Thank you, Deputy Morales. I appreciate you bringing her home instead of making this a criminal matter."

"After three months of being neighbors, don't you think you could call me Ruben?"

She didn't want anything that would bring them closer together but she didn't know how to avoid it. "Ruben, then. I appreciate the way you have handled things."

"I could have booked her for destruction of property. Technically it is the jurisdiction of the Haven Point PD but I was an officer on scene and could have made that call."

"Why didn't you?" She had to ask.

"I weighed the options, believe me. But when she seemed more frightened about coming home and facing you than she did at the prospect of going to the police station, I figured this was the better choice."

"You must think I'm the meanest mom in the world."

"Your daughter *should* be afraid of the consequences of her actions. She needs to fear disappointing her parents. In my professional life, I see too many cases where kids know their parents will never call them on their bad behavior. Guess what? That only leads to kids who don't know how to function in society."

"I will help her clean up the mess. Please find out the details of what we need to do. We'll make it right."

As if she needed one more thing to worry about in her life right now.

Oh, Silver. What have you done?

"I'll let you know," Ruben said. He was watching her with a strange expression, one of almost approval. Why?

She was the bad mother who hadn't even known where her child was that night. She had botched the whole thing, start to finish.

She had *no* business feeling this warmth seeping through her. She couldn't let herself be attracted to Ruben Morales. He was a law enforcement officer who would have absolutely no interest in her, once he knew the truth.

"All right. I'll be in touch tomorrow."

"Thank you."

He studied her for a long moment and she had to wonder what he saw. She had been watching a movie earlier with Mia, though that felt like hours ago. Her hair was probably messy where she had been leaning back against the sofa and she wore casual, comfortable clothes with no shape or style whatsoever.

"Doc? I know you're angry but try not to be too hard on Silver."

"Weren't you just telling me about the parents who never give their children consequences?"

"She definitely needs consequences. That's not what I'm saying. What she did was wrong, no doubt about it. But it might not hurt to remember she's at a tough age, trying to fit in to a new community, which can't be easy for anybody."

Dani was entirely too familiar with what that was like. "I'll be sure to keep that in mind," she said, forcing a polite smile. "Thanks again for your help. Good night, Ruben."

He smiled a little at her use of his first name but also

didn't appear to miss the direct hint, especially when she held open the door for him.

"Good night."

He reached down to give Winky another scratch behind her ears, then headed out into the night.

Dani closed the door and stood for a moment in her living room, feeling the heat of her little dog on her slippers. She wanted to sink down onto the floor of her entryway, gather Winky close and cry until she fell asleep, but that was the sort of thing she might have done as a lonely girl in foster care. She was a mother now, with a mother's responsibilities.

Right now, she needed to deal with her daughter.

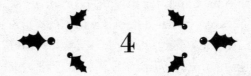

4

She made it as far as Silver's bedroom, then paused outside, still trying to process what had just happened.

How could her child have jeopardized everything like
this? Didn't she understand how precarious things were? If
Dani didn't do well in this internship, if they couldn't carve a
place for themselves here in Haven Point, she would have to
once more pick up her girls and start all over somewhere else.

They had a nice home here in a nice community. Where
would they go if Haven Point didn't work out?

The worry that always seemed to lurk at the edges of her
subconscious crept ever closer.

She took another deep breath, trying to beat it back again.

She had to do her best to be calm and collected when she spoke with Silver. Raging at her daughter would accomplish nothing.

Was this some kind of cry for help, tangible proof of everything Silver hadn't said? She wasn't happy here. That truth was becoming unavoidable. She didn't fit in because of her purple hair and her unique fashion sense and, most probably, because of her defensive attitude. She wanted to go back to Boston where she had friends, or even New York to live with Tommy's family.

A parent's job was to discern between a child's wants and her needs. In this case, Dani knew in her gut that her family needed a community like Haven Point.

When she pushed the door open, she found Silver facedown on her bed, the blanket up around her ears. The only light came from Silver's phone, which she was not supposed to have in her bedroom past 10:00 p.m. anyway.

She opened her mouth to yell about that but caught herself. She had other things to worry about right now.

Silver didn't look up when Dani came inside and moved to the bed. She waited her out, standing for a long moment until her daughter finally rolled over and held out her phone.

"Here. I know I'm not supposed to have it. I wasn't texting anyone. I was just looking at pictures of my friends back in Boston."

Dani's heart squeezed with sympathy, but she schooled her features so Silver didn't see.

"Thanks," she said calmly. "I'll put it on the charger in my room."

She said nothing else, just waited for Silver to speak first and explain herself. "Go ahead. Yell at me. I know you want to."

She did want to yell—to scream and rant and ask Silver what the hell she was thinking. The pain on her daughter's face held her back.

"I'm not going to yell."

"You're not?" Silver's shock was evident in her wide eyes.

"What would that do? It would only make both of us feel worse and wouldn't change what you've done."

"O-okay."

Dani turned on the bedside lamp then sat on the edge of the bed. "A deputy sheriff, though? Seriously? In what alternate reality would you ever think that was okay?"

Her daughter threw her forearm over her eyes, as protection from the light or to avoid her mother's gaze, Dani wasn't sure.

"I don't know," she admitted. "It was a stupid thing to do, okay? I know it was dumb. We... I wasn't thinking."

Dani didn't miss that telltale pronoun. She wanted to pounce on it and make Silver tell her who else had been involved, but somehow she sensed further interrogation would do nothing to move the conversation forward.

"Do you hate it here so much that you want to sabotage everything for all of us?"

A little tear leaked out of Silver's eye and dripped into the hair she had dyed herself. "I miss my friends," she said.

"You know the way to make the sort of friends you want to keep isn't to engage in criminal activity with them, right?"

"I know." She scratched a pattern into her quilt. "Nana says if I really hate it here, I can come live with her back in Queens."

Dani's insides twisted at the mention of her former mother-in-law. "When did you talk to your Grandma De-Luca?"

Silver looked more guilty about this than she had about showing up at the door with a deputy sheriff. "She messaged me and sent me her phone number a few months ago. After, you know. In case I wanted to talk to her about… about Dad and what happened. We've been texting on and off for a while now."

"You know I check your texts. I haven't seen anything like that."

Silver looked away. "I always delete them. I know you don't want me to talk to her. I can stop."

Again, Dani wanted to yell, but did her best to keep control. Silver loved her namesake grandmother, who had been an active part of their lives for her first few years, even babysitting her when Dani had classes.

Dani never would have made it through her undergraduate degree without Silvia DeLuca's help.

Their relationship had become strained after Dani filed for divorce six years ago, but even then she had allowed Silvia DeLuca to see her granddaughters, until the other woman started slyly undermining Dani to them. The final straw had come when Silvia dragged Silver to visit her father in prison without Dani's permission.

Silvia was one of those women who could never see her

child as he was. Tommy could do no wrong in her book. As far as she believed, anytime Tommy found himself in trouble, it was always someone else's fault.

She had been furious about the divorce and even more upset when Dani left for veterinary school in Boston. Their contact had dwindled to Christmas and birthday cards, which was exactly the way Dani preferred things.

"Are you mad that I've been texting Nana?"

"I'm mad that you've been hiding it. We can talk about that later, though. Right now, we need to focus on your actions tonight."

"I made a mistake. It was stupid. It won't happen again."

The words sounded far too well practiced to be sincere.

"No. It won't. You're grounded until further notice. That means extra chores here and at the clinic, no video games, no YouTube and no phone except at school."

Silver huffed but said nothing, obviously knowing she was on extremely thin ice. No doubt she could almost hear it cracking beneath her feet.

"Also, I need you to give me the names of the other girls involved so I can let their parents know and they can help you with the cleanup."

"I told you. It was just me."

They both knew that was a lie but Dani had no idea how to force the truth out of her.

"Fine. You can do the cleanup on your own."

"Fine," Silver said, her voice short. "Is that all?"

"For now."

With a sigh, Dani rose and squeezed Silver's arm. "You know I love you, Silverbell, right?"

Her daughter shrugged, not meeting her gaze.

"I brought you and Mia to Haven Point because we've been offered a chance to make a good life here, a place where you girls would be safe and healthy. A place with low crime, good schools and nice people."

"There were good schools and nice people in Boston. And in Queens before that."

"Agreed. We could have made a good life for ourselves somewhere else. This is the one that felt best. When I got this opportunity, you and Mia and I talked about it and we all agreed we wanted to give Haven Point a chance to become our home. I don't think any of us has really done a good job in that department. I'd like to try harder. What about you?"

"I guess," Silver said.

Dani reached down and hugged her daughter and after a moment, she felt small arms go around her.

Silver rested her head against Dani's chest, just above the thick nest of emotions there. She loved this beautiful, smart, contrary creature beyond words.

"Get some rest. Everything seems better in the morning."

She hoped, anyway. Because right now things seemed pretty bleak for Team Capelli.

"I get to be the candy cane in the school play. You should come see it! I get to sing a solo and everything. Can you come?"

"Wow. That's exciting." Ruben smiled down at Will

Montgomery, his boss's stepson and just about the most adorable kid he knew. "When is the play?"

"The Wednesday before Christmas at eleven." Will's mother, Andie Bailey—married to the sheriff and Ruben's boss, Marshall Bailey—sat in the visitor chair at his desk, waiting for Marsh to get off the phone so the sheriff could take her and their children to lunch on his break.

"Are you sure you don't want to join us for lunch?" she asked.

"Yeah," Will said. "You could sit by me and I could tell you all about my part."

"I hate to miss that kind invitation but I have some paperwork to finish."

The sheriff's department wasn't always a good place for kids, but Andie and the children had brought some shortbread cookies they had made that day to hand out to the other deputies in the office. Ruben had quickly secreted his plate in a desk drawer where everybody else better keep their hands off, if they knew what was good for them.

He loved seeing Will, his sister, Chloe, and their mother, Andie, together with Marshall. The four of them, along with Marshall's son Christopher made a solid, loving unit.

At the same time, his interactions with the family always left him a little…hollow. Not sad, precisely, only more aware than usual of his solitary state.

Ruben never thought he would be thirty-three and alone. He had always wanted a family, always imagined by this point in his life he would have a bunch of kids, a mortgage, a boat in the driveway and a kind, caring wife like Andie.

He had the boat and the mortgage, but not the rest.

"You might like my school program, too." Chloe gave him her sweetest smile, that one that always stole his heart. She was a few years older than Will but considerably more mature. Some of that had to do with her personality, though some might have been from the tough circumstances of a few summers ago, before her mother married Marshall.

"Are you a candy cane, too?"

"Ruben," she said in an exasperated voice. "We don't have candy canes in the sixth grade program. That's for the little kids. I'm in the choir."

"Let me know when it is and I'll see if I can arrange my schedule."

He had a nephew in her grade at Haven Point Elementary School, so would definitely try to make it.

"It's right after Will's class program."

"Easy enough. I'll add it to my schedule." Maybe that was his destiny, to always be the kindly uncle and friend.

He pushed away that depressing thought as Marshall finished his phone call and came out.

"Did I hear talk that somebody brought cookies?"

Will giggled. "We did! We've got some for you, too, Dad."

That was a new thing, the kids calling Marshall *dad*. Ruben had noticed it the last time he saw them all together. Their own father had been a police officer killed in the line of duty. Marshall had stepped up to take care of all of them and it was obvious the kids loved him.

He could tell Marshall was touched by the word. "Bring

them in here before somebody else eats them," he said gruffly.

Will and Chloe grabbed one of their remaining covered plates and charged into their stepfather's office, leaving Ruben with Andie.

"Those two," she said, shaking her head.

"They're wonderful."

"I can't argue with that. I'm enjoying them at this age, but who knows what trouble they'll bring me in about five years or so. Which reminds me, Marshall tells me you had some excitement at your place last night. Some vandalism on your beautiful new boat. How is *The Wonder*?"

He found himself reluctant to discuss Dani and her daughter with Andie, almost protectively so, which he knew was completely ridiculous.

"It was just kids messing around."

"I understand you caught one of them in the act. The new veterinarian's daughter, the one with the cool hair and the unusual name."

"Yes. But please don't spread that around." He really hoped the identity of his vandal wasn't common knowledge. He knew Andie would be discreet. She wasn't going to talk, not even to her friends at the Haven Point Helping Hands, a service and social organization in town.

"I won't," she assured him.

"Silver wasn't the only one involved, but she was the only one I caught. She won't tell me who else was there."

"Snitches get stitches," Andie said.

"Funny. She said the same thing."

71

"I understand her reticence to implicate others. She's probably worried about retribution. She's, what, thirteen? That's a hard age to start at a new school."

Andie could be a good source of information, he realized. The kids were busy helping Marshall shred some papers in his office so he decided now was as good a time as any to dig a little into his intriguing neighbors.

"What's their story? Dani and her kids? Do you know her at all?"

"She seems very nice and she's a good veterinarian. Right after she came to town, we went to her when Sadie got a bad bee sting in her eye."

"Ouch."

"Right? I would say Dani has a more abrupt bedside manner than your dad, but seemed very kind and caring."

"What about socially? Have you interacted much outside the veterinary clinic?"

Andie shrugged, though she looked intrigued at his line of questioning. Maybe he shouldn't have said anything. He didn't need his friend's wife matchmaking.

"Not really. She seems very...*private* is I guess the word I would use. She came to a few social events when they first moved to town. Again, she seemed nice enough but I'm afraid maybe we overwhelmed her. When McKenzie asked if she wanted to join the Helping Hands, she said no, that she was too busy with her girls and settling into a new town, starting a practice. Same thing when we asked her to join the book club."

"That's fair. Not everybody is a joiner."

"I get it, believe me. The women of this town can be in-timidating for even the toughest constitution."

"There are so many of you and you always travel in packs."

"Not always," she protested with a laugh.

"Most of the time, then."

Before she could answer, Marshall came out with the kids and Andie's face completely lit up.

Ruben was aware of a little pinch of discontent again as the two of them kissed. He did his best to ignore it. Marsh had been Ruben's friend long before he became his boss and Ruben was glad the sheriff and Andie seemed so happy together.

He was always aware when he was with them that if the two of them hadn't found each other first, Ruben definitely would have made a move. Andie was the kind of woman he had always thought he wanted—someone soft, warm, compassionate.

Worlds away from a certain prickly, cool, reserved vet-erinarian.

Somebody should probably tell that to his subconscious, which had filled his dreams with all kinds of inappropriate situations involving the woman the night before.

Friday was a long, difficult day. She would have liked to take the day off since the girls were out of school but her time off was limited as a new veterinarian.

She was lucky enough to have a few good caregivers in her rotation and Gloria, the clinic receptionist and office manager, had a daughter home from college for the holidays who was looking for a little extra cash.

Dani had hoped to be done by two, her usual schedule on Friday, but a bichon frise with an abdominal obstruction came in right as she was wrapping up for the day and the dog required emergency surgery.

The surgery had been much more complicated than she had expected and she had ended up calling on Frank to help. She found it demoralizing that she had needed his expertise, yet more evidence she wasn't up to the challenge of her new vocation, but Frank wouldn't let her beat herself up.

"Don't ever be embarrassed to ask for help." His eyes— so like his son's—were warm and kind. "I've been in the vet business for more than forty years. Just when I think I've seen everything under the sun, something new walks through the door to prove me wrong. You should never hesitate to call me, even after the practice is officially yours."

She wasn't sure that day would ever come—or ever *should* come. Who was she kidding, to think she had what it took to be a veterinarian? She was a failure. A nothing. Hadn't she heard that enough when she was growing up?

As usual when that negative self-talk intruded, she did her best to focus on how fiercely she had worked to get where she was. All the sleepless nights of studying, the hand cramps from propping a textbook in one hand while rocking a crying baby in the other, the many creative ways she had found to stretch a dollar.

We can do hard things. That was the message she tried to

reinforce to her girls. She couldn't help wondering when it would be her turn to do the easy things.

By the time she finally made it home just after five, three hours later than she'd planned, she was exhausted.

"Thank you for staying extra with them," she told Heidi, Gloria's youngest daughter.

"Not a problem. I need the extra cash. I'm saving up to get my belly button pierced."

Since the girl had four rows of pierced earrings and a ring in her lip, what was one more puncture wound? "Glad I could add to the pot, then. Have a good evening."

"Thanks, Dr. C. Silver's been in her room most of the afternoon doing homework and Mia is in the family room."

"Thanks."

After Dani let the babysitter out, she headed to find the easier of her children and found Mia playing quietly with her dolls.

"Hey, sweetie pie. How did your day go?"

Mia shrugged, without looking up at her.

"What's wrong, honey?"

"You said we should never lie but you lied."

Dani scanned over her day, trying to figure out where she had gone wrong this time.

"About what?"

"You said you would be home right after lunch and we could put our Christmas tree up today. Lunch was a long time ago and now it's almost dark and I bet you're going to say you're too tired to put up a Christmas tree."

Going through the hassle of putting up a tree was the absolute last thing she wanted to do right now. After the difficult day, her brain was mush and she wanted to collapse on the sofa and sleep for the rest of the evening.

She had made a promise, though, something she took very seriously.

She sat on the floor beside her daughter. "I'm sorry, Mia. I did tell you I would be home after lunch but then I had a dog emergency. Sometimes that happens when you're a veterinarian. We've talked about it before, remember? This time the emergency was a little bichon frise who had something stuck in her stomach. She was throwing up and couldn't eat or poop."

Her compassionate youngest child looked distressed at that. "Is she okay?"

"She is now. Dr. Morales came in and helped me fix things. It will take a day or two, but Princess Snowbear will be back to herself in a few days."

Apparently saving a dog's life warranted a few points in her book, at least where her youngest was concerned. Mia cuddled up to her. "I like Dr. Morales. He's nice."

"He is, indeed." She would have been in trouble without him during the surgery. What would she do when he finally retired?

She put that worry away for another day. "How's your sister been?"

Mia looked down the hall toward the bedrooms. "I don't know. She stayed in her room almost all day. Earlier, I asked if she wanted to play with my Shopkins and she told me they're stupid and I am, too."

Apparently at least one of her children had no problem being a snitch. "She shouldn't have said either of those things. You're not stupid and neither are your toys, honey."

The two girls were separated by seven years, which sometimes seemed such a vast chasm in their relationship. Sometimes Silver could be the sweetest thing to her sister and sometimes she barely tolerated Mia.

"What did you have for lunch?" Dani asked.

"Grilled cheese sandwiches, only Heidi left the crusts on and I had to cut them off myself."

"That's a hard day all around. Let's see what we can do to make the afternoon and evening better. What do you think about calzones for dinner?"

"I love calzones! Can I help you make them?"

"You got it, kid. Maybe we can talk Silver into helping us, too."

Mia looked doubtful but followed her down the hall. The doorbell rang before they reached Silver's bedroom door.

"Who's that?" Mia asked, looking nervous.

"I don't know. We'll have to answer it to see."

She looked through the peephole and saw a big, solid chest dressed in a brown sheriff's uniform. As she opened the door for Ruben Morales, she told herself it was only her exhaustion that had her feeling a little light-headed.

"Deputy Morales. Hello."

He smiled, looking big and dark and absolutely delicious— something she was furious with herself for noticing.

"Afternoon. I was on my way home but thought I should stop here first to let Silver know about the conversation I had with the graffiti specialist for the county and what it's going to take to clean up her artwork from last night."

Just once, couldn't she see the man when she wasn't exhausted and rumpled and feeling as if she'd been dragged behind his big boat for an hour?

"Come in," she said, holding the door for him. "I've only been home from the clinic for a few moments myself and haven't had a chance to talk to her yet. I'll grab her."

"Thanks. Hi there, Mia."

He smiled at her suddenly shy six-year-old, who somehow managed to give him a nervous smile in return. Dani stood there awkwardly for a long moment, then finally gave herself a mental head-slap and hurried down the hall. She expected Mia to follow her, but instead the girl opted to remain behind with Ruben.

"I told you I'm doing homework, Mia. What do you want?" Silver called out when Dani knocked on her door.

She could feel her shoulders tighten in response. If thirteen was this tough, how on earth was she going to survive the rest of the teenage years? she wondered for the bazillionth time.

"It's not Mia. It's me," Dani said, pushing open the door.

She found Silver on her bed, a notebook propped on pillows in front of her. No doubt she was writing in her journal, detailing how miserable her life was. Silver closed it quickly and while she didn't hide it under her bed, she looked as if she wanted to.

Dani released a breath. "Deputy Morales is here to speak with you."

For just an instant, Silver's mouth trembled with nerves. She looked down at the closed notebook in front of her and fiddled with her pen.

"I'm, um, in the middle of something here. I don't want to lose my train of thought. Can you just find out what he wants?"

"What he *wants* is to speak with you. Come on, honey. Might as well get it over with, right?"

"I guess." Silver sighed and climbed off her bed. She slipped the notebook into the drawer of her bedside table, wiped her hands down her jeans as if they were as sweaty as Dani's, then moved to the doorway.

When they returned to the living room, she found Ruben on the sofa with their dog, Winky, on his lap. Mia was showing him her vast collection of dolls and their wardrobe that Dani could swear was more fashionable than her own.

"What's this one's name?"

"That's Pia. She's my favorite. See, her hair is curly just like mine and her eyes are brown like mine. You have brown eyes, too."

"Yes I do."

"I named her Pia because it rhymes with Mia."

"Perfect. So if I had a doll, maybe I would have to name him Gruben."

Mia giggled, her shyness apparently all but gone, and Dani felt something hard and tight around her heart begin to crack apart a little.

No. She wouldn't let herself be drawn to him. She made

disastrous decisions in the men department and right now she couldn't afford another mistake.

"I have three outfits for her but this green dress is my favorite. You can get clothes to match your dolls if you want. I asked Santa for a green dress, too, but I don't know if I'll get it. Silver says it's too expensive and my mom has stupid loans."

"Does she?"

"I did not. I said she has student loans," Silver corrected.

"Though they're certainly stupid, too," Dani admitted.

Ruben looked up and flashed them both a smile that made her feel light-headed again.

"I'm sure they are. It can't be easy."

At the understanding in his voice, Dani was appalled to feel tears well up. She couldn't count the sleepless nights she'd had over the last thirteen years, worrying whether she would be able to provide for her daughters.

"It can be an adventure," she admitted. "It helps that your dad has kindly let us have this place rent-free."

"Dad's good about things like that," he said, then looked around her to where Silver was lurking.

"Hey, Silver. How's it going?"

She shrugged. "Fine. My mom said you wanted to talk to me. I've got a ton of homework, so…"

In other words, get on with it. Silver didn't say the words but she might as well have. Dani tried not to cringe at her rudeness.

"Right. Good for you, doing your homework on a Friday afternoon."

"Like I have a choice. I'm grounded from just about everything else."

"Look on the bright side. With all the studying you'll get, your next report card will be great."

"And if she keeps it up, maybe she'll get a scholarship when she's ready to go to college and won't need those stupid student loans," Dani said.

"Excellent point."

"Did you say you spoke with a graffiti cleanup specialist?"

"Yes." He rose and it seemed to Dani that all the oxygen in the room seemed to seep away. "There's a guy in the road department who takes care of that kind of trouble whenever any Lake Haven County property is vandalized. He's considered our expert. I took the spray can of paint to him and told him what kind of things you'd tagged with it and he's given me a couple of solvents that should work on my boat. For the other places, as I suspected, he says a new coat of paint will be cheaper and easier."

"Okay."

To Dani's relief, Silver seemed to lose a little of her attitude at the sharp reminder of her own actions and mistakes.

"I'm not scheduled for a shift tomorrow, so I figured it would be a good time to get started, especially since we're supposed to have unusually warm weather. Bob, the expert at the county, said we're better off jumping quickly on some of this cleanup. It will be easier now than if you wait a week or so, when the weather is colder."

"I don't know," Silver said. "Like I said, I have a lot of homework."

"She'll be there," Dani said firmly. "What time?"

"Why don't we say ten? We can start at my place and work our way to the neighbors after that. Oh, and bring a sack lunch."

"Seriously? This is going to take all day?"

"Maybe even longer. That's the problem with some poor choices. Cleaning up after yourself takes about ten times longer than the act itself."

Silver looked discouraged, as if she were scouting in her mind for some way out of the hole she had dug for herself.

"She'll be there," Dani repeated.

"Great. We're supposed to have a good day. Dress in layers. It might be chilly in the morning, then warm enough for shirtsleeves by the afternoon. With any luck, you can be done by dinnertime."

Silver's sigh was heavy. "Fine. I'll be there. Can I go now?"

Dani made a shooing motion with her hand and Silver escaped quickly.

"Thank you." Dani had to say it. "You've been much more understanding than I think I would have been in your shoes."

"I was thirteen myself once. I told you, I made plenty of my own stupid choices."

"You said that, but I still have a hard time believing it. You don't strike me as the troublemaker type."

When it came to graffiti, anyway. She could imagine him making all kinds of other trouble for the women of Haven Point.

"You might be surprised."

Mia was tugging on her jacket and it took Dani a moment to register it. "What is it, honey?" she asked.

"I can help Silver clean up," Mia said. Her features were so earnest, Dani felt that suspicious burning behind her eyes again.

"That is a very kind offer." Ruben smiled down at her girl with such sweetness it made Dani's heart ache, for reasons she didn't quite understand.

"Families stick together, no matter what," Mia informed him. "We help each other. That's what Mama says."

He glanced at Dani with that same warmth, which she knew she didn't deserve.

"I couldn't agree more, Miss Mia."

Dani did, too. While she wanted Silver to learn hard lessons about the consequences to her actions, she had thought all along that she would do what she could to help Silver clean up the graffiti, for her neighbors' sakes as much as her daughter's.

"That's a very good idea, sweetie. Yes. Mia and I can help with the cleanup. We'll come with you and Silver tomorrow, as the clinic is closed. We can meet you next door at ten with our work clothes on."

"Great. We'll make a party of it."

"Not *too* much of a party. Silver doesn't need fun, she needs consequences for her actions."

"A subdued party, then. It will be fun for us, but not nearly as fun for her."

He winked at Mia, who giggled with no trace of the shyness she had showed fifteen minutes earlier when he rang the doorbell.

How did he do it, win her over so easily?

Dani supposed it didn't matter. The only important thing, she thought as she let him out of the house, was to constantly be on guard and try her best to make sure he didn't win *her* over.

5

Ruben was in deep, deep trouble.

He was fiercely attracted to his neighbor. Something about Dani's complicated mix of vulnerability and chin-up defiance struck a chord deep inside, some place no one else had ever touched.

He didn't want to be attracted to her. She wasn't at all his type. He had always believed he preferred soft, sweet, gentle women—someone like Andie, someone giving and kind, not prickly and defensive.

He might tell himself that all day but it didn't change the fact that he found himself in this unlikely position where he couldn't stop thinking about her, dreaming about her, wondering about her.

What difference did that make? he asked himself as he finished gathering the supplies they would need to clean up his boat and waited for them to arrive.

Yeah, he was attracted to her, in a way he couldn't remember being to another woman, but that didn't mean he had to do anything about it.

They would be spending most of the day cleaning up graffiti. That's all. He only had to survive several hours in her company without making a fool of himself over her.

Maybe by the end of the day they would emerge as friends. Something told him Dani Capelli needed all the friends she could find.

As usual, his dogs were the first to inform him he had visitors. Ollie went on alert, his ears cocked for just a moment before he rocketed to the front door, Yukon close behind him.

They made it there about fifteen seconds before the doorbell rang.

Friends, he reminded himself. That didn't stop his heartbeat from kicking up a notch as he opened the door.

"Hi, policeman," Mia said, greeting him with her shy smile that stole his heart every time.

"Hi there, Miss Mia. Hi, Silver. Dani."

The other two females at his door didn't look nearly as happy to see him as the little girl was, but Ruben decided not to take it personally.

"You guys ready to do this?"

"Yep," Mia said.

"Yes. The sooner we can get started, the sooner we'll be done," Dani said.

"I know we talked about starting with my boat, but this morning I was thinking we should start with the other places while the weather is good and then make our way back here. Mine can wait, if we have to, plus I have the covered boathouse to protect from the elements a little. Does that work for you guys?"

"Whatever you think. Isn't that right, Silver?"

Her daughter looked like she would rather be anywhere else on earth. "Fine," she mumbled.

"Where do you want to go first?" Dani asked.

"Let's start at the Millers' house. The graffiti seems a little darker there and might take two coats of paint to cover. I talked to Mary this morning and she was able to find matching paint cans from when they had it repainted two years ago, so that should make things easier. I've got some painting supplies from when we redid this place. Rollers and paintbrushes here and a couple of trays."

"And I found a few things at our place, too." Dani gestured to a box at her feet.

"Great. We should be good, then. Silver, why don't you help me with this crate while I grab a few other things."

"That big thing?"

"Yeah. I think you can handle it."

He handed her the heavier of the two boxes, not out of spite but to again reinforce the message that her actions had consequences.

He picked up the other box, gave his usual orders to the dogs to behave, then closed the door behind him.

"You're not taking your dogs?" Mia asked. "They're cute. Maybe they can help us."

"Not today. I'm afraid they would mostly get in the way while we're trying to work. We kind of have to hurry to get two coats of paint on while the sun is shining."

"It is a beautiful day," Dani said. "One of the nicest we've had in weeks."

She was right, the weather was unseasonably warm for December, predicted to get into the high fifties, with no snow in the forecast for at least a few days. The morning sun felt almost warm on his shoulders.

"I'm glad. If it wasn't so nice, we would have to wait until spring to repaint. As it is, we might have to use some industrial space heaters so the paint will dry. We'll see how things go. I've got a couple buddies in construction who might be able to loan us some equipment for a few days."

Dani gave him a look he couldn't read, as if she couldn't quite figure him out. "You're going to a great deal of effort on Silver's behalf. I'm still not sure why."

He glanced at the girl, who walked with her head lowered as they made their way down the street toward the Millers' house.

"I don't know," he admitted, which was absolutely the truth. "I guess maybe this is one little way I can give back to repay all those who've helped me throughout my life. Besides that, around here, neighbors help each other. It's what we do."

She didn't look convinced but he changed the subject before she could press him for answers he couldn't provide.

"Have you met the Millers?" he asked as they approached the house.

"Briefly, when we first moved in. Mary brought us a pie with apples from her tree."

"That was her?" Silver asked, eyes shocked, as if she hadn't made the connection between a woman who would welcome them to the neighborhood with pie and the people whose property she had vandalized.

"Yes. Mary and Tom Miller," Dani said.

"They're very sweet," Ruben said. "She used to teach math at the high school and Tom worked at the post of-fice for years."

"The man who lives here yelled at us once," Mia said with a frown as they approached the house. "Silver and me weren't even doing anything. Just walking Winky past their house. It scared me."

Is that why Silver had picked this house to tag? Because the man who lived here had scared her little sister?

If it wasn't random vandalism, Ruben had to wonder again what *he* had done to earn her ire.

"He had a stroke a few years ago and sometimes he can be a little grumpy. I'm sorry that happened to you."

Silver met his gaze, shock in her eyes. "Oh. I didn't know."

"Sometimes when people have health problems, they be-come so focused on that, they aren't always aware of how their words or tone impact others."

"That must be difficult for Mary," Dani said, compassion in her voice.

"Yeah, but she's a trouper. I told her we were coming over. Silver, I thought you might have something you want to say to her."

Silver looked back down at the box in her hands and mumbled something he couldn't hear.

After he knocked on the door, Mary Miller answered wearing a ruffled apron with Christmas trees and candy canes on it. Out of the house wafted the delicious scents of sugar and cinnamon and butter.

"Hello, Ruben, dear."

He leaned in and kissed her wrinkled cheek. "Hi, Mary. I understand you've met Dani Capelli and her daughters, Mia and Silver. We're here to paint over the graffiti."

Her face softened and she reached both hands out and grasped his much bigger one in hers. "You told me on the phone you were coming but I wasn't sure you'd be able to make it. You're so busy! This is so kind of you, Ruben, but I'm not surprised. You've always been such a good boy."

He managed to refrain from rolling his eyes at Dani, who was watching this interchange with interest and, if he was not mistaken, considerable amusement.

"Who's here?" a gruff voice asked from the other room.

"Go back to your show, Tom," she said, her voice patient. "It's Ruben Morales here with that nice veterinarian who moved in down the street with her pretty girls."

Dani's amusement quickly shifted to discomfort when she

seemed to remember why they were there. "Silver, don't you have something you want to tell Mrs. Miller?"

The girl mumbled something incoherent, looking down at her sneakers.

"I'm sorry, dear. I don't hear as well as I used to. Could you repeat that?"

Silver looked up. "I'm very sorry I sprayed graffiti on your shed. It was a dumb thing to do. I made a mistake and I'm sorry."

As apologies went, that one was nicely done, Ruben had to admit.

"Well, you're making it right again. That's the important thing. We all make mistakes, choices we wish we hadn't. Why, just this morning, I poured buttermilk in my coffee when I meant to grab half-and-half. Let me tell you, that was quite a nasty surprise."

Ruben had to smile. Grabbing the wrong container out of the refrigerator didn't quite equate to vandalizing others' properties, but he appreciated her trying to make Silver feel better.

"It shouldn't take us long to paint over it, then we'll get out of your way."

"Thank you. The cans are right inside the shed. I don't know when I would have had the chance to clean it up my-self, and you know Tom likes the place to look tidy."

Silver winced a little, looking even more guilty. Good.

"Wait a minute. Before you go there to start work, you'd better try these snickerdoodles that just came out of the oven. I tried a new recipe this time and you would really help me out if you would taste them for me and give me your opinion."

"Oooh. I love snickerdoodles," Mia declared. "They're my favorite."

The elderly woman smiled down at the little girl. "Then you'll be the perfect one to try them out and tell me how you like the recipe."

She shuffled out of the hallway, shoulders bent from age and arthritis. A moment later, she returned with a plate piled high with cinnamon- and sugar-dusted cookies.

"They're a little more flat than my snickerdoodles usually turn out. I might need to add a tad more flour. Try them and tell me what you think."

Ruben took a bite, which was fluffy and sweet and delicious, as far as he could discern.

"Perfection," he said.

"Very tasty," Dani concurred.

"Yumalicious," Mia declared.

Silver nibbled hers, still with an odd expression on her features. "It's, um, really good. Thank you."

The woman beamed at them. "Oh, I'm so relieved. Here. You take these with you, to keep your strength up while you're painting."

She pulled plastic wrap over them and handed the plate to Mia, the only one of them who didn't have her hands full of painting supplies.

"That was nice of her, wasn't it?" Dani said to her daughter when they walked outside.

"I guess," Silver mumbled, her eyes still filled with confusion as they made their way to the shed.

Here, the vandals—he would never believe she acted alone—had covered the side of the shed with multiple huge spray-painted smiley faces and the words *Be Nice*.

"Oh, Silver," Dani exclaimed.

"I was dumb. I know. I don't need you to keep harping on it. Can we just move on now?"

"Good idea," Ruben said, taking pity on her discomfort. "We have a lot of work ahead of us. I brought some wire brushes. I think they're in the box you brought along. Our first step should probably be seeing if we can scrape some of it off before we try painting over it. Why don't you grab them, Silver?"

She didn't look thrilled at the assignment but nodded and started digging around in her crate until she pulled out the brushes.

"Is this what you wanted?"

"Exactly. Just start scraping away at the graffiti. I'm not sure if any will come off, but we can try."

They all went to work, Dani on one side, Silver in the middle and Ruben on the end.

He didn't mind painting and considered himself something of a pro. He'd spent many hours of his childhood earning spending money by helping his dad paint the concrete walls of the veterinary clinic. Those had been great times, where he'd been able to talk to his dad about girls, about life, about where he wanted to be in the future.

There was actually a Zen-like calm in the process, painting over the old and bringing in the new.

"Mommy, can I have another cookie?" Mia asked after a few moments. She was sitting on a garden bench, keeping watch over the cookies as if she expected Mary's garden gnomes to come to life and snatch them away.

"Just one. Let's save the rest for later."

Silver frowned as she continued working the wire brush against the wooden shed.

"What's wrong?" Ruben asked. "You seemed upset earlier about the cookies. Didn't you like them?"

"No. It's not that. They were great. It's just..." She looked down at the plate of cookies in her sister's hand then back at the tidy little house. "Why did she give us cookies?"

"She said she needed testers," Mia reminded her sister.

"But...I did a stupid thing and vandalized her property. Why is she so nice about it? I thought she would yell at me."

She gestured to the mess she had created on the shed. "I mean, if this were my place and some stupid kids, um, a stupid kid messed it up, I'd be seriously pissed."

"I suppose she sees that you're trying to make amends," Dani said. "That's what today is all about, to show our neighbors you're sorry for what you did, right?"

"I guess. I still don't get it."

"I don't care why," Mia said. "I just like the cookies. I'll eat them all if you don't want them."

"I never said I didn't want them," Silver protested, which made Ruben smile.

"She's a nice lady," he said. "Just like Mrs. Grimes, once

you get past her gruff shell. After you've been in Haven Point awhile, I think you'll find most people here are kind."

"If you say so," she muttered, looking not at all convinced.

"I do. In fact, in my experience, most people *everywhere* are kind. Sure, there are the selfish jerks out there. People who don't care about anyone but themselves and who are willing to do whatever it takes to get ahead, but they're usually far outnumbered by those willing to step up when they see a need."

"Wow. Do you need me to clean those rose-colored glasses for you?" Dani asked, looking at him as if he had just arrived from another planet filled with do-gooders.

He smiled. "I already polished them this morning, thanks. You can borrow them anytime you want, though."

"No thanks. I prefer to see the world as it is, not as some pretty picture with all the harsh edges blurred out."

Who had hurt her and left her so cynical? The girls' father? He wanted to ask but didn't dare with her daughters looking on.

"Mommy, if Silver doesn't want another cookie, can I have hers?"

"I said one more. Put them away for now. Maybe after lunch you can have another one."

She pouted but was easily distracted when Ruben told her he needed help holding the tray while he poured paint into it.

The little girl was adorable and he was thrilled she seemed to have lost her shyness with him so quickly.

With her curly dark hair and light olive-toned skin, she looked like something out of a Renaissance painting. Her mother and sister did as well. Throw their pictures up in a Venetian chapel and they would fit right in.

Okay, maybe they wouldn't fit in so well right *now* when they were wearing clothes suitable for paint and cleanup work. And Silver might need to lose the purple hair first.

"Do you have a ladder?" Dani asked a few moments later. "I can't quite reach the top."

"Over at my place. I'll grab it if necessary, but let me see if I can reach first."

"Use my brush. It has a longer handle."

She handed it over and their hands briefly connected. He attributed the little burst of heat that flared between them to the wire bristles of the brush conducting electricity. It was a nice theory but didn't quite explain the rosy blush climbing her high cheekbones.

Was it possible Dani was attracted to him, too? It was a fascinating idea, one he desperately wanted to explore, if not for her daughters looking on.

"Watch out," he said gruffly. "I don't want to shower down paint flakes on you."

She moved out of the way while he finished scraping the high spot and brushed off the flakes. When he finished, Ruben stepped back to look at the wall again.

"Good work. We might be able to get by with only one coat, which is good since it has to dry completely before the temperature drops tonight. Winter isn't a great time to clean up graffiti."

He didn't miss the guilt that flashed across Silver's expression. Good. Maybe if she felt guilty enough, she would come clean about who else had been involved with her in the vandalism.

"What now?" Silver asked, a new urgency in her voice.

"Brush off any remaining paint flakes, then you can start rolling on one side and I'll do the other. We'll meet in the middle. This shouldn't take us long."

"What can I do?" Dani asked.

"I've only brought the two rollers. You and Mia can be our cheerleaders."

She rolled her eyes, which led him to the not surprising conclusion that she probably wasn't the sort of girl who went in for short skirts and pom-poms.

"When we knocked earlier, I saw the woodpile close to the house is running a little low. Maybe you and Mia could grab the wheelbarrow and move some of the split logs closer to the house so she doesn't have to," he suggested.

Dani brightened at the suggestion. "That's a great job for us. Come on, Mia."

"Can I ride in the wheelbarrow?"

"Maybe on the way back from the house," Dani said.

For a few moments, he and Silver worked in silence.

"I don't get why we have to paint over the whole thing when the graffiti is only on part of it. Couldn't we just paint that?"

"If we only paint over the markings on the wall, we'll end up with a splotch of new paint that will look almost as bad as the graffiti. Painting the whole wall will hide it better."

She seemed to accept that, though it was obvious she didn't necessarily like it.

"Tell me about where you came from," he said after a few moments. "Boston, wasn't it? Did you like it there?"

"I guess. It was okay. My friends are cool."

"How long did you live there?"

"Since I was nine. That's when we moved from Queens so my mom could go to vet school."

Dani had loaded the wheelbarrow full of wood and was heading toward the house with Mia in the lead. He wanted to ask directly about Silver's father but didn't want to come across as too obvious.

"Just the three of you?" he asked, as unobtrusively as possible.

"And Winky. Her full name is Winky Stinksalot. The Winky part is from Harry Potter."

"Oh, right. The little house elf. You've had her a long time, then."

"We got her when I was a little girl. I found her in a park near our apartment in Queens. She was starving and dirty and didn't have a leash or anything. We put a sign up in the park but nobody ever came forward to claim her so Mom said we could keep her."

That was the most she had ever talked to him, the longest string of sentences he'd heard out of her mouth. He asked a few more questions about the things she liked to do in Boston and New York. Once Silver started, it was as if he had uncorked the bottle. She chattered as much as Mia had earlier, though mostly about her friends and the movies she liked and some of the places they liked to hang out in Boston.

In no time, they were finished with the wall and he had a much clearer picture of their family. They seemed to love each other very much, a message that came through in Silver's conversation.

He had also noticed the girl went to a great deal of effort not to mention her father, in what was an obviously deliberate effort to leave him out of the conversation.

Why? What was the big secret about the man?

"That looks great," Dani said, rejoining them. "I can't see any trace of graffiti. Do you think you'll need a second coat?"

"We may have to see what happens when it dries, but so far it looks like we've got good coverage. How did you two do?"

"We carried about a hundred logs over to the house." Mia slumped to the ground, apparently completely exhausted.

"Good work. Now Mrs. Miller won't have to walk all the way over here to refill her wood box for a week or two."

Mia looked happy about that, anyway.

"That should do it here. We'll check back later in a couple of hours to see if this will need a second coat. Meanwhile, let's head over to Mrs. Grimes's place and get started on her garage door. I'm warning you, it might be a little harder."

"We can do hard things," Mia said. "That's what our mama always says."

"Exactly right. Good thing we have snickerdoodles to help us keep up our strength."

★ ★ ★

Dani faced the garage door decorated with more of her daughter's handiwork, her heart sinking at the magnitude of the task ahead of them.

Gertrude Grimes hadn't been as sweet as the Millers. She had been terse and tight-lipped when Silver apologized for her actions. Dani had a feeling her daughter's English grade would *not* be very good this term.

Again, she had to wonder what Silver had been thinking. She couldn't understand her daughter. On what planet would she ever think destroying someone else's property would make her more liked, more popular, more *accepted* in their new community?

Dani sighed. How could she blame Silver, really? She had once been her, defiant and angry, trying to lash out at the world however she could.

Wasn't that the whole reason she had hooked up with Tommy DeLuca?

Tommy had seemed wild and reckless and dangerous, yes, but that had been a big part of his appeal when she was a needy, lonely sixteen-year-old girl.

He had been four years older, a twenty-year-old man who had no business hitting on a teenager, she could see that now. At the time, she hadn't thought anything was wrong with it, she had only been enthralled by his attention.

Like a thirsty, forgotten plant shriveling up in a corner, she had lapped up all of it desperately and had been pregnant with Silver when she graduated from high school.

Ruben Morales, on the other hand, was the complete opposite of her late ex-husband. Okay, except for the dangerous part. Something told her that for all his good-natured amiability, he would be fierce and protective if anything threatened those he loved.

What would it be like to have the love of a man like him?

That was a question she didn't have the courage to even consider.

"Do we need to use the wire brushes again here?" she asked him.

He stood beside her, studying Silver's handiwork.

"I'm afraid that would damage the garage door. I think our best bet here is to try the cleaning agent the county specialist suggested to see if we can get the paint to fade at all, then we'll repaint."

She watched as he reached into one of the crates of supplies for rags.

What was his story? The man was a complete mystery to her. She still didn't understand why he would want to spend an entire Saturday helping them clean up graffiti. So far, they had only worked at other people's houses, too. They hadn't even made it as far as his house to clean up his boat.

He was a fascinating enigma.

"Mia, there are some rags in that box there. Can you hand me a few?"

Her youngest rushed to help him, eager to please her new best friend. It worried her, this instant bond her youngest daughter seemed to have formed with the gorgeous deputy sheriff. Dani wasn't quite sure why Mia had glommed on to him, when she had been so shy around virtually everyone else since coming to Haven Point.

Funny, but Mia had the same reaction to Ruben's father. Usually around men, she was nervous, preferring to talk to them through Dani or Silver, or—more likely—not speak to them at all. Apparently, something about Frank Morales and his son set her at ease.

Dani wanted to think that was a good thing, but she wasn't quite sure.

After they wiped down the door with the cleaner, Ruben stood back to look. "I think some of it has faded, but it still might need two coats."

He grabbed a can of paint and the tray, and he and Silver went to work with the rollers.

"Good work," he said a few moments later. "You're really getting the hang of that paint roller. Maybe this summer, your mom can put you to work rolling a fresh coat of paint on the outside of the vet clinic. The last time it was painted was probably when I did it at your age."

"Did they even have paint in those days?" Silver asked with a sideways grin.

"Yes, but we had to make our own out of natural dyes from the plants we gathered around our covered wagons," Ruben said drily, which earned him an even wider grin from Silver.

"I'm not that old," he said. "Probably not much older than your mom."

"She'll be thirty-one in April," Silver offered, entirely too free with Dani's information.

"Thirty and already a doctor of veterinary medicine? That's impressive."

"Not that impressive. It took me five years to get my undergrad degree, since I was working full-time and had a child, and then another two years of working as a vet tech before I was able to get into veterinary school."

"I still think it's impressive," he said.

She told herself not to be warmed by his admiration but she couldn't seem to help it. Apparently some part of her was still that shriveled houseplant in the corner.

"That should do it," Ruben said a short time later.

"Are we done?" Silver asked.

"I think so. Depending on how this dries, we might not need a second coat here, either, but we'll have to check it for sure in a few hours."

"We still have to clean up your boat," Dani pointed out.

He made a face. "Believe me, I won't forget. *The Wonder* is only two months old. I've only had her in the water twice."

"I'm really sorry, Ruben," Silver said.

Apparently she was just as susceptible to the man's charm as her younger sister. Okay, and her mother.

"Good. You should be," he said, not unkindly. "Now let's go check the Millers' house and see if it's ready for another coat."

They packed all the supplies back into the crates and headed down the street. When they returned to the Millers', they found the paint on the shed had dried with good coverage.

"You lucked out," Ruben said. "Looks like we don't have

to do another coat here. Since that's the case, why don't we break for lunch, then meet back at my place in an hour or so to work on *The Wonder*?"

"Sounds good," Dani said.

"We're having chicken noodle soup," Mia informed him. "I helped put the carrots and the celery in the pot before we left."

"That sounds delicious."

"I bet you could have some," Mia said.

Dani didn't miss the sidelong look Ruben sent her. "That's very kind of you, but I don't want to take all your soup."

"Mom always make tons," Silver said. "You might as well eat with us."

Ruben didn't bother to hide his shock at her seconding her sister's invitation. His gaze met Dani's, a question in them, as if gauging her opinion about her daughters inviting him over. She shrugged.

"We do have plenty and you're welcome. It's the least we can do after all your help today, but don't feel obligated. You could probably use a break from having your ear talked off by one or more of us."

"I was going to grab a quick PB and J sandwich, but chicken noodle soup sounds way better. Listen, I've got a loaf of homemade bread at my place. Why don't I run home and check on the dogs, grab the bread and meet you at your house in fifteen minutes or so?"

In Boston, she might have found it unusual if a man had told her he had a loaf of homemade bread sitting around his house. Haven Point was another story. People did that here, just dropped off a loaf of warm, fragrant, scrumptious bread simply because they had baked extra and thought you might like it.

"That sounds delicious. We'll see you in a few moments. Come on, girls. We need to add the noodles to the soup."

She could have used a little distance from the man, a chance to rebuild all her defenses before spending the rest of the afternoon with him, but apparently she wouldn't be getting that right now.

While one coat of paint seemed to have covered over Silver's graffiti, Dani wasn't being nearly as effective when it came to resisting Ruben Morales.

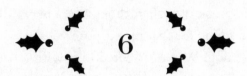

6

Twenty minutes later, Ruben rang the bell at Dani's house, the loaf of fresh bread under his arm.

The very adorable Mia opened the door for him immediately, almost as if she had been watching for him out the window.

"Hi." She beamed, showing off the gap in her front teeth. "The buzzer just went off, which means the soup is ready."

"Don't I have perfect timing, then?"

"You certainly do," Dani said from the doorway.

Twenty minutes. That's all the time they had been apart, but still, his heart seemed to kick in his chest at the sight of her, fresh and sweet and pretty.

In those twenty minutes, she had redone her hair, pulling back the loose strands that had slipped out of her ponytail throughout the morning as they worked. She looked lovely either way but he wondered how she would react if she knew he was suddenly battling a strong urge to start pulling those strands back out. He kind of preferred the tousled, sexy look of earlier, though he knew full well she hadn't been going for that on purpose.

Her little dog, Winky, greeted him with a friendly yip and Ruben diverted himself from that inappropriate hairstyle temptation by reaching down to scratch the dog's head.

"How were Ollie and Yukon?" Dani asked as she led the way to the kitchen, where plates and bowls had been set around the table.

"They're always happy to see me. Isn't that one of the best things about dogs? Ollie made it clear he didn't want me to leave again. Apparently he doesn't want me to do anything on the weekends but sit around and watch sports."

"I'm sorry we've messed up your routine."

"I'm not," he said truthfully. He said the words with a little more intensity than warranted, which might have been the reason he thought her color rose a little.

"Silver," she called down the hall. "Deputy Morales is here and lunch is ready."

"You and your girls don't have to call me Deputy Morales all the time, you know, like I told you the other day. I would prefer if you all call me Ruben, especially after we've already spent the entire day together."

"Right. Sorry. Habit." She gestured to the loaf of bread in his hand. "Would you like me to slice that?"

"That would be great. Thanks."

Silver came in and finished setting the table while Dani took his loaf of bread to a cutting board near the sink.

"Can I help do anything?"

"No. You're a guest. I'm afraid we only have water to drink. I should have warned you. I don't even have beer."

"Water's fine with me."

"Sit down," she ordered. "Anywhere is fine."

The moment he picked a seat, Mia joined him at the table, moving her chair closer to his. How could any guy not lose his heart to this one?

"You guys getting ready for Christmas yet? I didn't notice a Christmas tree."

"We took our old crappy tree to Goodwill when we moved," Silver said, pulling headphones off to drape around her neck.

"We took *all* our stuff to Goodwill," Mia added.

"Not everything," Dani protested. "Just the stuff we didn't want to move across country."

Silver rolled her eyes. "Everything that wouldn't fit in a little rented trailer the size of a bathtub. The Christmas tree didn't make the cut. Mom said we would pick up another one here but we haven't yet."

"I've been a little busy the last few weeks," Dani said tartly. "It doesn't help that I had to spend my one free day this week cleaning up graffiti, did it?"

"I didn't ask you to help. You offered. I could have done it by myself."

Dani's mouth tightened but she was busy dishing bowls of chicken noodle soup into chunky blue stoneware bowls and carrying them over to the table.

"Mama says we can get a real tree this year, as soon as we find one. I can't *wait*."

"There's a nice lot on the outskirts of Shelter Springs where they sell real trees. A friend of mine runs it, Carlos Urribe. He's a good guy."

"If we mention your name, will we get a discount?" Silver asked.

"Better not. He's still miffed at me over a bet he lost a few months back during the World Series."

"What about you?" Dani asked. "Do you decorate much for the holidays? I don't think I've noticed a tree at your place, either, when I've passed by."

"I love Christmas, don't get me wrong, but I live alone and it doesn't really seem like it's worth all the trouble just for me. I have a little tree in the front room. It's one of those prelit ones and I hang a dozen or so ornaments on it. If I didn't do *something*, I think my sister would probably come and decorate my whole house when I'm not looking."

"Would she really?" Dani looked as if she couldn't comprehend that sort of relationship.

"I've learned not to put anything past my family."

She sat down at the table finally, across from him. "Your family seems very close."

"Sometimes *too* close," he admitted.

She took a piece of bread and buttered it for Mia. "But you settled in Haven Point anyway."

"I lived in Boise when I was in college and when I went through the police academy, but when the job opened at the Lake Haven Sheriff's Department, I was glad to move back. I like it here."

"I do, too," Mia said.

He smiled at her, grateful he had at least one ally among the Capelli women.

"What about you?" he asked. "Do you come from a big family?"

"No," she said, her voice wooden. "Mia, don't slurp your noodles."

So family was a touchy subject. He filed that away for future reference, even as he was astonished at his urge to hold her close and kiss away the pain in her eyes.

"Small families are good, too," he said.

"They are. This is my family," she said, gesturing to her daughters.

"Except Nana," Silver said.

"Your mother?"

"My ex's mother. Late ex," she added quietly.

"I'm sorry."

She opened her mouth as if to say something, then apparently changed her mind. "Thanks," she mumbled.

So she was divorced and then the girls' father died. How sad for all of them. He wanted to ask about the man and what happened to him but decided this wasn't the appropriate time.

Dani changed the subject, asking him more about going through the police academy and why he wanted to go into law enforcement in the first place. He, in turn, talked to the girls about school and their favorite subjects. It turned into one of his most enjoyable meals in recent memory and gave him a much better picture of the family dynamics.

"Girls, hurry and finish your soup," Dani finally said. "We still have to help Ruben clean up his boat."

He thought about telling her he really didn't need her help. After speaking with the graffiti specialist for the county, he had found exactly the right solvent that would easily clean the paint off *The Wonder*. He had tested it the day before to be sure and it had worked like magic.

He *could* clean it himself. At the same time, he believed strongly that Silver needed to be involved in all aspects of the cleanup effort, including something he easily could handle on his own.

"It won't take us long," he assured her. "I can help you clear the table first. The soup was delicious, by the way. Thank you."

"You're welcome. And it's Silver's turn to load the dishwasher. You can help her."

Silver groaned but didn't push her luck.

Smart girl, he thought as he rose and picked up his soup bowl. He was beginning to like her, despite her attitude.

He liked *all* of them. Entirely too much. It was becoming too easy to forget his resolve about not dating women with children.

Not that he and Dani were dating, or anything close

to it. She was still brisk with him and somewhat distant, which made his undeniable fascination with her even more puzzling.

Dani refused to let herself be charmed by the man as she watched him tease Silver while the two of them cleaned up the few dishes in the kitchen.

What was his game? Why was he being so nice to them all?

He was an officer of the law and she had an inherent mistrust of him because of it. Growing up in the city, she saw too much corruption, too much inequality and bias and misuse of authority.

He appeared nothing like that. He seemed to be one of the good guys, a caring, dedicated sheriff's deputy who gave up an entire Saturday to help her daughter.

Still, Dani couldn't completely trust his motives.

She and the girls had secrets she would rather he not discover, secrets that might threaten her future here. The more time she spent around him, the likelier the chance that she might let some of those secrets slip to a trained investigator like Ruben.

If she wanted to make a better life for her girls here, she had to be wary about letting down her guard around him.

"Can I play with my dolls?" Mia asked.

"For a few minutes, then we need to head over and help Ruben and Silver clean up his boat. If we get done in time, we'll go pick out our Christmas tree."

"Yay!" Mia did a little circle in the air, which Winky promptly copied.

"Whoopee," Silver said, with no trace of excitement in her voice.

"You don't like Christmas?" Ruben asked.

"I like not having to go to school for two weeks," Silver said, "but the rest of it seems like a lot of work for limited payoff."

Silver's words stuck a little sharp-tipped thorn into Dani's heart. Had she failed her daughter when it came to instilling Christmas spirit in her?

She hadn't always loved the holiday, either. It was tough being in foster care at Christmas. If her foster family had other "real" children, there were always inherent inequities in the way she had been treated, especially among extended family members.

Most of the time, they probably weren't even aware of it. She had noticed, though, even as she understood. Why should grandparents extend the same effort and energy into finding the right gift for someone who could be gone from their lives the next day?

She had gotten used to it. What other choice had she been given? Eventually, Dani had come to treat Christmas as just another day to get through, this one with a little more chaos than most.

After she had Silver, though, Dani had gained an entirely new perspective.

She had this small, wonderful creature to think about

now and Christmas became far more magical when her focus shifted to providing memories for her child.

Dani had always tried to make up for the dearth of material things by giving her girls experiences they wouldn't forget: walking through a light display in a city park, going to the mall to see Santa, visiting nursing home residents who would otherwise be alone—both because it was kind and also to remind her girls that while they didn't have much, they had each other.

The last few years, she had been so insanely busy trying to survive the rigors of veterinary school, she was afraid she had failed in that arena, too.

This year had to be different.

While money was still tight thanks to all those loans she had taken out, gambling toward her future, she was more comfortable financially than she had been in years. That was in large part thanks to Ruben's father and his generosity both in the compensation he was providing her during her internship and his offer to let them live in this small but comfortable house on the lake.

She had been afraid this would be a hard Christmas. The stress and trauma of Tommy's death and the highly charged circumstances around it had taken their toll on her and on Silver. Mia was mostly oblivious, since her father had been a stranger to her, but Silver still grieved.

Despite everything, Dani had grieved as well. She had mourned the pipe dreams she'd cherished as a lonely, foolish teenage girl, swept off her feet by a fast-talking young man who had promised safety and security and the happily-ever-after she had always yearned after.

Those dream castles had turned to sawdust too quickly. His promises had all been an illusion, but at least her girls had come out of her marriage, the two most important things in her life.

In a way, she supposed Tommy had given her the thing she most needed, someone to love. Two amazing someones. She could regret many things about her marriage to a man who ultimately chose a life of crime over his family, but she would never regret her daughters.

She wanted to give them the best possible Christmas here in Haven Point.

Whatever game Ruben Morales might be playing, whether he was befriending them to dig deeper into her life in an effort to protect his father, or whether he genuinely wanted to know them better, she would be cautious around him. She had to be. Her girls had no one else to stand for them.

An hour later, she had to acknowledge that keeping her distance from Ruben Morales was easier said than done, especially when he was so very sweet to her daughters.

"Look at that," he said, standing back and admiring the work he and Silver had put in to clean away the graffiti. "It came off perfectly, just like the label on the cleanser said it would."

"You can't even tell it was ever there," Dani said, admiring the sleek, glossy gleam of his boat in the afternoon sunlight with the words *The Wonder* in small script near the stern.

"I'll admit, I was a little worried about damaging the finish, but this stuff is magic. I'm glad it worked so well."

"I do like your boat," Mia said. "It's pretty."

Ruben smiled down at her and Dani tried to ignore the little flutter of nerves inside her.

"Thanks. I think so, too. I never considered myself a boat guy but it kind of seemed a natural fit, since I own a house right on the water. I will say, next time I buy a boat, I'm going to do it at the beginning of the season, not at the end. I'm anxious to get out on her."

Silver rolled her eyes. "Why do guys always consider their boats girls?"

"Because we love them," he answered promptly. "And maybe because they're unpredictable and take more work than any guy ever expects."

This time Dani was the one who rolled her eyes. "And because men like to think they're the captains of them, but it's really the boat that makes all the rules," she told her daughter, then decided she would be wise to change the subject.

"You guys worked hard today. I'm impressed," Dani said. "I didn't think we would get everything cleaned up in one Saturday."

"Agreed," Ruben said. "I was worried the weather wouldn't hold, but we did it. Lucky for us, the shed at Mrs. Grimes's place didn't need a second coat, either."

"Yay us!" Mia said, beaming her gap-toothed grin.

"You didn't have much to do with it," Silver said.

"Not true," Ruben said. "She was the best cheerleader ever, plus she helped move firewood for the Millers and petted Mrs. Grimes's schnauzer."

Mia beamed at him, clearly smitten. Oh, Dani hoped her little girl didn't get her heart broken.

"Thank you for all your help," she said. "We never would have been able to make things right without it. You really went above and beyond."

"I can't believe I'm saying this, but it really was my pleasure. Despite the work involved, it was a fun day."

Dani was afraid to admit how very much she agreed with him. "Silver. Don't you have something you want to say to Deputy Morales?"

"Ruben," he insisted.

"Thanks again for helping us, Ruben," Silver mumbled. "And I'm sorry I tagged your girlfriend here."

Ruben grinned and patted the side of his sexy boat. "She forgives you. And so do I."

Dani could swear her daughter grinned back for just a moment but she concealed it quickly.

"The good news is, now she should be all ready for the Lights on the Lake Festival next week."

"I want to see that!" Mia said.

"You can watch the parade from your house, but it's more fun to go to Lake View Park downtown, where there are craft and food booths, live music and games for the kids. It's a big party. The biggest one of the season. You don't want to miss it."

Her first instinct was to tell him they would likely do better to watch from their house, but that seemed to play into her antisocial tendencies. She was trying to make a home here, which meant she needed to get out and mingle more.

"Thanks for the reminder. Can we help you clean up?"

"Not much to do. I should be fine."

Mia tugged on her sweatshirt. "Mama, can we go get our Christmas tree now?"

"Yes. Let's go home and clean up, then we'll drive to Shelter Springs and check out the lot Ruben was talking about."

"Do you have a tree stand and Christmas lights for your tree?" he asked.

She hadn't thought that far ahead. "No. I suppose I'll have to pick those up while we're in town."

"I might be able to help you out there, actually. My parents bought an artificial tree a few years ago and they've been storing their old things in my garage. There are a couple of tree stands and at least a half-dozen strings of lights. I can't guarantee they'll all work, but you're welcome to use what you can find."

His offer surprised and touched her, especially as she suddenly realized that purchasing multiple strings of lights and a new tree stand for a real tree might end up costing her more money than if she went ahead and bought a whole artificial tree.

"That's very nice of you. Thank you."

"Silver, come help me dig around in the garage for a minute, will you?"

"Ooh. That sounds fun," she said, her voice dripping with sarcasm. Still, she went with him toward the house and the attached garage, and Dani and Mia followed behind.

His garage was neatly kept and well organized, though not to the point where he seemed like a neat freak. He went to the back of the garage and pulled down a ladder from the ceiling, which made Mia's eyes go wide.

"That's cool! I want one of those in my room!"

"That would be great, except you don't have an attic above your room," Silver said. "Where would you go?"

"I don't care. I want one anyway. Can I have a pull-down ladder in my room, Mama?"

"Let's focus on the Christmas tree for now," she said.

"Can I go up?" Mia asked.

"Better let me handle this for now," Ruben said. "I haven't been up here for a bit and I'm not sure how stable some of the boxes are. But maybe another time."

She made a face but plopped onto the concrete floor to watch as he climbed the ladder then emerged a moment later with a green tree stand atop a box labeled Christmas Lights, which he held in one hand as he used the other to help in his descent.

"I saw one more box up there that might have some of my mom's old decorations. If you're interested in using them, I'm sure she won't mind."

"Oh, I couldn't."

"Let me grab the box anyway and you can decide after you take a look at what's inside."

He climbed the ladder again and she did her best not to

gawk through the fabric of the T-shirt he wore at the play of muscles in his shoulders and his back.

Just as he disappeared into the bonus room, she heard a polite woof and a moment later a yellow Lab wandered into the garage. He was on a leash and at the other end stood Ruben's father.

"Hi, Dr. Morales," Mia chirped. She immediately went to him for a hug, which seemed to thrill him.

"Hello. I wasn't expecting to find you in my son's garage," he told her. "What's all this about?"

"We're raiding your Christmas decorations," Silver told him. "Ruben said it was okay. We're getting a real tree this year and he said nobody is using your old tree stand."

"True enough. What a good idea! I'm sorry I didn't think of it first."

Ruben climbed down the ladder a moment later with another box under one arm.

"Hey, Dad." He set the box down and gave his father an affectionate hug, which made Dr. Morales smile and sent those blasted butterflies fluttering through Dani's insides.

She found it absolutely charming that he loved his parents and wasn't afraid to show it.

"What a kind thing, helping your lovely neighbors with their holiday decorations."

"I didn't think you and Mom would mind."

"Not at all. Not at all."

Frank smiled at them and Dani's heart warmed with gratitude for this man who had completely changed her life. She only hoped she could be worthy of his faith in her.

"I'll help you carry these things next door," he said. "Mia *corazón*, you don't mind holding Baxter's leash for me while I grab some boxes, do you?"

Mia giggled at the nickname he always called her. "Nope. Baxter is my friend."

She grabbed the dog's leash and petted him, giggling when he licked her.

"What have you all been up to on this beautiful, rare warm December gift of a day we've been given?"

Dani hesitated. She didn't want Frank knowing about Silver's vandalism but she didn't know how to avoid telling him.

Ruben sent her a sidelong look, as if he sensed exactly what was running through her mind.

"Just helping out some neighbors," he said with an easy smile.

Silver frowned and looked as if she wanted to spill the whole story to the veterinarian but she finally looked down at the ground, as if she was too embarrassed to confess to her mistakes.

"What about you?" Dani asked to change the subject.

"My beautiful bride and I went into Shelter Springs to do a little Christmas shopping this morning. I don't recommend it. The stores were a madhouse. But when you have eight grandchildren and four step-grandchildren, you have to start somewhere."

She loved the way Frank always referred to his wife. Myra was just as sweet as her husband and Dani had liked her instantly when they came to town.

"Were you out for a walk or did you stop by for something in particular?"

"A little of both. I won't deny Baxter and I both needed a walk along the lakeshore after all that shopping and those crowds, plus your mother wanted me to come over and remind you about your sister's big concert tomorrow."

"Oh, right."

"And I'm sure I don't need to remind you of this, but your mother is serving churros and chocolate at our house afterward."

"I'll definitely be there for that."

"No concert, no churros. You know the rule."

Ruben made a face. "It's a dumb rule."

"You can take that up with your mother, if you dare." Frank turned to Dani. "You're all invited, too, my dear. In fact, I was heading to your house next to tell you about it. Now you've saved me the trip."

"What concert?"

"My sister sings in a jazz band," Ruben explained. "They're pretty good, actually, and give a fun show, especially at Christmastime."

"That's nice."

"And they're doing a benefit concert at the Episcopal church tomorrow night," Frank explained. "The proceeds benefit the women's shelter. Afterward, Myra always throws a family party with hot chocolate and her famous churros."

Mia's eyes lit up. "I *love* churros," she declared. "Once I had them at school. They were *muy delicioso*."

Frank chuckled. "I've got a wonderful idea. Considering you live next door to each other, you could ride together."

She immediately wanted to protest but Ruben spoke up before she could. "That's a great idea, Dad. What do you say, Dani?"

She wanted to say no. She wanted to tell him to stop being so nice to her, to stop trying to confound her and twist up her insides and make her find him even more impossibly attractive.

"Can we, Mama? I love, love, love churros."

How was she supposed to refuse churros and chocolate with Ruben's family when it sounded so very appealing?

She forced a smile. "Sure. That sounds fun. What time is the concert?"

"It starts at seven, but there's no reserved seating, so you might want to be there early," Frank said.

"I'll pick you up about six fifteen. Does that work?"

"Sounds good. I guess we'll see you then."

She didn't see that she had much choice, when Mia and even Silver looked excited about the prospect.

"Thank you again for all your help today," she said to Ruben after Frank waved farewell to them all and continued on his way with his dog. "We would never have been able to take care of it all without you."

His smile left her entirely too breathless. "I was glad to help, this time. I hope I don't have to again," he said to Silver.

She, predictably, rolled her eyes. "You won't," she said. "I don't want to have to spend another Saturday cleaning up."

"Fair enough. Have fun tree shopping for your Christmas tree. If you need help stringing the lights, give me a call."

She wouldn't. Dani would stay up all night if she had to in order to finish the job. She didn't need to become more dependent on Ruben Morales for help with things she ought to be handling on her own.

"Thanks. Have a good evening."

She handed the box of lights to Silver, gave the tree stand to Mia, picked up the box of ornaments, then ushered her family out of the garage.

She couldn't afford to fall for Ruben, she told herself as they walked across their winter-dead lawn toward home.

Yes, he pushed all her buttons. He was big, sexy, sweet. Irresistible. But she would have to strengthen her defenses and do her best to keep a safe distance from him.

She couldn't risk a broken heart, too, not when her whole life here in Haven Point felt as if it were hanging by some fragile, silvery thread of tinsel.

7

Ruben knocked on Dani's door the next evening, trying to ignore the restless edge that settled on his shoulders like the gently falling snow that had finally come to Haven Point.

It was stupid to feel any nerves. This wasn't a date. He was simply being neighborly, giving Dani and her girls a ride to a concert. That knowledge didn't seem to take away the anticipation surging through his veins.

She didn't answer the door for a long moment. When she finally did, Ruben completely forgot that he needed to breathe in order to sustain life.

She looked stunning in a wine-colored skirt and a creamy

cable-knit sweater. Her dark hair hung in soft waves around her face, unlike the ponytail or messy bun he was used to seeing.

"Hi," she said. Her voice sounded a little raspy, though he wondered if that was his imagination.

He finally remembered he needed oxygen and sucked some into his lungs.

"Hi. I'm a little early, I'm afraid."

He didn't bother telling her he had been watching the clock for the last hour of his shift at the sheriff's office, while he sat at his desk finishing paperwork.

"Not a problem. We're all ready."

Before she finished speaking, cute little Mia peeked around her mother. "Hi, Deputy Ruben."

"Hello, Miss Mia. What a pretty dress. Does Pia have one like it?"

"Not this one," she said with a grin, twirling around to show off the red knit dress and her knee-high boots.

"Guess what? We got a Christmas tree but we can't make it stand up straight. Mom tried all afternoon and finally she said a bad word and threw her gloves at the wall."

"Thanks for sharing that, honey," Dani said, color climbing her high cheekbones.

Ruben laughed. "We've all been there. Don't worry about it. We've got a few minutes before we have to leave for the concert, if you'd like a little help."

"I had to take a thirty-minute shower to get all the sticky sap off earlier. I'm not anxious to go through that again, especially when I'm already dressed for the concert."

"You look lovely," he said, then wished he hadn't when wariness crept into her expression.

He wanted to tell her she was more than lovely, she was breathtaking. He caught the words just in time. He had a feeling if she had any hint that he dared consider this anything like a date, she would shove him back through the door, slam it in his face and forget the whole thing.

"Let me take a look and see if I can figure out where the problem is. Maybe I can get you straightened out."

"I'm fine," she said tartly. "It's the tree that needs work."

"That, too."

He smiled and after a moment, she sighed and led the way into her living room. The tree they had selected was a smallish Scotch pine with a pretty conical shape. It listed drunkenly to one side and he could see immediately why.

"The trunk on this one is too thin for the tree stand. You need a couple of plywood blocks to keep it in place. Any chance you have a hacksaw?"

"Sure. I keep it in my purse. A girl never knows when she's going to need a hacksaw."

He grinned, delighted with the sense of humor she hid too often. "Around here, you really do never know."

"I guess I'll have to get one, then."

"You can ask Santa to bring you one for Christmas," Mia said.

"Great idea." Dani ran a hand over her daughter's hair with a sweet smile that did funny things to him.

"I have one at home. When the concert's over, I'll stop and grab it."

"What about the churros?" Mia asked, brow furrowed with alarm.

"We won't miss them, I promise. We can fix your tree *after* the churros."

"Whew."

Dani looked at her tree, then back to him. "I don't want you to go to any trouble. I can probably figure it out."

"It will take me five minutes, I promise. Maybe less. And save you all kinds of frustration in the long run."

"You're undoubtedly right. I apparently don't have a high level of tolerance for Christmas tree aggravations."

"Who does?" He smiled. "I hope you've got more tolerance for Christmas concerts."

"Depends on the Christmas concert. But in general, yes. I like Christmas music."

"Good. Should we go?"

She called Silver to come out and the older girl actually greeted him with a smile, which he considered great progress in his relationship with the Capelli females.

Ruben Morales was entirely too appealing.

She watched him interact with his family at the concert, laughing down at his petite mother with the dark hair and bright eyes, at Dr. Morales, at his sister, Angela, who looked like a smaller, more feminine version of Ruben.

It had been a long time since she had been part of a big, noisy family, even on the periphery.

She hadn't really thought this through, the fact that his

entire family would be there when she and her girls arrived with Ruben.

She didn't miss the speculative look his mother and his sister gave her and then each other. They weren't the only ones, either. When she walked into the church with him, she saw a few raised eyebrows coming their direction from other people she had met since she and the girls came to town.

She did her best to ignore them but she wanted to immediately separate from his family and sit on the other side of the church. She really didn't need people thinking the two of them were seeing each other.

Her discomfort didn't ease when the lights dimmed. She found it just as difficult to ignore her awareness of him beside her, big and tough and gorgeous.

"It's nice, isn't it?" Ruben whispered after a few songs, his warm breath tickling her ear and doing funny things to her insides.

"Very," she whispered back truthfully. Did her voice sound as breathless as she felt? "Your sister has talent."

The jazz combo wouldn't have been out of place at the Blue Note or the Village Vanguard in New York, with a smoky sound that added an original twist to the Christmas classics.

"I'm not sure how she ended up with the singing gene, but she's the only one of the four of us who did."

On his other side, Ruben's mother shushed him and Dani winced. She didn't need Myra Morales on her bad side, so she settled back to enjoy the music.

When the concert ended and the performers gave their

final bows and left the small stage, the crowd rose and began milling around, with people moving to speak with acquaintances and calling out to friends.

"Wasn't that wonderful?" Myra exclaimed to Dani when Ruben moved into the aisle to talk to his brothers and Angela's husband, Reed, a lanky cowboy with a slow smile and a clearly defined hat line around his brown hair. "Gets you right in the holiday spirit, doesn't it?"

Dani thought with guilt about how she hadn't exactly been overflowing with holiday spirit the last few years, too busy dealing with her daughters and school. How sad that she had allowed the chaos of her life to steal that joy away from her.

"Yes," she said softly. "It really does. How kind of you and Dr. Morales to invite us."

To her shock, Myra reached out a hand to clasp Dani's. Her hand was warm, soft, and the kindness in the other woman's eyes stirred a lump in Dani's throat.

"I know I've said this before but I'm going to repeat myself. I can't thank you enough for taking a chance and coming here to Idaho to help Frank out at the clinic. I know it hasn't been easy for you and your girls and I wanted to tell you how much it means to me. He's not as young as he used to be. He thinks he can do everything he did when he was your age and he just can't. Having you here to take on some of the load has been wonderful for him."

Frank, she saw, had joined his sons and son-in-law and the men were laughing at something one of them had said. To her mind, he looked pretty hale and hearty, as if he could keep going for decades, but Dani was glad Myra thought her presence had been helpful.

"I'm grateful he took the chance on me," she said.

"From all accounts, you're doing a wonderful job."

She knew that wasn't completely true but she couldn't politely disagree. Before she could come up with an answer, they were joined by McKenzie Kilpatrick, the mayor of Haven Point.

The other woman was about the same age as Dani. She had always been kind and welcoming, but right now McKenzie was the last person in town Dani wanted to see.

McKenzie would have to know about Silver's little graffiti spree. Dani had the impression the woman made it a point to know everything going on in her town.

Was she coming to tell Dani and her spray paint–wielding daughter to go back to where they came from? Dani drew in a sharp breath and frowned, her shoulders suddenly stiff.

She had been waiting for someone in town to say something about the vandalism. Instead, McKenzie gave her a warm smile, greeted Dani with her usual friendliness, then turned to ask Myra a question about some scarves Ruben's mother was knitting to sell in a booth at the town festival the following weekend.

Dani felt her shoulders relax a little, but the tension didn't completely trickle away.

The easy familiarity between the two women was a firm reminder that Dani didn't quite belong here in this crowd full of people who had known each other for years.

She wasn't sure if she ever would.

★ ★ ★

A woman could get positively inebriated from that scent.

An hour later, Dani stood in the doorway to Myra's neat kitchen, inhaling the scent of chocolate and cinnamon and frying dough.

She wanted to stand here and simply let the scents flood through her, but she had spent too many years in foster care to be comfortable doing nothing while someone else was working.

"Is there something I can do to help?" she asked Myra.

The other woman looked up from the large six-burner stove where she was carefully piping dough from a pastry bag into hot oil for the churros.

"You're a guest. Guests don't have to work in my house. Sit down and visit."

"This guest would love nothing more than to help you. Please."

Myra shrugged. "You don't have to do a thing except sit back and enjoy yourself, but if you insist, you could roll these churros in the cinnamon and sugar."

"Sure. I can probably handle that."

Dani had learned early how to work in a kitchen in the various homes where she had stayed, though if she were honest, her best skill was washing dishes.

Rolling churros in cinnamon and sugar didn't sound particularly daunting.

She was in the middle of it when Ruben's older sister, Angela, came in. She did a double take when she spotted Dani at the counter. "Wow! How did you get so lucky?

Mom usually never lets anybody make the finishing touches on her churros."

"Oh, no pressure now," Dani said. While her words were flippant, she still felt a flutter of nerves, an age-old desire to please that she couldn't shake.

Angela grinned. "I'm just teasing. We're the most casual family around. Mom always told us we couldn't do anything wrong in the kitchen, as long as we were trying. Even if you burn something, it just means you'll know better next time."

Dani had spent several wonderful years in one foster home where a similar attitude had reigned. She had hoped to stay with Betsy Williams forever but the woman had become too ill to care for the foster children she had taken in. Leaving the woman's home had broken Dani's heart, the one she might have thought would have been indestructible by then.

How lucky for Ruben and his siblings, that their mother was so patient and loving.

"Grandma, can we have the first churro?"

Ruben's little nephew Charlie, who belonged to Angela and her husband, Reed, was about the same age as Mia and they had apparently become the best of friends. They leaned against the island, looking longingly at the plateful of churros.

"You can have the first ones," Myra said, "as long as you take the garbage out first."

"I can do that, Abuela," Charlie said.

"Me too, Abuela," Mia said, which made Myra smile,

and Dani give a little internal wince at how quickly her youngest child had been absorbed into the Morales family.

Silver, too, seemed to be enjoying herself. Ruben had a nephew and a niece around her age, Angela's son Zach who went to Sil's school and a girl, Esme, who apparently lived in Shelter Springs with her mother, Ruben's brother Javier's ex-wife, and went to school there. Last she had checked, the three of them were hanging out in a corner of the living room. Dani had even heard laughter coming from there several times.

One part of her was delighted that her daughter was making more friends, but she worried about both of her girls becoming too entangled in the family. She couldn't give them this big, noisy, happy family. Not forever. She knew what it was like to yearn for something she couldn't have and she didn't want her daughters to suffer that same pain.

"Thank you," Myra said with a delighted smile as the children returned from taking the full garbage bag out to the trash.

"*De nada*, Abuela," Charlie said.

"*De nada,*" Mia repeated with a giggle. "Now can we have a churro?"

"Don't forget the chocolate. That's the best part. There's a perfect spot for churros and chocolate at the table. Have a seat."

Using tongs provided by Myra, Dani rolled two long pastries in the cinnamon and sugar then set them on a plate. Myra ladled the thick, rich-looking hot chocolate into a mug and set it in the middle of the plate and carried the whole thing to the children.

"Here you go. Be careful. The chocolate is still a little warm."

The next few minutes were filled with sounds of exaggerated delight as the children enjoyed the sweet treat that drew the teenagers into the kitchen for theirs, followed soon after by everyone else.

Fifteen minutes later, Dani had dredged a dozen churros in cinnamon sugar and was looking for more when Myra handed her one on a plate. "This one is yours. Here. I insist. I've saved the best churro of the lot for you."

Dani went easier on the cinnamon sugar for her own. She wanted to eat it standing up there in the kitchen area of the open plan living space but Myra would have none of it.

"You've been on your feet long enough. Go sit down. I'm coming, too."

Dani moved out to the table and was dismayed that the only open seat was next to Ruben, almost as if he had been saving it for her.

He was in the middle of a conversation with his brother Javier, whom she had just met that evening, and his brother-in-law, Reed, but paused to give her a bright smile that nearly made her stumble and spill her hot chocolate all over the place.

Wouldn't that make a lovely impression on the Morales family?

Ruben patted the seat next to him and for a wild moment, she was tempted to race back into the kitchen, throw the dessert into the sink, grab her daughters and flee.

Her heart was in serious danger. She could easily see herself falling hard for Ruben. She might even be halfway there, a realization that filled her with panic.

She drew in a breath, gripped the warm handle of the mug and made herself move forward. She slipped into the chair beside him, aware as she did that it wasn't only the fried churro and the sugary chocolate drink that were bad for her in this family.

8

"I like your family very much," she said later as he held the door open for Silver and a sleepy Mia to load into the rear seats of his late-model pickup truck.

He smiled down at her and her pulse seemed to kick faster. "They're pretty great. I did okay in the family department."

She hoped he knew his family was much better than okay. Compared to the chaos of her childhood and adolescence, Ruben Morales won the family lottery.

"Did you have fun tonight?" Ruben asked when they were on the road heading the short distance to her house and his next door.

"I did," Mia said sleepily.

"What about you?" he asked Silver.

"The churros were good," she said.

"You seemed to be getting along well with Esme."

"She's nice," Silver said.

"She is. We don't see her as often as we'd like since she's with her mom most of the week. It's always a treat when she can come to family things. Too bad she doesn't go to Haven Point Middle School like you and Zach. I guess you probably know him from school."

"Yeah. I know him. We have English together and his locker is close to mine."

If Dani hadn't been turned around to check to see if Mia had fallen asleep, she might have missed the rather dreamy look on Silver's expression.

Oh, no. Apparently she and her daughter were both susceptible to the charm wielded by the men in the Morales family.

"You probably know he's on the middle school basketball team."

"Yes," she admitted, in a nonchalant sort of voice that didn't fool Dani for a moment. "It's kind of hard to miss since the cheerleaders decorate his locker every time we have a game. Everybody makes such a big deal over the basketball players in the halls and at the pep assemblies."

"Right. He's really busy this year with practices and games. Which actually brings me to something I need to talk to you about," he said as he pulled into Dani's driveway.

"To me?" Silver asked warily.

"All of you, really. But mostly you. Because of Zach's basketball practice and game schedule, I'm running into a little conflict. I think you might be just the person to help me out."

"With what?"

"The last few years, Zach has helped me with a little project my parents wrangled me into, but I think he's going to be too busy for the next few weeks to help me out. You would be the perfect person to step in and give me a hand."

"Again, with what?"

"I'll tell you, but I have to swear you to secrecy first."

"Do we have to take a blood oath or something?"

While Silver spoke with her usual edge of sarcasm, Dani could hear the curiosity underlying it.

"Pretty close."

"What's a blood oath?" Mia asked.

"Don't worry about that. It just means I need you to keep a big secret from everybody. Can you do that?"

Mia gave a sleepy frown. "Mommy says I'm not supposed to keep secrets from her."

"That is a good rule for life, kiddo. You can't go wrong if you tell your mom everything going on in your world."

Silver scoffed a little but hid it with a cough that didn't fool Dani for a moment—or Ruben, for that matter.

He and Dani shared a look, and she knew he was having the same thought. All teenagers kept things from their parents. It was as inevitable as acne.

She wasn't sure she liked these moments when their

thoughts seemed synchronized, almost as if they were a united front.

"Here's the thing, Miss Mia," Ruben went on. "Your mother will know this secret. In fact, I probably should have talked to her first before bringing it up."

"Too late for that now," Dani said.

He made a face. "Sorry about that. It's a good thing, I promise."

"Why don't we go inside so you don't have to do the big reveal out here in the car?"

"Good idea."

She didn't want to be charmed further by the man when he opened the rear door of his king cab to let Silver out, then made his way around the pickup to open Dani's door and scoop Mia into his arms.

This was a one-time thing. They were *not* a family unit.

Her house was warm and smelled piney from the frustrating Christmas tree that still leaned crookedly against the wall. Winky greeted them all with enthusiasm, moving from person to person to welcome them home.

Silver plopped onto the sofa and gathered the little dog onto her lap. "All right. What's the big secret?"

"I can tell all of you, as long as I can count on you to keep this under your hat."

"What if we don't want that kind of responsibility?" Dani asked.

"Too late for that now," he said, parroting her words from earlier and almost making her smile.

Oh, she liked him, entirely too much.

"Are you going to tell us or keep dragging out the drama?" Silver finally asked. "We swear we won't tell, okay?"

"All right. Here goes."

He glanced around the room as if checking for listening devices. "Every year, my family picks one or two households in town to be the recipients of a special family tradition."

"What's a tradition?" Mia asked from the floor, where she had settled to pet Winky.

Dani tamped down that darn maternal guilt that tended to creep out entirely too often, even when it was completely undeserved.

Yes, she had been busy trying to support her family and get through school but she still took time to do important things with her daughters, even if she perhaps hadn't articulated the reasons why as well as she should have to Mia.

Mia was just asking what a word meant, she wasn't impugning Dani's mothering skills.

Once in a while, Dani needed to give herself a break—which could be easier said than done.

"It's all the unique things we do together as a family," she said. "You know, like the Capelli Champion blue plate special, where one person gets to eat on the special plate on their birthday or whenever they do something amazing."

"Or how Mom always has you put out cookies for Santa," Silver said.

"And carrots for the reindeer," Mia reminded her.

"In my family, we have a few traditions."

"Churros and chocolate," Mia said.

"Exactly." His smile made Dani's toes tingle. Darn him.

"That's one of my favorites. Another one dates back to when I was Silver's age. Every year for twenty years, my parents have picked a few households in town and we deliver a little treat to them each day for twelve days leading up to Christmas."

"Oh. 'The Twelve Days of Christmas.' I love that song." Mia launched into exuberant song. "Four calling birds, three friendships, two turtlenecks, and a partridge in a pear tree."

Silver snickered at her sister's mangled lyrics, but for once didn't call her out on it.

"That's the one," Ruben said with a smile. "We start on December 13 and end on Christmas Eve."

"The twelve days of Christmas are supposed to run from Christmas Day to Epiphany on January 6. I learned that in, like, the fifth grade," Silver said.

"Technically, you're right. And if we wanted to be strict about it, that's the way we would do it, but ending on Christmas Eve is easier and a little more fun."

"What kind of treats do you leave?" Dani asked.

"Small things, like a hand-painted ornament, a Christmas book, a box of candy. Things like that. My mom does all the shopping for it and she assigns Angie one family and me the other one. Since Javi and Mateo both live in Shelter Springs, Mom lets them pick a family close to them to do with their kids now."

"That sounds like a nice tradition," Dani said. Anything that encouraged children to think about others was good, in her book.

"What does this have to do with us?" Silver asked.

"Usually, I tag Zach to help me out with mine but Angie told me tonight his schedule is packed every weeknight and that I couldn't use Andy, either, her middle boy, because he would be busy making *their* Secret Santa deliveries. I need help this year and it occurred to me I know the perfect person to make my deliveries."

"Me? Why would I want to do that?"

"Because you owe him, after what you did to his boat and all the help he gave you yesterday cleaning up your mess," Dani said sharply. "If he wants you to shovel his sidewalk from now until summer, you'll smile politely and say yes."

Silver didn't roll her eyes this time, but she did fold her arms across her chest and give her mother the skunk eye.

"It's not a tough job. You only have to drop off the gift, ring the doorbell, and hide until after they open the door and pick it up."

That caught Silver's attention and Dani could tell she looked intrigued.

"See?" Dani said. "Nothing all that different from what you and your friends used to do back in Boston. Except you never left a present behind."

Her daughter made a face. "We only did that a few times and only to the jerks in the neighborhood."

"There you go," Ruben said. "You've had practice at knock-and-runs already. This will be a piece of cake."

"Who are you giving the presents to?"

"I can only tell you that if you promise to help me. Otherwise I'll be breaching the strict confidentiality agreement."

Silver was silent for several seconds, looking out the window at the snow now fluttering down in big flakes.

"Okay. I guess I'll do it. I don't have much choice, do I?"

Ruben had a hard time not laughing at Silver's glum tone, as if she were being asked to pick between a week in the slammer or being put in stocks for the whole town to taunt.

He was fairly sure he had never been this dramatic when he was thirteen, but then he'd never had to move to a new town and try to make new friends there.

"I wouldn't say you don't have a choice. I can find something else for you to do but it probably wouldn't be as enjoyable. Cleaning out the cages at the clinic would be the first thing that comes to mind."

She groaned. "That's what my mom always makes me do when I'm in trouble."

He glanced at Dani beside him and she shrugged. "Low-hanging fruit. She hates it, so that's what I give her for punishment."

"There you go. We're on the same page. Helping me out with the Secret Santa project might take longer over the long haul—twelve days, compared to a few hours—but it will be much more fun."

"Can I help?" Mia asked. "I can run superfast."

She was the most adorable thing, one of those kids who couldn't help but bring sunshine into the world.

"I'm sure you do. That would be a big help, especially if Silver's legs get tired one night."

"We have to do this for twelve whole nights?"

"It will go by before you know it, don't worry," he assured her. "And you won't have to do it by yourself. I'll take care of some of the nights and maybe I can persuade Zach to come with us a night or two when he doesn't have practice or games."

Ruben hadn't missed the blush Silver wore whenever his handsome nephew was around. He had a feeling there was a crush simmering there, and if he wasn't mistaken, the interest was mutual. He wasn't above using puppy love for his own benefit.

"So you're in, right?"

"Like I said. I don't have much choice," she said, though much of the grumpiness had left her voice, as he had hoped, at the prospect of Zach helping them along the way.

"It will be fun. You'll see. We're taking it to a family that has had some rough times lately. There are four kids in the family including twins around your age."

"Oh?"

"Yeah. Do you know Ella and Emma Larkin?"

She shoved her hands in the pockets of her coat. "Yeah. I know them."

"Then you probably know their mom is in the middle of her second bout of cancer in three years."

Beside him, Dani made a small sound of distress. "Oh, that's terrible. I had no idea the twins' mom was going through that. Sil, why didn't you tell me?"

"How was I supposed to know? It's not like we talk about our moms all the time. Why would we?"

"I suppose that's true enough," Dani said.

"They've had a rough time," Ruben went on. "It can be scary for kids when a parent is sick."

"Yes, it can," Dani said. Her eyes looked haunted for a moment. Had she experienced something similar? Sympathy washed over him. If she had, he hoped she had someone to help her through it.

"My family figured this is a small thing that might help their holidays feel a little brighter while they're struggling. My mom has a way of finding exactly the right people who need a little lift."

"It's a very nice gesture," Dani said.

"So will you do it?"

"Yeah. I'll help you. It's better than cleaning out dog poop," Silver said. "Are we done? Can I go to my room now?"

Dani nodded and Silver disappeared in a flash down the hall, closing her door behind her.

Her mother gazed after the girl, frustration on her lovely features. "That girl. You'd think she'd never been taught manners. A goodbye and thank-you would have been nice."

"Don't be too hard on her. It's a tough age and she's dealing with a lot."

"That's no excuse. You've done so much for her and she should at least show a little gratitude. I'll make sure she does."

Dani was a good mother. She obviously loved her daughters and was doing her best to teach them how to be decent humans.

"And if she doesn't say it, let me. Thank you again for all

your help yesterday and for driving us tonight to join your family. It was a lovely evening."

"You're very welcome." He had enjoyed it, too, far more than he'd expected—in large part because Dani and her daughters had been along.

"We loved the treats, didn't we, Mia?"

"I love churros and chocolate. They're my new favorite thing in the whole world."

"I'm glad you liked it. I'll be sure to tell my mom."

"She's nice. And so is your dad. I wish they were my *abuela* and *abuelo*."

"Mia," Dani said, looking embarrassed. It made him wonder about her family situation. She was so closemouthed about everything. He knew her daughters had a grandmother on their late father's side, but Dani hadn't said anything about her own.

"I think they'd like to adopt you, too."

"Okay," she said happily, then gave a huge, ear-splitting yawn.

"Bedtime for you, missy. Come on. Say good-night to Ruben, then let's get in the tub."

"Good night, Ruben," she said, stealing his heart completely by throwing her arms around his waist. He lifted her up for a better hug then set her back down.

"Night, Miss Mia."

To Dani, he said, "While you're helping her to bed, why don't I straighten out that Christmas tree for you and maybe hang some of the lights?"

He could see the instant refusal leap into her expression.

Was she reluctant to accept *his* help or would she have the same reaction to anyone offering aid? He couldn't be completely sure, though he suspected the former.

"You don't have to do that. I'm sure the girls and I can figure it out tomorrow."

"I promised. I can have a hacksaw and a couple of plywood wedges here in five minutes and be in and out in half an hour."

"Please, Mama?" Mia joined her voice in the plea. "I want to decorate our Christmas tree!"

"Thirty minutes," Ruben pressed.

She gazed down at her daughter then up at him and sighed. "Fine. Thirty minutes. But you're not decorating the tree tonight, young lady. If Ruben hangs the lights, you can put the ornaments on tomorrow after school. Agreed?"

"What if I wake up early tomorrow and do it?" Mia negotiated.

"After school," she said firmly. "Right now it's past your bedtime. You need to jump in the tub and put on your pajamas."

Mia sighed, apparently knowing she had pushed her mother as far as she dared. "Fine."

Dani turned back to him as soon as Mia headed into her room. "You really don't have to do this."

"I want to. Your girls deserve a nice tree and I'm more than happy to help. You could simply say thank you."

"I suppose I can't be too angry with Silver for her lack of gratitude if I don't demonstrate it myself. Thank you. We would be very grateful for your help."

"You're welcome." He smiled. "I'll be back before you know it."

"I'll leave the door unlocked so you don't have to knock, just in case I'm busy with Mia's bath."

"Got it. See you in a minute."

He walked back out into the gently falling snow, unsettled at how relieved he was that the lovely evening and his time with Dani didn't yet have to end.

She did *not* want him in her house.

The entire time Dani helped Mia with her bath, she was aware of Ruben just a few rooms away, almost as if she could smell that spicy, leathery, outdoorsy scent of his soap from here.

How was it possible that his presence managed to fill the entire house? Yes, he was a big man, with strong shoulders and firm muscles. But he was still only one man.

"I'm not brushing my teeth with that!" Mia exclaimed suddenly, and Dani realized with chagrin that she had just squeezed hand lotion from the pump bottle in the bathroom onto Mia's toothbrush instead of the kids' toothpaste.

"Oh, man. I'm sorry. Well, I guess it was time for a new toothbrush anyway." She pulled one from the bottom drawer of the vanity where she kept a few extras and unboxed one for her daughter.

"It's purple! My favorite color! Thanks. You're the best mama ever."

If only. Silver would certainly not agree. Her older

daughter thought she was harsh and unfeeling, with arbitrary rules and unrealistic expectations.

Every mother needed a child like Mia in her life, though—one who saw the very best in her and was willing to overlook her mistakes and screwups. She prayed her daughter never grew out of this phase.

"And you're the very best Mia a mama could ever have," she said.

Mia threw her arms around Dani's neck, her hair wet and smelling of cherries from her shampoo.

"And Silver is the best Silver a mama could have, too, right?"

"That's exactly right," she answered. It was a good reminder. Yes, her older daughter was going through things. As Ruben said, this was a tough age and Dani had thrown her into a hard situation at the very same time she lost her father in a violent manner. They would get through it. She just had to remember the days when Silver was as sweet and loving as Mia.

"Can I go see the Christmas tree? I wonder if Ruben is done yet."

"Since that was the fastest bath on record and he had to go home to get some supplies, I highly doubt it's done, but you can go check the status."

While Mia raced out of the room, Dani took her time wiping up the water, putting away bath toys, cleaning the toothpaste off the sink.

She was stalling, she acknowledged, afraid to face Ruben again. She had a ridiculous crush on the man and was going to have to do something about it. She had no idea what that might be, though.

Finally she could avoid it no longer and made herself walk into the living room where she found the lights dimmed and Mia in one of Ruben's arms. She was gazing at the tree, her eyes soft with wonder.

"Look, Mama," Mia whispered when Dani walked into the room. "We have the most beautiful tree in the whole wide world."

Ruben's gaze met hers and Dani had to catch her breath at the expression in them, soft amusement and a warm tenderness.

"Don't you think it's beautiful?" Mia asked.

One would think they had never had a Christmas tree before. Maybe there was something special about this one, a sweet-smelling little pine in their new house beside a lake. Or maybe Mia was simply excited to have Ruben there.

"It is lovely. Look how straight you were able to get it. And I can't believe you hung all those lights already. That didn't take nearly as long as I would have expected."

"You picked a great tree."

"Except for the spindly trunk."

"Nothing's perfect," he said with a grin. "Other than that, this one is the right height and the branches aren't too thick. That made it much easier to string the lights. I'm not quite done. There's one more string I'd like to use for filling in the empty spots."

"It looks beautiful to me. Thank you."

"My pleasure." When he smiled at her like that, she forgot she had earned a doctorate of veterinary medicine. She forgot she was a single mother of two children and felt as if she were screwing up at every turn. She forgot about the fact that his father held her future in his hands and that ruining this opportunity Frank Morales had given her would be a disaster for her and her daughters.

Nothing else seemed to matter except the thick surge of blood in her veins, the butterflies suddenly swarming in her stomach, her overwhelming awareness of him.

She cleared her throat, appalled at herself. "Mia, now that you've seen the Christmas tree, you really do need to get to sleep. Tell Ruben good-night one more time, then head in."

Mia sighed and rested her cheek against his shoulder for a moment, as if she didn't want to leave him, either.

"Good night, Mia," he said.

"Okay. Good night." Mia threw her arms around his neck and hugged him, then kissed his cheek. "Thank you for putting the twinkly lights on my Christmas tree. It's the most beautiful thing I've ever seen."

"You're very welcome. I'll see you later."

The poor man looked completely enamored and Dani supposed she couldn't blame him. Mia had a great deal of her father's charm when she wanted to use it. The little girl smiled at him, waved and hurried out of the room.

"I need to tuck her in," she said. "You said you are almost done?"

"Yeah. It won't take me long to hang that last string. I can let myself out, if you have to help Mia with her bedtime routine."

"Thank you again for everything."

"I'm glad to help," he assured her with another smile that made her hurry down the hall to the girls' bedrooms with her heart pounding as if she'd never seen a gorgeous man smile.

In Mia's room, she read her daughter a short bedtime story and listened while she said her prayers.

"I sure like Deputy Ruben," Mia said sleepily when she finished.

Dani did, too. Entirely too much. "He's very nice, isn't he?"

"Why doesn't he have any little girls?"

That was an excellent question. Why hadn't the smart women of Haven Point snapped up a gorgeous, kind man like him years ago?

"I guess because he's not as lucky as I am," Dani said. She kissed her daughter on the forehead. "Good night, sweetie."

"Tomorrow, I get to decorate the tree," Mia said, already half-asleep.

"Yes, you do."

"I can't wait."

Dani couldn't help feeling a little envious as she left the room with Mia still smiling about the prospect. How long had it been since she treated each new day like an adventure?

She did love her job. Working with animals had always been her refuge, from the time before her mother got sick. She used to hide any stray cat and dog she found in her room, smuggling in food to it and making little beds on the floor.

Her mom would always find out and would shake her head.

"I'm sorry, but we can't keep it, *cara mia*," Sofia Capelli would say. "You know the rules about animals in the apartment and we can't afford to be evicted."

The two of them would take the subway to the nearest shelter, where Dani would say goodbye, then cry all the way back to their apartment.

That love for animals had sustained her through what she called in her head the "foster care years." In several of her placements, the families had pets, much to her delight. For reasons she couldn't fully explain, they always seemed to gravitate to Dani.

In her experience, animals could have amazing emotional instincts, sensing where they were needed most. Maybe they could tell she was bruised by life, lonely, afraid, and needed the steady, uncomplicated love of a dog or a cat.

Regardless, she loved caring for them and would always end up taking over responsibility for feeding them and cleaning up after them.

It had always been harder to say goodbye to the animals in each foster care placement than it had the people, even those who were kind to her.

Loving animals and having a calming way with them had led her to getting a part-time job in high school at that same shelter where she and her mother used to drop off the strays she gathered. Every day when she would take the subway, she would remember those trips with Sofia and miss her mother with a sharp, piercing ache.

She pushed away the memories. She no longer wallowed in self-pity, as she might have done when she was Silver's age.

Yes, her mom had died when she was a kid and she had ended up in foster care. That truly sucked. She had caught a bad break, like millions of other kids who found themselves in a similar situation, but she still had managed to create a good life for herself and her daughters.

Silver's bedroom light was out, she could see by the dark crack under the door, but Dani decided to say good-night anyway. She pushed open the door and, in the small glow from Silver's retro alarm clock picked up at a thrift store in Boston, she could see her daughter's hair and a pale blur of skin.

Silver shifted her gaze sleepily toward the door. "What do you want?" she asked, belligerence still threading through her voice.

Dani sighed. "Just checking on you. Do you need anything?"

"No," her daughter said after a moment, her tone a little less abrasive.

"Good night, then," Dani said softly. "I love you, Silverbell."

"Love you, too," Silver whispered, and Dani had to swallow away the emotions at those rare words that felt like a gift.

When she returned to the hallway, she assumed Ruben had finished and left already, until she heard the low murmur of a man's voice coming from the living room as Ruben said something to Winky.

She caught a hint of his outdoorsy soap above the overwhelming pine scent from the tree and she stood for a moment, eyes closed, trying to ignore the sudden jittery ache inside her.

She could do this. She only had to make it through saying good-night to him, then she could close the door behind him and do her best to push the man out of her head as easily as she did out of her house.

After sucking in a deep breath, she made her way to the living room, where she found Ruben on the sofa, winding an unused strand of lights around a plastic organizer that must have been inside the box from his father.

He had turned all the lights off so that only the Christmas tree glowed in the room, a kaleidoscope of colors gleaming against the walls and reflected in the window.

He smiled when he caught sight of her. "Nice, isn't it?"

"It's beautiful," she admitted, oddly emotional at the sight—or maybe at his kindness in helping put it up for her daughters.

"I feel as awestruck as Mia right now," she said. "There's something so magical about a Christmas tree, especially the first night or two when it feels new again but somehow familiar."

"Agreed. To me, a beautiful Christmas tree like this one represents hope and peace and the wonder of the season."

"Yet you still don't have one of your own."

"I can appreciate the beauty of something even when it's not mine."

She smiled, moving closer to the tree. "In a week or so,

I'll be tired of the needles and the sap and bored with having to water it every day, but right now I will simply enjoy it."

He gestured to the sofa beside him. She hesitated, everything inside her telling her it would be a bad idea, considering this awareness she couldn't seem to fight. She gave a mental shrug. She could live a little dangerously for a few more moments. Besides, she had something she needed to say to him and now seemed the perfect opportunity.

She sat next to him, aware of the heat coming from him. "I've been looking back across the last few days," she said slowly, not meeting his gaze, "and I have the sinking suspicion that, like Silver, I probably haven't acted as...grateful to you as I should have."

"For what it's worth, I don't have that impression at all."

She sighed. He was trying to be nice and she couldn't take the easy way out. Not when she was trying to teach the same lessons about expressing gratitude to her children.

"It's not easy for me, accepting help. You probably figured that out by now."

She finally dared to look at him in time to catch a slow, sweet smile that made her swallow hard.

"I may have had a hint or two," he drawled.

"I'm sorry. It's an ingrained reflex."

"Like Pavlov's dogs?"

She made a face at his reference to the classic psychological experiment. "Something like that. I've had to do most things on my own on and off for most of my girls' lives. Their father was...not around much."

She didn't tell him why, that the man she had married

the day before her eighteenth birthday had spent most of their married life in prison and that even after he came out, he couldn't wean himself away from the life.

"I've had to learn how to do everything, from fixing the garbage disposal to changing oil in my cars to setting up the Christmas tree."

"Seems like you've done a pretty good job so far."

For some reason, his words hit her hard. Dani thought of all her insecurities, all the lonely nights she sat up worrying for her daughters, all the things she couldn't give them, all the mistakes and fears and sorrows she couldn't heal.

She thought of the nights over the last three months where Silver had cried herself to sleep over her father, and her fear the time Mia had influenza, and the loneliness that sometimes had her tossing and turning in bed, longing for something that hadn't been part of her life in years.

Couldn't he see she was a disaster, barely holding the pieces of her life together?

"Sure. That's me. Totally in control. No problems here."

She laughed a little hysterically. The sound horrified her and she tried to cover her mouth with her hand but a sob escaped anyway.

"Are you okay?" he asked, setting aside the light string he had been holding.

"I..." She couldn't lie. Not to him and not to herself.

In the end, she didn't need to. He reached for her and, like Mia had earlier, she sank into the safety of his arms and the undeniable comfort of that wide, capable chest.

How long had it been since someone had offered to take

on her burdens, if only for a moment? It felt incredible to push them out of her mind and lay them down for now.

Another sob escaped and then another and before she knew it, her shoulders were shaking as she let out all the stress and turmoil that had been haunting her since the night he had brought Silver over with red spray paint on her hands.

Since much, much longer, if she were honest.

She couldn't have said how long she cried against him while the tree lights sparkled against the window and Winky snored softly at their feet. She couldn't have even said exactly why she was crying. It didn't really matter, she supposed, as reason intruded again and she came back to the reality that she was snuggled against Ruben, practically on his lap, and had just let him see a vulnerability she hid so carefully from the rest of the world. Even from herself.

She sniffled one last time, her breathing ragged, then pulled away slightly, too embarrassed to meet his gaze. "I can't believe I just completely lost it and blubbered all over your shirt. Can we just pretend the last few moments never happened?"

"If that would make you feel better."

She was not one of those lucky women who cried prettily, with delicate, diamond-shaped teardrops leaking out from under their perfect eyelashes.

When Dani cried, her nose ran, her skin went splotchy, her eyes turned as red-rimmed as Christmas ornaments.

"I don't think anything could make me feel better right now." There was a box of tissues on the side table, left there from the last time Mia had a cold when Dani had scattered them all over the house for her, and she reached for it gratefully, dabbing at her face even though she knew nothing she did would help fix what was likely a hideous mess.

"I never lose it like that. Ever. I can't remember the last time I cried."

"Then you were overdue," he said, with such kindness in his voice that she almost started up all over again.

"You must think I'm an idiot."

"I think you're a woman doing her best to raise two girls, trying to make a new life in a new town. I'm surprised you haven't had a dozen breakdowns since you came to Haven Point."

"I'll admit to three or four small ones, after the girls are in bed."

"If that's all, then I would say you're doing fine."

She didn't necessarily agree. If she was doing fine and things were going well, her daughter wouldn't have felt compelled to damage the property of three of their new neighbors.

Still, she appreciated his efforts to make her feel better.

"You're a very nice man, Deputy Morales. I imagine in your line of work you get plenty of experience dealing with irrational people."

"Sometimes. But there's a difference between being irrational and being emotionally exhausted and justifiably stressed. In my professional opinion, you fall in the latter category. There's no shame in needing someone to hold you once in a while."

She was in deep, deep danger of falling hard for this man. How in the world was she supposed to prevent it, when he could be so very sweet?

"Well, thank you. I appreciate you being so understanding."

"Anytime."

He spoke the word gruffly and she gazed at him, that hunger from earlier swirling back.

It had never really left, she realized.

If it felt so good to be held by him, how wonderful would it feel to kiss him?

One little kiss. What could that hurt?

She didn't give herself time to answer, only leaned forward to close the space between them and kissed the corner of his mouth. She told herself it was done only in gratitude, a small, rather insignificant gesture to let him know she appreciated all he had done for her family over the past few days and especially for doing his best to help her not feel like an idiot for the last few moments.

The moment her mouth touched warm male skin, however, she knew that for a lie. She was kissing him because she wanted to kiss him. Because she wanted *him*.

Ruben froze for only an instant and the moment seemed crystallized in time, like a pretty snow globe ornament hanging on the tree, then he shifted his mouth and kissed her fiercely, urgently, as if he had been waiting weeks for just this moment.

She hadn't been with a man since her divorce and only now did she admit how very much she had missed this surge of her blood, the catch in her breathing, the ache deep inside.

Everything she had so carefully stored away inside her after her marriage fell apart came roaring back, all her needs and hungers and aches.

His mouth was warm, firm, and she tasted hints of thick, rich chocolate and cinnamon sugar.

If she thought a woman could get drunk on the smell of his mother's kitchen, the taste of those same delicious flavors on his mouth against hers was a thousand times better.

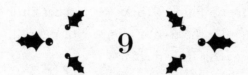

9

She didn't want the kiss to end.

It was magical, delicious, like a hundred dreams come true wrapped up in one heated embrace.

With the snow fluttering down outside and the Christmas tree lights gleaming beside them, the moment seemed perfect. Better than she ever could have imagined.

He didn't seem to want things to end, either. His mouth was fierce on hers, as if he couldn't get enough, and she could feel his racing pulse, his ragged breathing.

She had a wild urge to lead him down the hall to her bedroom, to keep kissing him—and more—all night, but she could never do that with her girls in the house. They risked disaster here, kissing in the front room where Silver or Mia might walk in on them at any moment.

The reminder of her daughters cast a shadow over the kiss, a shadow that darkened further when she felt a pressure against her leg that didn't feel quite right.

Her mouth still tangled with Ruben's, she shifted her gaze down and found Winky resting her chin on Dani's knee, watching the two of them with interest. They had an audience. Her little dog.

That was the distraction she needed, the one that effectively snapped her out of the heated embrace and back to reality.

She should *not* be doing this, kissing Ruben Morales as if her life depended on it.

What was she thinking?

Yes, he was a kind man. Big deal. She didn't need a kind man right now. She didn't need *any* man, but especially not *this* one, a law enforcement officer and her boss's son.

If she wanted a life for her daughters here in Haven Point, she needed to make it through this yearlong internship. She couldn't allow anything to threaten that. She especially couldn't let down her guard around Ruben.

She couldn't be foolish enough to think she might actually have a future with a man like him. Why would he want someone who had her history of poor judgment, who had been naive and stupid enough to marry a man capable of Tommy's crimes and have not one, but two children with him?

If Ruben knew the truth about Dani and her past, he wouldn't want her anywhere near him or his family.

That didn't change the fact that *she* wanted *him*, that she wanted to stay right here nestled against his hard chest and broad shoulders, where the past and her own mistakes seemed far enough away that they couldn't hurt her.

She sighed. The past always had a way of painting the present with its own ugly brush.

She pulled away, painfully aware of Ruben's ragged breathing, his dilated pupils.

"That was…"

The aroused rasp in his voice rippled down her spine but she firmly ignored it. "Not supposed to happen. I know. I think we're both acting a little irrationally tonight."

"Speak for yourself, Dr. Capelli. I knew exactly what I was doing."

What did he mean by *that*? She couldn't seem to make her brain cooperate enough to figure it out. Her face felt hot, her skin tight, her nerves as frayed as Winky's favorite blanket.

"Then you have to know that was a mistake. I shouldn't have… We shouldn't have… Oh. This is the most embarrassing night of my life."

He stopped her words by the simple yet profound gesture of grabbing her hand. "Would it make any difference if I told you I've been wanting to do that since you moved to town?"

Her fingers trembled in his. "You have not."

"I'm an officer of the law, Doc. I always speak the truth."

She managed to hold back a snort. "I don't believe that's a job requirement for any law enforcement officer I've ever met."

"Well, I'm sorry for that. In this case, I mean everything I say. You might as well know it. I've wanted to kiss you since we met. I'm afraid now that I've done it, I'm only going to want to kiss you more."

He might tell the truth all the time. She, on the other hand, was not only the ex-wife of a man who had been a convicted felon and worse, but she had been a juvenile delinquent in her own right when she had been a wild, angry foster kid lashing out at the world.

She had no such compunction toward honesty, especially when so very much depended on him believing her lie.

"Let's both do our best to forget what just happened. Tonight has been…strange, to say the least."

She rose, hoping against hope that he would get the hint. Dani was suddenly desperate for him to go. She needed time to figure out what had just happened here, how she could have been so stupid as to let him under her defenses, even for a moment.

To her relief, he rose as well and stood watching her for a long moment, the Christmas lights reflected in his eyes.

"I'm afraid I won't be able to forget the taste of you anytime soon," he said, his voice rough, and she had to curl her hands into fists against the urge to wrap them around his neck and go for round two.

What kind of masochistic fool was she?

"I'm afraid you'll just have to be content with your memories, Deputy Morales, because it won't happen again."

"Coming from any other woman, I would consider such a bold statement something of a challenge."

"I am not any other woman. I mean what I say."

Though her voice sounded firm enough, she wondered if he could see her hands tremble. With any luck, it was so dark in here, lit only by the Christmas tree, that he wouldn't have a clue.

To her vast relief, he seemed to take her words at face value. "You do know how to wound a man, don't you? I'll remind you that you kissed me first."

"I know. I shouldn't have."

"Why did you?"

She didn't have an answer for that, at least not one she understood herself.

"It doesn't matter. I'm grateful for all you've done this weekend. It was very kind of you to help us clean up the graffiti yesterday and to invite us to your sister's concert and your family party afterward, and I appreciate you letting me make a fool of myself by crying all over you tonight. Let's just say I let my emotions get the better of me."

His expression told her plainly that he didn't believe her but he didn't press. "Are you still willing to let Silver and Mia help me with the Secret Santa project?"

She had a feeling it would be in all of their best interests to restore a careful distance between her little family and Ruben Morales but she had already told him Silver would help.

She couldn't avoid him. They lived next door to each

other and his father was her boss. She tried for a casual tone, hoping to restore things to a more stable footing. "We're both adults here. Things don't have to be...awkward because we shared one little kiss, do they?"

He gave a rough laugh. "Again, you do know how to wound a man."

She wanted to tell him she didn't consider the kiss little, that it had rocked everything secure and safe in her world. She couldn't, of course, so she said nothing.

"Fine," he said after a moment. "If you're still good with Silver helping out, we'll start the Secret Santa campaign on the evening of the thirteenth. As soon as I figure out what time will work, I'll let you and Silver know."

"I'll have her ready. Thank you."

He gazed at her, his expression unreadable. He looked as if he wanted to say something more but he finally sighed. "Good night, then," he said.

"Good night."

He grabbed his coat off the back of the armchair, gave Winky one last pat, then headed out into the snow.

She closed the door behind him and fought the urge to sag against it, desperate for a moment to regain her composure. Instead, she made herself go into the kitchen to replace Winky's water and add a little more kibble to the bowl.

The dog deserved a big, juicy bone. If not for Winky, Dani might have let things go much further and made a terrible mistake.

She had to keep her distance from Ruben, no matter how difficult. The stakes were too great. After tonight and that heated kiss, she could no longer deny this attraction simmering between them. It wasn't only one-sided, that much was obvious. If she gave in to it, if she explored this heat and hunger between them, the results could be disastrous.

She had spent the last three days talking to Silver about how each action had consequences. It was an important lesson for Dani as well, one she couldn't afford to forget.

He couldn't get that kiss out of his head.

As Ruben pulled up in front of the veterinary clinic the following Thursday afternoon, he was uncomfortably aware of his sweaty palms and the low ache of anticipation curling through him.

He couldn't remember the last time a woman had left him so tied up in knots.

That kiss had haunted his dreams. *Dani* had haunted his dreams. Each time he closed his eyes, it seemed as if she was waiting for him, with her vulnerable eyes and her secrets and the sweetness she tried to conceal beneath a thin, crackly veneer of stiff reserve.

She worked so hard to hold herself apart. Why? Was it self-protectiveness on her part? What was she trying to hide?

He had stayed away as long as he could manage, until the need to see her again became too overwhelming, and so he had finally manufactured an excuse to see her again.

Now, as he sat in his patrol vehicle on his lunch hour, he wondered what the hell was wrong with him. She had made it clear she didn't want anything more than friendship with him, so why couldn't he manage to get her out of his head?

He was here now. He might as well go in and talk to her. That anticipation grew stronger as he climbed out of his vehicle and headed inside the clinic.

The reception area was empty except for Gloria McCoy, his dad's longtime receptionist. She smiled broadly when she spotted him. "Hey, Ruben honey. How are you?"

"Good. Good."

Gloria probably didn't need to know he hadn't slept well since Sunday because of a certain doctor of veterinary medicine who was somewhere in this very clinic right now.

He leaned on the reception counter. "How are you? How's your family?"

"Oh, you know. Hanging in there. Randy's wife is having my third grandbaby in a couple weeks."

"Oh, congratulations."

"And my Jen broke up with her boyfriend. Good riddance, I say. He was no good."

Her oldest daughter, Jen, was a few years younger than Ruben. Though she had grown into a lovely woman, he still always saw her as the pigtailed brat who used to throw snowballs at him and once rear-ended him in the school parking lot a few weeks after she got her driver's license.

"I saw her a few weeks ago at the hospital when I had to take an inmate at the jail in for an X-ray. She's a radiology technician, right? Does she enjoy it?"

"She loves it. She makes a good living, too." Gloria's features suddenly turned crafty. "Now that she's available again and has come to her senses, you may want to think about asking her out. She always had a little crush on you, you know."

He *hadn't* known that—and now he wished she had never told him. Jen probably wouldn't appreciate her mother spilling that particular can of beans. Ruben wasn't sure how comfortable he would be joking around with Jen, the next time he had to take an inmate in for medical care.

"I'll, uh, keep that in mind."

"You do that." Gloria beamed at him and Ruben shifted uncomfortably. He liked Jen but had never been particularly interested in her romantically—unlike a certain other woman he could name.

"If you're looking for your dad, he's not in today. You'll remember, this is one of his regular days off, since the new doc came. I think he and your mom were going Christmas shopping in Boise. Your mom said she needed another present for your brother's girl. Esme, right?"

Gloria always seem to know more about his family goings-on than Ruben did. "That's right. Thanks, but I'm actually not here for my dad. I was hoping to catch Dr. Capelli, unless she's gone home for her lunch hour."

Gloria gestured vaguely to the back rooms of the veterinary clinic. "That one rarely takes a lunch hour, unless her girls are out of school. You're more likely to find her eating a brown-bag lunch while she walks one of the dogs or cuddles a cat."

He couldn't discern from Gloria's tone what she thought about that behavior. He pictured Dani doing both those things and found the image rather adorable.

It suddenly occurred to Ruben that Gloria would likely be an incredibly helpful fount of information about the new veterinarian. She had worked with her since Dani came to town and Gloria wasn't known for being subtle about probing for information about a person.

She probably knew more about Dani than anyone else in Haven Point—including Ruben's dad.

He had dozens of questions he wanted to ask, but they all caught in his throat. He couldn't interrogate his father's nosy office manager, no matter how tempting. That would be inappropriate and intrusive. Right?

"Could you let her know I'm here?" he said instead.

"I'm waiting on a phone call from an insurance company. Do you mind just going on back and finding her? I imagine she's either in her office or in the treatment area. In case you didn't know, her office is right next to your father's."

"Thanks."

He went through the double doors leading from the reception-waiting area to the treatment rooms and offices. The door next to his father's office was open and the light was on but when Ruben poked his head inside, he found it empty. Down the hall, he could hear crooning, a sweet alto voice singing a Christmas carol.

He paused for a moment, enjoying the impromptu concert. Who would have guessed Dani Capelli sang Christmas music? She had a beautiful voice, too. Something gentle and tender unfurled in his chest as he paused there in the hallway. For all her sharp edges, this confirmed his suspicion that Dani was a softy at heart.

He received further proof when he walked farther down the hall to the doorway of the treatment room where animals were kept for observation postsurgery or if they were ill.

Dani sat on the floor in front of one of the cages that lined the wall. In her arms was the biggest bunny Ruben had ever seen, a soft gray with ears that flopped down. She was singing "Away in a Manger" and the rabbit seemed to be enjoying every note.

He had to smile. The woman was making it damn hard to resist her.

She didn't notice him at first, but continued singing to the creature. Ruben wondered for a moment if he ought to slip back out. He didn't want to scare Dani and, in turn, scare the creature.

He waited too long to decide, however. She must have sensed his presence, because she paused in her singing, looked up and gave a little gasp that did indeed have the rabbit jolting in her lap.

"Easy. Easy," she said, in a low, soothing voice that did ridiculous things to Ruben's insides. "I've got you, baby. I've got you."

In one graceful movement, she rose with the huge bunny in her arms and placed him back inside the largest of the cages. "There you go," she said in that same soothing tone, before closing the cage door and turning to face Ruben.

"Sorry I startled you." Taking his cue from her, he kept his voice low, unthreatening.

She moved closer. "It's not me you need to worry about. Cecil can be fierce."

"I'm assuming Cecil is the giant killer bunny."

"Not a killer. He's a particularly big French lop who had a little run-in with a bull terrier yesterday when he was out for a walk with his owner. I think Cecil is still suffering a little PTSD."

Ruben fought a smile, not sure why he found that amusing. Poor bunny. "How's he doing now?"

"Better. He should be ready to return to his family in another day or two."

"That's good. Who wants to be without their giant bunny at Christmastime?"

She made a face as she led him out of the room and into the hallway. "Your father's not here. He and your mother went Christmas shopping in Boise."

"That's what I hear. I'm not looking for my father, though."

"Oh?" He was almost positive he saw her blush. Her gaze danced to his mouth then quickly away and Ruben was instantly hot.

She remembered their kiss as well. He was certain of it.

"Have you had lunch? I was thinking about running over to Serrano's to grab a bite."

She looked briefly tempted, then shook her head. "I can't. I'm sorry. I have appointments scheduled again in twenty minutes."

"Another time, maybe. I should have asked in advance." It was a spur-of-the-moment invitation anyway.

"Guess I'll run home and grab a sandwich, then," he said.

She started to nibble her bottom lip then seemed to catch herself. "I have a turkey sandwich in my office. You can share it with me, if you want."

After more than a decade in law enforcement, few things had the power to astonish him anymore. Dani's lunch invitation would now top that list, especially after the way she had left things between them Sunday night. "That's very sweet of you. Thanks. I would love to take you up on it."

Looking as if she regretted saying anything, she went to the sink to wash her hands, then led the way back to her office. She gestured to the visitor chair before pulling a small insulated lunch bag out of a minirefrigerator in her office. The bag was decorated in vivid orange and pink flowers, offering a bright little spot of femininity in the otherwise clinical office.

She reached into the bag and emerged with a hoagie sandwich then handed him half.

"All I have to drink are water bottles. Do you mind?"

"It's perfect. I'm on duty anyway."

She handed him a cold one from the refrigerator, grabbed one for herself, then opened the cap and took a long drink.

"Thanks for this," he said. "I probably would have ended up buying fast food before I head back to Shelter Springs. This is a much healthier option."

"You're welcome. Oh, I have hummus and some vegetable sticks, too, if you want"

"Thanks. You're too generous."

She shrugged. "I always make too much lunch and end up wasting half of it."

He chewed a delicious bite, flavored with exactly the right ratio of mustard to mayonnaise, took a swig of his water bottle, then set down the water bottle, reminding himself he needed to get to the matter at hand.

"I really didn't come here for free lunch, I promise."

"I know."

"While this is delicious, I actually stopped by because today is the thirteenth."

She gave him a blank look for a moment before her confusion gave way to understanding. "Oh. Right. The Secret Santa project."

"According to my mother's long-standing tradition, we need to start giving out the gifts for the twelve days of Christmas today if we want to wrap things up by Christmas Eve. Are you still okay with Mia and Silver helping out?"

"I don't think I could stop that particular train now, even if I wanted to," she said ruefully. "They're planning on it. Mia, especially, is excited to help. She's talked about it every day since Sunday night."

Again, her cheeks suddenly seemed to turn a dusky rose and she avoided looking at him, focusing on the sandwich in front of her.

Was she remembering what else had happened Sunday night? He suspected so but couldn't be sure.

He certainly was remembering their kiss, especially when she nibbled on her delectable bottom lip again.

He wanted to be the one doing that.

Memories of those delicious few moments they had spent in her darkened living room pushed to the front of his mind. Her soft curves wrapped around him, her mouth sweet and eager against his, the soft, surprising peace he had found with her in his arms.

Too bad he also recalled so clearly what she had said afterward: *I'm afraid you'll just have to be content with your memories, Deputy Morales, because it won't happen again.*

She didn't want to kiss him again. He would have to be content with that. Something told him Dani needed a friend and if that was all she wanted from him, he would do his best to respect her wishes, no matter how tough that was to remember—especially when she was sweet enough to offer him half of her lunch.

"It should be fun for them," he said, returning to the real reason he told himself he was here in her office, to discuss the gift deliveries that night. "I'm not as fast as I used to be and it's become increasingly harder for a guy my size to hide behind a tree."

Her gaze danced over his chest and shoulders and, if he wasn't mistaken, she swallowed. "I imagine that's true."

"What time works best for you? I thought I would pick them up around six thirty tonight but I wouldn't want to interrupt your dinner or homework routine. I can adapt, if another time would be better."

"We usually eat dinner early to give the girls time to finish any homework. Six thirty should work fine."

"Do you want to come with us?" he asked on impulse. "When I do this with Zach, I usually drop him off a short distance away from the house we're hitting, then park around the corner or on the next block, where my vehicle isn't as suspicious. While Silver makes the delivery, you and Mia can wait with me, if you'd like."

"That might not be a bad idea, at least for the first night."

"Terrific. I'll pick everybody up, then."

He took another drink from the water bottle, touched again that she would be so unexpectedly generous with her lunch when she could be so prickly at other times.

"How's the Christmas tree?" he asked.

She gave a little laugh. "Completely over-the-top. You'll have to take a look when you come by tonight. I don't think there's a single branch that doesn't have an ornament or two on it. Mia went a little crazy."

"She's a great kid. You're very lucky."

"Believe me, I know." She took a bite of her sandwich, giving him a pensive look. "Why are you still single, Ruben? Seriously. You're great with kids and close to your own family. You're gorgeous—that goes without saying—have a good job and appear to have all your teeth. What am I missing?"

He shifted, not sure he registered anything after the word *gorgeous*. Both of them knew he wasn't. Inside, he still felt like the skinny Mexican kid who had been gangly and awkward in high school and didn't grow into his height until after college.

"I don't have a good answer to that. I was almost engaged about seven years ago, until we both realized we were together because it was convenient, not because of any grand passion. She's happily married now and has a couple of kids. I've dated on and off since then, somebody pretty seriously about six months ago, but nothing ever really clicked." He shrugged. "Maybe family life isn't in the cards for me."

The thought left him sad. He was thirty-three and was tired of coming home to a house filled only with his dogs, as much as he loved Ollie and Yukon.

At the same time, he wouldn't settle, not after the great example he had growing up of a loving, supportive family, with two parents who still adored each other.

"What about you? Do you see yourself marrying again?"

She suddenly looked as if she regretted bringing up the topic. "Been there, done that."

"You mentioned the girls' father is dead. I'm sorry."

She set down her sandwich. "Don't be. Mia and Silver are better off without Tommy. He broke their hearts, again and again. We had been divorced for years before he...died a few months ago."

It was recent, then. He hadn't expected that. He didn't miss the way she carefully phrased the sentence. What were the circumstances of his death? There was definitely a story there, one he wanted very much to learn.

He wanted to press her but was afraid now wasn't the time. She had clients coming in soon and he had to get back to work as well.

"I'm sorry," he said again. "Sounds like the guy was a lousy father, but it still couldn't have been easy on the girls to lose him at such young ages."

"They're doing fine. Mia never really knew him. Silver

struggles more, but I think she's mostly mourning the father she *should* have had, not the one she did."

"I get it." That didn't make the girl's grief any less intense, he was sure. No wonder Silver lashed out by vandalizing the neighbors' property. Compassion seeped through him.

"He...wasn't a good man, I'm sorry to say. My girls both deserved a father like you had. Someone like Frank, kind and caring," she said, mouth tight. "Unfortunately, that's not the kind of man I picked."

She blamed herself. He could hear the self-recrimination in her voice. It bothered him, made him wish he knew how to comfort her.

"Nobody makes it through this ride called life without making choices he or she regrets," Ruben said quietly.

She gave a raw-sounding little laugh and finally met his gaze. "True enough. You know, when I offered to share my sandwich, I didn't realize I would be rewarded with a bit of wise philosophy."

"It's on the house. Just my little way of repaying you for the food."

Her rueful smile seemed to arrow straight to his heart.

Her late ex-husband sounded like a royal bastard. Was he the reason Dani was so guarded, why she maintained such careful barriers between them? It seemed the logical conclusion. Ruben was angry on her behalf, both for the previous mistreatment and for the way her ex seemed to have left her bruised.

"Thank you," she said. "I enjoyed the philosophy *and* the

company. It's nice to eat lunch with someone who doesn't have four legs and a tail."

Before he could respond, Gloria appeared in the doorway. She looked startled to find them both there together. He had the feeling by her sudden dark look that she wasn't particularly pleased about it.

"Sorry to interrupt, Dr. Capelli, but your one o'clock is here. That Chihuahua with the runs."

Dani winced a little and set down the rest of her sandwich, from which she had maybe taken three total bites. "Thank you, Gloria. I'll be right out."

The receptionist headed back to the front office and Dani gave him an apologetic look. "Sorry about that. Gloria isn't always the most tactful person."

"You don't have to tell me that. She's worked for my dad since I was a kid. I know just what she's like."

"Of course." She rose and he had no choice but to do the same.

"Thanks for sharing your sandwich. I don't know when I've enjoyed a lunch more."

"So did I." She paused, nibbling that lip again. "Ruben, I..."

He had a feeling she was about to tell him all the reasons they shouldn't share lunch—or anything else—again. He didn't want to hear it, so he cut her off. "I'll see you tonight for the top-secret project."

"I... All right. Six thirty."

She suddenly looked so adorably flustered, so unlike her

usual reserved composure, he couldn't help himself. He leaned down and kissed the corner of her frown.

"Have a good afternoon," he murmured, then turned and walked down the hall already counting the moments until he could see her again.

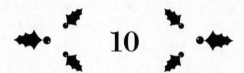

10

For the rest of the afternoon, Dani refused to let herself dwell on the strange interlude with Ruben or the weird, incongruous combination she felt around him, a mix of nervous awareness and a soft, seductive peace.

She was too busy taking care of the Chihuahua with abdominal distress, a black Lab who needed some porcupine quills pulled, Cecil the traumatized lop bunny and three Maine coons in need of checkups.

By the time she showed out her last patient and his human, she was exhausted. She finished her paperwork, grabbed her bag, put on her coat against the December chill and walked out to the waiting area to say goodbye to Gloria.

"That was a crazy afternoon. Thank you for helping everything to run smoothly. I don't know what I would have done without you."

"You're welcome." Gloria reached to shut down her computer for the evening, then returned a couple of files to the drawer to clear off her desk.

"Good thing you found time for a lunch break in there," she said. "By the way, I didn't realize you and Dr. Morales's son were such good friends."

There was a slight question on the end of her words, as if Gloria were trying to ascertain just how friendly the two were.

"We live next door to each other. It's impossible to avoid each other in a town as small as Haven Point."

"I suppose that's true." She paused. "He's a good guy, Dr. Capelli."

"I agree," she said, not liking Gloria's tone or her own defensive reaction to it. Why was it any of Gloria's business if Dani was friends with Dr. Morales's son?

"He's always been a hard worker, even when he was a kid who would come around here to make extra spending money. I thought maybe he would become a veterinarian like his dad, he was that good with the animals, but he had other ideas I guess."

"Kids often do."

"He's a good guy," she repeated. "I sure would hate to see him get hurt."

Was Gloria warning her away from Ruben? The idea would have been laughable if it wasn't so astonishing.

"Are you saying you think I would hurt him? Why would I do that?"

"I don't know. Maybe you'll decide things aren't working out for you here and you need to go back to the East Coast."

Did *Gloria* believe what she said, that things weren't working out here for Dani? All her doubts and insecurities seemed to crowd through her psyche, all the voices that told her she was better off staying a waitress instead of thinking she could ever build a solid future for her daughters doing something she loved.

"I appreciate the advice. I'll keep it in mind," she said stiffly.

She had thought Gloria liked her. The woman had been kind to her and was always more than patient with the girls. It hurt to know she questioned Dani's staying power.

"You should be relieved to know, then," she said, still in that tight voice, "that I'm not dating the man and I have no intention of changing that. Put your mind at ease. We're friends who happened to have lunch together today, that's all."

At her tone, Gloria looked regretful. "That didn't come out the way I meant. Sometimes my mouth blabs things before I really think them through. I've just known Ruben since he was little and, I'll admit, I've always thought he and my Jen would make a cute couple. I guess I was surprised when I saw you together earlier. Forget I said anything."

"It's forgotten." Dani forced a smile. "I'll see you tomorrow, Gloria. Have a good evening."

"Do you have any fun plans?" the woman asked, obviously trying to make up for her tactlessness of earlier.

I'm going to hang out with Ruben. You got a problem with that?

She almost said the words but decided not to pour fuel on the fire. Some day her own smart-ass mouth was going to get her in trouble here in this town full of nice people who might not expect it from her.

"Homework, dinner, bed. That's about it."

"Well, give those cute girls of yours a hug from me. Good night."

Dani tried not to dwell on Gloria's concerns as she followed that outline for her evening and helped Mia get in her nightly reading practice and hounded Silver about her math worksheet, then threw together one of the girls' favorites for dinner, her version of pasta *e fagioli* soup.

"When are we going? I can't wait. I can't wait," Mia said as she dried the dinner dishes while Dani washed. "When Ruben gets here, can I be the one who takes the present to the door?"

Dani frowned down at her daughter. "Why are you asking again, honey? We have talked about this all evening. Silver is going to do it this first time and check out the situation at the Larkin house. She's a really fast runner and should be able to figure out the best places to hide. After that, we can decide if she thinks you can do it."

Mia was too excited about the evening ahead of them and didn't appear dejected. "That's okay. It will be fun to wait in the truck with Ruben."

Dani wished she could agree. Instead, her stomach was in

knots, worrying about spending even a few moments in a vehicle with the man, especially with this soft, tensile connection that seemed to have formed between them when she wasn't looking.

Gloria's words kept ringing through her head. *He's a good guy. I sure would hate to see him get hurt.*

Gloria's unspoken message was that Dani was not the right kind of woman for him. She couldn't agree more. Both of them knew Dani was not the sort of woman who could make someone like Ruben happy.

She had no room in her life for any man right now, but especially a man who was a complete mismatch for her. Ruben was an officer of the law, for crying out loud. A squeaky-clean, make-the-world-a-better-place kind of man.

The moment he found out about Tommy, about his life of misdeeds and the chaos he had left in his wake and especially his last terrible acts, he wouldn't want anything to do with Dani or her girls.

There was a chance he already knew. She had told Frank right after it happened. She hadn't felt right about keeping something like that from the kindly veterinarian, even knowing it might ruin the opportunity for her.

Frank had assured her none of that mattered to him, which had only endeared the man more to her. She didn't *think* he would have told his son, but she couldn't be completely sure.

If he knew, would Ruben have been so kind and understanding to her and her girls?

Headlights suddenly flashed in her driveway before she

could come up with an answer to that. He was about fifteen minutes late, which seemed unusual for him.

Nerves fluttered through her and Mia's sudden squeal didn't help matters any.

"He's here! He's here!"

"Why do you always have to repeat everything you say?" Silver groused. "Do you think we didn't hear you the first time or something?"

"Enough, Sil. Will you just try to stow the attitude for five minutes tonight? I'll remind you, we're doing all of this because of you."

Silver slumped back into her chair, her mouth in a tight line. Dani wanted to think her words had some impact on her daughter, but she doubted it.

Had she been so difficult when she was thirteen? She didn't think so. Of course, that had been during the three relatively peaceful years she had lived with Betsy in that big brownstone in Flushing.

Though the woman had taken in three other girls around Dani's age, they each had their own rooms, a rarity during her years in the system. That big house by far had been the most comfortable of her placements and she had been on her best behavior during those years, until Betsy became ill and could no longer care for her charges.

All in all, thirteen had been a pretty good year. Maybe that's one of the reasons she had so little patience with her daughter at the same age, who had so much more than Dani had.

She didn't have time to dwell on the past, especially not

when the doorbell rang out through her house and Mia raced to it, her features glowing. At least one of them was excited about the prospect of a little holiday mischief.

"Hi, Deputy Morales" Dani heard her say cheerfully.

"Hey, Miss Mia," he answered.

Something was wrong. Even before she walked into the foyer to see his face, she could tell by the tone of his voice.

Seeing him only confirmed her suspicion. This afternoon when he had left her at lunchtime he had seemed cheerful, happy, his smile easy and warm. Now there was a closed-in quality to him, a tightness around his eyes and a deep sadness that seemed to have settled over him.

What was wrong? What had put that sudden bleak look in his eyes? It was all she could do to keep from asking and she had to fight the urge to place a comforting hand on his arm.

"Are you ready to go?" he asked.

"Yep." Mia beamed at him. "I can't wait!"

He didn't smile back. "Silver? Still up for this?"

Dani waited apprehensively for her teenager to make some sarcastic comment. *Not now, Silver,* she wanted to say.

To her vast relief, Sil was uncharacteristically subdued, almost as if she had picked up on Ruben's unspoken turmoil as well.

"I just need to put on my coat," her daughter said.

"Make sure it's a black or dark blue one, if possible. That will make it easier to hide in the bushes or behind trees, if you have to."

"I can't believe a sheriff's deputy is telling me to wear

dark clothing, the better to skulk around the neighborhood. What is the world coming to?"

This earned Silver a small smile, but it contained none of his usual warmth.

What was wrong? And how disconcerting, to realize how very dependent she was becoming on that smile and his usual cheery good humor. She was coming to crave it just as much as she yearned for a good plate of her favorite lasagna from Il Bambino's in Queens.

She had a horrible thought that left her cold. Had he somehow found out about Tommy? Had he gone back to the sheriff's department and put in a little research?

They didn't have the same name anymore so connecting the dots wouldn't be easy but it wouldn't be impossible.

There was also the chance he might have asked his father. Would Dr. Morales keep her secrets? She wanted to think so but couldn't be sure.

No. She gave him a closer look. Something told her his strange mood had nothing to do with her or her girls.

"You'll be skulking around this time for a good cause," he reminded Silver. "I wouldn't ask otherwise."

"What about us?" Mia asked. "Do we need dark clothes, too?"

His heavy mood seemed to lift a little as he smiled down at her youngest daughter. "You should be fine just the way you are."

"Good. I only have one winter coat, and it's this one."

She twirled around to show off the pink-and-purple coat she adored.

"It's very nice," Ruben said.

"Here, kiddo. Let's get your hat." Dani helped Mia put on the matching purple-and-pink beanie a friend back in Boston had knitted for her.

"I think we're ready now," Dani said after Silver joined them and Dani had the chance to put on her own coat.

"Great." He mustered a smile that again didn't quite reach his eyes.

What had happened?

"I've got tonight's gift in the truck already. It should be easy this time. The first few deliveries, the family won't be expecting you. After about the third night, they'll be on the lookout. Once, we delivered Secret Santa to a family that had six kids. They staked out the yard one night, trying to catch Mateo making the delivery. Fortunately he was a star on the track team and they could never see him."

"Silver is superfast, too," Mia said. "You should see how fast she runs. I can't even keep up with her. Neither can Mama."

"That's good." Ruben's smile seemed a little more genuine.

"You sure you're ready?" he asked Silver.

"As I'll ever be," she answered. To Dani's relief, she actually *did* look excited—from the anonymous gift-giving or from the risk involved, Dani didn't know but she supposed it didn't really matter.

"We'll use my pickup tonight since it's dark and unobtrusive," Ruben said. "But after a few days, we may want to switch things up, just to keep them guessing, in case somebody notices a strange vehicle in the neighborhood."

"Good heavens," Dani exclaimed. "I never realized this was more complicated than making a ransom drop."

"It can be, but the Morales family has had lots of experience, so you're in good hands."

The shiver rippling down her spine was due to the falling snow as they walked outside, not because her imagination was suddenly busy going off in all kinds of inappropriate directions.

After the previous unseasonably mild weekend, a storm system had moved in. Though it had only dropped a few inches, the snow was falling steadily, the kind of storm that could lay down a heavy blanket in only a few hours.

"Look how pretty the snow is, Mama." Mia lifted her face to the snow as she always did and held her tongue out to catch a snowflake.

"You're such a goon," Silver said, though it was said with more affection than malice.

"You are," Mia retorted.

"You both are. Get in Ruben's truck and let's do this," Dani said.

The girls climbed into the back row of his king cab again and Dani slid into the front seat. The vehicle smelled of him, that indefinable woodsy, sexy, masculine smell that did such ridiculous things to her insides and made her want to lean her head against the leather and inhale for a few hours.

"I guess you know where the Larkin girls live," Ruben said as he backed out of the driveway.

"I've been there a few times," Silver said.

Something had happened between Silver and the girls. Until a few weeks ago, the twins, Emma and Ella, had been among Silver's small circle of friends in town. Now whenever their names were mentioned, Silver behaved oddly, with a fine-edged tension Dani couldn't quite understand.

Ruben didn't appear to notice anything unusual. "Great. I'll drop you off at the end of their street and then pull down the road a little bit, where I'm out of view from their house. All you have to do is knock on the door or ring the doorbell—your choice—then hide around the side of their house or behind their shrubs until they answer. After they pick up the gift and go back inside, you can slip away and make your way around the corner to find us. You good with that?"

"I think I can handle it," she said drily.

"I have no doubt at all. I really appreciate your help with this. I'm getting a little too old to be hiding in the bushes and, as you put it, skulking around the neighborhood. If they're not home, by the way, just leave it."

His headlights illuminated the snow falling thickly as he drove to his destination. The street was quiet. Everyone with any sense was tucked in at home by the fire, safe from the increasing intensity of the weather.

Through the windows, she could see Christmas trees glowing through the winter night and several houses had lights outlining their windows and following their rooflines.

Inside, she could see shadows moving behind closed curtains and blinds. She wasn't a Peeping Tom but she did like to see houses all closed up against the night. It made her wonder about the people who lived inside. What they cooked for dinner, what they were watching on television, if they were laughing or having a party or playing video games.

When Silver was small, after Tommy went upstate the first time, Dani had left her with a babysitter in the evenings so she could go to night school after caring for her all day. She used to take the city bus to campus and back through a few quiet suburban neighborhoods.

She remembered coming home from class completely exhausted but with just enough energy to gaze at those houses and those closed curtains and the filtered blue light from the television screens. As she imagined people in their safe little cocoons, she would vow that she and Tommy would give their little Silvia a better childhood than their tiny fifth-floor walk-up apartment where they shared a bathroom with the apartment next door.

Through hard work and sacrifice and plenty of help along the way, she had come further than she'd ever dreamed. She was a veterinarian. They lived in a three-bedroom house on a beautiful mountain lake, something she couldn't even have imagined back then, when she had never been quite sure if she would have enough to feed her little girl.

Things weren't perfect. She would be the first one to admit that. She could be abrupt with the girls, more impatient than she wanted to be. But they knew, above all else, that their mother loved them.

She remembered hearing once that a person had two

chances to be part of a good parent-child relationship, once when they were children and once when they were parents. She had missed out on the first chance for a big portion of her childhood after her mother died, but she was doing her very best to make sure the second phase was filled with joy.

An important element of that was teaching her daughters to care about others, and participating in this little Christmas tradition with Ruben would help in that department.

"Here we are." He pulled to the side of the road in front of a vacant lot in a place where his pickup would not attract undue attention. From the console, he pulled out a small, neatly wrapped box and handed it to Silver in the back seat.

"Cute. Did you wrap it yourself?" she asked, with only a hint of sarcasm in her voice.

"My mom did this one, actually. She's done most of the prep work of buying and wrapping the gifts, since she knows her sons probably won't get to it."

Silver paused there, her glove on the door handle.

She was nervous, Dani realized.

"Nothing to worry about." Ruben gave a reassuring smile, picking up on Silver's apprehension, too. "Just go to the door, set the present down, ring the bell and run like he—, um, heck."

"Got it." Silver pushed open the door and stepped out into the snow.

Bundled in her dark coat, hat and the tightly wrapped scarf Dani had handed her before they left the house, Silver was all but unrecognizable, a blob of wool and down and GoreTex as she trudged to the corner and then out of sight.

"She's a good kid," Ruben said, watching after her.

His words warmed her far more than the heater of his pickup could. People couldn't always see past Silver's purple hair and attitude.

"She is," Dani murmured.

"I wish I could go with her." Mia's sigh from the back seat was deep and heartfelt.

Ruben turned around to smile at her. "Another night, okay? We'll make it happen for you."

"Promise?"

"Yes. Now, I'm going to turn off the engine and the lights so we don't look so suspicious sitting here. Are you okay with that?" he asked Dani. "It's only for a moment."

"We'll be fine, won't we, Mia?"

"I'm not cold one bit," she declared.

Ruben turned the key, plunging them into darkness and quiet. Outside, the snow fluttered down onto the landscape.

"This is fun," Mia said.

Ruben didn't answer and Dani frowned as he gazed out the windshield at the snow that began to pile up quickly.

"What's wrong?" she murmured softly. Something about the intimacy of the cab here in the dark gave her the courage to ask him. She didn't want anything that might tighten the growing bond between them, but she couldn't bear that he was obviously upset about something.

"What makes you think something is wrong?"

Though she felt stupid for presuming she knew the man, she wanted to think she had gained a little insight into him, especially over the last week or so.

"Instinct, I guess. You seem very different right now than you were at lunch. You're upset about something."

Did you find out about my ex-husband and what he did?

The words hovered on her tongue but she didn't dare ask him.

He was quiet for a long moment, so long that she thought he wasn't going to answer. Finally he gave her a searching look across the width of the pickup truck, then sighed.

"Let's just say it's been a long afternoon. This time of year can be tough on some people."

"And tough on those charged with looking after us," she answered.

"Unfortunately, that can be true." He was quiet again, listening to Mia humming Christmas songs softly in the back seat, always happy to entertain herself.

"I don't imagine you were all that thrilled about coming with us," he said after a moment. "But I'm selfishly glad you did. I needed this tonight."

"To sit in a cold pickup truck in the dark, waiting for my daughter to finish a knock-and-run?"

He smiled a little, and she wanted to think it was slightly more genuine. "That, yes, plus to have the chance to sit for a moment and think about some of the good things the holidays bring. The little kindnesses and the family time and the peace of a Lake Haven December night." He paused. "Too many people find this time of year lonely and sad. It breaks my heart sometimes."

Her own heart seemed to break a little and she wished that she could be the sort of woman who had the courage to hold him close and take away some of his pain, as he'd done for her the other night.

Gloria's words seemed to ring in her ears. Ruben was a good, caring man who deserved far better than somebody with her kind of baggage.

"I'm sorry your afternoon was hard." She didn't have any other words that seemed adequate.

"Nothing like a Chihuahua with diarrhea."

"Ew. Gross. You said *diarrhea*," Mia piped up from the back seat, making both of them smile.

That intimacy swirled around them again, that sense that they were alone here in the dark.

"I have to admit, I'm a little sad to find out you have to deal with rough things over the holidays. I'd like to believe a place like this is immune to that kind of thing."

"Believe me, Lake Haven County has its troubles, just like anywhere else. Otherwise, I wouldn't have a job."

"I suppose that's true. It doesn't make it any less sad."

Before he could answer, the back door opened and Silver jumped in. "Okay, that was fun!"

Ruben chuckled. "Did you get caught?"

"Almost. All the lights were on inside and I could tell they were home, but I was like a freaking ninja. You should have seen me. I crawled up the front porch steps and stayed low so they couldn't see me, then put the thingy down, rang the doorbell and took off as fast as I could around the side of the house. I thought for sure they were going to come looking for me, but then a minute later I heard the door close. After another minute or two, I peeked around the house and they had gone back inside."

"Did they take the gift?" Dani asked, struck by how long it had been since she had seen this kind of enthusiasm and excitement from her daughter.

She wanted to lean across the pickup truck cab and plant a great big smooch on Ruben Morales's cheek for giving her this little glimpse of the Silver she remembered from a few years earlier.

"Yeah. It wasn't there anymore, at least. I waited a few more moments to make sure no one was going to come back out, then I sneaked away and hurried back here."

"That sounds so fun!" Mia exclaimed. "I want to do it."

"Maybe we could both go tomorrow night," Silver said. "If I'm there with you, I can show you where to hide and wait for me while I go up to the door. You have to be fast."

"I can be. I promise. I'll run as fast as I can."

"That sounds like a plan." Ruben started up his pickup truck, turned the lights on and slowly drove back toward their houses. "From here on out, you'll have to be more careful. They'll be watching."

"Maybe we should mix up the time we go, just so they're not expecting us, watching for us."

"I was going to suggest exactly that," he said. "Let's go about seven thirty tomorrow, if that's not too late."

"Works for me," Silver said.

"The way this snow is coming down, you may have to run in boots."

"No problem for me. I went to school in Boston. You don't know snow until you've seen what we used to get."

By the time they reached Dani's house, another inch had fallen atop the two or three from earlier.

Ruben let them out and walked them up to the house. "Where's your snow shovel? I can clear some of this away. We're supposed to get a few more inches so you'll need to clear it again in the morning but I can at least start things off and take care of what's here now."

"That's totally not necessary. Silver and I can do it."

"I know you can, but you'll be doing me a favor. After my afternoon, I could use some kind of physical outlet."

She again wondered what had happened and wished she could ask him. If he could find a little release by clearing her driveway, she didn't see how she could refuse.

"The shovel is in the garage. Silver, will you show Ruben where it is while I get Mia to bed? You can leave it on the porch when you're done. And thank you. That's one more way I'm in your debt."

She was busy for the next twenty minutes with Mia's bath and bedtime routine. By the time her lights were out and Silver was in the shower, Dani figured Ruben would have been long gone. When she looked out the window, however, she spotted him leaning on her shovel handle, gazing out at the lake and the mountains that gleamed in the pale moonlight filtering through the storm clouds.

He looked so very desolate. On impulse, she grabbed a mug from the cupboard, heated some water in the microwave and mixed in some of her favorite gourmet hot cocoa, threw on her coat and boots, and walked out into the night.

He looked over when she approached him and the anguish in his eyes tore at her heart. He quickly schooled his expression.

"What's this?"

"Cocoa. It's not much, but you look like a man who could use something sweet."

She felt the chill from his ungloved hands as he took it from her. "Thanks. That's very thoughtful of you, Doc."

"You're welcome."

She thought about slipping back into the house but he had been extraordinarily kind to her the other night and she didn't see how she could walk away and leave him to his distress.

"Do you want to talk about what happened after you left the clinic? Just so you know, I'm tougher than I look. I've probably heard worse."

He gazed at her for a long moment, the steam from the cocoa curling between them. Finally he sighed. "I got a call about ten minutes after I left your clinic. I was there all afternoon and into the evening. A murder-suicide north of Shelter Springs."

"Oh, no," she murmured.

"It was an elderly couple in their eighties, both with health trouble. She had Alzheimer's and he was in heart failure."

"Did you know them?"

"Not really. They used to bring their little dogs to the

clinic when I was a kid and I remembered seeing them. My folks would know them better than I did. That didn't make it any easier. They had a daughter and she's the one who found them."

"Oh, poor thing."

"Right. I guess Al was getting sicker and could no longer take care of his wife's needs. He knew he was dying and he didn't want to leave her alone to go into a nursing home when something happened to him. That was all written in a note to his daughter. He shot his bride of more than sixty years, then laid down beside her, grabbed her hand and killed himself. I was first on the scene after the daughter called 911. It was…rough."

She ached at the raw, ragged edge to his voice.

"Oh, Ruben. I'm so sorry."

She reached a hand out to touch his arm through the soft down of his jacket. Before she even made contact, he set the mug of cocoa on the ground and wrapped his arms tightly around her. He needed this, the comfort of human contact. It was a small thing she could do. She hugged him close, wishing she could absorb all the cold of his skin and return it with heat.

He shuddered a little against her, not from the cold, she realized, but from being able to lean on someone else for a moment.

Some part of her had always considered law enforcement the enemy. Dani knew that probably traced back to her childhood, to the time when her mother died and the authorities came to take her away. A police officer enlisted by child welfare had dragged her away from her apartment, screaming for her mother. From then on, she had equated the police with loss and pain and unfeeling bureaucracy.

Then later, after she hooked up with Tommy, his choices and lifestyle had meant that any police officer posed a potential threat.

She felt stupid to realize how wrong she had been. They were human beings, doing a job. Some skated through, yes, and wielded the power of their position like a billy club. Others, like Ruben, were caring, dedicated, passionate law enforcement officers.

She held him for a long time while the snowflakes spit from the sky and the wind blew off the lake.

When he pulled away, he looked adorably embarrassed. "Thank you. I guess I needed a little human contact."

"There's no shame in needing someone to hold you once in a while, Deputy Morales. Somebody wise once told me that."

"Somebody should smack that know-it-all right in the mouth."

"Good idea," she murmured. Before she thought it through, she kissed him gently, intending only to offer comfort and solace. He seemed to catch his breath against her mouth and then he pulled her back into his arms and kissed her fiercely.

11

Somehow Dani's kiss pushed away the darkness that had hung over him all afternoon, since he had walked into that heartbreaking scene. He couldn't say she kissed him and made everything better, but at least he could focus on something else for now.

Her mouth was cold and tasted of chocolate. He wanted to savor every inch of it. It was crazy to kiss her out here, with the snow settling on his hair and his shoulders, and his feet cold in the snow, but he didn't care about any of that. She was here, in his arms again, as he had dreamed about all week.

She gave a soft little noise and wrapped her arms more

tightly around him and Ruben pulled her close, wishing he could absorb all the cold and give her back only heat.

He was falling for this woman. He never would have expected it, even a week ago, but Dani and her curious mix of vulnerability and defiance were somehow managing to wriggle into his heart.

He knew he couldn't keep her out here all night, not when the temperature was dropping and even now a fine layer of new snow covered where he had just shoveled, but he couldn't make himself end the kiss.

She was the one who finally pulled away after several long moments. Her nose and cheeks were rosy from the cold and she looked completely irresistible.

"I probably shouldn't have done that."

"You don't see me complaining, do you?" The only thing he wanted to complain about was that she had stopped.

She made a face. "You should be. I'm being completely irrational. I told you not even a week ago that we shouldn't kiss again, yet here I am breaking my own rule."

"You know what they say about rules. The only reason to make them is to break them."

She didn't smile, only continued looking at him with those shadows in her eyes. Was it really such a terrible thing that they had kissed again?

She shivered and he couldn't resist pulling her into his arms again, if only so he could steal a little more peace from having her in his arms. She nestled against him with a little sigh, her arms going around his waist and her cheek resting against his chest.

"Don't worry about it," he murmured. "That was a sympathy kiss. It doesn't count. I had a rough afternoon and you were only trying to help, which you did perfectly. I needed the reminder that I'm still alive and the world still contains magic and wonder, like Christmas trees and kisses from beautiful women. Thank you."

She gave a small half laugh he felt through the layers of his clothing. "Nice spin."

He did feel better. That heartbreaking scene would still haunt his dreams for nights to come, but she had helped counterbalance the tragedy through a bright, shining moment he would never forget.

He kissed the top of her head and she stayed there a few minutes longer, her arms around his waist while the snow swirled around them.

"I need to go inside."

"You do. It's freezing out here. I'm sorry I got distracted and didn't finish the hot cocoa you brought me."

She reached down and picked up the mug, already covered in a thin layer of snow. When she straightened, she gazed at him, eyes solemn and the wind tangling strands of her hair.

"I don't make smart decisions where men are concerned. I never have. I can't afford to let you be yet another mistake, Ruben. I have too much to lose here in Haven Point."

This wasn't the place he would have chosen for this conversation, outside in her driveway in the middle of a storm—especially not after the day he'd had, when his emotions were raw and exposed.

"What makes you think we would be a mistake?"

"Years of experience. Let's leave it at that. Look, I'm very attracted to you, Ruben. That is probably obvious. I'm having a very hard time resisting you."

"Good. For the record, I'm having a hard time resisting you, too."

She sighed. "We both have to try harder. I'm not good at relationships. Trust me when I say I'm not the kind of woman you need."

How could she know what kind of woman he needed, when he was only now beginning to realize it for himself?

She was shivering and he wanted to tuck her against him again, to keep her warm and safe against the elements and against those shadows in her eyes.

"We don't need to talk about this right now. Why don't you go inside and we can have this conversation another time?"

"I'd rather finish it now."

He didn't like the hard finality of her words. "Finish it?"

"I want to make a life here in Haven Point with my daughters. They deserve so much better than I've been able to provide to this point. Your father has given me a chance at a future for them I never imagined. I can't screw that up. I *won't* screw that up."

"You're saying a relationship with me would have the potential to damage your future."

"I'm saying I can't take that risk."

"I sure would like to know who hurt you so badly."

She gave a ragged-sounding laugh. "I could probably

come up with a long list, but at the top of it would be my-self and my own choices. I'm trying to make decisions with my head these days, not with my heart."

"We've all made poor decisions, Dani. At some point you might want to think about not beating yourself up about them any longer."

She gazed at him, the wind tangling her hair. When he saw she was shivering, he knew he couldn't push her about this now.

"Go on inside. I'll finish up out here and leave your snow shovel by the door."

"I... Thank you."

Gripping the mug of cocoa she had so sweetly fixed for him, she fled, leaving him outside in the cold.

Dani was absolutely the world's biggest sucker.

All day long, she had been telling herself she didn't need to go along with Ruben and the girls while they made that night's Secret Santa delivery. Her presence wasn't necessary anyway, and she really didn't want to be alone with him in his pickup truck.

Despite all that self-talk, here she was, trying her best to avoid Ruben's gaze while she put on her coat and gloves, Mia dancing around her.

She was the reason Dani was doing this, when she wanted to stay home where she would be safe. All afternoon, her daughter had begged and begged Dani to come with them.

You have to come, Mama. You have to.

She really didn't, but Mia was so excited at the prospect

of helping her sister with the gift drop-off, she was practically bouncing off the walls. She had spoken of nothing else all day.

Dani didn't want anything to spoil Mia's joy in the small act of service. If that meant Dani had to endure Ruben's company, she would figure out how to survive it.

"I can't wait," Mia said.

"You're going to have to be quiet, though," Silver reminded her. "I'm not sure you can do that."

"I can! I promise I can!"

"If you don't, you'll blow everything. They'll see us and the whole thing will be ruined."

Nervousness suddenly flitted across Mia's features, replacing any trace of excitement. "I think I can be quiet," she said, though her voice didn't seem remotely confident about the possibility.

Ruben knelt down to her level. "I have faith in you, sweetie. I know you can do it. You're going to be *great*."

Mia's exuberance returned and she threw her arms around his neck. Ruben gave a surprised laugh and hugged her back for a moment before he stood up.

"Everybody ready?"

No. Dani wasn't at all ready, but she had promised Mia.

"Let's go," she said, doing her best to ignore the simmering tension between them.

When she again climbed into his pickup truck, the familiar scent of him seemed to surround her like an embrace. She wanted to close her eyes and lean against the seat and simply savor it.

"I'll take you to the same place as last time," Ruben told Silver as he started up the truck. "Follow the same route you went last night. As I've said, from here on out, we'll probably have to mix things up a bit in case they're watching for you but I don't think you'll have trouble tonight, especially since we staggered the delivery time."

"Don't worry about this. We got it," Silver said, nudging her sister in the back seat.

Now that she had done it one night, Silver seemed to consider herself something of an expert. She was also more excited than she'd been the night before.

When Dani had asked her earlier if it had been difficult to keep quiet around her friends about the Secret Santa project, Silver had shrugged.

Not really, she had said. *I'm not hanging out with the twins much right now.*

Dani had tried to press, but Silver had become evasive, almost cagey.

They're busy with other friends right now, she'd finally said. *You're the one who told me friendships sometimes come and go at my age.*

Dani had said that, but she had also liked the twins and considered them a good influence on her daughter.

Oh, the capriciousness of teenage relationships. She had certainly seen that in her own life. It hadn't helped that she had moved schools so many times, with each different placement in the foster care system.

With luck, this would be Silver's final move during her school years. Her daughter would have plenty of time to make good and lasting friendships—unless Dani screwed everything up and they ended up having to leave Haven Point.

The storm of the night before had dropped about five inches of snow on Haven Point. Everything looked festive and charming, with icicles dripping off eaves and Christmas lights sparkling under a layer of white.

The sidewalks had been shoveled, which would make it easier for the girls to walk across the landscape.

"Good luck," Ruben said after parking in the same spot as the night before and turning off his lights.

"Here we go," Mia exclaimed as she climbed out of the vehicle.

"Remember," Silver said. "You have to zip your lips and keep up."

"I will," Mia promised.

Dani watched until they were out of sight, wishing she had gone with them. The time she dreaded was here. For the next ten minutes or so, she would have to be alone with Ruben.

She often had heard people say the phrase *the silence was deafening* but she had never really considered what that meant until right this moment. Usually she liked quiet moments of peace and reflection, but she would have described the hush inside Ruben's pickup truck at that moment as heavy, oppressive and excessively awkward.

She curled her fingers inside her gloves and was just about to say something banal about the weather when he spoke.

"Tell me about the girls' father."

The question coming out of the blue hit her like a punch to the gut. "Excuse me?"

"I don't even know the guy's name. I've been wondering all day about him and what he did to leave you so gun-shy about even kissing another man."

She caught her breath, not at all prepared for the question, for the world of pain and guilt it sent churning through her.

"He is not the reason I can't have a relationship with you, Ruben. At least not the only reason."

"But he's part of your past. A big part. What did he do to hurt you? Was he abusive?"

"I don't see how that's your business."

"You're putting something between us. If it's your husband, then it's my business."

"Maybe I just don't want a relationship right now. That's not a crime, Deputy Morales."

"No, it's not. But you've kissed me twice. There is something between us. I'd like to know the reason you're fighting it so hard."

"So because I kissed you twice, you think that gives you the right to know my entire life story?"

"Only the parts you want to tell me. I would like to get a clearer picture. You could at least tell me his name and how he died."

If she told him that, he would undoubtedly know everything—or at least could do an internet search and find the entire ugly picture.

She had legally changed her name and Silver's for a reason after her divorce. Mia had been born after that, so she had always been a Capelli.

Even then, she had worried that Tommy's choices, like toxic seaweed, would tangle up her and her girls and drag them under along with him.

Tommy had done nothing to support them. In fact, his choices had virtually guaranteed that he wouldn't be around to help raise his daughters, that he would be once more back in prison, paying for his crimes.

In her fury and hurt and fear, she had acted to protect herself and her daughters from being tarnished by their father's actions. Why should he have the right to share his name with his daughters?

It had seemed one more way to put distance between them. She had wanted no connection with him after he broke parole and was returned to prison. It had seemed easier for her and the girls to share the same name.

How grateful she had been for that fortuitous decision, especially after the events of three months earlier. It made it that much harder to trace a connection between Mia and Silver and their father. She didn't want them growing up under the cloud of having such a notorious man for a father.

She looked at Ruben now. She didn't want to tell him. It reflected so poorly on her and her own lousy judgment, that she had once been naive enough to fall for a man who turned out to be capable of such terrible things.

Ruben was a dogged investigator. Something told her he wouldn't rest until she told him. He would wrangle the information out of her, one way or another.

Somehow she knew he wouldn't interrogate the girls, but she also knew Silver might let something slip. Despite Tommy's poor choices, Silver had loved her father and missed him. Dani could envision a scenario where she mentioned his name, then Ruben would find the information out anyway.

Maybe it was better for her to tell him herself—not to control the narrative, but to be clear with Ruben about just how very bad she was for him.

She didn't want to tell him. Some part of her wanted to hold on to the last few moments of his good opinion, before he knew the truth. That was cowardly, though. She owed him honesty. He had been kind to her and to her daughters. She also trusted that he wouldn't spread the information around.

She let out a breath and gathered her courage.

"His name was Tommy," she said. "And he was—"

The rear doors of his pickup opened before she could complete the sentence. Mia and Silver climbed in, both out of breath and laughing, and the moment was gone.

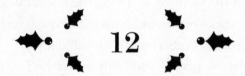

12

Her husband was *what?*

Ruben ground his teeth in frustration. What had she been about to tell him before the girls came back?

It was his own fault for bringing up the subject during a time when he knew they would only have limited opportunity to talk. What choice did he have, though, but to steal time when he found it? After the night before, she had been more than clear that she wasn't going to allow many private chats between them.

He felt as if he knew even less than he had before. All he had was a name, Tommy—and what the hell kind of grown man used a name like that, instead of Tom or Thomas?

He pushed his frustration aside for now. Maybe he would have an opportunity to suss out more information later.

"How did you do?" he asked Silver and Mia.

"That was the most fun *ever*!" Mia exclaimed.

"Did they see you?"

"Nope. Silver had me wait at the hiding place behind the bushes, then she went up and rang the doorbell, and ran so fast back to me. You should have seen how fast she ran!"

"That's great," Ruben said. "Good job."

"What did we give them?" Silver asked. "I forgot to ask you."

Ruben had to think back to the present his mother had showed him. "I think it was a CD of classic Christmas music to set the mood."

"Who even has CD players anymore?" Silver asked.

"I hope they do or they won't have any way of listening to it."

"Can I do it again tomorrow?" Mia asked.

"Well, here's the thing. Tomorrow night's going to be a busy time in Haven Point. It's the boat parade, if you'll remember, so I was thinking I would take care of tomorrow's delivery. Maybe I'll run over late tonight and leave it on their porch without ringing the bell so they find it first thing tomorrow morning when they go to get the newspaper."

"Who even gets a newspaper anymore?" Silver asked.

"You're killing me here," he said, which earned him only a grin in return.

She was, he thought as he started up the pickup and pulled away from the curb. When he wasn't looking, all of the Capelli females seemed to have wormed their way under his skin.

Silver was funny and smart, with a compassionate heart underneath all her brashness. Mia was completely adorable, with a joy for life and a generosity of spirit that he found completely irresistible.

And Dani.

He couldn't stop thinking about her. She haunted his dreams and his days. He looked forward to every moment he spent with her.

Yeah, he was falling hard for the woman and she was doing her very best to keep him at arm's length.

"I might do the same thing late Saturday night for Sunday's delivery, then we can get back to normal for Monday night. What do you think?"

"I guess," Mia said, disappointment threading through her voice. "I wanted to take their present to the door and ring the bell one time."

"We can see about that next week, okay? Anyway, you'll be having too much fun tomorrow at the boat parade to miss it too much. You're going, right? Trust me, this is something you don't want to miss."

"We're going, right, Mama? I want to see all the boats."

"I imagine we'll stop by at some point."

Dani had been subdued since she had told him the first name of the girls' father. Was what had happened to her marriage so very painful for her that she grieved at the mere mention of the man?

Ruben glanced across the cab as he pulled into their

driveway. He took a chance, though he had a feeling she wouldn't be happy with him. What was the difference? She was already doing her best to push him away.

"Here's a crazy idea. Do you guys want to be *in* the parade?"

"In the parade?" Mia exclaimed in an awed voice, as if he had just asked her if she wanted to move permanently into Cinderella's Castle at Disneyland. "Yes!"

"One problem," Silver pointed out. "We don't have a boat."

"Problem solved, then. I have one, as you may recall. A big one, with room for at least fifteen people. I'm signed up for the big parade. My nephews are helping me decorate *The Wonder* tomorrow and they'll be riding along as well as my brothers and possibly my mom and dad. There's plenty of room, if you'd like to join us."

Dani stared at him and Ruben met her gaze steadily. This was the sort of thing friends and neighbors did with one another. They hung out and went on boat rides and had fun together.

She opened her mouth to respond. He could tell before any words even came out that she was going to come up with an excuse. Before she could, Silver piped up.

"I wouldn't mind being in the parade," her daughter said in a deceptively casual tone. Dani shifted her stare to her daughter, her mouth sagging a little more.

"Great. That's two of you," Ruben said cheerfully. "Dani, I guess it's up to you. What do you say?"

It really wasn't fair to gang up on her but he figured it

was for a good cause. The girls *would* have fun participating in the boat parade and he would enjoy the chance to spend more time with them. Maybe he might even have the chance to find out a little more about this mysterious Tommy and the reason Dani looked so troubled when she spoke of him.

"Why would anybody want to take a boat ride in December with five inches of snow on the ground?" she asked.

"I have a good heater on the boat, with a cover that keeps out the elements. Plus, if it gets too cold, you can go down into the cabin, which is always toasty."

"Please, Mama? Please!" Mia begged.

"It really does sound fun." Silver added her voice.

Dani gazed at her girls in the back seat then sent him a sidelong look that told him she wasn't particularly pleased with him right now for dangling this possibility in front of her daughters before speaking with her about it.

"I don't know how I can say no. Even though I still think you're all crazy to want to be out on the water this time of year."

Anticipation curled through him, rich and delicious. "Great. Just make sure you bundle up. I owe you some hot cocoa so I'll make sure I have plenty on hand."

It was a deliberate reminder of their kiss the night before and he was rewarded by her delectable mouth tightening.

"What about churros?" Mia asked hopefully.

Ruben laughed. "I can't promise that, but I'll see what I can do about providing some kind of warm treat. The parade goes from the marina in Haven Point up to Shelter

Springs. I'm going to shuttle my pickup and boat trailer up there with Javi so we won't have to ride the boat back. I can drive you home afterward."

"This is the best Christmas ever," Mia exclaimed. "I can't wait!"

"I hope you enjoy it," Ruben said.

And I hope your mother can find some way to forgive me for roping you all into it.

Despite Dani's promise, Ruben wasn't sure she and her daughters would show up.

The next night as the sun began to slide behind the Redemption mountain range, he moved around his boat, checking that all was in order before the parade.

"Maybe they're not coming," his brother Javier said.

"Maybe not." He tried not to show his disappointment. He assumed Dani would at least call to tell him she wasn't coming, but maybe she got tied up with a weekend emergency at the clinic.

"The first boats are going to be taking off soon," Javi said. "How much longer do you want to wait?"

"A few more minutes. We still have to wait for Mom and Dad anyway."

He checked his watch and the dock where he had told Dani to meet him. Maybe she had decided her girls were better off watching from the shore at their first Lights on the Lake Festival. He couldn't blame her for that.

Suddenly he spied three figures racing toward them and the tension in his shoulders instantly released.

"There they are," he told Javi.

"We're coming," Silver called. "Don't leave yet."

Ruben couldn't hide his grin as the three of them hurried down the dock.

"Careful," he called. "Grab the rope railing. It's icy in spots."

Dani reached a hand down to grab Mia's hand and said something to Silver, who used the rope as well to make her way to the boat.

"Sorry we're late," Dani said, rather breathlessly. "Traffic was crazy and then I couldn't find a place to park."

"No problem. I should have warned you. Actually I should have had you ride with my mom and dad so you didn't have to park. Sorry I didn't think about it."

"We're here now. That's the important thing."

It was. While he was thrilled his family was coming along on this inaugural parade entry for *The Wonder*, he was aware of a deep joy that Dani and her girls were here, too.

Javi helped them aboard.

"Oh," Mia exclaimed, clapping her mittened hands together. "Your boat looks so pretty."

"Thanks. I had help from Esme, Zach and Andy. They're all hanging out below deck where the food is, if you want to join them," he said to Silver.

She seemed to blush, confirming his suspicion that she had a little crush on his nephew Zach. "Okay. I'll do that."

He gestured to the stairs that went down to the tiny cabin below deck. The space was barely big enough for a small galley, a table with two bench seats that folded down to a bed, a little closet-sized toilet room and a berth the size of a double bed.

The Wonder was a wild extravagance, but he figured his brothers could take it out with their families if they wanted. His father might even get in on the fun, once he was officially retired.

His family lived on a huge lake. It seemed only natural to have something more substantial than a few kayaks, paddleboards and his dad's small fishing boat. His nephews couldn't wait for him to take them out on overnight fishing trips.

"Are you sure you're ready for this?" he asked Dani now. "You should know I'm not a fan of boats."

"We'll be fine. I have life jackets for everybody. We'll be cruising just offshore so the parade watchers can see our lights and we'll be going slowly."

Another boat went past them, causing his to sway a little in the water, and Dani wobbled slightly. He caught her before she could fall. Heat kindled between them, even through her layers, and it was all he could do not to pull her into his arms.

Too bad they had an audience consisting of most of his close family members and hers.

"Your boat does look very nice. This must have taken some time." She took in the colored lights that outlined every angle and curve of the boat.

"Everybody came over early and helped me with the lights. Mateo is the one who insisted we bring along his light-up inflatable penguins."

"They're the perfect touch," she assured him. If he wasn't mistaken, that might almost be a smile he saw dancing there around her mouth. It made him want to kiss her again.

This was going to be a long boat ride if he had to spend the whole time keeping a tight rein on his impulses.

"I hope we all don't feel like we're in the North Pole, out on the water."

"Don't worry. Everything's warm below deck and inside the enclosure."

"Where do you want us?"

He had a feeling she wouldn't want to know the answer to that. "Let's grab you some life jackets, then you can choose where you want to sit. Wherever you're comfortable. We're only waiting for my parents."

"They're on the way," Javi said a moment later as Ruben was finding two life jackets in the right sizes that would fit over their outerwear. "Dad texted and said they were on their way from the parking lot. And here they are now."

Ruben saw his mother and father heading down the dock and had to sigh. Despite his repeated assurances to them that they needed to bring only themselves, his mother was carrying two large grocery bags in one hand and his father had a cooler. Ruben climbed down to help them onto the boat.

"Grab a seat, everybody," he said once they were on board, before taking his spot at the controls.

"Can I sit by you?" Mia asked. Without waiting for an answer, she plopped onto the seat next to his. "Mama, sit by me."

Dani looked at the other available seating some distance

away, then back at her daughter. With an almost audible sigh, she took a seat just on the other side of Mia.

Ruben didn't miss the way his mother did a double take when she spotted Dani and Mia sitting by him.

"Hello, Dr. Capelli. Miss Mia. How fun that you're joining us!"

"Darling Dani. Hello," his dad said. "I do hope there's no animal emergency in Haven Point, with both veterinarians on board for the next few hours."

Dani looked stricken. "Oh. I didn't even think of that. Maybe I should get off."

"I was only joking," his father said. "You are not getting off, young lady. The animals will be fine. We have good techs. I'm not sure which one is on call tonight, but I'm sure whoever it is can handle things so you can enjoy yourself tonight. If there's an emergency, they can always call the vets in Shelter Springs."

"Have you eaten?" Ruben's mother asked. "I've got all kinds of snacks. Popcorn, licorice, sugar cookies."

"I love sugar cookies," Mia said, with no attempt at subtlety whatsoever. "They're my favorite."

"Then you better grab the first one. Here you go, sweetie." Myra reached into one of her bags and pulled out a container. She opened it and passed it around.

Ruben reached for a cookie just as his radio went off with instructions for the parade.

"It's showtime," he said. "Everybody ready?"

"As I'll ever be," Dani muttered.

He gave her a reassuring smile and started up *The Wonder*.

★ ★ ★

Her girls were having the time of their lives.

Mia hadn't moved from Ruben's side all evening. Every once in a while he would let her take the steering wheel or helm or whatever it was called on a boat of this size. She would grin at her mother and then wave exuberantly at the parade watchers along the shoreline.

When Dani had checked on Silver and Ruben's niece and nephews, she found them all laughing hysterically while they played card games below deck. They weren't really getting into the spirit of the holiday event down there, but she supposed that didn't really matter. They were socializing in their own way. Silver was enjoying herself and actually having fun. Dani couldn't ask for anything more.

"This is wonderful, isn't it?" Myra said, pitching her voice loud enough to be heard over the low rumble of the boat.

"It really is."

"Can I let you in on a secret?"

"Um, sure."

"I've always wanted to ride on one of the boats during the light parade. For years, we've watched from the shore and it's been great fun to see all the decorations the boat owners put into the parade, but I secretly wanted to be out here on the water. I have a sneaking suspicion that might be one of the reasons Ruben bought this thing. There's a chance I may have mentioned it to him last Christmas."

A soft warmth unfurled inside her. "That's very sweet."

"He has always been a wonderful son. One day, he's going to make some lucky woman very, very happy."

Myra gave her a meaningful sort of smile and any warmth inside her seemed to crystallize and shatter. That lucky woman would *not* be Dani. It couldn't be. His mother had to see that, didn't she? Why on earth would she ever think Ruben might be interested in *Dani*—a divorced woman with two children, who was barely holding her life together?

His mother seemed to be waiting for her to answer. Dani shifted uncomfortably. "I'm sure that's true. He's a very kind man."

"He's wonderful with children, too."

She looked over to where Ruben was showing Mia something on the control panels of the boat. She caught her breath, more charmed than she wanted to admit by the sight of the two of them together, Ruben, tough and masculine, Mia so sweetly joyful.

Oh, she wanted something like this for her daughters. A man to care for them, watch over them, love them.

Her chest ached. How could she take that chance again, with her lousy track record?

"There's only one problem with riding in the parade," Myra said, interrupting her thoughts.

"What's that?"

"Now I can't decide whether it's more fun to be *in* the parade or to watch the parade."

"Maybe you can alternate," she suggested.

"Great idea. Next year, you and I can sit on the shore and wave to all the boats as they pass by."

Dani loved the idea of being there a year from now, after so many years of feeling as if her life was on hold. Wouldn't it be wonderful to throw down roots, to adopt some of these traditions for her own family? Maybe she would start a Secret Santa project for her girls next year, drawing upon the experience they were gaining this year through helping Ruben.

Where would they be a year from now? If they were still in Haven Point, she couldn't imagine they would be riding on *The Wonder* again. The thought filled her with an odd sort of loss. She shook it off, annoyed with herself. Even if Ruben never invited her out on his boat again, she and her girls were here now.

How ridiculous, to squander *this*—the people, the food, the magic of the season—because she was worrying about some nebulous future. She wouldn't do it, she decided. At least not tonight.

When they arrived in Shelter Springs, the scene at the marina was noisy and chaotic, with boats queuing up to be loaded onto trailers at the ramp or floating up to the docks to let out their passengers.

"It might have been faster just to take *The Wonder* back to Haven Point on the water," Frank said.

"I should have realized the backup we would face here," Ruben said. He gave Dani an apologetic look. "This might take a while. I'm sorry. I can let you off and you can ride back to Haven Point with my parents. They shuttled my mom's SUV here earlier."

"You can't load the boat onto the trailer by yourself," Frank reminded him.

"No, but Javi is here. He and I can do it together."

"That's a good plan. We can let everybody off and they can drive down to the festival while we take care of the boat." Ruben's normally quiet brother Javier spoke up. He had said little on the boat ride. The man was obviously going through something rough.

"Mama, can we go to the festival?" Mia said.

She should have thought this through better. Her car was parked at the marina in Haven Point, as Ruben had said he could give them a ride back to town after the parade. "I'm not sure if we'll be able to, by the time we're done helping Ruben with the boat. We'll see. If not, we'll make it next year."

"If you trust us to keep an eye on them, we could take your girls with us," Myra suggested.

Mia clapped her hands to show her approval of that idea and Dani didn't miss the way Silver nudged Esme with a grin and looked under her eyelashes at Zach.

"Are you sure?"

"Positive," Myra said. "We will *love* having them along with us. I only wish we had room to take you along, Dani, but we only have seat belts for seven in my SUV. I do hate for you to miss your first Lights on the Lake Festival."

"We still might make it in time," Ruben said. "Depends how long it takes to put out and drop the boat off at my place."

"Looks like there's a dock there where boats can let off their passengers. The queue is shorter there," his father suggested.

A few moments later, Ruben motored next to the dock and Javi jumped out to tie the boat and lend a hand while the passengers climbed out.

Dani's girls didn't seem too concerned about leaving her behind, too excited at the fun ahead of them. "Bye, Mama," Mia said.

"You have to promise me you'll behave yourselves and stick with Dr. and Mrs. Morales."

"I will and Silver will, too, won't you?"

"Sure thing," Silver said.

Her older daughter seemed actually...happy. Happier, at least, than she had been since they came to town. A tight band around Dani's heart seemed to ease a little and she smiled at Silver.

"Keep an eye on your sister, okay? Here's some spending money, if you need it."

"Thanks." Silver shoved the twenty she gave her into her pocket then bounded off the boat.

"They'll be just fine. I promise, we won't let either of them out of our sight. You have my number, right?" Myra asked.

"Yes. I have yours and Dr. Morales's, plus Silver's."

"If you make it to the festival before it closes, call and we'll let you know where we are. If not, we can drop the girls off at your house or they can wait at our house, whichever you prefer."

She waved them off, then settled back on the boat.

Javi was going to climb back on, then pointed to the lineup of boats still waiting for the ramp. "That's a good hour of waiting in the water. You could make it back to the marina in Haven Point in about half that. Want me to drive your truck and trailer back and meet you there?"

Ruben turned to Dani. "We'll let you decide. Are you tired of the water or can you handle another half hour in *The Wonder* back to Haven Point? It will be faster now that the parade is done and there's not so much traffic on the water."

"I'm game for a return trip. Sounds like that would be the easier course. My car is at the marina in Haven Point anyway."

"Good plan. I guess we'll let you out here, then, Javi."

His brother hopped onto the dock, untied the rigging and tossed it back onto the boat. "I'll see you back in Haven Point, then."

Ruben waved, maneuvered the boat away from the dock then slowly made his way around the other boats in the marina and out to the open water of the big lake.

The moment they were clear of everyone, Dani suddenly realized just what she had signed up for. Thirty minutes alone with Ruben on a romantic moonlight ride on his boat.

Heaven help her.

"The parade was fun, but I have to admit, I like this better."

The boat seemed much quieter now as Ruben motored steadily back to town. There was an intimacy under the moonlight. A few other boaters had opted to make the return trip so they weren't alone on the water, but they all seemed to keep their distance.

"Are you warm enough?" he asked her. She had moved up to sit beside him, much to his delight.

"I'm fine. You were right, it's cozy here with this all-weather cover."

"That was one of the selling points. When you live on a mountain lake, you've got a short boating season. Having a cover extends that, at least by a few months."

In the glow from the boat instruments, her features were a blur. What was she thinking? Did she think he had somehow arranged all of this to be alone with her? He hoped not—although he had to admit, he might have, if he'd been that smart.

"The girls seemed to have fun tonight. I think I even saw Silver laugh a time or two."

"Don't say anything," she said, "but I think my daughter has a crush on your nephew."

He smiled, remembering those innocent, uncomplicated days when liking a girl meant holding her hand between classes and maybe slipping notes into her locker.

"Zach is a good kid. Don't worry. Even if he likes her, too—which I think he does—he'll be respectful."

"Your family is pretty hard to resist."

"Then why keep trying so hard? They like you, too. As much as you let anybody like you, anyway."

She gave him a long look. "What is that supposed to mean?"

Now he'd done it. Opened his mouth, when he meant to simply enjoy the ride with her. "Never mind. Forget it."

"No. I'd like to know."

He sighed. "Only that you seem to go out of your way to keep people at a careful distance, almost as if you're afraid to let anybody get too close. My family. The women of the Haven Point Helping Hands. Andie told me they've invited you to join them, but you're really good at making excuses. I just wonder why you're trying so hard."

She gripped her hands tightly together in her lap. "I didn't grow up in a nice, safe place like Haven Point, where they have light parades to celebrate the holidays and everybody knows everybody else."

"I know. You grew up in Queens. But there are good people everywhere. Surely you had plenty of nice people around you there. Teachers. Neighbors. Friends. Your own family."

Her hands curled in her lap and she gazed out at the boat lights cutting through the water. "I'm not like you, Ruben, with a wonderful, warm, loving family that gets together on Sundays and spends holidays together and does nice things for neighbors, just for the fun of it. That's a completely foreign way of life to me. I'm...struggling to adjust."

"What was your childhood like, then?"

She looked out at the moonlight slicing across the cold lake. "Not pretty. I went into the foster care system when I was eight years old and stayed there until I got pregnant with Silver at seventeen, mostly to escape."

That explained so many things about her. Ruben's heart ached and he fought the urge to turn off the motor, float there in the water and just hold her, as she had done for him only a few nights earlier.

"What happened to your parents?"

"My father walked out when I was two. I have no idea where he went or why and to be honest, I don't care. He lost the right to be considered any kind of father a long time ago. Mom tried her best to keep things together until she got sick. Hepatitis C. It hit her hard and she died before she could get a liver transplant."

"I'm so sorry," he murmured.

"One day she wasn't at the apartment when I came home from school and a neighbor told me she collapsed on the stoop and was taken away in an ambulance. Social services came right after that and a cold stick of a woman told me my mother, my only remaining parent, had died. She told me to gather a few things I cared about so she and a police officer could take me to a new house."

His throat ached and he finally couldn't resist following up on his earlier impulse. He reached out a hand and pulled her closer to him. He thought she might yank away but after one frozen moment, she stayed there, cradled under one arm while he maneuvered *The Wonder* through the dark waves with the other.

"Was it…rough? Foster care, I mean." He had to ask.

"There was no physical or sexual abuse, if that's what you're wondering. I know that can happen but I suppose I was luckier than some. I had a few close calls in the latter area but I knew enough to sleep with a kitchen knife close by and nobody tried anything twice."

His hand tightened on the wheel as a mental picture

emerged of her, slim and dark and pretty, sleeping with a kitchen knife. He hated even thinking about it.

"Some of it was good. I spent three years with a wonderful woman who loved the foster children she cared for, until she became too frail to continue."

"It's good you had that, at least."

"It's tough on a kid, always knowing every situation is temporary. Wondering when the call would come and you'd have to grab your garbage bag of belongings and head to the next temporary place. With every new family, I would vow that I wouldn't cause trouble, but somehow it never quite worked out."

"Oh, Dani. I'm so sorry."

This glimpse into her past was both heartbreaking and illuminating. So many things about her made more sense now. She had a hard time making connections because deep down in her psyche some part of her was in a constant state of worry that they would be yanked away.

She had trusted him enough to tell him this part of her past, something he didn't think she shared very easily.

"You said you got pregnant with Silver at seventeen, mostly to escape."

Her shoulders tensed beneath his arm and she slipped away from him. Cool air rushed in to take her place.

"I was...looking for a happy ending. The safety and security I lost when I was eight."

"I take it you didn't find it."

She laughed, a sound without amusement. "You could say that. I might as well spill all my secrets. You want the ugly truth about me, Ruben. Fine. Here you go. I married an ex-convict."

He glanced over, sensing that wasn't the worst of what she wanted to tell him.

"Did you?" he said mildly.

"Tommy had served six months in jail for grand theft when we married. I knew that. He told me it was a misunderstanding, that he had made a mistake and trusted the wrong people, and I believed him. Mostly because I needed to believe him."

He had seen that in the loved ones of people who ran into trouble with the law. They convinced themselves all the evidence was wrong, that their loved one had a bad rap and the system was rigged against them.

Ruben knew there were cases where innocent people were convicted of crimes they didn't commit. They were the outliers, though. As a law enforcement officer, he wanted to believe that the system usually worked the way it was supposed to and those who committed crimes ended up right where they belonged.

"Tommy and I had two good years after Silver was born. I thought he had put the past behind him. He had a steady job as a mechanic and we were happy, I thought—until the day he was arrested along with three of his friends for organizing a luxury auto theft ring and chop shop in Jersey. Two members of the crew made the mistake of carjacking a Mercedes belonging to the wife of a federal judge, so this time Tommy was sent upstate. He wasn't actually part of the carjacking but because this was his second arrest as an adult after numerous juvenile offenses and because he was considered the leader of the enterprise, the one calling the shots, he was sentenced to five to ten years."

Not a small chunk. The charges must have been serious. "That's a stiff sentence."

"I tried to tell myself we could still make things work. That he would change and be the sweet man I knew when he got out again. I stayed married to him. I wrote to him every week while I was struggling to survive as a mom on my own, desperately trying to hang on to my scholarship and stay in college. Every Sunday, I would pack up Silver and we would take the train upstate to visit him."

He could picture her, defiantly resilient, trying to make the best of things. His heart ached for all the things she didn't say, the sacrifices she must have had to make and the loneliness she must have endured.

"He served four years. When he got out, I thought things would finally be different. That's what he promised me, over and over. He had vocational training as an electrician in prison and was going to make a new start."

"But he didn't?"

"You probably know how hard it is for felons on the outside. I think he tried for a while, but...something had changed in him. Or maybe I had changed during that time on my own. I don't know. Six months after he got out, I discovered he was hanging with his old crew, staying out late, being evasive about where he'd been. I kicked him out. I filed for divorce and left New York for Boston and vet school. Two months later, I found out I was pregnant with Mia, but by then Tommy was in trouble again and had been found in violation of his parole."

"He went back to prison?"

"For four more years." She was quiet. "He came to visit the girls once when he got out and I barely recognized him from the man I had once loved."

"That must have been tough, being on your own with two little girls while going through graduate school."

"Somehow the girls and I survived. During my second year of school, I started corresponding with your father and eventually he offered me this internship when I finished, with the potential to purchase his practice if I liked it here, so we moved here right after graduation. This was my chance to give the girls the life I always dreamed about."

"You're doing exactly that."

"I thought I was. But somehow the ghosts of our past mistakes never quite leave us alone, do they?"

He thought of his own mistakes on the job, the moments when he hadn't been fast enough to react or had misjudged a situation or underestimated a suspect.

"They don't. But life has a way of helping us eventually make our peace with them."

"I hope so. But I'm not there yet."

She was quiet. "I don't want to tell you, but I think you need to know the rest of it."

The rest of it? What more could there be? Judging by the way she twisted her hands in her lap and wouldn't meet his gaze, it had to be something she considered terrible. On impulse, he turned the boat engine off, wanting to focus on her without the distraction of having to maneuver the boat. They floated there on the water, rocking gently on the waves.

Under other circumstances, he would have found it restful and beautiful there on a cold December night, being safe and dry here inside the shelter, but the tension shimmered between them.

"There. Go ahead. Now I can give you my full attention."

"It's bad, Ruben. So bad."

"Tell me," he urged. He reached out for her hand and after a startled moment, she entwined her fingers through his.

"After that last visit a few years ago, I severed contact with Tommy," she said slowly. "I didn't know where he was until I heard his name on the news three months ago."

Three months ago. Right after she had come to Haven Point, around the time she began to shut herself off from participating in community events and started turning down invitations.

Her hand was trembling, he realized. All of her was trembling.

"Why was his name on the news?"

"You heard it, too, Ruben. Everyone in the country did. One lovely September afternoon, he walked into a bank in Brooklyn and pulled a gun on the tellers. He ended up killing a guard and two police officers in a shoot-out as he tried to escape, before he was eventually gunned down."

Ruben's gut clenched. He remembered that case, though

it happened across the country. Every member of law enforcement grieved when any of their own died in the line of duty and these deaths had seemed particularly senseless.

"Tommy DeLuca," he said.

"That's right. My ex-husband—the father of my beautiful girls—is Tommy DeLuca."

13

As she might have expected, Ruben went rigid at her words.

Three months earlier, Tommy's name had been bandied about on every news channel. He had been talked about in the same disgusted tones people used when discussing mass shooters, white supremacists, violent dictators.

He had become the current face of evil, a representative of everything wrong in the world—until the next newsmaker did something heinous and wiped him from memory.

Ruben remembered. She could tell by his reaction and the sudden tension that seemed to vibrate from his skin to hers where they held hands.

"DeLuca. Not Capelli," he said, his voice gruff.

She pulled her hand away and curled her fingers into a fist, wishing she could hold that heat inside. "I legally changed my name and Silver's back to my maiden name during the divorce proceedings, before Mia was born. I can't tell you how many times I've been grateful for that decision. Never more so than three months ago."

Water lapped against the boat. Normally the sound would have been calming, but not at this moment when her emotions were raw and exposed.

"I told your father the moment I heard the news, of course. When he first offered me the internship, I felt I had to tell him about Tommy—that he had served time during our marriage and some of the things he had done—but I don't know if I ever mentioned his name. I had to tell him everything after…after Tommy killed those men, who were only doing their job."

"What did my father say?"

That was yet another reason she adored Frank Morales, for his steady, kind support while she had been reeling in shock.

"He said I couldn't take on the burden of what my ex-husband had done. They were his choices, not mine. As far as your father was concerned, none of it mattered."

"Sounds about right."

"What else could he say? I was already here and had started working at the clinic."

"That wouldn't matter to my father. He says what he means."

"He is wonderful, yes. I was beyond grateful for his support, but he is the only other one who knows. You understand why I don't want this to get out. Imagine how people would treat the girls if they knew about their father."

He stared. "Why would anyone treat them any differently? They had nothing to do with Tommy's actions. None of it is their fault. Or yours, either."

"There you go, wearing those rose-colored glasses again. Of course people will treat me differently!"

"You've been divorced since before Mia was born. At least six years ago. And you've said he hasn't been part of your life in that time. How are you responsible for his actions?"

"You're being irrational if you don't think people will think less of my judgment for having married and had two children with a cop killer. Of course they will!"

He jaw hardened. "Then they're idiots. Idiots you don't need in your world. No one should blame you for your ex-husband's bad acts. If they do, they're not people you need in your life."

He couldn't really be that naive. He was in law enforcement. He had to know that even baseless whispers and finger-pointing about a person could ruin lives.

She had married Tommy. That fact was indisputable. She had been married to him for almost six years, together almost eight, though he had been in prison for more than half of that time. They had created two amazing daughters together.

No matter how she tried to excuse it in her own head by telling herself she was too young to know better, by comforting herself with the reminder that she had divorced him as soon as she realized he wasn't going to change, a grim fact remained.

She had once loved a man capable of terrible things.

"You and the girls are not responsible for what Tommy DeLuca might have done," Ruben said again.

"That's easy to say. You've never had people fire you from a job when they find out your husband was in prison. Or mothers in your apartment building not allow their children to play with yours. That was only when his crimes involved robbery. This is so much worse. He killed three people. Of course people will judge me and the girls for that. I don't sleep at night, worried if the next day will be the day someone figures it out and tells the...the world."

Her voice wobbled a bit on the last sentence, much to her chagrin. Ruben stepped closer, his expression intense.

"Small-minded people might want to tarnish you with the same brush. It's a natural hazard of living in a small town that one of the favorite pastimes is talking about your neighbors. I can't promise you or the girls won't ever face hurtful gossip, but I can promise it won't come from anybody you need in your life. No one should ever blame you or Silver or Mia for what their father did. My family won't. I certainly don't. Come here."

Before she realized what he intended, he pulled her into his arms, tugging her against his chest. She wouldn't let herself cry again, but thick, heavy emotions clogged her throat.

He was such a good man, kind and warm and generous. If everyone in Haven Point were like Ruben and his family, she would have no worries about telling people about her past. Some were, she knew. She had met other kind people here and wanted to give people the benefit of the doubt.

She was afraid. She knew it and was ashamed of it but couldn't seem to help it. She had spent so many years in foster care trying to be perfect that she was afraid to show people her imperfections, real and perceived.

What about those who could only see her ex-husband's crimes when they looked at her? She didn't want her girls to carry that stigma.

She let him hold her for a long moment, knowing this would be the last time she could allow it. His heat seeped through her coat and his arms enfolded her in strength and comfort.

How she wished things could be different, that she had made other choices at seventeen and didn't have this dark cloud hanging over her now because of those decisions.

"Ruben," she began, but whatever she intended to say was lost when he leaned down and silenced her with his mouth pressed against hers.

She should have immediately pulled away but she didn't have the strength. How could she possibly resist the temptation to kiss him one more time?

The boat rocked softly on the waves, pushing her toward him then away again, and she could hear the distant sound of other boats. Some part of her knew they needed to be heading back to Haven Point so she could find her children at the festival.

She pushed the knowledge aside for now. She could have this moment, couldn't she? A tiny slice of time to kiss this man who made her feel things she thought she had put away forever.

He deepened the kiss and she pressed herself against him, lost in the delicious sensations that pushed away the darkness.

They could make love, out here on the water.

The thought tangled her breath and left her light-headed.

There was a bed in the berth down below. She had seen it when she checked on Silver earlier. They could go below while the waves rocked the boat and she could be with him fully, as everything inside her ached for.

And then what?

They couldn't be together beyond this moment. It would be hard enough to push him away, as she knew she must. She couldn't make things harder on either of them by deepening their intimacy.

She closed her eyes, hating what she had to do but aware she had no choice. She wrenched her mouth away, though it was just about the hardest thing she'd ever done.

"Stop. Please, Ruben. Stop. We can't do this."

"Why not?"

"I told you. I make terrible decisions where men are concerned. Now you know just how terrible those decisions are. I can't drag you into my mess."

"I'm in it, like it or not. I care about you, Dani. I'd like to see where this goes between us."

She closed her eyes. "You have to be realistic here. Put away those glasses and look at me. What would the sheriff or others in the department think if they found out you were seeing a woman whose ex-husband had killed two of your own?"

That seemed to soak in. He let out a heavy breath and

straightened. "I hope they would be smart enough to know you can't be held responsible for the actions of someone who hasn't been part of your life for years."

"What if they don't see it that way?"

He gazed at her. "You're really going to let this come between us?"

"There is no *us*, except for a few kisses." Her hands were shaking and she folded them together, her heart aching. "That's all we have. All we'll ever have."

"Why? Because you made a mistake once and gave your heart to the wrong man?"

When she didn't answer, he reached for her hand, trapping her fingers before she could pull them away.

"Would it make a difference if I tell you I'm falling in love with you?"

His low words burst through her like Roman candles trailing a shower of sparks. She wanted to reach for them and hold on tight, to tuck them against her where she could treasure them forever.

Reality splashed over her just seconds later as if someone had doused her with that cold lake water.

"You're attracted to me. You're not in love with me."

"I'm thirty-three years old, Daniela. I've been attracted to plenty of women. I've never been in love with a single one of them, until now."

She wanted to believe him, to throw herself back into his arms right here on *The Wonder* and stay forever.

She couldn't do it. She didn't dare take the chance.

She never should have kissed him that first night. She

had somehow known this man had the potential to break her heart—not because of anything he did but because she didn't have the strength or courage to reach for the future they might have together.

She swallowed, hating herself all over again. "I'm flattered, believe me, but I...I'm not interested in a relationship," she lied. "Not with you and not with any man. You've been very kind to me and my daughters and I'm so grateful but...it has to end. I thought we could be friends but I can't see how that's possible. Not with this...this heat between us that we can never act upon."

"It's more than attraction and you damn well know it."

"I can't, Ruben. I'm sorry. Can you just take me back to Haven Point now? I need to find my daughters."

He gazed at her for a long moment. She couldn't see his expression through the dim light but she could feel the tension radiating off him.

She wanted to tell him she was sorry, that she didn't mean any of it. She wanted to step back into his arms and kiss him again until nothing else mattered. Instead, she forced herself to move away from him, to the other seat on the boat.

He opened his mouth to say something but closed it again and started up the boat, pulled up the anchor and headed back to Haven Point in silence.

Ruben usually enjoyed his regular visits to Haven Point Middle School, but he wasn't looking forward to this one. If he could have passed the emergency call off to someone else, he would have, but he was the school's liaison with the sheriff's department. It was his responsibility.

With only one more school day before Christmas vacation after this one, the anticipation at the school was as noticeable as the smell of corn dogs coming from the cafeteria. A big Christmas tree dominated the entryway, paper chain garlands were draped around the interior doorways and white paper snowflakes dangled from the ceilings.

He must have just missed the bell going off between classes, since the halls were clogged with students laughing, looking at their phones, shoving each other.

He saw at least a dozen Santa hats and as many ugly Christmas sweaters.

As he made his way to the office, he waved at several students he knew and fist-bumped a couple more. He was just about to push open one of the double glass doors into the office when Silver Capelli walked past.

"Oh!" she exclaimed. "Hey, Ruben." She actually smiled at him, which he considered amazing progress, considering where they had been a few weeks earlier.

He let the office door close again and moved out of the way of people going in and out so he could talk to her. "How's it going?"

"Pretty good. School is almost out for Christmas break. Only three periods and one day left, then we're off for two weeks."

He remembered that jubilation leading into a long break from school. Nothing else compared to it. How did grown-ups lose that excitement somewhere along the way?

Ruben looked around to make sure no one else was in earshot. "And only five more nights of our little project. How's that been going?"

She gave the same furtive scan of the area before shifting her gaze back to him. "Pretty good. I haven't been caught yet, if that's what you're asking. Mia and I are pretty sneaky."

Ruben had been shut out of his own Secret Santa deliveries a few days earlier, though he wasn't sure if the reason had more to do with his schedule becoming more chaotic leading up to the holidays or because Dani was purposely avoiding him.

He only knew that earlier in the week he had to work a late shift to cover for another deputy and asked if Silver could handle the delivery without him. Dani had suggested he leave all the gifts at their house so they could make the deliveries when it was convenient for her family's schedule, instead of his.

He couldn't manage to come up with a good argument. She was right, his work shifts had become crazy.

It made sense to hand it over to her and her girls. At least this way, the secret gifts his mother had prepared didn't all have to be delivered in the middle of the night when he was done with work.

Despite the logic, he couldn't help feeling excluded.

"Good job," he said to Silver. "My schedule should be a little more regular from now until Christmas Eve. Do you want me to take over now? I can probably handle the rest."

"No. I've got it," she said. "Mia would be heartbroken

if we couldn't finish out the whole twelve days. She gets a real kick out of it."

He had a feeling Mia wasn't the only one. "Well, let me know if you change your mind. I can take a night or two."

"I think we're good. I need to get to my English class before the tardy bell rings. I'll see you later, Ruben." She flashed him a quick smile. "Merry Christmas."

"Bye."

He watched her meet up with a couple of girls and start walking down the hall. She seemed to be talking and laughing with them, a far cry from the sullen girl she had been a few weeks earlier.

She had her mother's smile. He hadn't noticed it before, but now it made his heart ache.

He now knew what it felt like to bang his head against a wall again and again.

While her daughter was becoming friendlier and more comfortable around him, Dani had moved in the opposite direction. After their night on his boat during the Lights on the Lake Festival almost a week earlier, she had gone out of her way to avoid him. The warm, caring woman he had come to know over the past few weeks had once more become prickly and unapproachable.

He sighed. His life had seemed uncomplicated a few weeks ago. Now he was so tangled up over Dr. Daniela Capelli, he wasn't sleeping well, he was short-tempered, and he seemed to have lost any anticipation and joy for the upcoming holidays.

"Ruben. There you are."

The assistant principal at the middle school marched toward him, his features tight and his belly hanging over his belt.

Todd Andrews was around Ruben's age and they went to school together. Ruben remembered him as a sanctimonious jerk even in elementary school, when Todd used to volunteer every week to be the hall monitor so he could write up infractions committed by anybody he didn't like.

As far as Ruben was concerned, he hadn't changed much. If anything, a little power had made things worse.

"Hey, Todd," he said casually.

"I called in a report nearly forty minutes ago. What took you so long?"

The temper that seemed on a knife's edge these days threatened to flare. He had been working sixteen-hour days all week and was deep in the middle of an ugly domestic abuse case that was particularly heartbreaking this time of year. Not to mention that the middle school was a fifteen-minute drive from Shelter Springs in good weather and right now a storm was slowing traffic.

Apparently when the assistant principal of the middle school called, Ruben was supposed to speed over with his lights and siren blaring.

"Things are a little hectic this close to the holidays, Todd. I was on another call. What's going on? The dispatcher said you wanted to report another theft."

The middle school had been experiencing a rash of thefts, with the PE lockers being particularly hard hit since students often didn't bother to lock up their belongings.

"This is a little more than a missing cell phone! We have a serious situation. Maybe I need to speak to Sheriff Bailey."

"You could do that," Ruben said slowly, "but since I'm the department liaison to the middle and high schools in Haven Point, I'm afraid he would only pass your call on to me. You might as well start where you're going to end up. With me."

They had been over the subject of protocol and lines of authority before. It didn't seem to make any difference. Todd had always disliked Ruben and seemed to think going over his head to Marshall—someone he *also* disliked—would somehow solve all his problems.

"Since I'm here," Ruben said, "you might as well tell me what's going on, then I can consult with Sheriff Bailey."

He could tell by the other man's pursed lips that Todd didn't particularly like that idea. Too bad. Ruben had more important things to worry about than the man's ego. He was here to do his job.

Todd glowered. "I can't stress enough the gravity of this matter. The spirit club has been raising money to send to victims of the latest hurricane. We keep a jar in the office and people have been dropping off their extra change all month, until they had collected more than $250 in donations."

"That's impressive. Good for the spirit club."

"I would agree, except right after third hour, the whole jar disappeared. It was here before that, then it was gone. I thought perhaps a member of the spirit club leadership might have taken it to count the donations, since their fund-raising campaign ends today. They're supposed to talk to me first before handling the jar but students don't always follow procedure."

Much to Todd's dismay, Ruben was certain.

"I'm assuming you checked with them all."

"Of course I checked with them all! I called each one out of class and they assured me they hadn't seen the jar. Someone took it. Someone unauthorized. You need to move fast. I would suggest you put the whole school on lockdown until you find the culprit."

Ruben gave an inward groan. He couldn't put the whole school on lockdown over a missing jar of change. The very idea was ridiculous.

"Let's hold off on that while I ask a few questions first," he said. "Do you have any suspects?"

"I have four hundred suspects. They're called students."

Yeah. This was the reason he didn't like the guy. Todd always saw the bad in people, which Ruben considered a lousy character trait when it came to dealing with middle school students.

"Any chance you could narrow that down a little? You have security cameras in here, don't you?"

The other man's lips thinned further. "We do, but unfortunately they've been malfunctioning since last week and we haven't been able to get the district IT person in to take a look. Principal Garcia tried to call before she left town earlier this week and couldn't get anyone. Everybody seems to be backed up this time of year. Believe me, if the cameras were functional, I would have looked there first before involving the sheriff's department."

Ruben found this disheartening on several levels, especially the part about the principal being gone. Vicki Garcia was far more reasonable, with a kind heart and bucketloads of patience.

"That's too bad. I was hoping for an easier resolution."

"We need to search everyone. If you won't authorize a full lockdown, I think we should at least start a locker-by-locker search until we find the missing jar. It's a little big for students to hide under their shirts."

Ruben could think of several problems with that suggestion. While the law was vague about whether students had any expectation of privacy or protection from law enforcement against searches on school property and the school district had its own rules, the sheriff's department policy was clear. Without a warrant—or in this case, four hundred warrants—he could only search school lockers if he had strong and compelling evidence of wrongdoing.

Not only that, most of the students he knew kept all their belongings in backpacks and carried everything from class to class. He suspected half of them didn't even know their locker combinations.

Ruben tried to head off Todd's exuberance. "Let me do a little digging before we jump the gun. I need to talk to the office staff and see if they can give me some names of people who might have been in the office around the time the jar disappeared."

"Don't you think I've already asked the secretaries?" Todd demanded. "They don't know anything."

If he spoke to them with that kind of derogatory tone, Ruben completely understood why no one would want to tell the man what they knew. "I have to follow procedure. You, of all people, should appreciate that. Protocol demands I interview potential eyewitnesses myself, even if they have already been interviewed by school staff. I know it's a pain, but I can't break the rules."

The vice principal looked torn between his deep and abiding love for rules and his insistence that his way was the best. "It's a big waste of time, if you ask me," he finally said. "You would do better to at least search the backpacks and lockers of the ones we've had the most trouble with this year. The likeliest suspects. For instance, I hear you had some vandalism at your place a few weeks ago and that our new student from the East Coast was involved. Maybe you should start there."

Okay, now Ruben wanted to punch the bastard.

"Why would you think that?"

"There's a rumor going around that her family is connected—organized crime."

"Mafia? Really? Because she has an Italian surname? That's a little xenophobic and racist, don't you think, Todd? I'm surprised at you."

The other man flushed. "Setting aside the rumors I have picked up about her past and that her father was the leader of a crime syndicate, there remains the fact that she vandal-ized your home and that of one of our most beloved faculty members. Gertrude told me all about it. I don't think it's a coincidence that Miss Capelli moves to our school and suddenly we have a rash of thefts throughout the school year. And now this."

"I think you're jumping to conclusions with no basis in fact. Let me do my job, Todd. I'll start by talking with the office support staff and we can go from there."

He turned away without giving the man a chance to argue his point, hoping against hope that Silver Capelli had been at the exact opposite end of the school building when the jar of money disappeared.

"Any progress?" Marshall asked when Ruben called to check in an hour later.

"Nothing. I'm stumped. How do you want me to proceed?"

"Not with a lockdown and not with a person-by-person search, that's for sure. Your instincts are right on. Call in Todd's prime suspects and see if you get any hint of anything that doesn't feel right. These are kids. It should be pretty easy to tell if they're lying."

"You have kids. Can you always tell when Christopher isn't telling you the truth?"

"Good point," Marshall said. "Not always, but he usually has a tell or two. Watch for those who won't meet your gaze and also the overlong and too-complicated answers. You know the drill."

"Yeah. Thanks. I'll keep you posted."

He hung up from Marsh and looked over his list of suspects. He had spoken with all the staff and student office helpers, taking down names of everyone who had been in and out of the office around the time the jar had disappeared.

One name stood out. Silver Capelli. She had come in between classes during that time frame, claiming she had a verbal message from another student that one of the counselors wanted to speak with her about her schedule. That message, if it really had been given to Silver, appeared to have been a mistake. None of the three counselors claimed to have summoned her.

He had a grim, tight feeling in his chest. He had to find another suspect. If Silver had taken the donation jar, it would devastate her mother. He couldn't imagine having to be the one to tell Dani that Silver was on the hook for this.

With renewed determination, he headed out front to speak to the office staff one last time before he started going through the list of suspects and calling students back to speak with him.

Before he could reach the desk, the vice principal shoved open the double doors, carrying a large jar in one arm and dragging Silver behind him with the other.

"Ha! I found it," Todd declared, giving Ruben a triumphant look. "I haven't had time to count it but I hope it's all there, all $250 and change. And guess where I found it? In Miss Capelli's locker, where I suggested we look an hour ago, if you'll recall."

Ruben's heart dropped. She looked terrified and confused, but with that come-at-me defiance he had been used to seeing until lately.

"Sil," he said slowly. "Tell me you didn't do this."

The vice principal snorted "Of course she did it! The evidence was right there in her locker!"

"Did you have a warrant to search my locker?" she demanded.

"I don't need a warrant." He gave her an evil grin. "School administrators can search students' lockers and belongings at will, as long as they can show credible evidence of wrongdoing."

"What was your credible evidence?" Ruben asked calmly, trying his best to keep his temper contained. "This is the first I'm hearing of anything beyond suspicion."

The Silver he had come to know over the last few weeks wouldn't do something like that. Sure, she had vandalized *The Wonder* and a few other places. But she had also pitched in to clean up her mess. He sensed Silver used brashness and attitude to hide her inherent insecurities, like her mother did.

"While you were busy talking to the secretaries, I received an anonymous tip telling me exactly where to look for the missing money. Apparently someone saw her hiding it in her locker."

"How did you receive this so-called tip?" Ruben asked.

"A phone call in my office. And before you ask, no, I don't know the number. It was blocked. All I know is that the caller was a female student, obviously trying to disguise her voice by speaking in a false lower octave."

"It doesn't matter who called you," Silver said, her expression a mix of anger and fear. "They were lying. I didn't steal that stupid jar and I have no idea how it ended up in my locker."

Todd snorted. "So it just mysteriously appeared there and you had nothing to do with it. We're supposed to believe that?"

"I don't care what you believe. It's the truth. I didn't do it. And whose dumb idea was it anyway to leave a big jar full of money out in a public area full of middle school students? You should have just put a sign on it saying Take Me."

Ruben had to agree she had a point but Todd apparently saw things differently. His features turned an ugly shade of purple.

"That's quite enough out of you, young lady," he said, fierce dislike in his voice.

Why the hell did the man get a job in education when it was clear he couldn't stand the students? Todd was a bully, plain and simple. A clean-cut, by-the-rules bully. The only trouble was, with the more reasonable principal gone, this particular bully was calling the shots and Ruben didn't know what to do about it.

"I don't know how they did things where you came from," Todd said, "but here in Haven Point we don't tolerate this kind of behavior."

Silver folded her arms across her chest and gave him a scornful look. "Really? In my whole life, nobody ever told me it was against the rules to steal things. Back in Boston, we got extra credit for it."

"Silver, your sarcasm is not helping," Ruben said.

She turned a pleading look in his direction. "I didn't do this. I would *never*. I'm telling you, somebody had to have planted that in my locker."

Ruben was beginning to believe the same thing. He found it highly suspicious that she had been given a mysterious summons to speak with a counselor who never asked for her, right around the time the jar went missing.

Coincidences in his line of work were rarely that.

"Why would somebody set you up? Do you have any enemies?"

She gave him a pitying sort of look. "I'm new to the school when everybody else has been here their whole lives. I have an accent that's somewhere between Boston and Queens, I have purple hair and I wear clothes that won't catch on here for at least three years. Of *course* I have enemies!"

"If you have enemies, it's because you haven't tried to make friends," Todd said in a snide voice. "Face it, Miss Capelli, you've had a bad attitude since the first day you arrived at Haven Point Middle School."

Silver gave a little shuddering breath and Ruben knew instinctively she was close to tears. Damn it. She would *hate* crying in front of the vice principal, as much as her mother had hated crying in front of him.

He wanted to wrap his arms around her and promise her everything would be okay, that he would do everything he could to figure out a way to make this right, but he was helpless in the situation. All evidence pointed against her and at this point, Ruben had no proof someone else was behind the theft.

"Can you narrow that list down a little?" Ruben said. "Are you sure you can't identify the person who told you a counselor wanted to see you earlier?"

She shook her head. "I think it might have been a seventh grader. I didn't know her. She just said someone told her to tell the girl with purple hair that she had to go to the office, so I did."

"That's quite a convenient story," Todd said with a sneer.

"Ask Mrs. Hobbs, the counselor. I showed up and she didn't know a thing about me coming in, since she never asked anyone to get me."

"How do we know you didn't just make up the whole thing? It's more likely that you came up with some far-fetched story about someone telling someone to get you for Mrs. Hobbs, all so you could have an excuse to be in the office and steal the jar of money."

"But I didn't," she said. "Ruben, you believe me, don't you?"

He could say nothing, not with Todd there ready to jump on his every word.

"It looks pretty bad, kid."

"Stealing is grounds for immediate disciplinary action. Automatic suspension, at the very least, while we determine what charges will be filed in the criminal court."

"Criminal court? But I didn't take anything!"

"The proof was in your locker."

"I told you, someone else must have put that in there. It wasn't me."

Ruben believed her, without question, but he knew Todd wouldn't see things the same way. It was up to Ruben to prove her innocence, which was always much harder than proving guilt. He just had to find the person who set her up and convince them to admit to the truth.

No problem. Ha.

"Any idea who might have been able to do that? Who else would have your locker combination?"

For the first time, he saw her falter. She looked down at the ground then at her fingernails.

"I don't know," she finally said, her voice subdued, giving him the distinct impression she wasn't being completely truthful. "Maybe someone watched me get into my locker once and, I don't know, figured out my combination from that."

"Is there a master list on the computer of students and their combinations? Could someone have hacked into that?" Ruben asked Todd.

"That's ridiculous. Why would anybody do that?"

"To frame Silver, maybe."

"Highly unlikely."

"But not impossible."

"Nearly." The vice principal scowled. "We keep that information in a folder on the secretary's desk. But I can't imagine how a student could have access to that without being seen snooping, especially under my watch."

Someone had managed to steal a jar of money off the

counter without being seen under his watch but Ruben decided it might not be very politic right now to remind Todd of that.

"This is all a waste of time. Miss Capelli obviously stole that money. I am not surprised." He turned to her. "I'm just shocked that you would bring your ways to our school and think you can get away with it. We got you, didn't we?"

He grinned maliciously and Ruben again had to fight the urge to deck the little bastard. He could take him out with one good punch, but that would solve nothing and the paperwork would be a nightmare. He just had to figure out how he could fix this for Silver and for Dani.

Silver seemed to shrink in her chair and Ruben could see tears forming in her eyes.

"I am ordering suspension for the remainder of today and of course tomorrow, then I will consult with Principal Garcia during the break and we will determine the correct course of action from this point."

"The correct course of action would be to pull your head out and accept that I did not do this," she insisted.

Ruben wanted to tell her to stow it, that she was only making things worse for herself, but he could say nothing under the circumstances.

"I'm calling your mother right now. I'm sure Dr. Capelli will be shocked that her daughter could stoop to such terrible behavior."

"My mom? Why do you have to call my mom?"

"Because she needs to come and get you. As of this moment, you're suspended."

Silver sat back in the chair and covered her face with her hands and Ruben's heart broke for her.

"Given the seriousness of the situation, I don't think this is something that should be done in a phone call, Todd. I'm sure you agree with me on that."

The vice principal looked confused. "What are you suggesting?"

"I know Dr. Capelli. She works with my father, as I'm sure you're aware. Right now she's at the clinic. I think the best course of action would be for me to take Silver to her mother and speak with her there about what has happened today."

"I think it would be best if we call her in so I can tell her what kind of trouble Silver is in."

The anticipation in Todd's voice curdled his stomach. *So you can bully Dani, too, just like you're doing with her daughter? No chance in hell*, Ruben thought.

"Because of the seriousness of the matter, this is really a matter for law enforcement now. I'm afraid I need to take her into custody."

"What?" Silver said. She looked completely betrayed. He again wanted to assure her that everything would be okay but he couldn't say anything in front of the vice principal. Besides, he wasn't sure he could promise her anything of the sort, not when the evidence was so damning against her. It was hard to argue her innocence when the missing money was found in her locker.

"It would be best if I talk to her mother in person. Thank you for your help with the investigation but I'll take care of things from here." He met Silver's gaze, hoping she could see he was on her side. "Do you have everything you need? Your coat, your books?"

She lifted her backpack without meeting his gaze, her face crumpled as if she had lost faith in everything good and right in the world.

"Okay," he said in his most stern voice for Todd's benefit. "Let's go talk to your mother."

"You haven't finished your Christmas shopping yet? I've been done for *months*."

Dani cringed inwardly at the chiding tone from Gloria. Yet one more thing for her to feel guilty about. She had been a little busy the last few weeks trying to keep up with her work at the clinic and juggle being a mom to a troublesome teenager and an energetic six-year-old.

"I did most of mine online, which took so much hassle out of it," Gloria went on. "I'm afraid you're too late for online delivery now, though, especially up here in Haven Point. I always figure it takes things at least an extra day or two to make it over the mountains from Boise."

"You're probably right," Dani murmured. "I'm mostly done. I was thinking I would make a late-night trip to the big-box store in Shelter Springs after the girls are in bed tonight."

"You better finish before the weekend," Gloria advised. "I wouldn't be caught dead shopping on the last Saturday before the holiday. The crowds will be *insane*. People think

Black Friday is the biggest shopping day of the year, but it's not. It's the Saturday before Christmas."

She had lived in metropolitan areas all her life, first New York then Boston. Somehow she had a feeling her version of insane crowds and Gloria's version would be significantly different.

"I'll keep that in mind," Dani said. "Can you find my notes from my last appointment with McKenzie Kilpatrick's poodle? She's bringing her in again this afternoon for a follow-up appointment and I want to go over what we talked about last time."

The clinic door opened before Gloria had a chance to respond. Both of them turned to greet the newcomer but Dani's automatic polite smile of welcome never even had time to sprout at the sight of Ruben, in full, forbidding uniform complete with Stetson and coat, walking in with a subdued-looking Silver.

Dani's stomach plummeted. She could only think of a few reasons her daughter would be escorted home by a deputy sheriff, none of them good.

Oh, Silver. What kind of trouble are you in this time?

She straightened her spine, vertebra by vertebra. "What's going on? It's the middle of the school day. Are you sick?"

To her astonishment, Silver burst into tears and rushed through the door to the reception area. Dani barely had time for the shock to register before her daughter threw her arms around her, sobbing words she couldn't understand.

"Honey, it's okay. Whatever it is, it's going to be okay. We'll fix it."

"You can't fix this. I hate it here. Please, Mom, can I go back to Boston or New York? I could stay with Chelsea's family or...or Grandma DeLuca said I could live with her. Please, Mom."

There was no possible way on earth she was going to let Silver live with a friend or with Tommy's mother. "What's going on, Ruben? What's happened?"

Ruben glanced at Gloria, who was watching the whole proceeding avidly. "Can we go back to your office to discuss this somewhere more private?"

"It doesn't matter where we are," Silver said, her voice vibrating with emotion. "You can tell Gloria and everyone else. I don't care."

"Tell us what?" Dani asked, her sense of foreboding increasing.

"I've been suspended from school and now Ruben is going to arrest me."

14

Dani wasn't sure which was louder, her instinctive gasp or Gloria's sudden curse word, which wasn't at all fit for children's ears.

"Sorry. What?" She couldn't have heard Silver correctly. She *couldn't* have.

"Why don't we move this to your office," Ruben suggested again.

Through her shock, Dani looked at Gloria and then toward the front windows, where she could see a car pulling into the parking lot. Most likely it was McKenzie Kilpatrick with her beautiful standard poodle Paprika. Dani did *not* need the mayor of Haven Point hearing about Silver being in trouble, at least not until Dani herself knew what was going on.

"Gloria, will you please tell Mayor Kilpatrick I've been delayed but I'll be with her momentarily."

Dani's stomach curled with nausea as she led the way back to her small office. As usual, Ruben filled any space he occupied, but she didn't have time to focus on that.

She shut the door behind them all. "What is this about? Will someone please tell me what's going on?"

Silver only sobbed into her hands and Dani put an arm around her daughter's shoulders, giving Ruben an expectant look.

He sighed, his expression difficult to read. "Someone took a collection jar intended for disaster relief from the front office today. After the vice principal received a tip, he searched Silver's locker and found the jar there. I'm afraid she has been suspended for now and will likely face other disciplinary action when the principal returns after the New Year."

Dani felt as if someone had just touched dry ice to her insides. Everything seemed to shrivel and burn. First graffiti, now stealing a collection jar for charity. What was happening to her child? Was this the way Tommy had started? A poor choice here, a disastrous one there? First stealing spare change from school then moving on to a bank robbery and an eventual shoot-out with police?

The thought left her nauseous, grateful she was sitting down.

She thought when she came to Haven Point she was

doing the right thing for her children, trying to carve out a happy, warm life for them. Now everything was falling apart.

Dani looked at Silver's downcast head against her, the purple of her colored hair in vivid contrast to Dani's white lab coat.

No. No, she couldn't believe it. Emotions rose in her throat and as they did, she had a sudden unmistakable assurance.

Her daughter would not have done this.

She didn't care what kind of evidence Ruben thought he had against her. She knew her child and knew without any measure of doubt that Silver would not have stolen a collection jar intended for charity.

She would never believe it.

It wasn't simply that her daughter had a generous heart and always tried to help those in need, though she did. Silver was always the first one to make sandwiches and hand them out to the homeless or to empty her piggy bank to help out a cause she was passionate about.

Beyond that, Dani couldn't believe it simply because her daughter was entirely too street-smart to be part of something so ridiculously stupid, to think that she could get away with that kind of half-assed crime in full daylight, in a crowded school.

Dani had never wanted to be one of those parents who would never think ill of their own child and believed the whole world had it out for her. But in this case, she had to stand by Silver. She just couldn't accept it.

Her gaze shifted to Ruben and initial shock and dismay began to transform into something else—a deep sense of betrayal. He knew Silver. He had to know she would never be involved in something like this, no matter what kind of evidence he found.

"Honey, I need to speak with Deputy Morales out in the hallway," she said, careful to use his official title, not Ruben.

This man with a badge on his chest was not their sweet, kind friend who had taken them on boat rides and held her while she cried and delivered gifts to neighbors in need. This was a hard, immovable law enforcement officer.

Would it make a difference if I tell you I'm falling in love with you?

He had obviously come to his senses, as she had fully expected. He wouldn't be here, otherwise.

Pain and loss, her old familiar companions, sliced through her but she did her best to ignore them for now.

He followed her out into the hallway, his features remote.

Dani closed her office door with Silver on the other side and tried to keep her hands from trembling as she faced him. "You think she did this."

A muscle in his jaw flexed. "It's a little hard to defend her to the vice principal when the jar and the money were found in her locker."

"I can't believe you would let this happen."

"What was I supposed to do?" His voice had a bite to it but she ignored it and plowed forward.

"Have a little faith! You know Sil. You know she would

never do this. This is exactly what I was afraid would happen! I should never have told you about her father."

On some level, she knew she was being unfair, taking out her fear and frustration on him because she didn't know what else to do. In some strange way, his uniform had come to represent everything that seemed out of reach to her.

Security. Comfort. A safe haven.

She wanted that here in the aptly named Haven Point, but, as usual, she had screwed everything up. She was in love with Ruben and her heart ached at the impossibility of it all, the happiness that apparently would always remain just out of reach.

"I get it." Her voice sounded as cold as the rest of her felt. "Her dad is the worst sort of criminal, so of course Silver must be, too. She must have bad blood."

He continued to look down at her with stony features. "I never said or implied that."

"You didn't have to. I'm sure that's what you're thinking. The first moment anything goes wrong, it must be Silver's fault. Who else could be responsible?"

"You have a damn chip on your shoulder as big as Idaho, Dani. This has nothing to do with freaking Tommy De-Luca. The stolen money was in her locker. That's tough to explain away. Even you have to admit that."

For a moment, doubt flickered through her. Was it possible Silver had staged the whole thing knowing she would be caught? Was this some convoluted, underhanded way she had come up with to force Dani's hand and make her send Silver back to Boston or to New York and her grandmother?

No. She couldn't believe it. Sil would never do something like that. Her daughter was *not* her father, trying to manipulate every situation to her advantage.

Dani would never believe it and it hurt more than she ever imagined to discover that Ruben could.

"I know. You're only doing your job. I get it. The evidence was against her, plus there's the minor little matter of her father being a vicious cop killer. Why would you believe her when she said she didn't do it?"

"Can you just put down that chip and trust me for five freaking minutes?"

If her emotions weren't such a tangled mess, she might have laughed. Trust him. He had no idea what he was asking of her. She had spent her entire life trusting people, only to face betrayal after betrayal.

She couldn't have this out with him right now. She had a patient waiting. Unfortunately, McKenzie would simply have to wait a few moments longer. First, Dani had to do her best to comfort her heartbroken and frightened daughter.

"Thank you for bringing Silver here. I'm sure you didn't have to. I could have gone to the school to pick her up."

"The vice principal wanted you to, but I thought it would be better if I broke the news to you first myself."

She wanted to be grateful to him for that, at least, but she couldn't manage anything more than a stiff nod. "You've done that. Thanks. You can go now. I'll deal with things from this point."

"Dani—"

She didn't want to hear his apologies or explanations. Not

now. He should have stood up for her daughter. He had assured her that her past didn't matter a bit to him but at the first opportunity, Ruben was as quick as everyone else to judge and condemn.

"Under the circumstances, I'm afraid you'll have to take care of your own Secret Santa tradition tonight. My girls and I will be busy with other things."

Oh, she sounded like a bitch. She heard her own clipped words and wanted to call them back but this was for the best. Better to cut ties with him now, once and for all.

"I'll have Mia run over the rest of the gifts for the Larkin family and leave them on your porch. Excuse me, Deputy Morales. I have to focus on my daughter now."

She walked into her office and closed the door, feeling as if her heart had been sliced to pieces and was now lying on the floor under his boots.

A dark cloud seemed to have descended on their little house by the lake.

Silver had stayed in her room since the previous afternoon, periodically coming out like a shadowy wraith to use the bathroom, pick at her food, grab a drink, then return.

Mia didn't quite understand what was going on. Neither Silver nor Dani felt like she needed to know, but it was clear she sensed something serious was wrong. She was subdued, quiet, without her usual excited Christmas chatter or the songs she had been singing nonstop since her school program the day before.

Dani didn't sleep well, tossing and turning while she tried

to figure out what she could do to clear her child's name. Silver had told her all she knew, that someone she didn't know had told her a counselor wanted to see her. She had gone to the office, only to find out the message had been in error. Next thing she knew, the vice principal had been yanking her out of class and hauling her to the office to find Ruben there.

For reasons Dani didn't understand, her daughter didn't seem upset at Ruben. Far from it. She said he had tried to reason with the vice principal but the school had stood firm.

Perhaps Dani had been too hard on him. She remembered her bitter words and the abrupt way she had kicked him out of her office. He had asked her to trust him but she still didn't know how she could possibly do that.

She only knew this was the worst possible thing that could happen to Silver when she was trying to adapt to a new school. Guilty or not, she would be the subject of gossip at school. It was inevitable. She would be tried and convicted by all her peers. Dani was certain of it.

Maybe they would be better off picking up and going somewhere else. She was licensed to practice veterinary medicine anywhere in Idaho. They could move to a large community like Boise and she could practice there—or she could take the necessary licensing tests in another state and start over somewhere completely new. Maybe somewhere warm and beachy like California would be a nice change.

Some part of her was very much afraid that wouldn't do any good. How could they ever escape Tommy DeLuca's grim legacy? The past would follow them wherever they went.

She finally rose well before sunrise. After letting Winky out to do her business and then opening the door so she could come inside again, Dani sat with her dog in her lap next to the Christmas tree Ruben had helped them put up.

There, alone, she wept for the mistakes she couldn't change, the decisions she couldn't undo and the ripple effect those choices continued to have in the lives of those she loved.

At last, she brushed herself off, dried her tears and rose. Her daughters needed her and she needed to focus on that.

After sending Mia off to school, Dani persuaded Silver to go into the clinic with her while she worked her Friday half day.

Silver wanted to stay home and hide away by herself but Dani didn't feel like that would be the best option for her. Better to give her something constructive to do and help focus her attention outward, so she told Silver she would pay her to walk and cuddle some of the dogs and cats they were boarding over the holidays.

It seemed to work. Animals always had a way of working their calming magic and Silver was in a much better frame of mind by the time they left the clinic.

As she and her daughter were driving home through the snow-covered pines and firs that lined the road beside the lake, inspiration struck. "Mia will be getting out early today for Christmas break. I think we should drive to Shelter Springs, finish our Christmas shopping, have a nice dinner somewhere in town and then go to see *The Nutcracker.*

I believe tonight is the last night we can catch the amateur ballet troupe's production there. What do you think?"

"I guess, as long as we won't see anybody from my school."

Dani briefly shifted her gaze from the road, her heart breaking all over again for her daughter. "I can't promise you that. I'm sorry. There's a good chance we might see someone from school. I understand why you would want to avoid everyone. Never mind. We can go to the ballet next year. Tonight, let's just stay home and watch a movie or something."

Silver chewed her lip, a habit Dani knew her daughter had picked up from her. "No," she said after a moment, her voice resolute. "I didn't do anything wrong, so I shouldn't be the one hiding at home like I'm ashamed or something."

"Good call," Dani said around the lump in her throat. "We'll go and have a great time together, just the three of us. Anybody who has a problem with it can take it up with somebody who gives a rat's ass."

Silver giggled, the sound so sweet that Dani didn't even feel guilty for swearing.

As Dani might have expected, Mia was thrilled with the idea of dinner and the ballet, especially as it meant dressing up a little more than usual.

Dani had just finished putting on her favorite red sweater and piling her hair up into an easy updo when the doorbell rang.

"Who could that be?" Mia asked, dancing to the door with her best ballerina pirouette. She opened it before Dani could make it to the door herself to check the peephole first.

Mia beamed at the person on the other side. "Hi, Ruben! Guess what? We're going to see *The Nutcracker*. I watched it once on TV but now we get to see the real thing, with real people dancing. Like this."

She did another pirouette, twirling her doll around in her arms.

"You're both very good. May we come in? We need to talk to your mom and to Silver."

We? Who was here with him? Dani moved farther into the living room, sticking the last pin in her hair. Her hands froze and slowly lowered when she spotted two girls with him, Emma and Ella Larkin.

They were the friends of Silver whose mother had cancer, the family who had been receiving all the Secret Santa gifts delivered by Silver and Mia for Ruben over the past week.

The girls didn't meet her gaze, just looked down at the ground, and Dani frowned in confusion.

Why were they there? Had they found out about the gifts? Oh, she hoped not. Silver and Mia had taken such care to avoid discovery. It would be too bad if the surprise had been ruined.

It must be that. What else would bring them here, in Ruben's company? They were certainly having an odd reaction, though.

"We need to speak with Silver, too," Ruben said. He glanced at her, his features so grim and remote that her heart ached. He was wearing his uniform again and the silvery badge at his chest reflected the lights of the Christmas tree he had helped them with.

She wanted to tell him no, that Silver was unavailable, but her daughter popped her head out of her bedroom before Dani had the chance.

Silver had the same reaction Dani had to the twins' appearance. She froze, then frowned in confusion. "Oh," she said. "Hi."

Dani could detect no warmth whatsoever in her voice, which surprised her. Until the last few weeks, the three girls had been friends.

"Silver, could you come in here and sit down?" Ruben said. "Emma and Ella have something they need to tell you."

"It doesn't matter," Silver said quickly.

"Yes, it does."

Though she looked as if she wanted to flee back into her room and slam the door, she finally moved slowly into the living room, her hands curled at her sides and her features tense. She perched on the edge of the sofa and Dani sat beside her.

"What is this about?" she asked.

"Go ahead, girls," Ruben said, in that same solemn voice.

Dani couldn't tell the girls apart. She thought Silver had once told her Emma had a mole on her cheek. Or was that Ella? Either way, with their fine blond hair and blue eyes, the girls looked so much alike, Dani wondered if their own mother knew which was which.

Today, they both looked as if they had been crying, she realized. Their eyes were red, with little makeup streaks on their splotchy cheeks.

What on earth was going on?

One of them stepped forward a little. "We…we owe you an apology," she said, speaking quickly as if the words were being forced out of her. "Emma and I were the ones who stole the spirit club's donation jar. *I* stole it, anyway. It was easy, since I'm an aide in the office. I just put it in one of those empty boxes of paper reams from the copy machine, when the secretaries were back in the staff room having a treat. Then I offered to take all the empty boxes to the re-cycling outside."

"Except she didn't," the other girl said. "El made up a fake note so she could call me out of class and I opened your locker and we put it in there. And we're sorry."

Dani stared at the girls, completely astonished. She had always thought them such nice girls. They had been kind to Silver since they moved to Haven Point, the two girls Dani had considered Silver's closest friends.

Why would they do something like this?

She looked over at Silver and was further shocked to re-alize her daughter didn't seem particularly surprised, almost as if she had been expecting something like this.

"How did you know my combination?"

Emma spoke up. "You gave it to me that time when I needed extra space to put all that stuff for my country pre-sentation in Spanish class about Mexico, remember? The piñata and the sombrero and the sodas we bought at the market."

"She still had the combination on her phone," Ella con-fessed. "We just opened your locker before third hour and stuck it in there."

"And then I called Vice Principal Andrews with the anonymous tip," Emma said, her voice breaking a little. "It was a dumb thing to do and we're really sorry."

"Super sorry," Ella said. She looked at her sister's distress and tears began to leak out of her eyes, too. Their reactions appeared genuine, but Dani was still so stunned, she couldn't be quite sure.

"We thought maybe you would get detention and that's all."

"We never thought you'd be suspended," Ella said. "When I heard Vice Principal Andrews telling the secretaries this morning that you would probably have to go to juvie after the New Year, I thought I was going to throw up."

"Is that when you decided to tell the truth?" Dani asked, still reeling.

The girls looked at each other, then at Ruben. "N–not exactly," Ella admitted.

"But we probably *would* have told the truth, even if Officer Morales hadn't pulled us out of class after lunch and took us into the office so he could tell us he knew we did it."

"He gave us a big lecture about how bad it was to let somebody else suffer for something we did. It was really scary."

"He said how disappointed our mom would be in us to know that while she is fighting for her life, we are doing bad stuff with the life we've been given and blaming other people." Emma started to cry again and her twin squeezed her fingers.

"He said how, if we had any character at all, we would

tell the truth about stealing the money jar and…and everything else."

"Everything else?" Silver looked stunned and, if Dani wasn't mistaken, guilty.

Emma sniffled. "Yeah. He said we should tell him everything. We had to, if we wanted to make things right."

"We didn't want to but…but it was the right thing to do. So we told him we were with you that night with the spray paint and that it was our idea in the first place."

Dani sat back, not sure she could take any more surprises. "Ella and Emma were the girls out with you that night."

Of course. She should have realized. She remembered Silver telling her they weren't hanging out anymore. Maybe they felt guilty that Silver had been caught while they had gotten off scot-free.

"It was all our fault, Dr. Capelli," Ella said.

"Sil didn't want to go, but we made her. We told her she was a baby if she didn't and we…we were going to tell everyone at school about her dad."

Her dad. Silver had told them about Tommy and the girls had used the truth about his crimes as a weapon against her.

Dani closed her eyes and cursed a blue streak in her head, the words she didn't say anymore. This was worse than she could have imagined. Far worse.

She opened her eyes and realized Mia was sitting on the chair closest to the Christmas tree, watching the whole proceeding with a kind of baffled interest.

Dani didn't want her here for this discussion. She was only six years old, an innocent who still believed in Santa

Claus and Christmas miracles and happy endings. She didn't need this kind of ugliness in her world.

"Mia, honey, would you go in your room and play with Wink and Pia for a little while?"

Her chin jutted out. "But I want to talk to Ruben."

"I really need you to watch Wink. Just for a minute, pumpkin, okay?"

She huffed out a breath but picked up her doll. "Come on, Winky," she said, and dragged both doll and dog to her room, where she closed the door.

When Mia was out of earshot, Dani turned to her older daughter. "You told them about your father."

Silver's chin trembled and her eyes looked guilty. "I know you told me I shouldn't tell anyone, but I was at their house one day and the TV news was on and they did a story about one of the kids whose dad was killed going back to school and…and I felt so awful and…and sad it all slipped out. But they promised not to tell."

"We didn't," Emma assured her. "We only said that so she would come with us that night, but we would never tell, I promise, Dr. Capelli."

The word would get out. They might think they weren't breaking a confidence by telling one girl. And then that girl would tell another and that girl would tell another, and in a flash the entire school would know the horrible truth.

Dani tried not to panic. This wasn't the time for it.

Some part of her wondered if it would be better to come clean with everyone in town about Tommy and take their chances about how people might react. Getting in front of the truth might be better than this constant fear of exposure.

She suspected Ruben was right. There would certainly be people in town who would inevitably think less of her, who would lump her and her daughters in with Tommy and his horrible final acts. To certain people, like perhaps the vice principal at the middle school and others like him, Silver would always be considered poisoned fruit dangling from a criminally inclined tree.

Dani accepted her own culpability in ever hooking up with Tommy in the first place when she was a needy, starved-for-love teenager, but she absolutely hated the idea of anyone thinking less of her daughters, who were truly innocent of the entire situation.

She wanted to think most people would be like Frank and Myra Morales. They wouldn't blame her or her girls for the actions of a man who hadn't been part of their lives in years.

It wouldn't be a universally held position, she knew, but maybe they were tough enough to handle the whispers and gossip of the few.

She could worry about that later. Right now, she needed to hear what these girls had come here with Ruben to tell them.

"All right. So you were there that night on the little graffiti spree. I still don't understand why you stole the money jar and tried to pin it on Silver."

The girls started to cry again, so hard that Ruben placed a hand on each shoulder. Just as it did for Dani, his presence seemed to steady them, even when he was being stern and forbidding.

"It was so stupid and mean and *wrong* and we should never have done it," Ella said through her sobs.

"We thought she had told on us for the vandalism, especially when we saw your family with Deputy Morales at the boat parade."

"We kept thinking you were going to come and arrest us," Ella said with another sniffle.

"We...we thought that if Silver got in trouble for something else, nobody would believe her if she said the graffiti was our idea."

"We just didn't want our mom to know we did such a bad thing. Dad made us promise we wouldn't do anything to upset our mom, so we could have the best Christmas for her."

"It might be our last one with her and we...we didn't want to get caught," Emma said. "But we just made everything worse."

Dani swallowed. Their convoluted reasoning made no sense, but then, she wasn't thirteen years old, dealing with a seriously ill parent.

She wanted to be furious with the girls, and some part of her was, but she couldn't help a deep sense of sorrow for the hard times their family was going through. She had been younger than Emma and Ella but she vividly remembered that terrible, helpless feeling as her mother grew more and more ill.

"Here's the thing, girls," Ruben said, his voice solemn.

"Silver never once told me who was with her the night of the vandalism. She took all the blame and did all the cleanup by herself."

If possible, the girls looked even more guilty.

"I asked her a dozen times and she would never say a word," he continued. "She protected you. She insisted she was by herself, even though I heard you guys that night and knew she wasn't alone."

"We're so sorry, Sil," Emma said.

"Really, really sorry," her sister added.

"We shouldn't have said that about your dad, that we would tell people. We would never do that, I swear."

"I still don't know why you care if people know, though," Ella said. "It's not like what he did is your fault. I mean, you're just a kid and you barely knew him. How can anybody blame you?"

"It's not your fault, any more than it's our fault our mom has cancer. It might make you sad and stuff, and that's okay, but it's not your fault."

Dani felt as if Emma's words suddenly unlocked a door in front of her, showing her something profound and simple on the other side.

Ruben had tried to tell her but she hadn't let the truth seep in. Somehow hearing it from these young girls made her see the situation with stronger clarity.

Tommy's choices were not *her* fault and they weren't Silver's. She didn't want her daughters to carry guilt over them for the rest of their lives, to forever feel as if they were somehow tarnished because of their father's actions.

She didn't want it for her daughters and she didn't want it for herself.

And if she wanted them to be free of Tommy forever, she couldn't hide in fear from the things he had done as if she—or they—were somehow responsible.

She wasn't.

Silver wasn't.

Mia certainly wasn't.

Part of being free of the past meant owning it. Not hiding in fear but being open with those who cared about them, trusting that they would accept that inviolable truth as well.

Since coming to Haven Point, Dani had been so afraid to trust anyone. She could blame it on her insecure foster care upbringing or her own bad choice in relationships, but the result was isolation and loneliness.

At some point, she would have to take that leap, as much as it scared her.

"We're really sorry," Emma said. "After we told Deputy Morales the truth, we told Vice Principal Andrews. He didn't want to believe us at first."

"Yeah, he said we were only covering up for our friend."

Emma grinned a little through her tears. "But then Deputy Morales yelled at him and told him he was a small-minded swear word and if he didn't do everything possible to clear your name, Deputy Morales would personally see to it that he was demoted back to teaching health class."

"You did that?" Silver looked stunned.

Ruben shifted. "You were innocent and he refused to

accept it. I couldn't allow him to continue smearing your reputation at school."

"Wow. Thanks." Silver smiled at him with the same kind of adoration her sister might have offered.

Ruben cleared his throat. "Okay, girls. You've apologized. Your dad is waiting out in the car for you."

"What's going to happen now?" Silver asked.

"It's a little too early to say for sure. I don't believe the county attorney will want to charge them with anything, especially because the money was all accounted for and has already been sent to the charity for hurricane relief. I'll talk to him and see if we can avoid charges, as long as you girls agree to community service for the vandalism, the theft of the donation jar and your attempts to pin it on an innocent friend."

"Yes, sir," they both said together. The girls appeared contrite, chastened by the reality of what they had done. Dani hoped they were.

"Will...will you ever forgive us, Silver?" Emma asked.

Beside Dani, her daughter gave a little shrug. "Probably. For now, I still want to be mad and hurt for a couple of days."

Ruben's gaze met hers and Dani saw an amusement that matched her own over Silver's honesty. His amusement quickly faded, replaced by something stark and unbearably sad.

She ached, knowing she had caused that look.

"Our dad took our phones for, like, ever when he had to pick us up at the school," Ella said. "We can't call you, but maybe we could come over during Christmas break and hang out and stuff. We can try to borrow our dad's phone and call you."

"Maybe," Silver said, with little enthusiasm.

The girls seemed to accept that. "Okay," Emma said. "I guess we'll see you later."

Ruben walked them to the door and watched as they climbed into a waiting vehicle in the driveway before turning back to Silver and Dani.

"How did you finally figure out it wasn't me?" Silver asked after the door closed behind the Larkin twins.

"I *never* thought it was you. Not for a single second," Ruben said. "You told me yesterday you didn't do it and I believed you. That's what I said on the way to the vet clinic, remember?"

"I thought you were just saying that." Silver looked as if reality still hadn't sunk in.

"I wish you had trusted me. It's kind of my job to get to the bottom of things, remember? I told you I would figure out who really stole the jar."

Dani felt sick inside all over again, remembering how she had accused Ruben of jumping to conclusions because of Tommy.

"I should have believed you," Silver said.

"You should have. It's never a sign of weakness to trust somebody to help you out when you need it."

Silver reached out and hugged him tightly. "Thanks."

He hugged her back, eyes soft. "You're welcome, kiddo."

"Seriously. How did you know it was them?" Silver asked.

Ruben gave a rough-sounding laugh. "If you want the truth, I didn't have any idea who was behind it yesterday, I only knew it wasn't you. Then something happened last night."

"What was it?" Dani had to ask.

He gazed at her, his expression guarded. "Because somebody was mad at me, I had to do the Secret Santa delivery by myself. While I was out there lurking about, I happened to notice that the Larkin's mailbox was spray painted red. The exact shade of red I cleaned off *The Wonder* a few weeks ago. I couldn't believe I hadn't noticed it before, but maybe it was because I wasn't the one doing the deliveries this year."

"I never even noticed that," Silver admitted.

"Again, it's my job to notice things. I knew it couldn't be a coincidence. I guessed that they were the ones who provided the spray paint. I imagine they found it in their garage or something."

Silver flushed a little. "I didn't want to do the graffiti. I thought it was dumb but they really wanted to, for some reason. They were mad at Miss Grimes because she sent Ella to detention. I thought that's all we were going to do, then they wanted to do the other places and I...I didn't say no. So that makes it my fault as much as theirs. My mom always says going along is the same as saying yes."

"Your mom is right about that," Ruben said gruffly. "I also remembered your strange reaction when I told you the Larkins would be the family we planned to help with the twelve days of Christmas. You mentioned something about how you weren't really hanging out with the twins anymore. With that kind of response, I had to suspect something must have happened between you and them."

"They were afraid I was going to tell on them, even though I didn't. I thought they were just being wussies. I didn't even think about how maybe they were worried about upsetting their mom."

"Even though you guys were mad at each other, you stepped up to do the Secret Santa deliveries for them anyway. That took guts, kiddo."

Dani thought she had been proud of her daughter for holding her head up against unjust accusations earlier, but that paled in comparison to this moment, knowing her daughter had been willing to do a kind thing for two girls who had treated her abominably.

Silver had taken the high road, focusing not on her own hurt feelings but on the tough time the Larkins were going through because of their mother's illness.

Dani hugged her and for once, Silver didn't pull away but leaned her head on her mother's shoulder.

"So you figured out Ella and Emma were likely involved with the graffiti. I still don't understand how you were able to make the leap from the spray paint to them stealing the collection jar," Dani said.

"Last night when I couldn't sleep, I went over the list the school had given me of all the students who had been in the office around the time the money disappeared. I discovered Ella was an office aide the hour just before the disappearance, which gave her plenty of access and opportunity. I told you before, I don't believe in coincidences. I couldn't figure out a motive at that point, but I thought if I talked to the girls, I could maybe get there."

He gave a slight chuckle. "For the record, Vice Principal Andrews was not in favor of me taking the girls out of class and questioning them, but I went ahead and did it anyway. I don't think I'm going to be on his Christmas list this year."

Silver and Ruben grinned at each other and Dani felt emotion swell up in her throat.

She wanted to throw her arms around him, to thank him from the bottom of her heart for believing in her child when he had every reason not to. They owed him so much. She couldn't even hope to find the right words.

"Ruben, I..."

Before she could complete the sentence, she heard Winky's claws on the hardwood floors of the hall and a moment later the dog came into the room, trying desperately to shake off the Santa hat Mia must have put on her.

"Can we come out now? We've been in there *forever.*"

Oh. Poor Mia. "Yes. I'm sorry. You can come out."

Ruben seemed to take that as his cue. He shoved on his Stetson. "I've got to run. We're shorthanded this time of year and I've been gone long enough. Have fun at *The Nutcracker.*"

"We will now," Silver said.

"If I don't see you again before the holidays, merry Christmas."

That reserve was back in his gaze, Dani saw. She had put it there and she didn't know how to fix things. She desperately missed the warmth she had become used to seeing.

"Merry Christmas," she murmured. She wanted to say so many other things but now didn't seem the time. He didn't give her a chance anyway. He patted Winky, who had taken the Santa hat off by now and was chewing on the pom-pom, then gave Mia a quick hug, smiled at Silver and walked out the door, without even looking at Dani.

15

"That was so fun, Mama. Thank you for taking me."
Dani smiled at a sleepy Mia cuddled in her bed with her dark-haired doppelgänger doll beside her and the handsome new nutcracker she had purchased at the play tucked in beside Pia. Mia hummed a few bars of the music they had enjoyed, lilting and lovely and classically familiar.

"You're welcome, honey. I'm glad you had fun."

"Can we go see the ballet again next year? Maybe it can be our family tradition."

"What a terrific idea."

"All families need traditions. That's what you said."

"We do need them."

"And can we do our own Secret Santa next year to someone? That was Silver's idea and I want to do it, too."

Her heart softened at these girls who liked the feeling of reaching out and helping others and wanted it to continue.

"I think that's an excellent idea. We don't have to only do nice things in December. We also need to think all year long about people around us who might need something happy in their world."

Mia smiled, already almost asleep and Dani hugged her one more time then turned out the light.

Traditions were necessary, she thought as she walked out into the hall. Her girls needed that sense of continuity. Would they find that if she picked up and moved to a new state to practice veterinary medicine?

For too much of her life, she had been focused on the next thing. Getting out of foster care and being on her own. Having a baby. Tommy's release date. Final exams, the next semester's classes, earning her degree.

She wasn't working toward anything now, except being the best veterinarian, mother and *person* she could be.

It was past time she stopped thinking everything would be perfect at some point in the future—when she could afford a better house, when her student loans were paid off—and started focusing on how she could make this moment the best possible.

She needed to commit to Haven Point, to building a life here and fully integrating into the community. Tonight, she had bumped into several families from Haven Point at the ballet and everyone had been more than kind to her.

She and the girls had even been invited to a family New Year's Eve party at Eliza and Aidan Caine's house in Snow Angel Cove.

Dani had given a vague, noncommittal answer at the time, but she would call Eliza the next day to accept, she decided. It seemed like a monumental step, but one she felt good about.

When she walked into the living room, she discovered Silver, hair wet from her shower and in her pajamas, lying on the floor and gazing at the Christmas tree. Winky rested on her stomach, perfectly content.

Silver had turned on Christmas music and it played softly in the background. The tree seemed particularly fragrant tonight, its piney scent capturing the magic of the season perfectly.

Dani tried to imprint the sweetness of the moment in her mind so she could take out the memory to enjoy during those times when Silver inevitably tested her patience.

She sat beside her on the floor, leaning back against the sofa. "Are you okay?"

Silver nodded. "Just enjoying the Christmas tree. It's so peaceful here, watching all the colors. Remember how I used to do this when I was a little kid back in Queens, in our crappy apartment? We had that ugly little fake tree but I still always wanted to lie on the floor and dream about Christmas."

Those early Christmases had been meager indeed, with Tommy in prison and Dani in school and working various part-time jobs. She had felt like such a failure as a mom, unable to provide more for her daughter, but when she reflected on it now, she remembered only the joy on Silver's face at whatever few small presents she found under that ugly fake tree.

"Did you enjoy the ballet? It was fun to see Ruben's parents there, along with his nephews and niece."

Silver moved to a sitting position, her back against the sofa like Dani's, and settled Winky into a more comfortable spot on her lap. "Zach said their grandparents take them every year to see *The Nutcracker* during the holiday season."

"Ah. Another Morales tradition." She sent Silver a sideways look. "What else did Zach have to say? You talked to him for most of the intermission."

"He asked me what was going on, why I wasn't in school today. He said a kid in his geometry class told him I had been arrested, so Zach got all up in his face and told the kid to stop telling lies about me." Silver grinned a little but quickly hid it by turning her face away.

"That's sweet of him to stand up for you. Did you tell him what really happened?"

"No. It didn't seem right to rat out Ella and Em. I told him it was just a misunderstanding and I would be back after Christmas. He seemed happy about that."

Dani smiled. "I think he likes you."

This time Silver didn't bother to hide her grin. "Maybe."

They sat in a companionable silence, listening to a jazzy version of "Silent Night."

"Ruben's pretty great, isn't he?" Silver said out of the blue. "He believed in me the whole time."

The torrent of emotions Dani had done her best to dam up all evening seemed to break free and she had to close her eyes at the sheer force of them. "Yes. He is pretty great."

"If he didn't keep investigating, I might still be suspended." Silver sent her a sidelong look. "You know why he went to all that effort to clear my name, right?"

"Because he's an excellent judge of character," Dani replied.

Her daughter grinned. "Well, yeah. But also because *he* likes *you*."

Would it make a difference if I tell you I'm falling in love with you?

She thought of those moments in his arms on the boat, the sheer joy of being with him. Had she ruined everything between them? How could she make it right?

"I need to ask you something," she said to Silver. "Something serious. Do you really hate it here? If you do, I can look into practicing somewhere else. I would like to stay in Haven Point and build our future here, but not if you're going to be miserable."

Silver pulled Winky higher in her arms and tucked the dog's little head under her chin. "I'm sorry I've been unhappy. It was…everything with Ella and Emma, plus missing my friends back in Boston and stuff. I don't really hate it here."

"But could you ever love it?"

"Yeah. I think I could. It's pretty here. There's maybe not as much to do as Boston or New York, but we can always go back and visit those places when we want."

"That's right. I'm okay with you going back to stay with

your friends on a visit. Maybe you can start saving your money for a plane ticket by doing extra work at the clinic."

"That would be good." Silver paused. "I have friends here. There are good people everywhere and there are jerks, too. Ruben told me the trick is to surround yourself with the first kind of people and do your best to ignore the second."

Yet more wisdom from the man. How could she help but love him?

"And don't forget, you have to start by *being* a good person yourself, instead of a jerk."

Silver was quiet for a moment and seemed content watching the Christmas tree and petting their fluffy dog. "Hey, do you think Ruben might let Mia and me do the last few Secret Santa deliveries?"

"You still want to, after the trouble Ella and Emma caused you?"

"I like taking the gifts. It makes me feel good inside and it's a small thing I can do for someone else. Besides, their mom might die. I think they made some stupid choices because they're afraid, which I would be, too, I guess, if there was any chance I might lose you."

Oh. Just when Dani thought she had her emotions under control, her daughter had to go and say something like that. Emotions clogged her throat and her eyes welled up with tears.

Yes, the bulk of the teen years were still ahead of them, but Dani hoped she never lost sight of how amazing her daughter was.

"I'll talk to Ruben. I don't think he'll mind. You should probably get to bed now. It's late."

"Yeah. I'm tired."

They both rose and to Dani's delight, her daughter wrapped her arms around her waist. "Merry almost Christmas, Mom. I think it's going to be our best one ever."

That Silver could say those words after the trauma of the last three months and the final horrible, desperate choices her father had made filled Dani with joy.

After Silver went to bed, taking Wink with her, Dani sat for a long time there in the darkness illuminated only by the Christmas tree.

She knew what she had to do—she needed only to find the courage for it.

It was nearly midnight when she saw the lights of a vehicle pulling into the driveway next door. Ruben must have worked a late shift, after doing his best to clear her daughter's name all morning.

She needed to speak with the man and suddenly she knew it wouldn't wait another moment.

Heart pounding, she pulled on her boots. She didn't bother with her coat, just grabbed the knit throw from the chair and draped it around her shoulders like a wrap before heading outside.

The December night felt like a precious gift. It was snowing gently, big, puffy flakes that landed in her hair and on the wrap. In the moonlight, she could make out the vastness of the lake and the steep mountains rising up on the other side. The hushed beauty of the scene humbled her and made her infinitely grateful she could witness it.

She was nervous about talking to Ruben, but there was also a sense of...*peace*. That was the only word she could use to describe it. Silver had described the experience of gazing at the Christmas tree using that same word and it fit here, too.

She felt a deep sense of peace.

At his door, she didn't hesitate for an instant, simply knocked softly. From inside, she heard a well-mannered deep-throated bark she recognized as Yukon's and another little yip from Ollie and then the door opened.

Ruben looked as if he had been in the process of taking off his uniform when she knocked. He wore the dark khaki pants but only a white T-shirt and none of the other things that always hung on his belt—his weapon, his radio, his Taser. All the things that made him appear so dangerous.

She had a feeling they probably weren't far away, though. He wasn't the sort of man who would answer the door in the middle of the night without being ready for anything.

His eyes widened in shock when he spotted her. The dogs rushed out, tails wagging to greet her.

"Dani! What are you doing here? Come in."

As she went inside with Yukon and Ollie sticking close to her, she realized she had never been in his house in all the months she had lived next door to him.

Now she looked around with interest. It was comfortable, masculine, with Mission-style furniture and photographs of Haven Point and its surroundings on the walls.

It smelled like him, too, that outdoorsy, cedary scent she found so delicious.

His house seemed to fit him, somehow.

"What's going on? Are the girls okay?"

"The girls are fine. Everyone is fine." She petted Yukon. Maybe she should have waited until morning. What had seemed urgent to her might not appear the same to him when he was tired from a long day at work.

"I came for two reasons. Three, really."

He studied her and some of his tension seemed to seep away. "That sounds serious. Sit down."

He gestured to the sofa but she shook her head. "I won't take long. The girls are home alone. They're in bed, but I probably should have told Silver where I was going."

Her daughter might figure it out, given their conversation earlier. She wasn't sure how she felt about that.

She hadn't really thought this through, intent only on sharing some of the thoughts running through her mind.

"She's one of the reasons I'm here. Silver would like to finish up the Secret Santa deliveries to the Larkins and I told her I would ask you about it."

He blinked those incredibly long eyelashes. "After everything the twins did to Sil, she still wants to be part of that?"

Dani laughed a little. "I know. I had the same reaction. She says she likes giving the presents and likes the way it makes her feel to be doing something nice for them."

"She's a great kid."

"She is. I sometimes forget that in the day to day. It's important that I don't lose sight of it. I'm trying to do better."

He smiled and her knees turned suddenly wobbly for some reason. She thought about taking a seat, but decided she felt a little more in control on her feet, wobbly or not.

"As I said, Silver is only one of the reasons I'm here."

"Oh?"

"I think I was so stunned this afternoon that I didn't properly thank you for going to bat for her like you did."

His T-shirt rippled as he shrugged his shoulders. "What else could I do? I knew Sil wouldn't have taken that money. She said she didn't and I believed her. None of it made sense. I'm just glad I could figure it out before the school moved forward with pressing charges."

She was, too, more appreciative than she could ever tell him. She would have hated knowing her daughter had a juvenile record.

"I didn't say it this afternoon but I'm deeply grateful for your instincts and your investigative skills. We would have been lost without you."

"I'm glad it worked out the way it did." He gave her a careful look. "You said you had three reasons for stopping by. What's the third?"

The peace she felt earlier seemed to have evaporated now. For one crazy instant, she was tempted to tell him she had miscounted and her work here was done.

That would be cowardly, though. If her daughter could show such strength and grace, Dani could do nothing less. She drew in a deep breath for courage and stepped forward. "I...I would like to give you something."

He raised an eyebrow, looking so gorgeous that everything inside her seemed to sigh.

"An early Christmas present?"

"Something like that."

Gathering her nerves, she took another step, raised up on her toes and pressed her mouth to his.

At once, all of her nerves fled and that peace returned. This was right. *They* were right. She was so foolish to have doubted it for a moment.

After a heart-stopping moment of hesitation when she began to wonder if she was too late, he wrapped his arms tightly around her and kissed her with a ferocity that stole her breath.

She gave a little laugh and entwined her own arms around his neck, loving the taste of him and the overwhelming sense of joy exploding like those Roman candles again.

Love coursed through her, sweet and beautiful, like a cleansing storm.

He kissed her until her knees were weak again, until she couldn't think straight and her breathing was ragged and she was a quivering, aching bundle of desire.

"Have I mentioned before how much I love Christmas presents?" he murmured against her mouth.

It took her dazzled brain a moment to make the connection back to what he had said earlier. She laughed, loving him more than she ever imagined possible.

"That was more an apology than a Christmas present, I guess."

"You don't owe me any apology."

"I do. You bared your heart to me last week. At the time, I wasn't in a good place to hear it. But I haven't been able to think about anything else since then and…I'm sorry for the way I reacted."

"You're forgiven," he murmured.

"You make it too easy." She stepped away a little, knowing she had to get through this, no matter how difficult, and she couldn't seem to string together a coherent thought while she was in his arms. "When you told me you were falling in love with me, I…panicked."

"I'm sorry."

"It's not your fault. I wasn't looking for this when I moved to Haven Point but I think I fell hard right around the time we met. I was sure of it that day you held me when I had a breakdown, when you were so very kind to me, and I've been fighting it ever since."

"How's that working out for you?"

She made a face and took one more deep breath for courage. "Terribly. I don't want to fight it anymore. I love you, Ruben. I love how kind you are with my children, I love seeing you with your family, I love the way I seem to lose my head completely when you kiss me."

He seemed to take that as incentive to kiss her again and Dani wanted to sink into him, to stay here forever in the shelter of his arms.

"Yes. Like that," she said, her voice thready and aroused.

He smiled and kissed the corner of her mouth and she had to wonder just why she had been fighting this for so long.

"I had long ago told myself I would be better off forgetting about romance entirely and only focusing on my girls and my career. And then I met you. You made me laugh and cry and feel things I thought I never would again. You helped me realize I still have so much love inside me to give to the right man."

He held her and she listened to his heartbeat, knowing she didn't want to be anywhere else in the world except right here. "You are the right man, Ruben. Good, decent, caring. The kind of man I think I've finally managed to convince myself I deserve. More than that, the kind of man I need."

This time, she kissed him and the fierce emotion in his eyes was all the answer she needed.

They kissed for a long time, until they were on the sofa, wrapped together under the throw she had brought over. The snow was falling gently outside the window and she could see the Christmas tree he had helped set up gleaming through the night from her house next door.

He had brought light and color to her world, in so many ways.

"I can't stay," she said with deep regret. "I have to get back to the girls."

"I know." He kissed her again then stood up and pulled her to her feet, rearranging the sweater he had been in the process of tangling.

He wrapped the woven throw back around her shoulders with a soft tenderness that stole her heart all over again. "I love you, Daniela Capelli."

She laughed a little. "Nobody calls me Daniela. How did you even know that's my full name?"

"My dad mentioned it long before you came here. He told me years ago he had met a lovely veterinary student with a beautiful name to match. I could never have imagined during that passing conversation that one day I would be completely enamored with that woman—and with her daughters, I should add."

What would her girls think about the idea of her and Ruben together? She felt a tiny flutter of misgiving but pushed it away. Silver and Mia both loved him and would be thrilled.

"I'll walk you back," he said.

"You don't have to."

He raised an eyebrow in answer, grabbed his down coat from the closet by the door and reached for her hand.

Ollie and Yukon came with them, their advance guard, sniffing every patch of the sidewalk as Dani walked hand in hand through the falling snow toward her little house along the lakeshore with the man she loved.

Epilogue

R uben started up *The Wonder*, the thrum of her motor familiar and beloved to him now after the past year.

"Here we go." Beside him, Dani gave a smile that was even more familiar and beloved.

"Last chance. Are you sure you don't want to stay on dry land and watch the parade with the girls and my parents? I still feel a little guilty that you haven't seen the whole Haven Point Lights on the Lake boat parade in all its glory."

She shook her head. "I'll have other chances to see it. Right now, I'm exactly where I want to be."

Though it was almost time for the parade to start, he couldn't resist stealing a moment to kiss his beautiful bride of three months, there at the Haven Point marina on a cold December night.

"I'm glad you're here with me."

"So am I. I've been looking forward to it for weeks. I still can't believe everybody bailed at the last minute and it's just the two of us."

After the big party of the previous year, everybody in his family had ended up staying on shore for various reasons. Angie had obligations with the Haven Point Helping Hands booth, Silver had been invited to ride on a friend's boat and his parents had been persuaded by Mia to watch the whole parade from the park in town.

He didn't mind. Between his job, the girls and her increased responsibilities at the clinic now that his father had officially retired, these moments alone together were as rare as they were cherished.

"The dogs are ready," she said, laughing at their trio of canines who were sprawled out on the foredeck, waiting for the fun to begin.

Okay, they weren't completely alone. Ollie, Yukon and Winky—who had formed their own little pack over the past year—never missed a chance to go out on *The Wonder*.

The dogs, like Dani and the girls, had become seasoned sailors after a summer spent out on the water every chance they could find.

The past year had been the happiest of Ruben's life. Every moment seemed an adventure, from cross-country skiing the previous winter, to helping Dani and the girls plant and nurture their first garden in the springtime, to the gorgeous

September day when they all had merged their lives together in a beautiful ceremony in the little church in town.

Each week seemed better than the one before.

Ruben had always loved the changing seasons along the lake—the new life in the spring, the recreational opportunities of the summer, the quiet and peace of the fall.

He had a feeling this season, Christmastime, would always be his favorite. This was the time of year when he had found the woman beside him, the one who filled his life with more joy than he ever could have imagined.

"You don't think they'll be too cold out there, do you?" she asked, with a worried look at the dogs as the parade started and Ruben guided the boat behind the watercraft in front of *The Wonder*.

"It's at least twenty degrees warmer out there with the radiant heat off all the lights the kids strung around," he assured her.

His poor boat looked like a floating casino at this point, with Christmas lights dangling from every possible spot. A floating casino from the South Pole, he amended. The two giant light-up inflatable penguins from last year had been joined by one more and all three bobbed around maniacally as *The Wonder* churned through the water.

He never would have guessed when he bought the cabin cruiser a little more than a year ago that the boat could end up changing his life. Without it, or more accurately, without a night of mischief by three teenage girls when they spray painted her, he wasn't sure he and Dani would have found their way to each other.

As he thought about how empty his life would be without her and the girls, thick emotion welled up in his chest.

Dani, always in tune to his mood, gave him a concerned look. "Are you okay?"

"Perfect," he said. "I was just thinking about how my world has changed since we did this last Christmas."

Her features softened with a tender look that humbled him. "What a gift this year has been."

He reached a hand out and she rose to join him at the wheel. He kissed her briefly but didn't want to take his attention too far from the boat controls when there was so much traffic on the water. He also didn't want to let her go so he tucked her in front of him, his arms on either side and her back nestled against his front.

Keeping his eyes on the water illuminated by his boat lights, he kissed the back of her neck and was rewarded with a shiver. That was one of her most sensitive spots—and how lucky was he to have discovered most of them over the past year?

"Careful, or you're going to make me wish we weren't in this parade at all," she murmured. "Are you sure we can't sneak off and dock at home for a bit while the girls are gone? Nobody would know."

He grinned. "In case you missed it, Doc, we have three eight-foot-tall light-up inflatable penguins aboard. I think they might draw a little attention, parked at our dock for a few hours."

"Too bad."

Ruben tightened his arms around her and whispered a

suggestion for later, something that made her laugh and the dogs look over at them with a resigned sort of curiosity.

They had plenty of time.

They had forever.

★ ★ ★ ★ ★